Side Quest

Stephanie K Clemens

Adventures with Ink

Copyright © 2026 by Stephanie K. Clemens

All rights reserved.

No part of this publication may be reproduced, distributed, or transmitted in any form or by any means, including photocopying, recording, or other electronic or mechanical methods, without the prior written permission of the publisher, except as permitted by U.S. copyright law. For permission requests, contact Stephanie K. Clemens.

The story, all names, characters, and incidents portrayed in this production are fictitious. No identification with actual persons (living or deceased), places, buildings, and products is intended or should be inferred.

Book Cover by Covers and Berries

To anyone who has tried to stay on task and finished thirteen other projects, but not the one you needed to get done.

Contents

1. The Thorn and the Throne — 1
2. A Goat, a God, and a Bad Decision — 11
3. Spellbinding Is Not Consent — 27
4. Sidekick: Unwanted, Uninvited, Unbreakable — 37
5. The Chicken Must Die — 45
6. Potions of Regret (Now with Extra Honesty) — 60
7. The Bard That Wept — 70
8. Ruins of Regret — 79
9. The Wishing Well, Not Well — 87
10. Campfire Promises — 96
11. Bones, Brothers, and Unfinished Business — 104
12. Brew or Die (The Dwarven Ale Trials) — 114
13. One Accidental Love Elixir Later — 124
14. There's Only One Bed (Please Don't Make It Weird) — 135
15. The Map That Personally Hates Me — 148

16.	The Cult of Never Finishing Anything	158
17.	Escape by Goat-Drawn Pie Catapult	172
18.	Blood and Bets at the Black Fang	181
19.	Spines and Bindings	194
20.	Spines, Sighs, and Other Dangerous Things	203
21.	The Sourdough of Destiny	212
22.	The Library of Unwritten Recipes	225
23.	The Ballad of Thorn and Flame	238
24.	Almost Confessed: Then a Kraken Happened	254
25.	Percival the Uncatchable	265
26.	Team Chaos Rides Again (Almost)	277
27.	Drafts, Daggers, and Dangerous Truths	287
28.	Gala of Gowns, Daggers, and Hidden Keys	301
29.	A Dance Before the Fall	314
30.	The Crown Is a Lie	324
31.	Shadow Guild Reunion (With Betrayal Punch)	335
32.	How to Stage a Regicide (Without Dying)	343
33.	Ink, Blood, and an Unwritten Crown	353
34.	Ashes, Aftermath, and Goodbye	359
35.	The Tavern on the Edge of the World	371
36.	You Stayed	378
37.	Final Side Quest (Just One More)	384

Field Guides	387
APPENDIX: A LESS-THAN-OFFICIAL ADVENTURER'S COMPENDIUM	399
Acknowledgements	413
About the author	416
Also by	417

of Side Quest

- Midlands
- The Bookstore Cafe
- Library of Unwritten Recipes
- Duskmire
- Tavern at edge of the World
- White Fang Paverspines & Bindings
- Eldreach
- Market

1

The Thorn and the Throne

"All great quests begin with a blade, a secret, and the deeply incorrect assumption that nothing will go wrong."

Have you come to hear a tale of adventure, daring, and perhaps . . . love? If that's the case, you're in luck. I've got just the story—heroism, hijinks, and heartbreak in equal measure. Now, how shall I begin? Hmm. Let's try something traditional this time . . .

Once upon a time, a deadly assassin was hired to kill a tyrant king. She would have done it, too—swiftly, silently, and without an ounce of fuss—if the universe hadn't conspired to throw fifteen goats, three haunted taverns, one chatty mage, and precisely one cursed chicken in her way. Honestly, she deserved better.

Kaelin Thorn was sitting in her favorite oversized and overstuffed chair, boots off, feet up, glass of cold foamy ale on the table beside her, reading—yes, you heard that right, reading.

It was one of her favorite things to do when she wasn't on a mission. There was something about escaping into a world of heroes and damsels filled with yearning and romance that made her happy, not that she would ever admit it. In fact, Kaelin read about love the way some people study battlefield strategy—objectively, and with the underlying suspicion that it might get her killed. Despite that tendency, it was how she relaxed.

Pounding on the door dared to interrupt the cozy atmosphere she'd created for herself: a warm fire crackling in the stone fireplace she'd built herself years ago, a worn quilt thrown halfway to the side covering very little of her, but there if she decided she needed it, and her dog, Timber, curled up just below her feet.

Timber looked like a cross between a wolf and a raccoon, with one blue eye and one hazel. When she arrived on Kaelin's doorstep a year ago, it was a competition over who was most feral. Kaelin proved it was her within a week. Timber respected that, hence the loyalty. But that's neither here nor there. Let's get back to the story, shall we?

Where was I . . . Oh yes, pounding.

Kaelin sighed, carefully folding over the corner of the last page she read before closing her book, setting it down, and standing. She made her way to the door, intending to open it when an envelope slid underneath.

"Not another mission," she muttered to herself, or maybe Timber (it was difficult to tell in situations like this) before picking up the envelope.

She turned the rough paper over in her hand, noting the crimson wax seal of the Shadow Guild before sliding her dagger (named Mercy, if anyone is interested) under the flap and slicing it open.

Dear Thorn,

(Ugh. Off to a grand start.)

(Or should I call you Thorn of the North),

(Absolutely not. Who told him that? I will find them.)

A new, shall we say, situation has arisen, and it needs your particular skill set to be remedied.

(He says 'situation' like it's a kitchen spill, not regicide.)

King Varric of Eldreach has become a tyrant, and that's putting it nicely, and he needs to be removed from power.

(Oh good. A king. Because the last three times went so smoothly.)

You've proven time and time again that you can handle matters such as this, as difficult as they are.

(Translation: 'I don't know how you survive, but I'd like to take credit for it.')

If you succeed in fixing our little problem, there is a substantial reward. Let's just say never working again would be an option.

(Bold of him to assume I'd stop working. Or that he has that kind of money.)

Meet me at the Last Wish tomorrow at dusk to accept the job and receive further instructions.

(Because nothing says 'classified assassination contract' like a tavern that smells like old blood and bad decisions.)

Dangerously Yours,
(... *He did not.*)
Professor M. Mortimer
(*He did.*)
(*He actually signed it that way.*)
(*I need a drink.*)

Kaelin rolled her eyes at the end of the letter.

As she should have. Who signs a letter 'dangerously yours'?

Professor Mundice Mortimer hadn't been in the field for at least ten years, and he definitely wasn't spending any time keeping his skills intact. He might be the main recruiter for the Shadow Guild, but he wasn't a threat to anyone anymore.

After reading the missive a second time and committing it to memory, Kaelin threw the parchment into the fire and watched it curl, then blacken as it turned to ash.

She curled back into her chair and picked up her book.

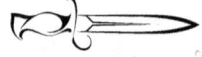

Before I move on to her meeting tomorrow, perhaps I should tell you a little more about our protagonist.

Kaelin Thorn had twenty-six confirmed kills, a dagger collection named after extinct flowers, and the emotional availability of a scorched cabbage. This, of course, made her wildly popular in the assassin guilds and completely incapable of handling sincere compliments.

Fifteen years ago was when it all started. Kaelin, a rowdy fifteen-year-old girl with black hair and eyes so blue they looked violet in certain light, attempted to pickpocket the wrong person. She would have known better if she had had any sense of self preservation, but after the tragic loss of her parents, the destruction of the orphanage she was placed in, and the labor the last family she lived with forced her into, she felt pretty invincible. I mean, she'd proven she was a survivor, or at least that's what she thought. Until she cut the purse strings of Dame Anwyn Stride, otherwise known as the Harrowmistress of the Inner Circle. It is true that Kaelin was caught in her attempt to relieve Dame Stride of her precious belongings; it is also true that she was not caught until the goods were in her hands, having successfully removed them from Dame Stride's person. Most individuals who knew Dame Anwyn Stride would consider Kaelin's theft a success. Kaelin did not; it did, however, change the course of her life. It was also the reason why, at thirty, our protagonist had twenty-six confirmed kills, a permanent scowl, and trust issues deeper than the Radbin Straights, which, as of now, no one had ever seen the bottom of.

To call the Last Wish a tavern was . . . generous. Words like den of iniquity, reckoning of the soulless, or the place livers go to die, would be far more accurate. The only individuals who chose to enter its hallowed filth-encrusted walls were bloodthirsty brigands and heavily armed assassins, which was why Kaelin never chose it as a meeting place. Not to mention, it reeked. Inside. Outside. Possibly in another dimension. Like the smell of evil rot had permeated the wood, the stones, the very soul of the place. It wafted into the surrounding block like a sentient warning sign for anyone with standards. Or maybe its goal was to turn the entire area into an attraction for any and all hedonistic and criminal activities.

Which was why Kaelin was still standing outside the door, face covered to protect her nostrils from the scent of stale beer, dried blood, and broken dreams.

No, I don't know what broken dreams smell like, but it sounded good, didn't it?

With a sigh and a roll of her shoulders, she pushed the door open and entered the dark smoke-drenched room. She nearly gagged. She let her eyes adjust before moving farther into the . . . tavern. Criminals drank and laughed and argued like they were normal law-abiding citizens. They weren't. No one who entered the Last Wish followed rules.

Kaelin found a table in the corner—back to the wall, always. It was an old rule of hers, born from nearly dying twice in one week over a decade ago. You couldn't watch everyone if you were in the middle of a room.

Since Mortimer wasn't there yet (of course he wasn't), she claimed the table for herself. Leave it to the recruiter to set a meeting time and be late for it. Just another way he illustrated how important he believed himself to be.

The door opened again.

Light streamed into the room like it was trying to rescue someone.

And in walked Professor Mundice Mortimer, round glasses reflecting the last of the day, wispy white hair ruffled like he'd lost a duel with humidity, and a cloak so melodramatic it belonged in a theater troupe.

Because of course he wore a cloak. The man took 'cloak and dagger' a bit too literally. But at least he was here, and only marginally late.

"Aw, Thorn. A pleasure to see you again." He dragged a chair across the sticky floor, the legs screeching like tortured banshees. The entire tavern glanced over at them, winced, and returned to their legally questionable business.

Kaelin leaned forward.

She wanted details. The mission. The pay. The dangers the Guild would bother to tell her about—if they told Mortimer anything at all, which was doubtful. But even now, Kaelin sometimes forgot that hope was a waste of energy, and she was better off without it.

She locked eyes with him and waited.

Mortimer blinked. Smiled. Waited back.

She said nothing.

He waited, then waited some more, clearly expecting her to speak. But she wasn't one to extend pleasantries to anyone, much less the pompous fool sitting in front of her. You could call it rude, but she wouldn't care.

Mortimer cleared his throat. "Well then, we might as well get started." He paused.

She arched her eyebrow. A threat in micro-expression form.

"King Varric is not the king he was expected to be," Mortimer said, each word enunciated as if he feared she wouldn't understand plain speech. "At the very least, he is a tyrant. At worst, an evil despot. The Guild has decided it's time to do something about it."

Kaelin did not blink.

If Mortimer knew what she was thinking—or how many ways she knew to silence pompous men—he wouldn't be sitting across from her so comfortably.

But Mortimer didn't know. Mortimer never knew.

He couldn't even dispose of a half-dead informant without backup.

Kaelin, however . . .

Well. There was still that one incident in Saltmere.

Let's just say the town no longer held festivals.

"Continue," Kaelin said, casually picking her teeth with Mercy—a dagger, not a metaphor, though it might as well be.

What you don't know is that Mercy was the only blade Kaelin had never used to kill anyone. A line in the sand she drew a long time ago.

A shame, really, that no one tells you the tide always comes.

Mortimer took off his glasses and polished them with his sleeve.

"There's concern," he said, "that the king is . . . well, he's gone a bit . . . you know . . ."

"Are you trying to say he's mentally unwell?" Kaelin asked flatly.

He nodded, his white wispy curls fluttering with every move. "Yes, that's it. Anyway, it's become a problem, and he needs disposing of. And the Hallowmistress insisted that you do it. For a generous sum, of course."

Kaelin's expression didn't change.

But when Mortimer spoke the number, her knuckles went still.

It was a very large number.

Years of training meant Kaelin Thorn didn't betray emotions easily. She didn't twitch. Didn't flinch. Didn't let hope breathe.

But her brain—traitorous thing that it was—whispered:

That would be enough.

Enough to stop running. Enough to buy land. Enough to open—

No.

Absolutely not.

Kaelin Thorn didn't dream.

She most certainly did not dream about a quiet little bookshop and tea house with loose-leaf brews and shelves full of tragic romances.

She had never told anyone. She refused to tell herself.

And yet.

She met Mortimer's gaze again.

Flat. Cold. Assassin-like.

"Fine," she said.

2

A GOAT, A GOD, AND A BAD DECISION

"Some side quests you choose. Others come with horns and a vengeance kink."

Three days.

Kaelin had left the Last Wish three days ago, and everything had already turned to shambles. After packing, she'd left Timber a side of venison, knowing full well the dog (questionable species, status pending) could take care of herself if the mission ran long. Still, Timber had grown soft this past year—*domesticated*, if Kaelin was being dramatic—and Kaelin worried she wouldn't last long on her own.

Not that our assassin would ever admit she cared about the animal's well-being. She can lie to herself all she wants. We know better. Never mind that her mentor taught her that affection was weakness. Especially when it comes with fur and trust issues. Kaelin had definitely developed a fondness for Timber.

To stay out of sight—and therefore out of mind—Kaelin made camp the first night. She shouldn't have.

The Great Winds of Anderboke arrived uninvited, tore through the clearing like a bored storm god with something to prove, and a single rogue spark from her fire found the canvas of her tent.

The tent burned.

So did her camp roll.

Her pack.

All her clothes.

All her food.

Including the hard cheese.

She hadn't packed much (there were towns along the way), but still—losing a wedge of hard cheese to the flames felt particularly cruel. So, instead of weeping like a normal person, she walked through the night with soot in her hair and murder in her heart. At a stream, she stopped just long enough to refill her water flask and contemplate her life choices.

Which was when the sky opened up in a deluge of rain and—because of course it did—lightning struck her coin purse.

Yes. Her coin purse.

All her gold, silver, and copper fused into one gloriously useless nugget of melted metal. A shimmering lump of failure.

To say our assassin was having a hard time would be an understatement. A more accurate description might involve the words 'cosmically hexed.'

This is what happens when you laugh at fate. It laughs back—with lightning.

She stumbled into some small town that probably had a name. Not that Kaelin had bothered to learn it. It smelled like onions, and the mayor had sideburns shaped like question marks—those were her only takeaways.

Unable to pay for a room at the inn, Kaelin did what any resourceful, sleep-deprived assassin would do: she broke into the stable and slept in the loft with the hay.

Unfortunately, the stable hand woke up at dawn, opened the loft hatch, and Kaelin fell through like a sack of vengeful potatoes. Right next to a startled horse.

The horse bolted.

The stable hand screamed.

Kaelin was immediately accused of horse theft.

She half-snuck, half-ran out of town before the local law could grab their boots.

The only bright side? The horse didn't go far. And really, she reasoned, since she was already branded a thief . . .

"Might as well make it worth their while," Kaelin said to herself. She was, after all, morally grey and marginally hungry.

Now, it was the morning of the third day, and she rode her ill-gotten steed into the cheery little town of Raven's Hollow—a place so wholesome-looking it mismatched her mood like her ex used to mismatch their socks.

Her goals?

- Find a mage eccentric enough to un-glob her coins.

- Trade said un-globbed metal for food and supplies.

- Finally get back to the actual mission: assassinate the king. You know, that tiny little quest she was supposed to be on.

Little does Kaelin know that she was two goats and one demigod away from forgetting she's an assassin entirely. And we're only on chapter two.

It needs to be said—not everything is a trial for Kaelin.

She found her mage without any problems. He was exactly where someone had said he'd be (for once), and not only did he separate her unfortunate glob of coin metal, he even allocated the results into neat little chunks by original denomination.

A miracle. She almost said thank you.

(Almost.)

Unfortunately, that was the only thing that went smoothly.

The market was a bustling center of capitalism, chaos, and far too much shouting. Yes, it had what she needed, but every merchant wanted to haggle—and Kaelin was in no mood to play that game. She scowled. They raised prices. She scowled harder. They smiled and raised them more.

This is what happens when you try to intimidate people who make a living selling fake wands and candied rat tails.

Eventually, the stalemate broke. She danced the back-and-forth bartering ballet, kept (mostly) within budget, and crossed every item off her list. Almost.

The closures on her new packs needed sewing, so she was stuck in town waiting for the final bits to be finished. With nothing to do but sit. And wait. And avoid thinking about a little bookshop that didn't exist yet.

And that's when she heard it.

A child.

Crying.

Her body tensed on instinct. Fight or flight? Definitely flight. Preferably through a wall. But the child saw her. Big, red-rimmed eyes. Tear-streaked cheeks. He waved.

She could still run.

But what kind of monster turns their back on a crying child?

Spoiler: not our assassin. Not today.

Kaelin sighed, shoulders already slumping in defeat. She weaved through the milling townsfolk, none of whom seemed to notice the boy—like they'd trained their eyes to slide past small, sad things. When she reached him, she crouched low and asked, with exactly zero ceremony: "Why are you crying?"

The boy hiccupped. "My goat, Marzipan, is missing. I've looked everywhere for her."

Yes, this is the first of the two goats that made Kaelin question all of her life choices. The second had better aim.

Kaelin blinked. "What's your name? Where are your parents? Maybe we can get them to help you find your goat."

Totally reasonable suggestion. Completely ignored.

"Thimble," he said. "And my parents are gone. There's no one to help me."

There it was. A tiny tug at the very last heartstring Kaelin hadn't burned through. Dammit.

"Maybe I could help you find your goat," she said, already regretting the words.

Thimble's whole face lit up like a sunrise. "Really? You'll help me save Marzipan?"

Kaelin sighed again, this time with more soul.

"Yeah," she muttered. "I'll help you find your goat."

And so, begins the saga of Marzipan the Goat, Kaelin the Reluctant, and the terrible, terrible decision to care.

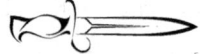

She left Thimble in town under the care of one of the shopkeepers. It cost her more coin, which was regrettable. But adventures like these were no place for a small child. You never knew when a goblin would jump out of a cavern and demand new shoes.

Which left Kaelin alone, exactly how she liked it, following goat tracks into mists that did not look natural. Honestly, that's never a good sign.

As soon as she entered the mists, things started to happen, or stopped happening, depending on how you looked at it.

Birds stopped chirping. In a forest surrounded by trees, nary a bird chirped.

Those same trees seemed like they were breathing. Kaelin tripped over a root and reached out to stabilize herself. The bark pulsed beneath her palm. It felt . . . wrong. Like the tree was inhaling and exhaling. Or digesting. She quickly removed her hand, not wanting to become its next meal.

It's completely unnecessary to mention that the trail looped around on itself, bringing Kaelin back to the beginning, not once, not twice, not even three times. By the fourth lap around this 'mystical woodland death maze,' Kaelin was ready to stab geometry; instead, she finally found the path that led deeper into the forest.

That the path appeared in front of her was a more accurate description, but I thought I'd be nice and let her take the credit, this time.

The trees were lucky she never took out her anger on nature, no matter how stabby she was feeling.

None of those things caused her to question this little side quest any more than she already was, but when the trees started whispering her name, she muttered profanities, fluently, in three different languages before she continued deeper into the forest.

It wasn't long after the whispers started that she reached a clearing with stone ruins and—yes—Marzipan standing proudly on a moss-covered altar, chewing on vines like she owned the place.

"Come here, Marzipan," Kaelin called. "It's time to go home to Thimble. That kid really misses you."

The goat stared at her and continued its chewing.

"Dammit, you (bleep, bleepity, bleep) from the underworld. Get your ass down here. You don't want to find out what happens if I have to drag you out of here." Kaelin's short fuse was burned to a crisp. She wanted cheese, a soft bed, and to be done with this distraction.

And don't we all?

Except maybe the goat, she seemed deeply connected to her aesthetic.

Of course, Kaelin rarely got what she wanted.

A loud pop echoed throughout the forest. The ground beneath the stone ruins cracked open.

An ancient spirit—Alron of the Hollow, a demigod of thresholds, guardianship, and occasionally revenge—emerged. He was part stag, part stormcloud, and very annoyed about being awakened by a goat.

"Who dares disturb the sanctum of Alron the Hollow?" the ancient spirit bellowed. Paused. ". . . Is that goat eating my altar?" he asked, quieter, his tone quizzical.

"You've got to be kidding me?" were Kaelin's exact words as she witnessed the spectacle in front of her.

Alron stared at the goat in disbelief. How could it be standing there calmly munching on his altar? A goat does what a goat wants to do. There's no question about it.

There was no time for this nonsense, so Kaelin did what any unreasonably impatient person would do when faced with a stubborn goat and the demigod that was pondering its existence: she opened her mouth when she should have kept it closed.

"I'll just take the goat and be on my way." She sauntered up to the goat, her mind racing as she tried to decide how she was going to convince Marzipan to listen to her.

Alron's eyes left the goat and focused on her. "Who dares to disturb my slumber?"

Technically, it was Marzipan, but goats don't give a (bleep) about demigods. Alron was very much aware of this fact.

Kaelin looked to her right, then to her left. If the demigod wasn't going to blame the goat, she was the only other being around to blame.

"Your trespass"—he pointed a finger at her—"has disturbed my eternal slumber; therefore, you must pay. I demand an offering of blood or bond."

Marzipan bleated. It was clear she refused to be part of any offering.

Kaelin tried diplomacy first. It wasn't her strongest of skills, but when saving a goat for a child, it seemed like the appropriate choice.

"Alron, can I call you Alron?" she started, taking her time as she determined what she could negotiate with. "Why don't we sit down, chat, and strike a deal? There's no need for blood or bonding. I'm here to save a child's goat."

The look she tossed Marzipan would have frozen a lesser man, but Marzipan didn't care one iota; after all, she was a female goat.

"No," Alron thundered.

Kaelin did her best not to roll her eyes. She failed to hide her annoyance. "I'm sure there's something you want, maybe someone you want disposed of." She took a beat to ponder her next words. "Let me guess. Someone stole your crown. Slept on your moss. Looked at you wrong during a thunderstorm? I take jobs like that all the time. Tell me who, and I'll take care of that after I return the goat."

She didn't need another mission, but when one negotiates with a demigod, it's best not to hold anything back.

"No."

"Now you're just being unreasonable." (Said with a tone that really should've triggered smiting.)

Marzipan bleated in agreement.

"I could just take the goat; it's not like you'd give me too much trouble." Her snark was set on offensive with a side of let's-piss-him-off.

It was not a wise decision, but when diplomacy failed Kaelin, as it always did, her next tactic was always sarcasm and snarkiness, because angering the being that had what you wanted was always a good idea. (I'm also proficient in sarcasm.)

"What did you say?" Alron bellowed, shaking the leaves off trees with his booming incredulity.

"Oh, nothing, just that I could leave here with the goat, and that there's nothing you could do about it." She turned to leave as soon as she saw Marzipan take a step towards her.

Alron galloped until he stood in front of her, blocking her exit. When she tried to take another route, he was in front of her in the blink of an eye, preventing her, once again, from leaving.

"Not so easy to get past me, is it?" He chuckled.

Kaelin sighed. "I didn't want to do this, but you've given me no choice."

This was when she turned to her most successful tactic of getting what she wanted: violence.

I'm not going to lie to you. The battle was epic. Really, one for the ages. It was the kind of fight bards exaggerate and scholars pretend didn't happen. There were lawsuits.

Kaelin drew her daggers, specifically Moonveil and Whisperthorn, two of her favorite daggers. Both very sharp and very pointy. She circled Alron, waiting and watching for the exact moment she should make her move.

Alron struck first, sending lightning arcing through the trees, followed by throwing moss-covered stones faster than Kaelin had ever seen stones thrown. They rained down on her, one after another. It would have broken her spirit, but the moss covering softened their impact.

Lightning arced, moss flew, and somewhere, a tree wept.

There was a pause in the chaos. It was less than a second, but she countered with some impressive knife work, managing to draw blood from several unimportant places. There was a lucky roll where she managed to escape a lightning arc. The ground was truly singed right where she had been standing.

Kaelin deflected a vine whip with Moonveil and cursed herself for wearing non-slip boots when she didn't glide across the grass like she'd planned, causing her swipe with Whisperthorn to miss its mark.

And then, out of the blue, a creature, one that looked vaguely familiar, leapt in, snarled at the demigod, distracting him long enough for Kaelin to regain her footing before disappearing.

None of it was enough, and it looked like Kaelin wasn't going to survive. Alron raised his hand to smite her, when Marzipan charged the demigod, head-butting him at just the right moment.

Begrudgingly impressed by the fact the goat involved itself, Alron halted the fight.

"Instead of fighting to the death, I have decided to let the Hollow's ancient rite decide your fate," Alron proclaimed while standing with his hands on his hips, assured of his own importance.

Kaelin was not convinced, even more annoyed, and angry that this was going to take her even longer than she planned.

"This rite involves three tests of guardianship." Alron projected his voice as if there was an audience to impress instead of just Kaelin and the goat. "If you succeed, you, and that goat"—the demigod thrust his chin towards Marzipan—"shall walk free. If you fail, your soul will be bound here, and you will become the Hollow's next guardian."

Why the demigod would want a failure of a guardian to protect the Hollow is beyond me, Kaelin, and the goat. But those were his rules.

She looked up at the sky. "I should have left the damn goat."

"Since this baffling creature is so important to you, protect it." He clapped.

The forest filled with sticky fog. And for the second time on her journey, the sky opened up, thunder cracked, and water pelted her. Lucky for her, and our story, Kaelin was a quick thinker.

She whipped her belt off and wrapped it around Marzipan's neck seconds before the goat attempted to bolt. Leather ripped through her hand. The searing pain brought tears to her eyes, but she held on. Trees shifted through the mist, creating a maze of trails impossible to navigate on a sunny day, but during a thunderstorm and in a fog that clung to you, it was worse than impossible. (Whatever that word was. I apologize; it seems to have escaped me.)

But Kaelin didn't believe in impossible tasks, so she weaved her way through the maze, dragging the damn goat behind her every step of the way, all while ensuring it wasn't struck by lightning. Eventually, the storm stopped and the fog cleared, leaving them standing in the clearing in front of Alron.

"Hmm, that was supposed to be a challenge. But you not only made it through; the two of you are unscathed." He stroked the point of his goatee. "The next test requires more than just perseverance."

A stone sentinel appeared in front of Kaelin, who stood there dripping water, staring at Alron with murder in her eyes.

"You must answer the sentinel's riddle or . . ."

Kaelin interrupted. "Yeah, yeah, yeah. You've already said. Can we just get on with this whole rite thing? I have better things to do with my time."

Aghast, Alron raised his brows. "Fine, your riddle awaits."

The stone sentinel began to spout out his riddle, but Kaelin swiped Whisperthorn across the sentinel's neck. Then punched him in the face, sending his stone head rolling across the clearing.

Whisperthorn was the perfect dagger to use in this particular instance because the now-extinct flower it was named after helped people hear things never said.

"The answer is 'a shadow,' " she said, her glare stronger than ever.

Alron glared right back. "I should disqualify you for cheating."

"Is my answer correct?" She raised an eyebrow.

You see, whenever there's a test with a riddle, everyone always used the same one. It would have been amusing if it weren't so foolish.

"You know it is," he grumbled. "The last test is a memory of your own guardianship."

Her eyes burned as a memory infiltrated her mind. She almost resigned herself to becoming the Hollow's guardian. It had to be better than dredging up old memories.

"You want story time? Is that really my last test?" Her tone made it sound as if it would be easy. But the last thing Kaelin wanted to do was relive one of the many events in her life that caused her to keep her emotions better protected than a dragon's hoard.

Alron rubbed his hands. "You could just accept the consequences of failing and give me your soul."

"I'd rather not." Kaelin took a deep breath. Short and sweet—that was the way to go. "I was on a mission about ten years ago, and it went terribly wrong. My fellow assassin was caught in the crossfire of a crossbow battle. She was hit. I entered the fray, basically weaponless." She'd brought a knife to a crossbow fight. "And dragged her body back to safety. She lived long enough to thank me for my kindness. But not long enough to see what I did to the individuals that hurt her."

She pushed her hair out of her eyes. It definitely wasn't tears she was wiping away; we all know the Thorn of the North would never be seen crying.

Alron was moved by her story and the vulnerability she would never admit to showing.

He cleared his throat and declared Kaelin the Hollow's Chosen: Guardian of Thresholds, Speaker of Silent Vows, She Who Keeps the Lost, Watcher of Goats, Accidentally Divine, Wielder of Mild Inconvenience, before disappearing into a swirl of mist and stag antlers, leaving behind a map.

Without thinking about it, Kaelin picked up the map and muttered, "That better not be a title I have to put down on paperwork."

Marzipan nuzzled her as the moss glowed with golden light, vines uncurled like waking snakes, and pale blossoms bloomed between Marzipan's hooves.

Kaelin returned the goat to Thimble, waving away any words of gratitude.

The villagers whispered as she got the hell out of town. A woman threw a garland of turnips at her feet. A man tried to hand her a baby. She did not make eye contact. It wasn't until she was well on the road that she realized she had forgotten to pick up the cheese she'd purchased.

3

SPELLBINDING IS NOT CONSENT

"Magical contracts are like tattoos: permanent, usually regretted, and often acquired during moments of panic."

Still muddy, tired, and tragically cheese-less, Kaelin was well outside the town limits of Raven's Hollow and back on track to finish her original Guild assignment. As she rode atop the stolen horse, she vowed not to be derailed by another side quest.

Kaelin should have known better than to make a vow that promised anything. A vow was the one thing that would cause everything to go wrong.

There was no time for shenanigans. And yet, here she was—neck-deep in goat-related detours. The Shadow Guild liked to send multiple assassins to do a job when just one would do. They thought competition brought out the best in everyone they employed. Little did they know, it just caused a dip in morale every time one of the assassins found out they weren't the only one hired for the job.

And here she was, set on finishing the job, and she let herself get waylaid by a goat. What *was* wrong with her—letting a watery-eyed kid reroute her entire deadly agenda?

Kaelin liked to act like she was surprised every time she went off to save someone; let's just say she was the only one that was shocked by her actions.

The horse's ears perked, twisting towards a sound off to the left. Was that a human scream? She should ignore it. She didn't need another distraction.

Another scream pierced the air. Birds flew out of a nearby bush, disturbed by the calamitous wailing. At least I assume that's why they left; birds aren't known for thinking things through.

"Dammit," she cursed, directing the horse towards the sound of suffering.

There's something wrong with Kaelin. It's called a conscience. Highly inconvenient for assassins.

Crashing through the trees with dramatic aplomb, she found herself staring at a youngish man (he was definitely somewhere between the ages of twenty-nine and a hundred), dressed in the most flamboyant mage robes that had ever assaulted her eyes. Really, why do people insist on standing out when it's so much more useful to blend into the shadows?

Yes, she noticed the robes first. It took a moment before she actually saw why the man was screaming.

The mage was being held by his neck by a vine, apparently a sentient one with a grudge.

"Oh, thank the gods, someone to help me." The man's eyes were pleading while his hands were the only thing keeping the plant from finishing him off.

Kaelin contemplated her life at this point. Should she just turn around and leave? Anyone being strangled by a vine probably did something to deserve it. Vines weren't known for their tempers. She pulled the reins of her stolen horse. Another side quest wasn't on her schedule for today.

"Please, if you leave, I'll be soulbound to a vine demon with commitment issues," the man begged, his magenta and lime green robes swirled around his feet. "I swear there's a perfectly good reason I'm in this predicament."

The horse turned back. Not Kaelin, but the horse. She sighed, it appeared she was going to have to save the mage. Looking around, figuring out the best approach, she noticed a scroll.

(Was that romantic binding language in ancient Arcanum?)

I can assure you, not only was it ancient Arcanum, it was also a soulbinding spell. The mage was definitely the cause of his current situation.

"Dammit, you did this, didn't you?" she half yelled, half muttered, already knowing the answer.

Taking a step forward, she brandished Moonveil in an attempt to get the vine to let go of the man's neck. Of course, it was futile, and she had to use the dagger to cut him free.

Thankfully, her swiping actions somehow banished the last of the magical effects. When someone says love hurts, they definitely mean it: just look at what happened to the poor vine. It slithered off to go nurse its wounds and maybe propagate. Kaelin watched until she was sure the danger was over.

The mage took a knee and bowed his head. He looked up, and words Kaelin never wanted to hear left his mouth. "You saved me, that means we're fate-bound companions now."

"No." She walked backwards away from him. "Absolutely not. Whatever spell you cast. Undo it. now!"

Stomping around the small clearing, Kaelin muttered every single spell that had even an inkling of being able to break the bond. Unfortunately, she really sucked at magic. It never ended in a catastrophe; it just never really worked. It was kind of like baking: even if you have all the right ingredients, things just go wrong.

She turned to the mage. "Fix this or I'm going to use my least favorite dagger on you."

Kaelin didn't have a favorite, or a least favorite; she loved all her daggers equally. However, the mage didn't know that.

He scrambled to undo the spell. Instead, lightning would have struck him, had Kaelin not shoved him out of the way. She really needed to make up her mind. If she'd let the lightning strike him, the spell might've broken—assuming he didn't survive. Which was a risk she was almost willing to accept.

Then there was a grey cloud that hovered over her and wouldn't leave her alone. She got an unexpected shower when she poked it with Mercy.

The mage was about to try again when, out of nowhere, a howl reverberated through the woods. A howl Kaelin recognized made the no longer strangled mage nearly jump out of his robes, and sent the horse rearing like it'd just seen a tax collector and was ready to bolt into the next kingdom.

She grabbed the horse's reins before his hooves hit the ground, glared at the mage with daggers in her eyes (not literal ones, in case you were confused) and cursed her animal companion.

"I left you an entire side of venison and told you to stay home." Her exasperation was visible in every inch of her body.

Timber loped into view, looking like a majestic feral gremlin, if you ignored her tongue hanging out the side of her mouth—or maybe the tongue was what really brought home her vibe.

She approached Kaelin, sat in front of her, and offered a paw while staring the assassin down with a very stereotypical wolfdog stare.

"Oh my, she's magnificent." The mage stared at Timber. His eyes glowing with shock and admiration. "Does she accept bribes? I have some dried mangoes."

Dogs always know where the story's going. That's why they show up right before it gets worse—with smug paws and excellent timing.

"Don't cast another spell." Kaelin stood there, dripping wet, eyes darting between the mage and her dog, unsure what to do with either one of them.

"But you said . . ."

Kaelin rolled her eyes. "I know what I said. But if you continue, one of us is going to die, and I don't want it to be me, or my dog."

She didn't want to, but she reached down and petted Timber. The lolling tongue was too much to resist.

"And no, she doesn't accept bribes, especially not mangoes. No matter what she tells herself." Kaelin crossed her arms. It was meant to look tough; it almost succeeded. The dog rolling on its back at Kaelin's feet really wasn't helping with the image.

"Well then, if I'm along for the journey, I might as well introduce myself." He held out his hand.

Kaelin stared at it. She didn't shake it. She didn't move. She just . . . stared.

Timber, however, padded over and sat on his feet. The mage wobbled, flailed, and landed on his arse in the mud. Normally, Kaelin would feel sorry for his clothes, but the mud could only make them look better.

He looked up at her, robes soaked and smile unwavering. "I'm Tobias Fenwick. Sorcerer mage extraordinaire at your service. Or at least, that's the goal."

He attempted a bow from the ground. The wind rustled his sleeves as if they were in on the performance.

"You're extraordinarily bad at magic. That's for sure," Kaelin said. It wasn't very nice of her, but she was ready to move on, done with this interlude.

Tobias grinned, unaware or unwilling to acknowledge her insult. "I'm a work in progress. I left the world of magical academia to develop my skills and learn real magic. Not that Academy fluff they insist on teaching you."

"You should probably go back. I think the fluff might suit you."

Tobias just shook his head. "It didn't, and then I found this." He held up the scroll. The scroll was just one of the items he found. The more interesting one was the forbidden Spellbook of Binding and Benevolence. But he wasn't ready to talk about that. "I was trying a spell to help convince people to like me, just a little. But things went awry rather quickly."

She just stared. Then blinked. "Really, you tried to cast a spell that overrides consent? No wonder it went so very wrong."

"It didn't go that badly. I wanted to find someone with protective instincts, and you showed up. It was like the spell brought you to me."

Kaelin rolled her eyes. "Trust me, it didn't. The scream did, sticking me with another damn side quest."

"Oh, are you on a quest? I can help. You should bring me along. I can be your sidekick. I'm very good at sidekick things."

The scroll glowed like it was happy. It had no right to be happy—scrolls that orchestrate magical life-bonding shenanigans should at least have the decency to sulk.

"This isn't a buddy adventure," Kaelin ground out. "I work alone."

The presence of the horse and the dog undercut her words. Tobias was intelligent enough not to point that out.

He grinned. "Okay, I'll try to break the spell again. There's gotta be something that will work."

He stroked his chin, pondering what words would do the trick. If he had stayed at the Academy, he would have known her rescuing him twice cemented the bonding. But he had dropped out before he got to that lesson.

He grabbed his wand from a pocket hidden somewhere in his robes. Tobias flourished once . . . twice . . . thrice—*BOOM*. A glitter bomb exploded across the clearing.

Kaelin recoiled like it was acid. "Nope. Absolutely not. I draw the line at glitter."

"Oops," Tobias said brightly. "Wrong incantation."

His second attempt? All their rations turned into cupcakes.

Timber and Tobias each ate one.

Kaelin muttered, "Why couldn't it be cheese?"

Tobias glanced over at her. "So, you like cheese. What do you know, I like cheese too." He smiled so wide Kaelin thought his face might break. He was so happy they had something in common. But really, doesn't everyone like cheese?

"Don't try—"

It was too late; Tobias had already tried to break the spell again, this time turning Timber's fur a sparkly shade of purple. It was a good look for her. Not that Timber thought so, she growled. Tobias quaked. The spell wore off. He offered the dog a piece of jerky as an apology.

Kaelin couldn't take another attempt at breaking this forsaken bond, a curse she was stuck with. She gritted her teeth and gave in.

"I guess I'm stuck with you for now," she ground out.

Tobias might have clapped with joy. (Sorry, I turned my back for a moment.) He was looking forward to the adventure and getting to know his new companions.

Kaelin allowed the mage to ride the stolen horse. She figured her clothing was more suited for walking.

"I shall call this magnificent steed 'Edelwhin the Valiant.' " An epic name for a pretty standard horse.

"Edelwhin? Sounds like the kind of horse that wears embroidered saddle blankets and recites poetry. I'm calling him Ed."

Timber snorted, which either meant she agreed, or she just really hated embroidered saddle blankets. Hard to say with her. But for the record, *Ed* got a tail wag. 'Edelwhin the Valiant' got a raised leg and suspicious sniff.

As they continued on their way, Tobias chatted. Kaelin grumbled. Timber happily accepted jerky from the mage, tail wagging like he'd just solved world peace.

Tobias might even be her new favorite person—though Kaelin suspected it was just the snacks.

Still, it was annoying. Almost as annoying as the mage's nonstop talking.

She sighed and wondered how long it would take before she regretted every decision that led her to this moment.

Spoiler: not long.

And thus, the assassin, the mage, and the slightly judgmental dog set out towards destiny—or more likely, another horrible side quest.

4

Sidekick: Unwanted, Uninvited, Unbreakable

"Fate rarely asks for your opinion. Especially when assigning sidekicks."

They had only been on the road for a day and a half. Just thirty-six hours. Or to put it another way, two thousand one hundred and sixty minutes—each one dragging longer than a poet reciting their own work before lighting the funeral pyre. However, for Kaelin, it felt less like a journey and more like the opening scene of eternal damnation.

Tobias chattered incessantly—there was no other way to chatter, really—and she had ridden ahead purely for survival. Not far enough, though. His low murmur still carried on the wind as he narrated every rock, leaf, and slightly interesting patch of dirt to Timber.

Timber, traitor that she was, had chosen him over her. And Kaelin wasn't sure which betrayal stung more: the abandonment or the beef jerky. Kaelin told herself it didn't bother her.

But it did. Almost as much as Tobias's ability to find personal meaning in moss.

What Kaelin didn't know was that Timber was sticking close to Tobias out of spite for being left behind. Loyalty had its price, and apparently today the price was cured meat and a three-hour commentary on lichen.

If Timber had been less patient with humans, she might have bitten him already, just a nip, nothing fatal. It still wasn't completely out of the question; she was saving it as her secret weapon. Very useful, should he begin another dissertation on bark textures and their importance in potion work. And honestly? I wouldn't blame her. Have you ever listened to anyone talk about tree bark? Exactly. Torture.

"Timber, look there!" He pointed to teal flowers cascading down the cliffside. "That's Water's Mist. It's incredibly rare. Look how it tumbles down its vine, resembling a waterfall in motion. And the blue-green color—it practically shimmers. It's stunning, isn't it?"

Kaelin slowed despite herself. His excitement crashed through the bond between them, infectious and irritating all at once. But you want to know what was even worse, at least to her? She felt her own interest stirring. She'd always loved flowers—the stranger, the better—and she'd only ever seen the Water's Mist once before.

Which was how, despite spending the last four hours calculating how many days she had to wait before she could ditch him without triggering some cosmic retribution (five and a half, if she was creative), she found herself easing her horse up beside him.

All because she wanted to know more about a flower.

It was infuriating.

Numerous pontifications on various fauna and flora along their route, several contemplations of which dagger would end the nature chatter most clearly, and too many hours to count—they arrived at a crumbling toll station swarmed by clerics.

Kaelin sighed. Timber groaned. Tobias gasped at the ivy-covered stonework as if it was a rare relic of architectural wonder.

Someone should have told him: nothing good ever came of running into a group of clerics.

"Halt." The tallest of the clerics ordered, his long robes spilling over his body like a muddy waterfall. "According to the laws of passage, only those who qualify under subsection twenty-one(b) of chapter two hundred and fourteen are permitted to cross without providing proper papers."

"Papers?" Tobias blinked. "I've crossed here before—no one ever mentioned paperwork."

Kaelin tried to push her way past the gate, only to slam into a wall that buzzed with sanctimonious energy. "Let me pass. I don't have time for bureaucratic nonsense."

Timber walked up to each of the clerics, sniffed, then moved on. She sat next to Kaelin with all the judgment of a goddess, tail flicking in irritation. Not a single one of the clerics smelled of beef jerky.

"Let us pass, or you'll get to meet Glassfire." Kaelin ground her teeth. "I promise you won't like it."

Tobias held up his hand. "They're just doing their job." He turned back to the clerics. "Who are you and what's the basis for your authority?"

The leader took a step forward, chest puffed. "We are the Order of Binding Contracts. Guardians of paperwork. Scribes of legality. Champions of subsection clarity. Heralds of paragraph precision. Defenders of proper formatting. None shall pass without filing a Form of Purpose."

For a brief moment Kaelin thought the cleric looked familiar. The thought disappeared as her irritation bubbled to the surface. "I have your form right here." She drew one of her many blades and tapped it against her palm.

A second cleric stepped forward. "I'm afraid that doesn't qualify as an exception to the Form of Purpose." He unrolled a scroll. It hit the dirt with a thud and unrolled for yards. "You must fill out this form . . . in triplicate." His tone was solemn, as if he'd just pronounced a death sentence.

What the clerics forgot—along with everyone else in the region—was that the Order of Binding Contracts was cursed to only speak in legalese, never give direct answers, and create endless amounts of paperwork wherever they went.

Tobias leaned over, examining the scroll. "Look at the handwriting. Immaculate. The calligraphy is truly inspiring. The flourishes on the serifs are absolutely sublime. But is this parchment . . . weeping?"

The ink dripped like black tears.

"If it's not, it will be soon." Kaelin mentally moved Tobias to the top of her dagger list.

Timber yawned, walked over, circled three times, and laid herself down on the bottom third of the scroll. The clerics gasped as though she'd destroyed a holy relic.

Tobias stepped towards the clerics. "I'm so sorry for our companion. She's impatient when it comes to paperwork."

"How dare you make excuses for that . . . that . . . beast." The leader paced back and forth, polished head gleaming. "It has committed an unspeakable crime: obstructing subsection legibility."

Kaelin's grip tightened on her dagger. No one insulted Timber. No one.

Tobias grabbed her shoulder. She shook him off, but didn't attack the clerics. It was a test of her self-control. A test no one was sure she was going to pass.

The mage placed himself between her and the clerics. He really didn't want her to kill anyone today, and she seemed irritated enough to do so.

"I can handle this," Tobias whispered before addressing the clerics. "Is there another form, a shorter one perhaps, that would allow us to pass?"

One of the clerics chimed in, "What about subsection fourteen (h) of chapter thirty-two entitled 'Emergency Crossings?'"

"We don't know that this is an emergency," another one responded.

One cleric adjusted his spectacles. "We cannot declare an emergency without first filing the Emergency Declaration Addendum."

"It's going to be an emergency if they don't let us pass," Kaelin muttered.

Timber howled in solidarity—or possibly just out of sheer boredom.

"Are there any exceptions that don't require any paperwork?" Tobias asked.

Kaelin rolled her eyes as the thought that there were daggers less sharp than Tobias's ability to miss the point flew through her mind.

The collective gasp from the clerics was so dramatic it nearly summoned a thunderstorm. Instead, it summoned something worse: a paper elemental—an unholy mass of shredded contracts, stamped seals, and ink that bled like open wounds.

The thing rose from the scroll pile, towering over them. Its parchment skin glowed with fine print. Its first cry was the sound of forty quills scratching in unison.

"Oh no," Tobias whispered. Sweat dripped down his temple. "It's bound in subclauses!"

Kaelin groaned and drew Mercy. "Does everything you touch conjure a monster?"

"That's unfair. Sometimes I conjure explosions."

The elemental lashed out, slapping Kaelin across the chest with a massive sheet stamped in crimson: denied. She staggered back, spitting out paper fibers.

Then came the red tape. Actual red tape. It shot out like tentacles, binding her arms in regulations so tight she could practically *hear* the legalese squeaking. Timber barked, lunged, and shredded the tape into confetti. The clerics gasped as though she'd desecrated their holy texts.

Tobias raised his staff. "Don't worry, I've got this!"

His spell fizzled, then exploded into shimmering gold dust. The ink on the elemental turned to glitter, cascading in fabulous, sparkling tears.

"Really?" Kaelin ducked as the elemental threw a cascade of parchment like throwing stars. "You made it fabulous?"

"Accidentally!" he squeaked. "But also—look how it catches the light!"

The elemental shrieked in contract jargon, flinging notarized seals like coins at a wedding. One hit Tobias square on the forehead. It stuck there, sizzling: see appendix b.

Timber, goddess that she was, waded straight into the mess, grabbed the scrolly core, and shook it violently like a chew toy. With each thrash, legal citations rained down like snow. The clerics wailed, clutching their beads of bureaucracy.

Finally, with a decisive *snap* of her jaws, Timber shredded the last binding clause. The enchantment broke. The elemental collapsed into a sad heap of bureaucratic dust. The cursed scroll shriveled, curled, and vanished with the faintest sound of a filing cabinet slamming shut.

The invisible wall shimmered, then vanished.

"Fine," the lead cleric said, brushing glitter from his robes with deep bureaucratic resignation. "We shall grant you a special dispensation to pass."

Timber trotted across first, tail high, glitter clinging to her fur like she was born for the runway. Tobias followed, looking far too pleased with the outcome.

Kaelin hesitated, Mercy still in her hand. She looked at the glitter, at the clerics, at Tobias's proud face. Then—against all odds—she grinned. Once. Maybe.

Tobias froze, wide-eyed. "Did you just— Was that— Did you smile?"

"No."

Timber sneezed glitter like even she didn't believe it.

That moment was Kaelin smiling. No, really. It was like an eclipse: brief, strange, and likely to trigger the end of days.

5

THE CHICKEN MUST DIE

"Legends speak of dragons and demons. No one warns you about poultry and pyromancy."

By the time the clerics let them through, Kaelin had sworn three new oaths never to step foot near parchment again. They weren't written down; if they were, she would have set them on fire and scattered the ashes just to be sure they were truly destroyed. Now, all she wanted to do was get as far away from the toll station as possible. She might have been tired, but if she was forced to deal with any more bureaucracy today, she would be leaving Mercy sheathed and using another one of her daggers. Whisperthorn was feeling neglected lately.

"Look, a stream!" Tobias pointed like a kid spotting his first unicorn. "We have to stay here for the night. It's so relaxing. Just what we need after, well, you know."

She considered slipping away while he was distracted. It wouldn't be hard—her shadow vanished quieter than most people's footsteps. But Timber had already committed treason by splashing happily in the stream like a puppy. Tobias threw a stick. Her dog swam after it, snapping the stick in two instead of bringing it back.

Kaelin sighed. It appeared the decision of where to sleep had been made for her. It was a rather picturesque spot, not that she'd admit it to anyone, not even herself.

"You should rest." Tobias tried to help her with her pack.

She shrugged him off. It's not like she needed his help. Travel companions made her wary, too many bodies to keep safe.

"I can at least cook for us."

He could not cook for them. This was a skill that Tobias did not possess. He struggled in a well-appointed kitchen, so cooking over a campfire was a challenge he was not prepared to handle.

The smell of scorched bacon drifted across the camp like a warning. Kaelin briefly considered adding Tobias to her list of things she'd kill before breakfast—right between mercenaries and bureaucrats. Instead, she sighed the sigh of the tragically overworked and took over. Years of being on the road, camping in random places, had helped her develop certain skills, like cooking an edible dinner on an open fire. She finished cooking what was left of the bacon, toasted some bread, and constructed a pretty tasty sandwich.

"So, since we're stuck together, why don't we get to know each other?" Tobias needed to fill the silence with something. "I'll go first. I was attending university for mages, but it was all so theoretical. Five years ago, I left to learn magic out in the world. You know, the hands-on approach."

Kaelin deadpanned, "Congratulations. You've burned the bacon. Consider yourself graduated."

"My family is still disappointed with me. Convinced I made the worst decision ever." Tobias took a bite of his dinner. "What about you? Why are you on the road?"

She stared at him. Said nothing. Took a bite of her sandwich.

Ah yes, the classic companion dinner. One offers a confession about life's purpose, the other contributes bread, bacon, and brooding. Balanced. Really.

Timber stole the rest of Tobias's sandwich before padding over to lay down next to Kaelin, laying her head in the assassin's lap. Kaelin pretended not to notice. She didn't smile. She definitely didn't. If anyone suggested she had, she would stab them. With Whisperthorn, for variety's sake. The poor dagger deserved attention.

Kaelin was ready early the next morning. Not only was she ready, she was impatient to get going. If things had gone as planned, she'd be in Eldreach in the next two days. Instead, she was still over a week away; she had an incompetent new companion, a disloyal dog, and was still lacking in her favorite snack, cheese.

A quick glance around the camp confirmed everyone was still asleep. She growled in frustration but stuck around, all while silently listing everything she could stab in her vicinity and which of her daggers she would use to do so. Her dagger, Glassfire, was thought of a lot.

I'm not sure why Kaelin didn't leave everyone behind. Actually, I do know, but it's more fun watching her pretend she doesn't.

"Did you say something?" Tobias stepped out of his tent, stretching like a cat in the sun after an extremely satisfying afternoon nap.

Kaelin rolled her eyes. "It's time to get on the road."

She turned to put her pack on Ed. Ed is the horse, in case you've forgotten. Kaelin certainly hadn't—he was the only one who listened without arguing.

"Can we . . ," Tobias started. "About five years ago, I was in a town. There was a fire-breathing chicken. They contained it, but maybe we can check."

Her head moved so fast a muscle in her neck protested. "Did you say fire-breathing chicken?"

"Yes, I think his name was Percival." He rubbed the back of his neck.

"Why in the world would I care what the chicken's name is?" She crossed her arms, intrigued despite knowing better. And by 'knowing better,' I mean: she's done this exact thing before and it ended with scorch marks and stitches. Did she learn? No. But don't tell her I said that.

Tobias smiled. "He's Skritch's mascot." He delivered the response with the smooth indifference of someone who has clearly never been attacked by livestock.

Kaelin's glare was sharper than her extra dagger. "You want me to go to a town that's made the decision that a fire-breathing chicken is its mascot?"

The goofy grin and careless shrug had her counting the number of ways she could use Moonveil, another dagger named after another extinct flower, to cause pain without killing him.

"They have an excellent cheese shop there too," Tobias added as if a good smoked gouda was the deciding factor for her to risk third-degree burns from poultry.

Kaelin stopped, hand frozen mid-air as the conflict between her desire for murder or mozzarella created an internal debate that left Moonveil alone in its sheath. Cheese was not just a snack; it was perfection, some might even say destiny, aged for twelve months and wrapped in wax. Timber's head popped up, clearly not actually sleeping, despite the raucous snoring that had been the soundtrack of the morning.

It was quite apparent that the two shared a love of cheese. While Timber did prefer bacon, her next favorite food was a sharp cheddar.

Kaelin would never admit it aloud, but cheese was her Achilles heel. Well, that and emotionally vulnerable conversations. The cheese was more likely to kill her.

Which was why, after only a brief moment of hesitation, these words fell from her lips: "We might as well head into Skritch."

Tobias, quite literally, jumped with joy, tripped over his cloak, stumbled three steps directly into Timber, who he tried to avoid. But she leapt to her feet, moved directly into the path he was careening down, causing him to flip arse-over-head, landing on his back, staring at the sky. And thus, Tobias began his morning ritual of gravity appreciation.

"Enthusiasm only causes trouble. Let's go, so we have time for che—the chicken." Kaelin didn't laugh. She wanted to, but laughing was a chink in her armor that she would never abide. She led Ed away from the campsite so no one could see her struggle—with her pack, her patience, or the undeniable pull of dairy products.

She was still leading Ed when they passed the NOW ENTERING SKRITCH sign. Not that she needed it to know exactly where she was. The oversized rooster burning down winter solstice decorations with a singing *CAW-CAW* clued her in.

The fire brigade, two gnomes and a goat, were trying to stop the destruction. But they were no match for a bird three times the size of a golden retriever.

Kaelin rolled her eyes as she took one step towards the melee in front of her. But she was almost run over by someone in a chef's hat. Finlo Quickwhisk ran after the pyrotechnic poultry yelling, "I swear I didn't use magic this time." He waved a wooden spoon over his head as if he wielded a dangerous weapon. "It was a cream-based casserole; it shouldn't have caused flames, indigestion maybe, but not fire."

Brenna Birchbake stood in the doorway of her cheese shop, arms folded, shaking her head. The only sign of her amusement was a quick twitch of her lips before she sighed and chased after her husband.

You might not know Finlo and Brenna—Kaelin certainly didn't—but I'm told the T.A.L.E.S. Librarian has a copy of their story, or as I like to call it, Percival's origin story. Yes, the fire-breathing rooster was the great Percival, town mascot of Skritch, whether he liked it or not. Most days he didn't mind; today was not most days.

Kaelin sighed. She wanted to ignore the foul fowl, go to the cheese shop, and buy some Havarti. After all, her goals here were much like her goals everywhere else: stab it, buy cheese, leave town.

Her hand hovered over her dagger as the poultry approached the cheese shop. There wasn't much that would force her to act—except protecting a pound of provolone. That, apparently, ranked higher than most people. Provolone always kept its promises with its beautiful nutty flavor and creamy texture.

The padding of paws stopped beside her. Timber eyed the cheese shop and howled, which did nothing to bring attention to them. After all, the tinsel was singed and all that was left of the snowman was a sad puddle with a smoking corn-cob pipe. Watching the destruction didn't bother the assassin, but she could tell it bothered the townfolk. Especially when all that remained of the decorated tree was a pile of ash and a cinnamon-smelling puff of smoke.

The town fire brigade was racing towards the open fire. Well, the goat was. The two gnomes were moving much slower, wary of what Percival would do next. The gnomes' reluctance was the main reason the goat was in charge, despite his habit of chasing his tail in an emergency. At least he wasn't afraid of the rooster. Auntie Thyme was screaming about turning Finlo into a scone, for real this time.

No one noticed Kaelin, her companion creature, or Ed standing there. Not many people noticed her, and if they did, the black hood normally convinced them to pretend they didn't.

Tobias let out a low whistle as he stumbled his way towards her, brushing soot from his cloak and only managing to smear it worse. He shaded his eyes like a man admiring a sunrise, not a rooster-induced inferno. "This is worse than I hoped."

"Was it worse than you expected?" she muttered.

He grinned, fishing through his pockets until he found his notebook. He squinted through a haze of smoke as he flipped through the pages until he found whatever he was looking for.

Snapping the book closed, he looked up at her. "Expected? Oh, I never expect the worst. I only hope. Hoping's shinier."

Her glare promised the pain of a thousand paper cuts. "That's a good way to get yourself killed."

"Maybe," Tobias said as he reached into his pocket. When he pulled it out, his fingers shimmered, and he flicked glitter from his thumb so it sparkled in the smoky air. "But at least I'll die fabulous."

Kaelin's dagger hand twitched. She avoided glitter the same way she avoided feelings—they were both messy, lingering, impossible to scrape off. Provolone was one thing. Glittered poultry was another.

Then Tobias did the most Tobias thing: he reached for her hand, gentle, earnest. "You can't stab Percival."

Kaelin froze. She didn't notice touch—never had. And Tobias seemed to realize it too, because the moment stretched a beat too long—until awareness flickered, sharp as a blade. Safer thought: stab him. Simpler. Daggers never asked what a touch meant.

"Why did you bring me here if it wasn't to kill the chicken?" she snapped, voice sharp enough to cover the unsettling flicker of awareness.

And here, dear reader, we have what most romance scholars call a *moment*. Please don't tell Kaelin that; she might stab me too.

"We can take care of Percival, not kill him. The town would never forgive us." He dropped her hand as if it burned him, and instinctively patted Ed's flank. The glittered handprint he'd left on the horse's hide made Kaelin consider not only stabbing him but also burning his fashion sense.

She kept her dagger sheathed. For now.

"If I'm not allowed to stab the chicken, what do you suggest I do?"

I wish I could say Tobias had a plan, but that would be a lie, and there's no reason to lie ... yet.

"Something to extinguish the fire?" Tobias snapped his fingers over his head as if he had said something revolutionary. "A dessert? Custard maybe? It helps with dragons, it could work on chickens."

"Sounds too simple." Her tone was as flat as an abandoned pancake after Sunday brunch.

It was at this point that Brenna heard the newcomers and dragged Finlo over to them. "I hate to interrupt, but we've tried tarts, donuts, even a soufflé, even after that one incident." She eyed Finlo. "But that's neither here nor there. The fire breathing always returns."

"You don't have to tell everyone about the sentient soufflés. It's been years since that happened." Finlo sighed, eyeing the rooster warily.

Brenna smiled. "I didn't tell them. You did."

"I remember you two." Tobias bounced from one foot to another. "This all started because of your savory tart. And you ..." He pointed at Brenna. "You own the cheese shop."

Kaelin's head snapped towards the young woman like she'd just whispered the holy word: cheese. Timber sat at her feet, eyes wide with canine devotion. Both assassin and hound realized their dreams of dairy might come true. For Kaelin, she was now determined to disarm Percival. Timber, on the other hand, hoped her woeful eyes would do the trick.

"Follow me." Brenna waved the group on. "That is, if you're serious about helping with Percival."

Timber followed first, then Kaelin, leading Ed along with her. Tobias had been distracted, so he scurried to catch up.

"Why would anyone name a rooster?" Kaelin muttered. "Especially when they're nothing but trouble."

"You named the horse Ed." Tobias pointed out.

Kaelin stroked the hilt of her dagger. Tobias gulped.

"You named him Edelwhin. I refused to call him by such a ridiculous name."

And thus, dear reader, our assassin chose cheese over poultry, restraint over stabbing, and reality over ridiculous names. For now.

Kaelin had followed Brenna under the holy conviction that they were heading to the cheese shop. Instead, she found herself in a kitchen where the utensils seemed to judge her life choices. For once, she didn't bother hiding the disappointment.

Brenna noticed the sag in the assassin's shoulders and the sad eyes of the woman's companion creature. "Were you hoping for something different?"

Timber pawed at Brenna, unleashing a whine so tragic it belonged in an opera about lost cheese.

"No, it's best if we get to work neutralizing the chicken."

Finlo lunged for a spoon; it dodged with the disdain of a fencing master. "He's a rooster," he added primly, as if taxonomy mattered when things were on fire.

Kaelin's eyes bored into him, sharp as Whisperthorn and just as deadly.

He cleared his throat. "Chicken's fine."

"This is wonderful, vibrating with magic. Where should we start?" Tobias tilted his head. "She won't admit it," he all but sang, "but Kaelin's hoping for cheese."

And there, dear reader, he committed the most dangerous act in existence: telling the truth about Kaelin out loud.

"That's easy enough to do." Brenna smiled before disappearing into the pantry.

Tobias tripped over a table leg and stumbled towards the counter. When he reached out to steady himself, he accidentally touched a whisk, which had the audacity to whack him on the hand as he was still careening towards a wooden chair. Somehow, he landed arse-first in the chair, looking smug, as though the whole routine had been intentional. Kaelin's lip twitched before she buried the smile. He didn't deserve encouragement.

A giggle escaped before he pulled himself together. "I think I have a magic spell that we can infuse the custard with. It should nullify whatever is causing Percival to breathe fire."

"No magic!" Brenna and Finlo yelled together.

She came back with a tray so glorious it deserved its own choir—cheeses of every type and scent, some Kaelin didn't even recognize. For a heartbeat, she forgot the rooster, the fire, even Tobias. Almost.

She pulled her gaze away from the mountain of goodness that was presented before her. "Why no magic?"

Finlo sighed, finding great interest in something on the floor. "Cooking and spells don't mix. Especially not with dragon peppers. That's . . . how we got the pyrotechnic Percival."

"Should be fine, we won't be using any dragon peppers." Tobias rubbed his chin. "I've never caused anything to become a pyromaniac before."

"There's always a first time," Kaelin added. It wasn't a helpful comment, but it was the first thing that popped into her head.

Tobias grinned, his expression didn't match his words. "You're not helping."

Everyone joined Tobias at the table, including the cheese plate. Outside, the sky lit up as a loud *caw-caw* echoed through the air.

"I don't think we can do this without magic," Tobias said. "We should avoid the dragon peppers though. Try something a little less spicy."

"Make the custard," Kaelin ordered. "Infuse it with something that doesn't include a binding spell, coating Percival in magenta glitter, or calling forth any type of demon." She popped a piece of cheddar into her mouth. "I'm going to see what the damn rooster is up to now."

She took another handful of cheese and headed outside. Things were . . . calm. Normal even. An old woman walked by, the one who had chased Finlo earlier. Kaelin stopped her.

"Where's the rooster?"

Auntie Thyme shrugged. "Left. And good riddance. I don't know why the mayor insisted on a town mascot. We're better off without him. That chicken was a menace before he ate Finlo's galette."

Kaelin didn't say a word. She turned back towards the house, walked straight into the kitchen where everyone except Timber was working diligently on a custard-filled donut.

Tobias stirred the custard, sprinkling a potion in as he did so. "I think the custard donut will soothe Percival; I know it would soothe me."

"We have a problem," Kaelin said.

Brenna looked up. "Worse than Percival?"

"Percival is gone."

As if to confirm, a deafening *CAW-CAW* split the sky, followed by a suspiciously rooster-shaped shadow streaking past the window.

"Gone where?" Tobias asked.

Kaelin grabbed another fistful of cheddar. "Wherever chickens go before disaster."

Tobias turned back to the custard and continued to stir.

And there it was, dear reader: the moment when everything should have stopped. Should have. Instead, Tobias added more sugar, Finlo scolded him, and Kaelin realized she was the only person in the room who understood that the apocalypse was already loose . . . feathered, furious, and probably flammable.

6

POTIONS OF REGRET (NOW WITH EXTRA HONESTY)

"Truth, when distilled, is best served in very small doses. Preferably not on an empty stomach. Or with traveling companions. Or at all, really."

"Are you finished with your custard bombs, or whatever it is you're insisting on calling them?" Kaelin paced the length of Finlo's home, itching to stab something and leave—find Percival, disable the rooster, and get back to the mission she'd been hired to carry out.

Tobias looked up, his hair dusted with flour. "I think so. I've added a preservative spell that uses rosemary for aroma . . ." He paused before muttering, "or maybe immortality . . . This is on top of the extinguishing tonic we added to the custard."

"Fine, does that mean we can leave?" She stopped, hands on her hips. "I have things I should be doing, but you insisted on this side quest."

Finlo looked up from the bag he was filling with donuts. "I hope this works. I let Tobias handle the magic; food and magic don't really go together for me."

Brenna put her hand on his shoulder as if to say thank you, but they didn't need to know that. Tobias sneezed, creating a cloud of flour that hid Kaelin's eye roll.

Timber looked longingly at the bag.

"Those are not for you. Unless you start breathing fire."

Timber raised an eyebrow, suggesting that could be arranged.

"Don't even think of it. I'll leave you behind somewhere like the deserts of Saltmere."

The dog sighed, pressing her snout into Kaelin's empty hand. The assassin rubbed the top of Timber's head without a conscious thought.

Finlo handed her the bag. Tobias muttered something about ingredients for a healing tonic and snagged a vial of something. Kaelin stared longingly at the barely touched cheese tray as if it was the last bastion of goodness in an otherwise desolate world.

Brenna stepped towards her. "I packed this for you. It's a rind of smoked gouda, in case of an emergency."

Timber's tail thumped against the floor, its rhythm steady enough to start a contra dance party.

If fate had been paying attention, it would have sent them home. Unfortunately, fate was too busy laughing. And thus they departed, armed with pastries and poor decisions. And emergency cheese, how could I forget that important detail?

When Tobias tripped over a root, Kaelin caught his elbow without thinking. He blinked, surprised, as if she'd just performed a miracle instead of basic physics.

"Don't make it a moment," she warned.

He made it a moment anyway.

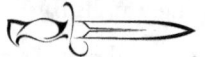

One day and two nights passed, and the only sign of Percival was the burned remnants he had left in his wake. But the rooster, nowhere to be found.

Kaelin stood with a town looming before her. Ed on her left, Timber on her right, she tossed a dagger into the air, caught it on repeat. This time it was Aurora's End—named for a flower that looked merciful until it wasn't. The only thing missing from the scene was her cloak blowing in the wind. It would have looked majestic. Unfortunately, Tobias had turned the garment into a ferret, the ferret had run away, and now the assassin needed a new cloak.

The breeze carried the scent of cinnamon and sanctimony from the town. Kaelin scowled. A town shouldn't smell like snickerdoodles. Timber's tongue lolled out of her mouth; she didn't agree with her human. In fact, a cookie sounded really good right about now.

"I should have picked up a health tonic before leaving Skritch," Kaelin muttered to herself and anyone who chose to listen.

Tobias shuffled up, carrying two plates of something that looked almost edible. "Cloverbite is right there. We could stop."

Timber sniffed. The acrid smell emanating from the plate had the dog questioning whether it should be consumed.

"As long as it doesn't delay us. There's a rampaging rooster on the loose—not to mention my actual mission. The longer it takes me to get to King Varric, the more damage he's going to do." Kaelin mounted Ed.

Tobias hesitated for half a beat, but he couldn't stop himself from asking the question. "What is your mission?"

"You don't want to know." Kaelin clicked her tongue, and Ed surged forward.

Ah, deflection, a necessary skill of the trade.

They trotted in silence until they were no longer looking at the town from a distance but had arrived and stood in front of a building that leaned precariously to the left, almost touching the shop next door. A sign creaking in the wind labeled the toppling building as the apothecary. The letters were barely visible, faded from years of unpredictable weather.

"Let's go in." Tobias inched towards the door. "Didn't you say something about wanting a healing spell? And look, they're having a sale."

Kaelin raised an eyebrow. The shop in front of her looked like it had been dragged through a portal and rebuilt by someone who hated right angles and customer safety. She held her hand up to stop Tobias from entering, but the door had already screeched its betrayal. With a roll of her eyes, she followed him inside.

Timber took one sniff, shook her head, and curled up next to Ed. The shop was no place for a sane dog.

Kaelin squinted as her eyes adjusted to the dim lighting and dust motes disturbed by their entrance. Apothecaries should smell like sage and salvation. This one smelled more like burned sugar and bad decisions. She should have turned around and left. Instead, she perused the potions, healing salves, elixirs, and tinctures that could double as weapons. She would have shopped longer, but various teapots whistled every time she walked by.

"Look at all these potions. There's one for hair growth—ooh look, emotional stability, and there's your health repair." Tobias turned from one shelf of vials to the next. His excitement vibrated from him in waves. "Is that a buy-two-get-one-curse-free sale?"

He picked up a heart-shaped bottle. "This one's for love."

"Then put it down before it attacks you," Kaelin said.

He grinned. "You think I'm irresistible even to potions?"

"No, I think you're allergic to good decisions."

She thought she heard him mutter something that sounded like concern over so many half-off tinctures and possets, but she couldn't be sure.

A wizened woman stepped out from behind the shelves, her bones audibly creaking with her steps. "Marne has what you're looking for, some things you aren't, and at least three things that should be left well enough alone."

"Just the healing salve and this," Kaelin responded, slipping the family-sized headache potion into the pile. It was almost impossible to ignore the smell of lavender and mothballs emanating from the woman, but Kaelin managed it. Too bad not breathing wasn't a possibility.

If only it had stopped there, but Tobias flitted from shelf to shelf, picking up one bottle after another—only to have them rearrange themselves the moment he set them down. He paused briefly, his eyes flicking to the assassin. Her glare promised consequences. He knew that look—but curiosity was louder than his survival instinct, so he darted from one aisle to the next as eager tonics whispered, "Buy me."

However, he managed to ignore the pleas and approached the counter with only a small pouch of what looked like tea in his hand.

"We'll take this, too." Tobias tossed the pouch onto the counter. He thought it was a protection tea labeled: VERITAS ESSENCE: FOR WHEN EMOTIONAL SUPPRESSION ISN'T YOUR VIBE.

So many things would have been avoided if he had carefully read the label. Sometimes it's too late to learn that one should never buy a potion based solely on its aroma.

Marne looked at their goods, hesitating over the bag of dried something or other Tobias had decided on.

"Truth is best in small doses," she muttered.

My dear reader, foreshadowing rarely comes so clearly labeled.

For a moment, Tobias thought about returning the tea to whatever shelf wanted it. "Is it chamomile?"

"If it was, it wouldn't require courage to drink it," Marne responded, cryptic as always. She then turned to Kaelin. "That will be one silver piece."

Kaelin glared but paid anyway. "I thought this was a sale—more like highway robbery."

"Highways only rob the easy targets," the old woman sniffed. "Potions rob everyone. And they never show remorse."

Outside, Timber snored.

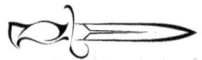

Shockingly, our assassin and her merry band made it out of Cloverbite unscathed. Or so she believed.

Kaelin walked the perimeter of their camp as Tobias set about making tea to go along with some scones and sandwiches he managed to purchase without her noticing. Well, he didn't think she'd noticed, but she had—and decided to let him have this one. Anything to avoid a burned campfire meal for one night. What she didn't notice was that he used the tea from the apothecary or that it had a warning label about unwanted revelations. If she had, things might have turned out differently. Instead, she finished her patrol, sat on a log, took a sip of tea, and set it down before grabbing a beef and cheddar sandwich. Timber lapped up the bitter drink when Kaelin wasn't looking.

It wasn't long before everyone had a cup in hand. At first, there was nothing. Just silence as each one chewed their food.

"You scare the void out of me," blurted Tobias. Words meant to stay in his head now reverberated throughout the camp, breaking the companionable silence.

Kaelin stared at him, eyes wide. His words sounded like emotion. She didn't do emotions.

Tobias's voice cracked like a spell miscast. He clamped a hand over his mouth, eyes wide in horror. Kaelin blinked once. Twice. Somewhere, a cricket began a slow death sonata.

Tobias wanted to stop, not to say anything more. However, his mouth had other ideas. "I can't stop watching you, because I've never felt safer with anyone."

She wanted to glare. Instead, her eyes burned. She hastily swiped away any evidence that she had feelings.

"That's terrifying, Kaelin." He clapped both hands over his mouth, trying to physically hold back the words that wouldn't stop tumbling out.

Her hand twitched. Tobias worried she was deciding which dagger would be best to silence him forever. If only he had known his words might have created a crack in her armor.

The campground was quiet, the only sounds being the incessant chirping of an unwanted insect and the sound of their breathing. Kaelin went to stand. Hesitated.

Her throat tightened. This wasn't a battle. This was worse. "I don't want to be alone anymore. I've told myself I do ... But lately I've wondered what it would be like to belong. To ..." She looked down at her empty hands. "Matter to someone." Her voice was raw, barely louder than a whisper.

For a heartbeat, Tobias forgot how to breathe. The assassin who could silence armies had just whispered loneliness into existence. It was more dangerous than any dagger she'd ever drawn.

As soon as the words passed her lips, she reached for Whisperthorn. As if she could duel her own emotions, which, for her, would be better than acknowledging them.

There it is, dear reader—the thing Kaelin would kill to keep hidden. Possibly literally.

Timber looked from the assassin to the mage and back. She plodded over, circled twice, and lay down on Tobias's feet, resting her head on Kaelin's lap. It was her way of saying, *you're both disasters, but you're my disasters.* She then closed her eyes and snored so loudly the fire sputtered, ending the moment and causing a sigh of relief, but neither of them moved.

Kaelin muttered, "Even the dog knows how to ruin a moment."

"Or save one," Tobias said softly. She pretended not to hear him.

Kaelin yanked her cloak around her like armor, glaring at the embers as they burned out. Tobias muttered something about needing new tea.

When Tobias finally fell asleep, the faint light of the moon cast shadows across Kaelin's face. She reached for her dagger, hesitated, then set it back down. Her armor was heavier when no one was trying to break through it. Across the camp, Tobias dreamed of a voice saying his name in the dark, and for once, it didn't sound like a warning.

Neither of them ever mentioned what passed between them in that moment. At least not out loud. Which, as we all know, meant it lived rent-free in both of their heads.

Just when the moment calcified into awkwardness, her satchel glowed. The map (yes, the one from the demigod) lit up. Kaelin stomped over and ripped it out of the bag. Runes sparkled across the surface and then faded until the only thing illuminated was the town of Gravemire—a haunted place of cursed forests, tax-collecting undead, and deeply unfriendly librarians.

Disturbed from her slumber, Timber growled at it, then promptly peed on the edge.

Kaelin shrugged. "That's fair."

And with that, their next disaster announced itself with glowing runes and dog pee.

7

THE BARD THAT WEPT

"Not all songs are born of love. Some are born of beer, questionable bets, and the poor life choices of assassins."

The next morning came like all mornings do, too fast and too soon.

Kaelin would have overslept if it hadn't been for the loud *caw-caw* that had the audacity to interrupt her sleep, reminding her of an unfinished quest involving a chicken who should not be ignored. Her nightmares had featured feathers, glowing eyes, and one very smug cluck. The rooster apparently wanted an encore.

The message was solidified when she stepped out of her tent and a rooster-shaped shadow streaked across the sky towards parts unknown. Of course, it was also in that moment that the urine-stained map glowed once more.

Some quests waited patiently in line. Others burned down three villages and demanded your attention. And then there were those that simply glowed until you paid attention.

Kaelin's head felt like someone had used it to test sword sharpness. Emotional hangovers were worse than ale's—they didn't fade with time, just waited for eye contact and small talk to reappear. And Tobias's brand of earnestness was the emotional equivalent of standing barefoot on sincerity.

Timber trotted past her with the smug satisfaction of someone who had slept soundly and knew it.

"Let's go. Gravemire awaits." Kaelin was gruffer than usual this morning, a normal side effect after unwanted emotional intimacy. Worse than poison. Harder to cure. And far more persistent.

Tobias nodded as he shoved the last of his things into his pack. His usual chipperness was muted as they started their daily journey. He kept stealing glances at her, like he was afraid she might evaporate if he looked away too long. She pretended not to notice, which fooled neither of them.

Timber looked from one to the other, shook her head, and went to stand by Ed. At least the horse had the emotional range to cope. The other two—questionable.

Every step squelched like an insult. The trees leaned close, whispering opinions they couldn't prove. Tobias opened his mouth once, twice, then wisely decided the sound of rain was safer company. The silence was thick enough to drown in.

They trudged. Yes, it was one of those days. The ground was muddy, the weather grim, and the mood tense enough to require a massage. The silence that followed them down the road was as thick as fog. Rain clung to their cloaks, turning the dirt to sludge. Then a golden glow cut through the gloom. When the tavern's noise reached them, Kaelin was almost grateful for it—noise was easier than thought.

The Winking Wyvern awaited, a bustling roadside tavern, probably haunted, where bad ideas blossomed into even worse decisions. Laughter spilled from the windows, mingling with the smell of ale, roasted nuts, and sorrow. This tavern, like so many others, was a favorite stop for mercenaries, adventurers, and people who owed taxes in at least three kingdoms.

Instead of entering with caution and nose plugs, they scurried toward it like people trying to hide from their own thoughts. The sign above the door winked. Literally. Tobias stopped to wink back. The sign looked offended.

Every tavern, dear reader, claims to be the heart of adventure. Most are closer to its liver. The Wyvern's walls leaned inward from too many stories being told at once. Somewhere in the rafters, something laughed—or possibly hatched.

They had no idea that before the night was over, someone would cry into a mug, swear eternal loyalty, and start composing their legend—badly.

The tavern hosted the infamous Midwinter Drinking Gauntlet—a contest where no one survived with their dignity intact.

It was midwinter. They were doomed.

The door swung open, welcoming the ragged travelers. Tobias immediately found an excuse to flee—something about a lute, claiming it had magical properties. It was, of course, on the other side of the room. Timber sniffed, smelled meat, and started to fill her belly. This left the assassin standing there, alone.

"I see we have a new contestant for the Midwinter Drinking Gauntlet," proclaimed a busty tavern wench as she raised Kaelin's arm up as if she'd volunteered.

Kaelin ripped her hand away, shaking her head, but stopped. Maybe a barrel full of ale was just what she needed. Entering the contest didn't mean she had to win.

Of course she had to win; the Thorn of the North always won.

"Fine. I'll do it." The chair she grabbed scraped the floor as she moved it into place.

An orc turned towards her, their horns capped with silver tips. "A worthy challenger. I'm Brug Ironthroat. Undefeated at the Winking Wyvern, traveling bard and purveyor of regret." Their voice could shatter glass or lull a child to sleep. "I only lose to legends."

They raised their mug in salute, and the tavern roared approval. Someone in the corner fainted from excitement or alcohol—it was hard to tell which.

And sometimes people mistake rage-drinking for strategy. But, dear reader, it is how most friendships start—and most legends stumble into being.

Challengers chosen, the contest began with all the grace of a tavern brawl wearing its Sunday best. Tankards slammed against tables, ale sloshed across wooden floors, and the crowd roared with the kind of enthusiasm only found in the deeply inebriated.

Someone started a betting pool. The odds shifted wildly every time Kaelin scowled. A gnome shouted for "Team Murderface." Tobias, of course, placed his bet on Kaelin's survival, not her victory—an important distinction.

Kaelin looked at the foaming tankard of ale in front of her. As much as she thought she didn't need to win, what she saw before her was another mission. She studied each gulp like a tactical maneuver, calculating head tilt, breathing intervals, and splash radius.

Brug took a very different approach. Singing between each swig, weaving epic verses about their own magnificence. One tale involved pink horns, a shimmering gown, and a plethora of backup dancers no one else could see. Tobias started clapping in rhythm. Kaelin's glare silenced him by the second verse. He mouthed "sorry"—then immediately clapped again.

Tobias, unable to stay away from the assassin for long—whether from spellbinding or sheer fascination—stood, watching her drink.

His attempts to cheer her on were unique, to say the least.

"Don't die!" he shouted at one point, followed by the ever-helpful advice: "Drink like you're hydrating after cardio!"

Kaelin ignored him with the focus of a general plotting a siege. Each gulp felt like defiance—of gravity, destiny, and common sense.

Against all odds—and alcohol content—Kaelin outlasted Brug. The bard collapsed with the kind of drama that suggested both heartbreak and performance art. Moments later, they rose again, tears streaming, already composing a ballad about their 'noble demise.'

Kaelin didn't know it was orc bardic tradition that losing a drinking contest meant pledging eternal artistic servitude, which was how she found herself the unwilling muse of a bard who rhymed 'destiny' with 'ale and me.'

Now Brug was on verse two, Kaelin sat shaking her head as the song continued on and on.

The crowd erupted with applause as Brug finished and knelt before Kaelin. She tried to scootch away, but she was trapped by everyone who wanted to congratulate her.

"You are my muse." They clutched their heart as the silver on the horns caught the light. "My undying loyalty is yours, as is my continued song."

Kaelin's eyes darted around the room, looking for an escape route, a trapdoor, maybe even divine intervention—anything to end this moment.

Brug stood, raising their hand and horns to the sky. "I will chronicle your every deed, triumph, and dramatic sigh."

"What about my exasperated eye rolls?" she muttered. "I don't want a bard, a follower, or a living reminder of my 'heroics.'"

Timber put her paws on Brug's chest and licked their face. Tobias clapped his hands like this was the best thing he'd ever heard.

He looked at Kaelin, pride softening into something dangerously fond. "You inspire loyalty," he said quietly. "Even when you don't mean to."

She nearly choked on her ale. Kaelin had been praised before—by generals, by clients, by corpses—but never like this. Praise without expectation felt heavier than any blade. Tobias saw it too, the flicker of something human beneath her scowl.

And thus, dear reader, destiny acquired a background vocalist.

And thus, Team Chaos acquired a soundtrack. Whether Kaelin liked it or not.

She nodded, an acceptance of fate. She would have preferred stabbing it, but that didn't seem to be an option.

Unfortunately, or fortunately depending on your perspective, Brug sang their first ode to Kaelin, a ballad so heartfelt and ridiculously poetic that it moved half the tavern to tears.

The mage wept openly. "It's definitely the onions." He sniffled into his sleeve. It was not the onions.

Kaelin glared daggers; at least she didn't unsheathe any of them. But some small part of her—a traitorous part—liked what she heard. Because, for the first time, someone was praising her not as a tool. Not as a blade. But as a person.

She didn't know what to do with that. So, she ordered another drink.

And somewhere behind her, Brug began verse two.

The night—and Kaelin's tolerance for affection—would never be the same. Neither, unfortunately, would be the volume of her mornings.

The tavern smelled of stale triumph and regret. Timber was halfway through someone's breakfast by the time Kaelin finished packing.

"You're quiet," Tobias said. "Plotting or hungover?"

"Yes," she replied.

Kaelin went from one hangover to another—but she much preferred the one caused by too much ale. What she didn't appreciate was the singing orc, who followed her out of the tavern cheerfully, joining the group as if it was a foregone conclusion.

"What are you doing here?" She tightened the straps on Ed's saddle.

Brug bowed with a sweeping gesture. "Last night I swore to sing your acts of heroism! Which, by binding oath and creative inspiration, means you're stuck with me."

Kaelin sighed. "Not another one."

"Can I sing with you?" Tobias asked, slinging his pack over his shoulder.

They gasped, clutching their heart, tears filling their eyes. "I would be honored if you joined me."

"This is going to be so much fun." Tobias clapped—there might have been glitter. There was always glitter. No one ever knew where he got it.

Before Kaelin could stop them, the orc scooped Tobias up and spun him in a circle.

Timber lunged forward, stopping when Brug set Tobias down.

"And who are you?" They dug through their pouch. "Do you like jerky? I have some extra here somewhere. Ah, there it is."

And just like that, Timber accepted the bard onto their team. As they rode out together, Brug began strumming a new song: 'The Assassin That Outdrank the World.'

Every found family begins with a mistake. Some with blood. This one, mercifully, began with ale—and the faint promise of harmony, though no one believed it yet.

8

RUINS OF REGRET

"Even assassins bleed. They're just better at hiding it."

"Your satchel is glowing again, Kaelin," Tobias observed—in that deeply unhelpful way only he could pull off. "Do you think it's tracking Percival?"

Kaelin didn't even look at the map. "It's illuminating Gravemire again . . . still. It clearly wants us there now, but we're going to have to deal with the Order of Binding Contracts if we stay on our current route."

Tobias sighed—he might have even rolled his eyes. "Are we going to have to face them again?"

"Who exactly is the Order of Binding Contracts?" Brug asked, harmonizing with nature and all the sounds it had to offer.

"Bureaucracy at its most painful," Kaelin answered.

"Did you just sing that?" Tobias tilted his head.

Timber howled.

Kaelin put one foot in front of the other. "I agree, Timber, we need another way."

Ed shook his head and neighed.

"What's that, Ed? You have a suggestion?" Tobias asked, knowing the horse wouldn't respond.

Brug stopped. "I was told of a shortcut back at the Winking Wyvern. We could make our way through the Petrified Forest of Veyra, and straight into the Ruins of Regret." Their eyes gleamed. "Just think of the verses, the tragedy, the perfectly timed key changes."

Tobias paused. "The Ruins of Regret? That sounds ... ominous."

"How much time could we save?" Kaelin tapped the toe of her boot in the dirt.

"If this Order of Binding Contracts is as bad as you say, half a fortnight, maybe more." Brug shrugged.

Kaelin nodded, indicating the orc should lead the way.

They might avoid paperwork, but the emotional tax would be unavoidable.

They followed the bard when they turned off the main road, leading them down a narrow path where vines reached out to stop them, or give them high fives, depending on the time of day. Kaelin swatted one away before it could decide.

Hours later, as the sun dipped low and Brug's songs turned from triumphant ballads to haunting hums, they found a clearing. Tobias scorched dinner. Kaelin and Timber hung back, watching it all. She was itching to continue on her journey, but it was time to rest before they walked into the Petrified Forest.

The next morning came fast and furious. No one was ready to get up and start moving.

"Come on, guys, we have a forest to visit and ruins to conquer," Tobias said with his normal enthusiasm before stretching. "Are we really headed to a place where every tree has turned to stone?"

Brug stepped out of their tent, polishing the silver on their tusk. "It's better than just stone trees. The locals say the forest remembers fear. The same curse that turned the trees to stone can do the same to travelers—showing them their deepest regrets before it claims them."

"Sounds like a good time." Kaelin led Ed to the trail, not waiting for anyone to follow. Not surprisingly, Timber was right by her side.

Brug quietly played their lute as they made their way to the forest, past singing flowers, dancing dryads, and one babbling brook. Before long, they stood in front of stone trees.

"This place hums in a minor key." Brug strummed.

"Sounds more like screaming to me," Kaelin muttered.

Timber pushed her snout into Brug's pouch and walked away with a giant piece of jerky.

Tobias tried to collect a sample, accidentally chipping a tree. The moan that reverberated around them came from somewhere within the stone grain.

The air thickened, heavy with the kind of silence that even made Timber stop panting.

It wasn't just quiet—it was listening.

Never trust forests that don't move in the wind. Stillness isn't natural.

The forest thinned into ruins—ancient stone half-swallowed by petrified roots. The air itself hummed, alive with old illusion magic.

"This is . . . academically invigorating," Tobias said, voice climbing half an octave too high.

"I wonder what the acoustics are like?" Brug didn't wait for an answer before strumming a chord that echoed through the ruins like laughter in a tomb.

"Pretty sure the acoustics are perfect for screaming," Kaelin muttered.

Timber padded along beside her. The dog could feel everyone's unease, but wasn't sure what was causing it.

"This will save time. It'll be worth it," she insisted.

Shortcuts never save time.

The air shifted—pressure, static, the kind that prickles along your spine. They all felt it, though no one said a word. But each of them saw something. It began as echoes in the stones surrounding them—shadows flickering through petrified trunks.

The illusions solidified into each person's deepest fears.

Kaelin saw her younger self kneeling before a failed target, blade trembling—the sound of her own ragged breathing echoing like someone else's. Then Stride appeared—too vivid, too close—finishing the job with effortless precision.

"I taught you to be unbreakable." Stride's condemnation was soft, but cruel. "You're a disappointment. A waste of my time. Worthless."

Kaelin turned away, swiping at her face before the tears could fall. It was the easiest way to escape. Or so she thought. But everywhere she looked she saw herself mid-failure. Each memory calcified before her eyes, trapped forever in grey stone. She unsheathed one dagger after the next, tossing them at each of her failures.

Tobias, journal and quill in hand, attempted to document the cursed trees, but one hissed at him in a woman's voice that accosted his ears. He fainted. Brug immediately began composing "Lullaby for a Scholar," but was soon drawn away from their fallen friend.

The mage regained consciousness surrounded by petrified trees. Leaping to his feet, he spun, desperate to escape what each tree reflected towards him. Everywhere he turned was an unfinished spell. Each one whispered, "You'll always ruin the magic you touch."

He spun until he collapsed, surrounded by spells that hissed his failures back at him. Every spell cracked and turned to stone around him, brittle with disappointment.

Somewhere between panic and silence, Brug's voice rose—fragile at first, then defiant. They sang of heroes far and wide. The trees became their audience—stone-faced, unblinking. One by one, they turned away. The silence that followed was the loudest sound Brug had ever heard—and it was perfectly in pitch.

Fear, when properly aged, was like a fine wine: addictive and likely to make you do foolish things.

Timber, having finished her stolen jerky, trotted deeper into the ruins' quiet. Her head snapped from Kaelin frozen on her knees, to Tobias running in circles like he was chasing his tail, to Brug sobbing while they sang a soulful ballad.

The thing about a loyal animal companion is they're allowed to mess with the humans they've claimed, but no one or nothing else has the same permission.

Timber howled, then snarled—it wasn't loud, but low and certain. It promised violence, the immediate kind. She lunged through the illusion tormenting Kaelin, teeth flashing as she tore through the petrified assassin statue. The stone shattered like brittle bones.

The assassin blinked, dazed for a moment, before shoving the lingering dread back where it belonged, somewhere easy to ignore and likely to be forgotten. Aurora's End found its way into her hand. For one treacherous beat, Stride's words echoed inside her, and she wanted to believe them. Instead, she moved, her muscle memory taking over, even while her mind froze. With one practiced flick, her dagger flew, shattering the illusion's hold on Tobias. He halted mid-circle, panting as if he'd run a marathon, possibly while standing still.

Timber tore through the illusion holding Brug captive. The bard strummed a discordant chord on their lute that vibrated through the trees. The chord rippled through the ruins, snapping the spell's hold. Each of them shook off the visions that would haunt them for years—and buried them deep in the kind of place no one names out loud.

Illusions are easiest broken by those who've already accepted reality. Dogs, for instance.

Kaelin retrieved her dagger, wiping it on her thigh before returning it to its sheath. Tobias, hands shaking, walked to the center of the ruins, drawn there by a mosaic surrounded by petrified trees. Timber padded after him, followed by the rest of the group.

Sprawled before them was a mosaic of a doomed empire devouring itself as thrones toppled and palaces burned, outlined by a gold chain that weaved into a familiar symbol shining in the top center. The chain wrapped itself around a quill that bled ink. Under it, the words ALL BONDS BLEED pulsed, as if they remembered every oath ever taken. The image burned its way into her brain. She lingered, suddenly ill from the dread of recognizing something she wished she hadn't.

Some symbols don't fade with empires—they just change stationery.

"The quill and chain—it reminds me of something." Tobias stroked his chin with a trembling hand. "Where have I seen it before?"

Brug hummed a slow, mournful tune. The sound vibrated in the stone trunks, echoing like trapped memories.

The symbol burned itself into Kaelin's mind. She'd seen that mark before—carved into contracts, pressed into wax, written into her life before she'd learned how to read it. It shouldn't be here, it belonged to shadows and contracts, not ruins and empires. But lies travel well.

She turned—running away from what she'd seen and everything it meant. The ruins faded behind them as they stepped into a forest. A normal one, with no scared trees in sight.

"Next time, we take the road that doesn't obsess over our failures." Kaelin tried to mask her shaken state with sarcasm. The only person she fooled was herself.

Tobias nodded, clutching his notes. "I think that was quite productive!" His tone was chipper even though his voice shook.

"In trauma or melody?" Brug asked.

And so, our intrepid party carried on—slightly more traumatized, moderately less dignified, and with considerably more respect for dogs. Onward, then, to Gravemire, where bureaucracy flirts with necromancy. And both require you to sign in triplicate.

What could possibly go wrong?

9

The Wishing Well, Not Well

"Be careful what you wish for—especially if the wishing well hisses back."

A shroud of quiet settled over the weary travelers as they continued to follow the map, whose relentless glow pointed them in a single unyielding direction. Was Gravemire on the way to Eldreach? If Kaelin tilted the map just right—and ignored things like scale, geography, and basic reasoning—it was almost on the way. Almost. But in reality, it was another delay, pushing Kaelin even closer to missing the deadline for assassinating the king.

"If the map's so intent on glowing," Tobias said, "perhaps it could glow us somewhere less cold and muddy."

"You're the one who trusted a map that smells like goat," Kaelin shot back.

"It's reliable," he protested.

"It's damp," she countered.

And thus began round thirty-seven of the same argument, slightly wetter than before.

"It's not the map's fault you can't read it," Kaelin muttered.

"It literally glows when we go in the 'right' direction. Reading it isn't the problem," Tobias quipped, a sure sign they had been on the road for too long.

"Then stop arguing with it." She glared.

Tobias pushed his hair out of his eyes. "I'm arguing with you."

"Exactly," she said before stomping off. Or squelching off, the mud was really unbearable.

With the final word having been said, silence reigned over the weary travelers.

The chaotic ruckus of someone stumbling snatched Kaelin out of her reverie. She looked up to see Tobias fall next to a quaint stone well. The well was too perfect—stones uncracked, moss trimmed, a single beam of sunlight spotlighting its charm. It looked welcoming, as if it were awaiting a bard's ballad, but after the Petrified Forest of Veyra, trust issues ran deeper than ever. At least for some of the party—others were still susceptible to architectural optimism.

The clearing around the well was unnaturally quiet. No birds. No wind. Even the insects seemed to hold their breath. Magic hung in the air like humidity—thick, invisible, and impossible to ignore. The kind of quiet that makes you think something's waiting. It usually is.

Brug, instantly fascinated, clapped their hands. "A wishing well! Finally, something worthy of a bard's song. This one will be joyous—and probably poorly advised."

Tobias stood, brushing debris off his coat. "You should be careful, Brug. Enchanted wells are statistically uncooperative. Rarely do you get what you wish for, and sometimes the well wishes back."

"Careful?" Brug echoed, affronted. "I'm a bard. We dine on danger, and occasionally regret."

"Mostly regret," Tobias muttered. "And not listening."

Kaelin sighed. "Bad decisions. Don't forget those."

"Bad decisions lead to beautiful songs," Brug said. "We need beautiful songs."

Kaelin rolled her eyes and muttered, "We need cheese, not a lecture on magical plumbing."

Ed took the respite to munch on some grass. Timber sniffed the rocks, barked at the well, and trotted away, searching for a tasty snack—anything but the greenery the horse was enjoying.

Dear reader, if you've ever seen a bard at a wishing well, you know where this is going. If you haven't . . . congratulations, you're about to find out.

The air stilled, thick around them. The map's glow dimmed, as if it wanted to hide from whatever was about to happen. Or maybe it just didn't approve of their pace slowing.

Before anyone could stop them, Brug skipped to the well—yes, they skipped—and emptied their half-full flask. Hands raised to the sky, they bellowed, "I wish for a real adventure. Something worth remembering, something worthy of a song."

Tobias groaned.

"You fool," Kaelin muttered.

Ed munched.

Timber yipped, excited for whatever was going to happen.

The well glowed ominously. Purple steam rose from its depths.

The ground rumbled—a warning, ignored.

Water splashed out, black as ink, turning into shadowy figures climbing from regions better left unsaid.

Tobias shook his head, his curls flopping over one eye. "Oh look, consequences."

Kaelin didn't say a word. She drew Whisperthorn and Glassfire; this situation called for a dagger in each hand.

Timber smiled, her tongue lolling to one side as she eyed the creatures with something akin to glee. She really loved a true adventure—she might have been the only one.

Shadow beasts emerged from the well. Wolf-like creatures made of smoke and claws, illusions given a violent form.

While they appeared related to our unique canine, they were not. Although, they did share an unusual love for jerky.

Kaelin leapt into the fray—strategic, precise, furious—slicing through smoke faster than it could reform. It didn't help. Which, naturally, only made her angrier.

Tobias flung his hand towards the shadows. "Don't worry! I've almost got the right incantation!"

"That's what you said before you turned my cloak into a ferret!" Kaelin shouted back.

"In fairness, it was an excellent ferret." He smiled wide.

Kaelin ducked a swipe of smoke. "If you explode us, I'm haunting you."

"You already do," Tobias said cheerfully.

Tobias, in an attempt to save them all, cast a light spell. It was, in theory, a well-thought-out plan. After all, they were fighting shadows. Unfortunately, the spell blinded everyone except the shadows. A fragment of the spell caught the mage's cloak on fire.

As they stumbled around, the well's minions surrounded them. The bard, fascinated by it all, pulled out their lute and composed a new ballad.

Tobias cast another spell—the creatures closest to them burst into a cloud of gold glitter. It helped, momentarily, even if Kaelin preferred a less shimmery solution. It was a dazzling failure, but thematically consistent.

Brug, trapped by their own wish, belted a battle song so loud it physically rattled the shadows. A few even attempted to cover their ears. It didn't help.

Alas, this was the opening Kaelin needed. She drew Aurora's End, slicing and dicing any creature close enough for her blade to reach. Next to her, Timber lunged, tearing through the shadows, proving once again dogs are greater than shadow magic.

When the last shadow dissolved, the well exhaled a long, low sigh that sounded far too human. The mist it left behind shimmered purple, curling into the air like regret before fading.

Tobias limped over, wiping soot off his cheek. "See? Perfectly manageable chaos."

Kaelin arched a brow. "You were on fire for half the fight."

"Contained fire," he corrected.

There's a difference, apparently.

As the last shadow dissolved, a symbol shimmered on the stone, so faint it was almost imperceptible, but there it was—visible to anyone paying attention—a solitary quill wrapped in a gold chain.

Kaelin crouched, tracing the faint outline with her gloved finger. "I've seen this before," she whispered. The symbol was an integral part of her life, on every secret missive she'd ever received. But it did not belong here. Timber growled softly beside her, the sound low and certain—as if the dog knew what Kaelin refused to admit.

With the battle over, Brug collapsed on the rock, panting. "I didn't think the wish would work. I assumed you had to use a coin to activate a well," they admitted—half proud, half guilty.

"Next time, ask for cheese." Kaelin turned away from the fading symbol and glared as she collected her daggers.

Timber howled in agreement, eyes wide as she contemplated cheese monsters.

Seriously, it was an idea so good she almost went to the well and wished for it herself.

Tobias pushed his hand through his hair, serious—maybe for the first time since he'd met Kaelin. "Brug, don't wish for things you aren't ready to survive."

It caught her off guard every time he looked like that—focused, unguarded, completely devoid of irony. It made her want to look away, and not because of embarrassment. She simply didn't know what to do with sincerity.

The bard kicked a rock and stubbed their toe when it didn't move. The hopping that followed was as dramatic as expected. They stopped. "But isn't that what adventure is?" they said, quieter than anyone had ever heard them.

Tobias paused mid-quill chew. Kaelin didn't answer aloud, but her silence agreed. Some wishes deserved an audience, others only a witness.

Everything stilled around them for a second time. Whispers rose from the well—promises, temptations, bargains. Everything that they wanted, and everything they should ignore. Despite herself, even Kaelin took a step closer.

Tobias grabbed her arm. "I'm sure this well is cursed. Tied to old magic. It's best we leave it alone."

She looked at his hand gripping her forearm. Then at him. Nodding, she tossed her dagger in briefly—anything to get the well to shut up. It worked. Moments later, Glassfire was spat out. Of course the dagger came back—Glassfire always does.

Some wells grant water.

Others grant nightmares.

This one? Both, depending on the coin.

They didn't speak as they packed up. The ground still hissed faintly, like the well was sulking. Tobias muttered something about 'statistical anomalies in wish fulfillment,' while Brug swore an oath never to drink from anything that rhymed with 'spell.'

Timber sneezed—a clear canine verdict of 'idiots.' The wind carried it away like punctuation.

Kaelin adjusted her hood. "Progress," she said.

Without saying a word, the group moved on, exhausted, but unwilling to set up camp next to the cursed wishing well. So, they moved on, slow and steady, until they were far enough away that the well's whispers were no longer heard.

Before they were even settled for the night, Brug started writing verses about their glorious victory. It was a fantastic piece of melodrama, lacking in nothing except actual facts.

"You can't sing that anywhere. That's not even close to what happened." Tobias handed out the dinner he'd burned. "Hand those over, and I'll edit them for factual accuracy."

Brug reluctantly handed over their journal. Why would they want to get bogged down by accuracy when they could make it so much more interesting? "Since you insist."

Journal in hand, overcooked meal momentarily forgotten, Tobias sat on the ground and chewed on the point of his quill, scratching out verses here and there, changing words in the chorus, rewriting an entire bridge.

Offended by the mage's officious nature, Brug tried to get their journal back, but it was too late—Tobias was on a roll.

Off to the side, away from the antagonistic camaraderie happening in front of her, Kaelin munched on her burned dinner. Under her breath, she muttered something about 'stabbing them.'

But her words lacked conviction—a rare occurrence. The assassin took issuing threats very seriously, and never issued one unless she intended on following through.

Timber curled up at Kaelin's feet. She absentmindedly stroked the dog's fur, and her mind lingered on Brug's wish as the night pressed in—quiet, heavy, and uncomfortably patient.

A real adventure. One worth remembering. She stayed silent, almost invisible under the cover of a moonless night. But she admitted to herself alone that she wanted the same thing as Brug. And that thought terrified her more than any shadow creatures they might face.

Timber, of course, knew better. Wells were trouble. Wishes were worse. But she was just a dog, and dogs weren't consulted about plot decisions.

10

Campfire Promises

"This, dear reader, is what we call 'emotional foreshadowing.' Or flirting, if you're feeling generous."

Brug had wanted a grand adventure. What they got was a lot of traipsing. Day after day, the group traipsed through forests, down muddy paths, up mountains, then down mountains. The rhythm of a story that refused to reach its chorus—a march through mud towards something, if only they knew what. The damp air smelled of pine and disappointment. It was routine for Kaelin, eye-opening for Tobias, and boring for Brug. There was nothing to sing about unless you counted how the sun filtered through pine needles.

"How much farther until we reach civilization?" Tobias asked.

"Define civilization," Kaelin replied. "If you mean a roof, three days. If you mean people who don't try to stab us, never."

"So . . . three days, then."

Question answered, Tobias went back to examining everything in the forest and expounding on it.

"The interesting thing about coniferous needles is how well they work in protection spells." Tobias lectured anyone who listened—at the moment, no one paid him any attention. He didn't let that stop him from his pontification—nothing short of death or applause ever did. And even death was debatable.

Timber stopped, sniffing the air. The air stilled, heavy, oppressive even. Her ears flicked back. She froze, every hair on her back a raised flag of warning. The forest held its breath, waiting. She let out a plaintive howl. A warning, not that anyone recognized it for what it was.

Kaelin assumed the dog's dramatics were cheese related. "I know, Timber. It's been days since we ran out of Brenna's emergency cheese." She patted her four-legged companion's head. "I want more too."

Tobias raised a brow. "You talk to her like she's going to answer."

"She does," Kaelin said. "You just don't speak dog."

He grinned. "Working on it."

Timber shook the assassin's hand off her head before running around her and over to Tobias. She howled again, louder this time.

"All right, General," Tobias said softly, lowering his head to Timber's level. "Lead on."

Ed stopped. He reared up on his hind legs. Kaelin grabbed the reins before the horse could dart. His hooves clattered—proof that even the horse had better instincts than the assassin.

Somewhere above them, the clouds gathered like gossipmongers—quiet at first, then vicious. A single droplet fell on Tobias's nose.

"Harmless," he said. Famous last words.

Somewhere thunder grumbled—a throat clearing before a catastrophe. The temperature dropped, water fell from the sky, softly at first. But before long, it sharpened into knives, piercing through their cloaks and freezing their bones. The wind howled through the trees louder than Timber had ever howled in her life.

Timber yipped, Kaelin flipped her hood on and followed, dragging Ed along with her. The others fell in step behind her. Tobias blocked the wind with his arm. Brug contemplated pulling out their lute to write a song, but the thought of the water ruining it made them think twice.

Growth, dear reader, comes at unexpected times. So does pneumonia, but that's less poetic.

In front of them, a half-collapsed hunter's cabin appeared like a beacon of hope as frigid water soaked every inch of their clothing.

"We'll camp here for the night. Wait out the storm," Kaelin hollered over the screaming of the wind.

Timber shook her head before strutting inside. She curled up like a barrier of fur and warmth, clearly content to be away from the weather outside.

"Define shelter?" Tobias yelled as a roof beam collapsed at his feet. He sketched a small sigil and the wind at the doorway dropped half a pitch—quieter, not gone. The kind of spell that respected both storms and doorframes.

In tales of grand adventure, storms are metaphors for inner turmoil. In real life, they symbolize wet socks, mildew, and the creeping suspicion your destiny is laughing at you.

Inside, Tobias headed straight to the fireplace. He muttered an incantation, a flame burst and then fizzled like enthusiasm on a Sunday night. Another attempt ended in another failure, this time with a puff of pink smoke. At least there wasn't glitter. This story has had so much glitter, and we aren't even to the midpoint.

Kaelin silently took over—because competence was louder than commentary. She built an actual fire, the old-fashioned way, with flint and steel, no magic necessary. A fire caught in an instant, warming the structure. It caused the place to almost feel homey.

The fire roared, and for the first time all day, the cabin smelled of something other than wet misery—woodsmoke, burned bread, and damp wool. The storm's howling softened into a muffled heartbeat against the roof. For a rare moment, the world outside didn't matter.

Tobias set his pack beside hers—deliberately, not crowding—then produced dry socks from some impossible corner. He didn't hand them to her; he set them within reach, like a question she could answer later.

"May I?" he asked, palm hovering over a cracked window frame. At her nod, a faint thread of mending stitched along the worst of the gaps. Not heat—shelter.

She took herself to a corner of the room, sharpening her daggers. Tobias offered her food without saying a word. Unusual for him. She took it reluctantly. It was burned, like every other meal he cooked. She didn't mock him for it. Unusual. Disarming. Terrifying in its own quiet way.

"If I die of damp, please write a tragic ballad of my grand adventure," Brug mumbled from their chair near the fire.

"You'd die of melodrama first," Kaelin said.

Meal finished, clothes mostly dried, Brug couldn't help themselves—they were a bard, after all. For a few moments, singing filled the cabin, but only for a few moments. They quickly nodded off mid-verse, their song replaced with snoring that shook the walls.

Kaelin stood, intending to clean her plate. Instead, Tobias took it from her.

"You don't have to do everything yourself, you know?" The words were quiet, more to himself than to her.

She didn't answer, but she didn't take the plate back either—which, for Kaelin, was practically a love letter.

"You say that as if anyone else is going to do it right," she muttered as she moved closer to the fire, and by default, joined the group.

Silence stretched between them—the comfortable kind, if you ignored the daggers.

Tobias stared into the fire, the reflection turning his eyes to molten gold. His fingers traced the rim of his mug like he was measuring his courage. For once, he wasn't trying to fill the silence—he was trying to survive it.

He took the seat next to her and fidgeted. His mouth opened and closed over and over again.

"What?"

"It's nothing. You don't want to hear any of it."

"Maybe, maybe not. The only way to find out is to spit it out." The words shocked Kaelin.

Tobias gave a small, shaky laugh—one that didn't survive the journey out of his throat. He looked down, shoulders curling inward as if bracing for impact.

He shrugged as if to dismiss the importance of anything said after that. "My family never trusted my magic, or me." The words left him in a rush, like he'd been holding his breath for years. "All they cared about was whether I'd bring ruin or shame to the family. As much as I craved adventure, I couldn't stay with my family, letting them tear me down every single day."

The confession sat between them, flickering in the firelight, too heavy to joke about and too fragile to touch. Tobias stood and poked at the embers with a stick, pretending not to care, but his hand trembled.

Kaelin didn't know how to respond, so she let the silence stretch on.

"It's true, though. I am a walking disaster." The words were supposed to sound light, joke-like, but his voice cracked enough to show how deep the wounds ran.

"You take careful steps," she said, surprising them both. "Then you run when you should walk. It's . . . fixable." The last word sounded like an admission she hadn't meant to make.

Quiet filled the space. Kaelin crossed her arms, forming a wall of protection against the emotional onslaught. "You're not the only one people walk away from." She looked away. "At least you could leave," she said. "You're more than a pawn in someone else's game."

Everything about the assassin was defensive in that moment; her words were sharp, her body rigid. She hated how easily his honesty disarmed her. Words like that were dangerous—they lingered. They softened stone and rebuilt walls that shouldn't exist. Kaelin knew better than to trust softness. Softness broke.

She was moments away from running out of the room.

Timber got up and slowly padded her way over, sitting back down and resting her head on Kaelin's lap. She was an anchor in the emotional storm the assassin was experiencing.

"If you decide you don't want me here, say so. I'll leave when the spell fades." Tobias paused. "But I won't leave you just because you're sharp around the edges."

She didn't reply in words. She sheathed her dagger, moving closer to the fire. "Don't make promises you can't keep."

He didn't answer—didn't need to. For the first time, his silence said more than his spells ever could.

And there it is—not love, not yet. But something akin to hope, dangerously so.

Outside, the rain softened to a whisper, the storm exhausted by its own drama.

From the rafters, something chittered. A bedraggled squirrel stared down at them like a furious landlord, dropped a pinecone on Brug's head, and vanished. Even the wildlife had notes.

Inside, peace took shape: a bard, a mage, an assassin, and a dog. Every legend starts somewhere—usually right after everyone falls asleep.

Brug mumbled something about epic storms before resuming their earth-shattering snoring. Timber flopped between them, a peace treaty in fur. Within moments, she was snoring in harmony with Brug. Hope, it seems, comes with its own soundtrack.

11

Bones, Brothers, and Unfinished Business

"Death is not the end. It's just the start of very complicated paperwork."

Kaelin strapped down the last of their gear onto Ed. One horse for three travelers and a dog really wasn't enough. Shrugging, she checked the buckles one last time before turning away.

"You know, I'm not a packhorse. I should be carrying heroes, not their belongings," an unfamiliar voice said. "I'd even settle for having a villain ride me if it meant getting rid of this baggage."

"Unfortunately, one horse for three people means none of us gets to ride . . ." She stopped, and her eyes darted around the area, from the hunter's cabin, to tree, to another tree. The only one around was the horse. "Tobias, what did you do to Ed?"

The mage stumbled out of the cabin, one arm in his coat, the other struggling to find the hole, hair flopping over one eye. His sleeve was dusted with flour, and a faint smell of rosemary clung to him.

"What's wrong?" he asked, blinking like a man who hadn't yet had enough caffeine—or sense.

"Ed is talking," Kaelin said flatly. "Horses don't talk."

"Don't blame Tobias, I've always been able to speak; I normally choose to stay silent," Ed interrupted, his tone debonair, polished even.

Kaelin stared at him for a full heartbeat. "Great, next thing will be poetry and a manifesto."

Tobias raised both hands defensively. "I—uh—didn't do anything. Well, maybe a tiny whisper-warmth charm and a mild protection spell, but neither should've caused . . . vocabulary."

Kaelin squinted, halfway between disbelief and resignation. "You know, I used to think the weirdest part of my life was killing kings. But no, it's the horse."

Tobias stared. Kaelin thumbed her dagger. Brug stepped out of the cabin, strumming their lute.

"Are we ready to go?" they asked.

Ed's head swung to look at the orc. "I take it back. I think they're too large to ride me. The pack is fine, for now."

Brug plucked a triumphant chord anyway. "This one will be the chorus that saves kingdoms!"

Ed sighed. "That tone will haunt me in my sleep. Preferably after a nap."

Which, to be fair, is how most diplomatic conversations start.

The horse wandered down the path, just far enough not to hear Brug's musical talents.

Timber padded over, brushing her head against Kaelin's hand.

The assassin looked down. "Don't even think about actually speaking. I might just stab you."

Tobias, voice low and soft, said, "She won't. Not without a reason." He knelt next to Timber, offered her a morsel before scratching behind her ears.

Ed paused mid-step, glancing over his shoulder. "There are old oaths stitched into the road," he murmured. "I've been quiet about them." Then, as if realizing he'd said too much, he snorted and continued walking.

Kaelin frowned. "Wonderful. The horse is cryptic now."

And with that, the party set off again—one assassin, one bard, one over-caffeinated mage, one possibly cursed horse, and a dog with better instincts than all of them combined.

If you think this sounds like the beginning of trouble, you'd be right. But let's be honest—it's been trouble since breakfast.

Thankfully, or maybe not, depending on how you looked at it, they were closer to Gravemire than they thought.

The day started off like most days after a storm, with the exception of the talking horse: sun shining, birds singing, wind whispering through the trees. The orchestra of nature combined with soft strumming and light humming. But like all things, it was not meant to last.

The road ahead coiled through the forest like something that had forgotten how to die properly. Trees grew thinner, their bark paling to the color of old parchment. Moss crept higher, smothering everything it could reach—stones, roots, and the faint hope that following a glowing map was actually a good idea.

Even the air grew heavier—thick with the taste of iron and old prayers. The mist clung like memory, and somewhere in it, armor sighed.

Brug hummed under their breath, a tune somewhere between a dirge and a drinking song. Tobias tried to join in, but rhythm fled from him the way common sense usually did. Even Ed fell quiet, his hooves dull against the cobblestones.

"Is it me," Tobias whispered, "or does it feel like we're walking into a story that doesn't end well?"

"You're in it," Kaelin replied. "So yes."

And indeed, dear reader, this was the part of the story where laughter began to echo differently—like it knew it was trespassing.

By the time the last scrap of sunlight gave up and fled behind the horizon, mist had rolled in—thick, sour, and alive. The map pulsed faintly from Kaelin's satchel, the word Gravemire glowing like a warning label written by the overconfident dead.

Before them stretched a battlefield. Ruins better left in times long gone emerged in front of them, haunted by the past and forgotten by the future.

Kaelin's hand twitched towards her dagger—habit more than threat—before Brug's quill even moved.

Ahead, a figure waited at the edge of the fog—armor tarnished, posture noble, a skeletal knight whose bones caught the moonlight like glass.

Ed stopped abruptly. "Well," the horse said, "I'd bow, but that seems in poor taste."

Brug gasped, scribbling furiously. "Finally! The ghost of a hero! This song will be magnificent—tragedy, valor, and the faint smell of mildew!"

Kaelin rolled her shoulders, readying her daggers. "Let's hope the dead are better conversationalists than the living."

Yes, he is both skeleton and knight. No, you may not question the logistics of sword-wielding with bony fingers. He makes it work.

The knight turned towards them, and in a voice of both echo and elegy, said, "Welcome, travelers. You walk roads haunted by oaths."

Which, to be fair, was not the worst greeting they'd received that week.

"Not more talk of oaths," Kaelin muttered, glaring at the horse.

The skeletal knight bowed. "I'm Sir Harlow. A knight of the oblong table, once revered for heroic feats, but alas, those days have passed."

Brug stopped mid-strum. "Wait, Sir Harlow—as in the Harlow from the Briarwick campaigns? You were a woman then—Harriet the Heroic. At least I believe that's what they called you."

The knight gave a soft hollow laugh, bones shifting like wind through chimes. "They did, but I preferred Harlow. A mage in the capital owed me a favor—I claimed it before I died."

Tobias blinked. "You mean . . ."

"I mean, I was granted the body that matched the soul I'd already lived as. Death merely preserved it."

Tobias's expression softened, awe flickering behind his eyes. "That's incredible," he murmured. "To keep who you are, even past death."

Kaelin tilted her head. "So, you died as yourself."

"Finally," said Harlow.

For once, even Kaelin didn't have a retort. The fog pressed close, as if giving the knight privacy to breathe—or the illusion of it.

For once, dear reader, I thought about not interrupting, but if death had a silver lining, it's self-actualization with style.

"I thought my struggles would end there, but now I've been searching for my estranged brother. We had a falling out centuries ago, but I made an oath to save him, and I will."

Brug sat, quill and paper in hand, furiously writing down every word, searching for the right melody.

"I've held on to that oath, perhaps too tightly," Sir Harlow continued. "My brother sought immortality—instead he found undeath. Now his soul rots in Gravemire. I would see him freed."

"You mean he's a lich." Tobias's eyes widened. He wasn't fond of liches, evil intelligence combined with the smell of rot. Just the thought made him want to gag. A flicker of disgust passed through him, but beneath it—pity. Even monsters, he thought, started as people who wanted more time.

"A powerful mage who didn't want to age. Bound their soul, to become immortal." Brug sang. "Oh, I like the rhyming pattern."

"Yes, a lich. A stubborn one," Sir Harlow responded. "A family trait."

Nothing ruins a family reunion like necromancy. Or family, really.

"He lingers still," Harlow said softly. "Bound not by magic, but by guilt. I intend to free him—if you'll lend me your blades."

"You're asking assassins to save a lich," Kaelin said.

"I'm asking heroes," Harlow corrected.

Which, in Kaelin's opinion, was clearly the first mistake.

Brug stood, pacing. "There should be something about 'bones of valor' or maybe 'songs of marrow.'"

To everyone's shock and probably dismay, Sir Harlow responded with his own awkward, but elegant verse.

Tobias leaned towards Kaelin. "Are they flirting in rhyme?"

"If they start a metaphor about bones, I'm leaving," she muttered.

Delighted, Brug launched into the beginnings of a ballad. When they paused, the knight would add his own words.

Going from a request for assistance to an impromptu poetry duel—half heartfelt, mostly ridiculous.

And thus, dear reader, the rarest of sights: two poets courting each other with metaphors about mortality. Try not to swoon.

Tobias couldn't stop himself from gazing at Kaelin, touched by the night before and the flirtation in front of him. She caught him staring. He pretended to gag.

"I need more cheese if I'm going to survive this," she muttered.

Timber circled, lay down, and yawned. Patiently waiting for the duel to end.

The fog thickened, curling like an audience leaning closer to hear the next stanza. For all its gloom, Gravemire was listening.

"I will put this in a song, and it will live on forever," Brug proclaimed.

Sir Harlow bowed, bones creaking. "I would be honored. However, saving my brother would make an even better ballad."

"If I'm going to help, I need to know what I'm getting myself into," Kaelin said.

Tobias muffled a laugh. "When have you ever known what you're getting yourself into?"

She glared. It didn't even faze him.

"My brother, Malrik, wanted immortality and power. He felt the only way to get what he wanted was to become a lich. I opposed it." Harlow's shoulder bones slumped. "It led to a fight that eventually was the cause of my death."

Kaelin rolled her shoulders. "Does he even want to be saved?"

Harlow shook his head. "I don't know. I'm not sure he will forgive me. But I long for reconciliation. It's the only thing missing in my death."

Kaelin, pragmatic as ever, pointed out the obvious. "Liches don't usually do tea and forgiveness."

Tobias, idealistic as ever, said, "But maybe they should. Maybe that's why the map brought us here."

Harlow looked at him with something close to admiration. "Then the map has more mercy than most men I've met."

Harlow studied Kaelin, quietly hopeful. "Would you . . . help me?"

All eyes turned towards her, begging, even Timber's.

"Fine," she agreed reluctantly. "This is just another delay."

"Thank you." Sir Harlow's bony hands grabbed hers. "Follow me."

They followed him through the battlefield until they arrived at the edge of an ancient crypt-library. The door moaned as it opened before them. Inside, shadowy wards and bone guardians blocked the path.

Kaelin and Tobias fought them off, Timber ran away with a femur, and Brug and Harlow exchanged couplets—even as they fought.

A spark of eerie blue flame lit the chamber, throwing long shadows that trembled with every heartbeat. The air reeked of dust and devotion left too long unspoken.

A booming voice echoed through the crypt-library. "Brother . . . you return to me with mere mortals?"

It wasn't a voice so much as a collapse of warmth—the sound of time remembering what it lost.

Harlow steeled himself, but faltered. "I can't do this right now. I can't face him."

Kaelin froze, half turning towards him. The knight who'd faced death twice was trembling. That, more than any lich, made her uneasy.

"Wait . . . What?" Kaelin stopped.

The knight turned towards her. "I need time. But thank you—for giving me hope this might be possible."

Brug solemnly declared, "Then let us write the ballad of reconciliation yet to come."

Kaelin groaned. "God save me from poets."

"Oh, you'll be in the ballad too. Probably as the tragic dagger-wielding heartbreaker." Tobias smirked.

For the first time all day, Kaelin didn't argue. She just sighed—because sometimes being feared was easier than being seen.

They backed out of the crypt and camped outside; the mist cleared, but the tension lingered. Kaelin watched Harlow sit by the fireless night, staring at the stars.

And if hope were contagious, she decided she was already showing symptoms.

12

BREW OR DIE (THE DWARVEN ALE TRIALS)

"Some cultures test heroes with monsters. Dwarves use beer, fire, and disappointing uncles."

The morning came sooner than anyone wanted and later than anyone needed. The battle had passed, but something of it clung to them—an ache behind the eyes, a silence that refused to leave. A war left unfinished. The ghosts of Gravemire might have gone for the moment, but they'd left their fingerprints on the air. It was easier to keep moving than to think about what lingered.

"Would you mind if I joined you for a few days?" Sir Harlow asked, his tone careful, as though he were still learning how to speak among the living. "There's still a debt I owe the living, and I'd rather not face the road alone."

Brug grabbed their heart. "It would be joyous indeed if you came along."

"I guess that settles that," Kaelin said under her breath. She told herself it was temporary. Everything was, until it wasn't.

Tobias shrugged. "The more, the merrier."

"Just one more person not riding me," Ed muttered.

Timber sniffed, then howled—a low sound, almost like a question. It was one thing to accept the dead among the living at night, but it felt less natural under sunlight.

With the decision made, it wasn't long before they were on the road, the battlefield long behind them. They traveled in the hush that followed unfinished conversations. Every clang of Harlow's armor seemed to measure the distance between grief and whatever came next. Tobias tried to fill the silence with optimism once or twice, but even his magic couldn't raise a ghost's spirit, or Kaelin's. Harlow was the quietest of them all, even though he clinked with each step, a quiet metronome for the group's uneasy truce with fate.

The road weaved its way around rocks, trees, and streams until they stood in front of Myrkspire Mountain Gate—the only way to get through the mountain. Going over it wasn't an option. The closer they came, the louder it became—music, hammering, and the unmistakable smell of hops wrestling with smoke. The kind of chaos that promised either celebration or catastrophe—sometimes both. The echo of laughter drifted down the valley before they saw the source.

They expected guards or trolls—instead, they stumbled into a raucous dwarven brew festival. A keg exploded in the distance.

Someone cheered. Someone else was on fire. A goat in a tiny judge's hat bleated approval.

Tobias whispered, "Is this a trial or a cult?"

Kaelin didn't bother answering; cults usually had better organization.

The gatekeeper, a redheaded dwarf of indeterminate age, approached them. He was loud, proud, and perpetually disappointed, and he was there to explain the rules of passage. He puffed out his chest, beard glinting with droplets of spilled ale, and grinned the way only a man with zero self-awareness could.

"I'm Uncle Borin Emberforge, Master of the Gate, Keeper of the Keg, and—depending on the day—the family disappointment. I'm here to tell you, if ye can't brew, ye can't pass. It's tradition. Don't ask who started it. We've forgotten, but it sounds important."

Instantly fascinated, Tobias clapped his hands. "Is there a rule book?"

"It's too bad I can't stab tradition," Kaelin said. "It would make things so much easier."

Sir Harlow shook his head. "In my day, we had gates that required passwords, not pints."

"Progress," Ed said flatly. "Now everyone dies drunk instead of honorable."

Borin Emberforge climbed onto a table and spread his arms. "Welcome to the Ale Trials!" he bellowed. "There are three parts. First, you must create an original ale with local ingredients. Second, you must temper and bless the ale over the forge fire. And finally, you must drink the brew and remain conscious."

"Imagine the ballad I could write about our victory," Brug declared.

Miri Emberforge, Borin's niece, stepped forward. "There's no way this group can beat an Emberforge—especially not a walking relic from the afterparty."

Kaelin sighed. "I liked her better before she said anything."

Brug heard her disparaging remarks and signed the group up without asking.

Harlow banged his skeletal fist on his armor. "If the living must prove their worth, I should prove I'm still among them."

Kaelin glared at anyone and everyone around her but didn't object—mostly because she was too tired to fight dwarven bureaucracy. Besides, if she was going to be dragged into another mess, at least this one came with alcohol.

Tables were set, ingredients laid out. The smell of malt and smoke curled through the air like a challenge. Dwarves shouted recipes, insults, and marriage proposals in equal measure. The forge's heat turned the air thick enough to chew.

Tobias approached the brew like a magical experiment. Kaelin thought of it like a battlefield. Harlow watched, amused and faintly nostalgic.

"I remember enjoying a pint. Those were the days," Sir Harlow reminisced.

"If we survive this," Tobias said, eyes bright, "I'm writing a paper on cross-disciplinary brewing methods."

"If we survive this," she replied, "I'm setting the paper on fire."

It wasn't flirtation. Not exactly. But it was close enough that Timber sighed and walked away.

Tobias looked at the ingredients before suggesting. "We could use enchanted yeast for flavor amplification."

Kaelin eyed him for a beat. "Or we could use poisonous mushrooms for balance."

"Now is not the time to poison the judges," Tobias muttered.

"Are you sure? It seems like the right time to me," Kaelin replied.

Tobias looked over at Brug. "If we lose, I want it on record I was against homicide."

"Noted," Brug chimed in. "I'll rhyme it with ale."

Kaelin hid her grin behind her cup. He noticed details, rules, how to stay alive—and then completely ignored all of them five seconds later. It was infuriating. It was . . . consistent.

"In life, I once brewed a restorative stout for wounded soldiers. The secret is patience—and rosemary. It's a natural preservative." Sir Harlow added.

Tobias nodded. He added rosemary in honor of the advice.

Timber taste-tested the concoction and passed out immediately. Brug wrote an ode to her sacrifice, temporary as it was.

They named their final concoction 'The Widow's Warmth' with the slogan 'One Sip, and You'll See the Afterlife—or It'll See You.'

Harlow stirred the brew with careful precision. His undead hands kept the temperature perfectly steady. Even the steam curled respectfully away from him, unwilling to test the patience of the dead.

There's something to be said for unintentional magical contributions.

Tobias was impressed by the knight's fortitude.

Kaelin muttered, "Finally, being dead's useful."

"Careful," Tobias said. "He might start charging for it."

And somewhere in the background, Brug began tuning their lute, certain that nothing improved a near-fatal brewing attempt like music.

The forge roared like a dragon with indigestion. The heat pressed against them like an angry god. Tobias's runes flared gold, then red. The air shimmered thick enough to taste—bitter, metallic, alive. Sparks leapt into Tobias's hair; Kaelin swore, steadying the cauldron as if daring the mountain to blink first. Heat shimmered between them like the pause before bad decisions.

"Don't panic," Kaelin snapped, which, of course, made Tobias panic more.

Harlow braced the cauldron, unflinching, bones glinting gold in the firelight. The roar of the forge swallowed the sound of their arguments and almost made them sound like a team.

When the eruption came, it singed Borin's beard and nearly vaporized Tobias's eyebrows. Thankfully, it didn't kill anyone. Kaelin preferred her deaths intentional and well-deserved.

Tobias and Kaelin exchanged an almost-smile—almost. She hated how easy it was starting to feel. The moment flickered like the forge light—bright, reckless, gone too soon. But she caught herself wanting to chase it anyway, which was worse than any curse.

Harlow quietly remarked, "You two balance chaos and purpose better than most living kingdoms."

Kaelin snorted. "That's generous. Mostly, I stop him from dying."

Tobias added, "And she reminds me not to blow up the moral high ground."

It wasn't harmony, but it was rhythm—and that was new.

Brug turned Harlow's statement into a verse immediately. "Chaos and purpose, drunk and nervous," they sang. "Perfect rhyme. I'm calling this song 'The Ale That Almost Killed Us All.' Working title."

"It's now time for the final stage of the Ale Trials. The contestants must drink their brew," Borin announced.

The crowd cheered and chanted. There was clapping and stomping. They were lucky the mountain didn't tumble down on them. It was loud enough to cause seismic activity.

Kaelin downed hers like she was swallowing regret.

Tobias sipped it slowly, then swished it in his mouth. "I taste notes of charred honey and mild death." He paused for a beat. "It pairs nicely with hope or despair."

Samples were taken to the judges, a bunch of goats. Goats were surprisingly good judges of beer. One bleated appreciatively. It sounded like a combination of indigestion and applause.

The ale glowed and released harmless magical illusions. Everyone had a vision of what they wanted most.

Kaelin watched herself in a room surrounded by books. She didn't see anyone else there, but she could feel that she wasn't alone. For once, the quiet didn't feel lonely.

Tobias closed his eyes, and Kaelin was there in front of him, smiling at him. He pretended not to see it. Hope, as inconvenient as ever, refused to stay gone.

Harlow looked at his brother and himself, embracing each other in forgiveness. The image flickered as fragile as a flame.

The goats declared their brew the winner.

"Ye've brewed hope and despair in the same mug! That's artistry!" Borin declared.

Brug immediately hummed a victory tune loud enough to wake a mountain.

The gates opened with the help of the goats. The dwarves granted them safe passage through the mountain. Borin added a cask of Elderfire Ale for the road.

"Just more for me to carry that I can't enjoy," Ed complained.

Sir Harlow lingered behind, staring into the mountain tunnels. "There's an old saying—'the deeper you go, the more ghosts you find.' I think mine waits below."

"Your brother?" Tobias asked.

The knight nodded. "Aye. Gravemire was only at the edge of his reach. I can feel his pull."

Kaelin put her hand on his shoulder. "You don't have to face him alone."

Harlow smiled. It was both sad and serene under his helm. "That's what every hero says before they learn why some battles must be faced alone." He turned, the dwarven fire reflecting off his armor like sunlight.

"Before you go, one last toast, for luck." Brug poured each of them a pint, except for Timber; she got cheese.

Harlow lifted his mug. "Consider my debt to the living repaid. Keep walking forward, no matter the ghosts behind." He turned towards the tunnels. His lantern glowed faintly blue. "Thank you for reminding me I'm still part of the living, even if it's not a conventional life."

The air cooled as he walked away. The scent of hops and smoke followed him down the dark tunnel until only the sound of his footsteps remained.

They watched him disappear into the dark.

Brug plucked a somber tune, promising to come back to write the words later. Everyone needed to hear "The Knight Who Brewed His Last Goodbye."

Tobias watched until the light flickered out of sight. "He'll come back."

Kaelin didn't watch the knight walk away. "Maybe," she said. "Or maybe that's not the point."

And so, the heroes of questionable repute, freshly crowned as dwarven brewmasters, continued their march into destiny.

It smelled faintly of beer, regret, and something uncomfortably close to hope.

13

ONE ACCIDENTAL LOVE ELIXIR LATER

"Alchemy is 10% ingredients, 20% precision, and 70% catastrophic overconfidence."

The tunnels of Myrkspire Pass lit up for our drunken travelers, illuminating their path through to the other side and away from both Sir Harlow and the remnants of the Ale Trials. Some adventures end with glory. Others end with hangovers, regret, and mild spelunking.

The amber lights flickered along the walls, pulsing like a heartbeat—as if the mountain itself had drunk too much and was trying to steady itself.

They stopped stumbling when the tunnel widened enough to set up camp. It took twice as long as it should have, but half the time Ed expected it to take. Water dripped rhythmically from the ceiling, providing the beat for the chaos below. Truly, if there were a soundtrack for bad decisions, it would be this: uneven footsteps, dripping water, and the faint hiss of something starting to burn.

Tobias rummaged through the bag Borin had given them. "Look, I have enough ingredients to make a healing tonic!" Which, of course, he began doing immediately.

To be fair, Tobias's 'healing tonics' usually did more for the soul than the body—mostly because the body didn't survive long enough to complain.

"The last time you said that," Kaelin muttered, "we lost half a frying pan and gained a mild haunting."

It didn't take long for Tobias to finish. In fact, Kaelin had just finished setting up the tents when the mage handed her a mug, smiling with the earnestness of a man who'd never learned from history. For half a heartbeat, she forgot to be careful. She clocked the way he had laid out everything in precise rows, labeled every cork so no one died of a mix-up. Competence was a dangerous flirtation. That's when she remembered herself, armor clanking back into place—metaphorically, but only just.

She took a sip. "You mean another drink that'll kill us slower."

Tobias slid the waterskin across the log to her without comment—his action said more than any words ever could. It said, "I know you like caution, it's yours if you want it."

"I will immortalize our Ale Trial victory in song," Brug declared. They grabbed their lute, but every time they started to sing, they drifted off, the words leaving their head before the verse was fully formed. They strummed a single note, then asked no one in particular, "Does anyone remember the rhyme for fermentation?"

It was a fair question. Scholars have debated it for centuries. Brug, however, intended to solve it while half-conscious and tipsy—an approach common among great poets and poor planners alike.

"This actually tastes good," Tobias slurred before pouring himself another mug. He stood, tilting one way and then the next before sitting back down. "Is it just me, or are the tunnels spinning?"

Ed's head swung from Tobias to the gifted barrel of ale. "Great. Now I'm going to have to carry the mage and a keg."

Kaelin leaned against the tunnel wall, watching the mage's grin soften in the flickering light. She thought about smiling back—but then she remembered she had standards. And survival instincts. Both were in short supply lately, even though she'd been rationing them since Tobias started mixing drinks and potions. Still, there was something about that grin—unguarded, uncalculated—that made her forget, just for a breath, that getting attached was a terrible idea.

Timber sniffed the ground as if anticipating trouble. Her hackles bristled and ears twitched as she stared at the brew bubbling a little too cheerfully. If experience had taught her anything, it was that when liquid starts looking pleased with itself, run. Unfortunately, she was surrounded by bipeds that couldn't take a hint.

And yet, somehow, they survived the night. Which, frankly, surprised everyone—including the mountain. Especially the mountain.

SIDE QUEST

They emerged on the other side of Myrkspire into an old-growth cedar forest, surrounded by trees with bases larger than some houses. The sunlight stabbed at them with cruel enthusiasm. Tobias, hungover from his so-called 'healing elixir,' immediately started taking notes on everything around him.

"I've never seen anything like these trees," he said, awe softening his voice. "They're giants among us. Do you think there are dryads here?"

"That would be fun," Brug said brightly.

"Gods, I hope not. They're mischievous little creatures," Kaelin replied, rubbing her temple.

She didn't elaborate, but somewhere in her past was a story involving a stolen boot, a tree with opinions, and one very embarrassing misunderstanding.

Ed stopped in the clearing. "I need a break. Will you three drink this ale already?"

Kaelin sighed. Another delay, but if she was being honest, she didn't feel like going any farther today. "Fine. We'll set up camp here."

Tobias grabbed his alchemy kit. He mixed herbs, including some rosemary—after all, it worked with their ale. He scanned the camp, and his eyes lit up when they landed on the barrel of ale. When he poured in a splash, mist rose from the mixture.

You'd think a man who had just survived an exploding brewery would know when to stop. You'd be wrong.

"Nothing Tobias brews ever ends quietly," Kaelin said, scratching Timber's ears, waiting for whatever happened next.

If she'd learned anything, it was that 'quietly' was rarely on the menu.

Brug sauntered by the cauldron, trying not to look suspicious. If anyone was watching, they would have failed. Their eyes darted from one person to another before they added a fairy flower to the mix. "This will improve the aroma."

The mist thickened; tendrils curled towards the horse. Ed sneezed, bumping into Timber, who knocked down one of the stakes holding the cauldron in place. The mixture spilled. It shimmered, pinkish steam rising before vanishing into the air.

Tobias flicked two fingers, and a thin wind ward shivered into place, nudging the worst of the steam away from Timber and Kaelin. Not flashy. Just . . . thoughtful. The kind of magic that noticed where you stood.

Tobias began to sweat. He tried to contain it before declaring, "It's fine. Definitely not cursed."

Historically speaking, those words have never been followed by anything fine. Or uncursed.

Kaelin crossed her arms. "Where have I heard that before?"

The answer, dear reader, was 'every single time he opened his mouth.'

"Statistically," Tobias muttered, "this is where something explodes."

"At least you're learning," she said, and it felt dangerously like a private joke.

The strumming of the lute sounded like romance. The assassin held her breath, waiting for something to happen. The mage crossed his fingers, praying he was right and everything would be fine. On the other hand, Brug waited, impatiently, for the adventure to begin. Nothing happened. Everyone ate their dinner and went to sleep.

Honestly, dear reader, it was a let down for everyone, except Tobias. I saw him breathe a sigh of relief.

Morning came with birds chirping and sunlight filtering through the giant trees. It was cold but beautiful, cheerful even. Mornings shouldn't be that happy.

Someone—*not* Kaelin—had set her boots nearer the fire so they'd be warm. She didn't comment. Gratitude was a habit she was still learning to wear without itching.

She stretched, bones aching, mind foggy. For a moment, the forest was just quiet—no explosions, no magic, no idiots brewing disaster. Then Tobias opened his mouth, and peace died a swift death.

"Let's get . . . ," Kaelin started.

". . . On the road," Tobias finished.

They looked at each other for a moment. Shocked.

Tobias winced. "Is that—annoying?"

"It's inconvenient," she said. *Paused*. "But not . . . awful."

He nodded like she'd handed him a map with three safe roads.

Brug just smiled. "It's happening." They clapped their hands.

"What's happening?" Kaelin asked, unsure if she really wanted their answer.

"Love." They spun in a circle. "It's in the air. All around us. The air hums with it. Even the trees are whispering about it."

"Trees don't whisper," she replied. Her lack of emotion countered Brug's enthusiasm.

Tobias stepped in. "They do . . ."

"They don't," she tried to interrupt.

But Tobias continued over her dissent. "If you listen closely."

She glared.

Brug sighed with hearts in their eyes. They hugged a cedar tree. "You understand me, don't you?" they whispered. "You've seen so much, been around so long. Deep roots, strong. I can feel our connection."

The tree creaked in the wind.

"It's shy," Brug explained.

It was a tree. It was not shy. It was, however, enduring the most awkward love confession in arboreal history.

Tobias rubbed the back of his neck. "Do you feel strange?" He avoided making eye contact with Kaelin.

"Define strange?" she asked flatly.

He hesitated. "I don't know. Like everything is too alive . . . Too bright, too colorful?"

"Congrats. You've discovered emotions or hallucinogens." She turned away. "Now pack up before Brug marries the local fauna." She tossed the words over her shoulders.

Love spells don't work on a schedule; they prefer to wait until the most inconvenient moment before kicking in.

And in this case, they apparently started with light flirting and forest humidity.

As they traveled, the terrain changed from giant trees to normal-sized redwoods bordering cliffs over the ocean. Ferns and flowers covered the forest floor, happy, bright, and colorful.

Tobias pointed to his left, away from the sea. "Look at those—"

"—lovely purple flowers," Kaelin finished. She shook her head. "What did I just say?" Her tone was laced with confusion.

"We can shut it down," Tobias offered quietly. "The finishing-each-other's-sentences thing. If you want."

"I want control," she said. Then, softer, "I'll let you know when I don't."

Consent, negotiated like travel routes.

Brug smiled, whistling as they strolled down the path.

"Maybe I should name—"

"—one of your daggers after it. I believe it's a heart-shaped fairy flower," the mage pointed out.

Kaelin didn't understand why they were finishing each other's sentences. She didn't know how she felt about it.

The space between them hummed—annoying, unfamiliar, and far too aware of itself. She pretended not to notice.

Timber sidled up next to Tobias, growling anytime the wind blew the wrong way.

Every rabbit, fox, and deer walked next to Ed, flirting with the horse in each animal's native tongue. Pushing and shoving the other animals out of the way, vying for Ed's attention.

It was like watching nature's most confusing mating ritual. All. Day. Long.

As did Tobias and Kaelin finishing each other's sentences, Timber barking at anything and everything that got too close to the mage, and Brug writing sonnets to the flora and fauna declaring their undying love over and over again.

Evening came, the forest was less enchanted or more exhausted.

By the time they decided to set up camp, Tobias was flustered, and Kaelin was irritable. Brug had hearts in their eyes.

And Timber decided that love, like alchemy, was better observed from afar.

The sun set while they settled into camp. By the time they were done, stars shone overhead like fairies dancing in the clouds. It was a night made for hand-holding and romantic confessions. There was only one orc okay with those emotions, and they were busy confessing their feelings to a tree as the potion's magic was about to peak.

"Brug, come have a seat. I just finished dinner, and it's only slightly burned." Tobias waved the orc over.

The bard sashayed over with an extra kick-ball-change. They pirouetted onto a log and waited for their plate. "Ah, a delicious meal served by a handsome mage. What a glorious night!"

"It's quite vibrant," Tobias admitted. He shrugged to dismiss the odd feelings he'd had all day. His feelings didn't stop him from handing Kaelin a plate or from sitting next to her.

They ate to the music of their bard and Timber. At least the dog was howling in key.

When the meal was over, Kaelin cleaned up. When she was done, she could have sat anywhere, but instead, she found her way back to Tobias. Their hands were so close they might as well have been touching.

"Here okay?" he asked, not moving closer until she answered.

"For now," she said, which was the bravest yes she could give a person and still survive it.

The space between them buzzed, warm and irritatingly alive. She told herself it was the ale—or proximity—or the universe mocking her again.

Tobias looked at their hands. "I don't know why I feel this way around you."

Kaelin's pulse jumped, not because of the words, but because he meant them. People rarely did. She hated how that mattered.

"Airborne alchemy. It's the only explanation." She shrugged before folding her hands in her lap.

"But I felt it before last night."

"You're wrong," she denied with unusual force. "Probably still that stupid spellbinding spell."

Tobias whispered, "That faded a while ago." He didn't mean for her to hear.

She did. "But you're still here."

"I'll always be here, as long as you'll let me." The words tumbled out. He wasn't sure if he wanted to say them or not, but now that they were out, he felt relief. Promises were cheap. Staying was expensive. He kept paying in small coins—warm boots, wind wards, questions he didn't force her to answer.

The universe held its breath, which was concerning because last time it did that, something exploded.

She looked at him—steady hands, hopeful eyes, absolutely terrible judgment. The worst part was how much she trusted him anyway.

"How about I test an antidote on you?" she threatened before she stood. All she wanted was someone's loyalty, but now that it was within reach, it felt too close, too bright—like staring straight into sunlight.

Ed nosed the cauldron towards the assassin.

Animals: always trying to hint at humans instead of making announcements.

"What now?" She couldn't handle any more confessions, especially not if they came from her.

There was a label stuck to the bottom of the cauldron. She peeled it off and read it. " 'Elixir of Emotional Amplification—not for social situations.' Tobias!"

She thrust the label towards him. He read it and blushed.

"I didn't . . . That is . . . It was an . . ," he stammered.

"Never mind. Hopefully, we can sleep it off." Kaelin stormed off to her tent.

They would not, in fact, sleep it off.

14

There's Only One Bed (Please Don't Make It Weird)

"Proximity does things to people. So do emotional wounds, warm fires, and unresolved tension."

T he next morning came early, and it was bright. Still too pretty, with too many birds chirping, lights streaming through branches, and dust motes sparkling. It was the sort of morning that mocked you for having feelings the night before.

Kaelin stepped out of the tent, squinting as the sun burrowed into her brain like gophers in the dirt. It didn't help that she was also groggy, annoyed the world dared to be cheerful when she would rather vomit on someone's shoes—not hers, she really liked her boots.

The forest hummed with lingering magic, like the emotional equivalent of static cling. It clung worse than Tobias's optimism and was twice as hard to get rid of.

Tobias looked just as miserable when he emerged from his tent. He rubbed the back of his neck, looked at her, looked away, and then did the worst thing possible—smiled shyly. He had the decency to look guilty about it, which somehow made it worse. Kaelin promptly decided she hated mornings, sunlight, and all known forms of human interaction.

After last night, he continually glanced over at the assassin when he believed she wasn't looking. She, of course, noticed every glance, catalogued them for future avoidance, and pretended it didn't matter. It absolutely mattered.

"I'm sorry about last night." Tobias might have been talking to Kaelin, but he couldn't look at her.

"What for?" she asked. "Did something happen last night?"

Tobias's head whipped towards her. She raised an eyebrow.

"I don't know but, you know I'm always messing something up." He wiped his hands on his pants. It was a useless gesture; regret doesn't come off that easily.

They were both convinced the other one didn't remember anything important—they were both wrong.

"So . . . feeling less emotionally compromised this morning?" He made the mistake of undermining their denial.

Kaelin almost ignored him. "Define less."

Ah, the traditional morning-after dance: denial in three-four time. Two steps back, one step sideways, and absolutely no eye contact.

Brug joined them for a morning coffee, chipper as soon as they heard the birds chirping. They continued to serenade the trees, deeply in love with a particularly shapely oak tree. The oak, for its part, swayed seductively in the wind. Tobias swore he heard it giggle.

All while Ed was trailed by a lovesick family of rabbits and a goat. No one knew where the goat had come from. The goat wore the expression of someone who'd made a terrible romantic decision and was now committed out of pride.

Timber ignored everyone, muttering with body language that she preferred them before they had all caught feelings. She was worried they were contagious. If Timber could have rolled her eyes, she would have. Instead, she sighed—a sound that somehow managed to convey the word 'unbelievable.'

If hangovers were an art form, this group could have been a museum exhibition. EMOTIONAL RESIDUE, CIRCA CHAOS, the plaque would read. Medium: regret, glitter, and poor impulse control.

Together, they sat around what was left of the campfire eating breakfast. Mostly quiet, at least as quiet as this group ever was now. Kaelin watched as Tobias ate his food absentmindedly, his focus on whatever it was he furiously scribbled into his journal. Curious, not that she would admit it if anyone asked, she used collecting their dirty dishes as an excuse to get closer. It worked, for the most part.

"I don't know what went wrong, was it a dosage error?" he asked himself. After all, he'd yet to realize anyone else was near him.

She realized he thought yesterday was a scientific mishap. It was easier for her if she pretended to believe him. Easier to call it alchemy than vulnerability. Easier to call it a spell than a choice.

"I have written the greatest love ballad of all time," Brug announced, to who, no one knew. "Last night was inspirational."

They began to sing; it was objectively terrible, but something about it made Timber howl in harmony.

The assassin, always capable of ignoring the things she didn't want to think about, blocked out the music as she finished packing.

"Do you want to talk about last night?" Tobias approached gently.

Her pack fell to the ground.

She glared at it. He stepped back with a shake of his head. He'd learned to recognize when proximity became peril.

She didn't discuss feelings. Even though his words echoed in her head. Was he really promising her his loyalty, that he wouldn't abandon her? She rolled her shoulders. He couldn't be, it was just the potion. Nothing more. But that didn't stop his words from echoing in her head.

"Let's go." Her tone was sharp, sharper than it needed to be. But she was raw around the edges, which made her stabby and there was nothing around her to stab. Stomping off, she decided walking alone was the only way she would survive. But Tobias followed her with some muttered excuse about map navigation.

She pretended to be annoyed. The pretending took effort. He pretended not to notice, which was worse. Somewhere between them, affection curled up like a cat—uninvited, persistent, and absolutely refusing to leave.

* * *

The road wound its way to the shore. It was one of those places where the cliffs met the ocean. Beautiful, breathtaking, and impossible to navigate, especially when there was fog and a consistent drizzle, a perfect recipe for romance or tragedy, depending on who was holding the map.

"Oh look, a waterfall!" Brug pointed to where water cascaded over a cliff before drifting into the ocean. "It's so romantic."

"Is that an inn built into the cliff next to it?" Tobias looked at the structure longingly. It had been forever since he'd slept on something other than a bedroll.

Kaelin saw the look and caved before she even knew it was happening. "Why don't we stay there for the night?"

Timber looked at her and raised one doggy eyebrow. The assassin raised one eyebrow back. The bark that followed said it all. Roughly translated: 'Bad idea, you emotionally compromised gremlin.' Not that it had an effect on what was about to happen.

Tobias skipped, yes, skipped to the inn's entrance. There was no way he was going to allow anything to happen to change Kaelin's mind. Somewhere in the universe, destiny took notes and snickered.

For once, the door was silent as it opened, and they stepped inside. The air smelled of salt, smoke, and something recognizable, but unidentifiable. Lanterns hung crooked on all the walls, their flames guttering every few seconds, like they were constantly considering giving up and deciding even that was too much effort. The wallpaper, once floral, had somehow fossilized. Somewhere a pipe dripped in perfect time with Tobias's optimism. Ed took one glance and found his way to the stables without a word. Apparently, the horse was done talking, for the moment.

The inn was shabby, and not the chic sort of shabby that trends every so often. Everything about the place had seen better days, including the innkeeper. A gnome of indeterminate age, like most gnomes, stood behind the front desk looking weary and weathered—as though he'd been personally betrayed by gravity.

The wind outside whistled through cracks in the walls, bringing with it the smell of seaweed and wet rope—the sort of scent that promised mold and adventure in equal measure.

"Tell me what you need before you drip all over my floor." The gnome's gruff voice broke the silence.

"Something with mood lighting," Brug demanded.

The innkeeper stared, then blinked once. "There's one room with one slightly cursed bed."

"Sounds perfect! We'll take it." Brug tossed some coins onto the desk.

Tobias looked from the innkeeper to Brug and back. "Did you say cursed?"

"Pay it no mind. Just ignore the whispers," he said. "It's just the mattress remembering things." The key appeared while the coin disappeared.

Kaelin snatched the key off the desk. "I guess that's settled then." It wasn't, but she wasn't about to admit she'd already lost control of the situation.

The stairs, unlike the silent door, creaked. Each step moaned beneath their weight, a symphony of creaks and complaints. The corridor narrowed as they climbed. The walls bowed inward as though the whole place was conspiring to shove them closer together.

She unlocked the door and swung it open. The room itself was small enough to qualify as a large cupboard. A single candle flickered in a sconce, throwing shadows that looked suspiciously sentient. The bed dominated the space, carved from dark wood and upholstered in regret. Its sheets were faded rose-colored—romantic once, tragic now. The whisper came from beneath the pillow, a sigh that sounded uncomfortably like 'welcome back.'

Tobias, more flustered than he'd ever been, said, "You can have the bed."

"Nope." She shook her head, obviously uncomfortable for the first time. If emotions were landmines, this was a field she had no intention of crossing barefoot.

She insisted she didn't need comfort. He insisted he didn't need sleep. They were both lying. Poorly.

Timber, ever pragmatic, claimed the floor by one side of the bed. She gave Tobias a look that said, 'I'm watching you,' and he believed her.

"I'm going to find somewhere romantic to sleep." Brug left the room with a swoosh.

Where they went, no one knew; it was likely by another tree though.

Kaelin looked at the bed. "There's room for both of us." She sat on the side of the bed, near Timber.

"Are you sure? It's awfully small." Tobias took a step back and ran into a wall. He briefly considered apologizing to the wall.

She sighed. "Look, it's a bed, I know you want to sleep on something other than a bedroll. It's fine." The statement was followed by her signature murder glare.

He sat immediately. "Okay. We should get some sleep then."

Timber stood, padded over to the side Tobias was on, circled, and lay down. Her canine chaperone instincts were on high alert. There would be no smiting under her watch.

Kaelin nodded and unsheathed all her daggers. It took more than a moment. Then she lay down, her back to him. He followed her lead, as uncomfortable as it was.

She told herself it was just exhaustion, that warmth wasn't safety and quiet wasn't peace. But the space between them didn't feel empty anymore, and that was dangerous enough.

It's not that Kaelin disliked sharing. She just preferred her personal space to be unoccupied, unexamined, and entirely unswooned in. The bed creaked softly, whispering something that sounded suspiciously like 'finally.' Neither of them dared move again.

* * *

The candle flickered out hours before light found its way into the room through the crack in the walls and the one minuscule window. The air was heavy with old salt and sleep, the kind that clung to everything, including thoughts best left unexamined. It might have forced the assassin and the mage to wake up, but that would assume that either of them slept.

Kaelin stared at the ceiling beams, counting cracks and pretending each one was a continent she'd rather be conquering. Beside her, Tobias was too still to be asleep. Every time he exhaled, the mattress whispered something obscene about 'tension.'

Timber snored, still asleep on the floor next to Tobias. Every few seconds, her paw twitched—chasing dream rabbits or emotional stability, hard to say which.

Unable to stay still any longer, Kaelin twisted in place, or at least she thought she had. She was wrong. Her hand brushed his arm, and she froze. Tobias held his breath, waiting to feel her reaction. When nothing happened, he rolled onto his back. His shoulder just barely touched her back.

Proximity, the world's most efficient torture.

The dog's dreamy barks filled the silence. Her dreams were the only thing not filled with the tension occupying the space between the two in bed.

Tobias, ever the overthinker, whispered, "I can't tell if you're awake or plotting my death."

"Can't it be both?" She rolled onto her back. Their shoulders fully touched. She didn't move away.

He turned to face her. "So, awake and not plotting my death. You don't scare me like you used to."

She hated how well he knew her. How soft his words sounded. She hated even more that his words somehow made her chest stutter.

The silence was a precipice, one she wasn't sure she was ready to leap off. Still, she turned towards him. They were so close, inches away from each other.

Her pulse echoed in the quiet, syncing with his breathing, an accidental rhythm that felt far too deliberate.

The one candle sputtered back to life. After all, the room was cursed.

They locked eyes, their first unguarded look.

She almost leaned in. She almost let herself trust. To feel it. He almost did the same.

There was a loud crash. The door swung open. "I found waffles, pumpkin spice with cream cheese, my dear lovebirds."

Timber snapped awake, barked, growled, and drooled. Tobias flinched and jumped out of the bed. Kaelin stabbed the pillow. It was an accident, or so she claimed.

The cursed bed sighed. "Finally."

"We're leaving immediately," she muttered before storming out of the room.

Ah yes, flight—humanity's oldest coping mechanism. Hope, unfortunately, is harder to outrun.

Behind her, Tobias lingered a second too long in the doorway, staring at the dent her dagger left in the pillow.

Kaelin stopped as soon as she reached the bottom of the stairs. Outside the room, the hall was too bright, the air too clean. The world had no right to smell normal after a night like that. Then the smell of bacon, not burned, and breakfast sweets with a bit of cloves, nutmeg, and cinnamon added in, wafted out of the inn's pub. Without a single thought, she wandered inside.

"Table for one?" a cheerful gnome with pigtails asked.

Kaelin glanced over her shoulder. "I wish. But make it for three, four if you count the dog."

The gnome smiled, gesturing for her to follow. "I'm Maggie Mae. I'll be helping you this morning."

Kaelin grunted her agreement.

As she took her seat, Timber clambered down the stairs, followed by Brug's heavy steps, and a tiptoeing Tobias.

"I'll have the pumpkin spice waffles and bacon. They'll have . . . " She pointed to the rest of the group with her chin ". . . everything else."

Brug took their seat, humming something joyous. Tobias sulked, slouching in his chair. Kaelin pretended to sharpen her knives, but was actually desperately trying to steady her thoughts.

Her mind circled back to the room, the one bed, the moment. Outwardly, she acted cold and dismissive.

She didn't want to kill the moment. She wanted to understand it. That was worse.

"Look at you two lovebirds." Brug rested their chin in their hands.

Timber growled.

Brug batted their eyelashes. "So cute the morning after one bed, so scandalous."

Kaelin ignored them. Tobias felt a deep need to talk.

"I'm sorry. For earlier, for that moment, or maybe for all the things I said, or maybe didn't say." Tobias used so many words to say nothing at all.

Kaelin stopped him, or at least tried. "We're fine. Stop talking."

They were not fine. He did not stop talking.

Breakfast came, was consumed, and now it was time to leave.

Tobias unrolled their map. It immediately sighed, folded itself in half, and burst into flames.

Kaelin groaned. "Oh good. The map hates us again."

"It doesn't hate us—it's temperamental parchment!" Tobias exclaimed.

Brug looked at the map. "It's love parchment! Look, it burned a heart shape."

There are few things more dangerous than magical cartography and romantic subplots. Our heroes now had both.

"Okay, lovebirds. It's time to go where the map takes you." Brug grabbed the map.

Timber growled. She really didn't like the word 'lovebirds.'

Kaelin stomped off, again.

A faint sound echoed from the trees—a distant, indignant crow of fire.

Timber's ears perked up.

Somewhere out there, a certain rooster was awake. And it was personal. Destiny apparently had a thing for bad timing and poultry.

15

The Map That Personally Hates Me

"Magical maps are notoriously unreliable. Much like hope, or ex-boyfriends."

The group left the inn behind, having drunk too much coffee, got too little sleep, and once again feeling emotionally compromised. The morning mist clung to their cloaks like gossip, damp and persistent. The coastal road carved its way along a cliff that couldn't decide whether it was land or sea, with spray crashing below and fog curling overhead. It was beautiful in the way disasters sometimes are—picturesque right before someone slips.

Tobias looked over the map, first one way then the next. For the moment, the parchment was silent and no longer glowing. Suspiciously silent.

Kaelin snatched the map out of his hands and walked several paces away. The amount of noise she made with the map was truly impressive—if passive aggression was an Olympic sport, she'd have medaled. The wind snatched the corners, flapping it like it protested her handling. The parchment crackled like it wanted to file a complaint. Disgusted with the map, or herself (and honestly, what was the difference?), she rolled it up and shoved it into Tobias's pack like it owed her rent.

Both of them were pretending not to think about 'The Almost Kiss That Didn't Happen (and Thank the Gods for That).' Both of them were failing.

Kaelin pretended the icy wind helped; it didn't. Tobias pretended to study the map; it wasn't cooperating either. He kept glancing sideways at her, as if eye contact might rewrite history or at least improve their sense of direction. It didn't do either.

He eventually gave the map back to her, annoyed with the stubborn paper.

It didn't help that Brug sang a new love ballad they titled "Two Hearts, One Mattress." They were about as subtle as a dragon in a library. The dragon, for the record, would have had more restraint.

Timber growled every time they rhymed 'love' with 'dove,' which was unfortunately often. On the third growl, Brug switched to 'love' and 'above,' which was somehow worse.

The group marched away in silence, if you didn't count the singing, the passive-aggressive map rustling, and Tobias's attempt to look like he hadn't fallen off a bed of emotions. Seabirds wheeled overhead, squawking in what sounded suspiciously like laughter. Even nature had a sense of irony today.

It didn't take long for them to hike back up to the cliffside trail. The ocean crashed below them, a metronome to their day.

Salt clung to everything—boots, cloaks, unresolved tension. A distant lighthouse blinked through the fog like a tired god keeping watch, or judging them. Probably both.

They crested a bend and found a roadside shrine: a weathered pillar of driftwood and brass nailed with tiny compasses and coils of red thread. A tarnished plaque read, TO THE NAVIGATRIX, WHO SAVES FOOLS FROM MAPS AND MAPS FROM FOOLS. Someone had left an offering—three sardines in a shell bowl and a shot of cheap rum. Kaelin paused, then flicked a copper into the bowl with a slight flick of her wrist that said, 'superstition is for other people' and also 'absolutely not taking chances today.'

"Let me check the map again." Tobias held out his hand, already braced for impact. "Why isn't it giving us a new location?"

She slapped the rolled paper into his hand.

This time when he unrolled it, the map sighed audibly.

"Oh, it's you again," the map said, its tone tinged with sarcasm.

"Great, now it talks, and it's judging us," Kaelin muttered.

Brug sauntered over, for once not singing. "I will charm the map with a song," they announced grandly before belting out something that sounded suspiciously like an apology set to opera.

The map was not charmed. It folded itself shut and smacked the orc across their face.

"It's fine." Brug's nose bled slightly. "It's just playing hard to get."

Tobias took the map back. "Now's the time to show us where to go next."

"Maybe point us in the direction of the king or the flaming poultry." Kaelin threw her braid over her shoulder.

Nothing happened. Kaelin looked at the map. One route highlighted, then another, and one more.

"This is pointless," she muttered, tossing the map to the mage.

He got out his wand, chanted something with multiple syllables, and tapped the map. Nothing happened.

She looked over his shoulders, and the paper rerouted three times. "If we follow the map, we're going to travel in circles."

"Maybe it's a metaphor," Tobias said.

"For what?" She raised an eyebrow.

"For our entire relationship," he whispered, loud enough to be heard.

The map sniffed—actually sniffed—and crinkled petulantly.

"There are few things worse than a vindictive piece of parchment," Tobias said.

"Except maybe the person who enchanted it," Kaelin replied.

"Or the person who broke up with it," Brug added, wiggling their eyebrows.

Kaelin blinked. "You think someone dated the map?"

Brug grinned. "Wouldn't be the strangest ex I've heard of."

"It's Guild-work," Tobias murmured, tapping a faint watermark. "See the ouroboros compass embossing? That's Ourochart—Eldreach cartomancers. They lace temperament into terrain. Rumor says they charge double to chart matters of the heart."

"So, we're paying with my sanity," Kaelin said. "Good. I was overstocked."

Passive-aggressive maps focused on love were extra frustrating. They knew all the wrong turns and had the emotional maturity of a teenage oracle. Which, unfortunately, meant it fit right in with the rest of them.

They continued on without the map's help. Ed stayed silent as the group wandered until they found a clearing surrounded by fog and ferns. The air smelled faintly of moss and lament—the scent of people who once thought camping would be 'fun.'

"Let's take a break. Maybe I can reason with the map." Tobias offered a solution.

"You can't reason with paper," Kaelin responded. "I've tried. Contracts mostly."

"Also receipts," Brug added. "Tried to argue sales tax with a shop in Northwode once. Lost to parchment."

They all stared at the map. It was finally glowing again. Soft, pulse-like light spread across the parchment, illuminating faded ink and an unfamiliar symbol in the corner—a compass shaped like a serpent biting its own tail.

"Back to Myrkspire," Tobias read.

The words shimmered across the map like bad news delivered politely.

Timber offered to pee on it again.

"Not now, Timber," Kaelin commanded.

Brug looked over their shoulders. "Are we going back to Myrkspire? You lovebirds could use another party."

"No," Kaelin and Tobias said at the same time, then looked at each other. Was the elixir still affecting them?

"It's sulking," Tobias groaned. "I think it wants an apology."

Kaelin refused on principle—and possibly out of spite. "I don't apologize to inanimate objects."

This was demonstrably false. She had apologized to a teapot once, but that had been strategic.

"Maybe you should apologize," Tobias suggested. "Not because the map deserves it, but because I can't read it without your cooperation."

She glared. Timber glared. Brug hummed.

"Fine." She relented, muttering something vaguely resembling an apology.

The map purred. It purred like a smug cat that had just witnessed emotional growth and disapproved.

It was official. The map had imprinted on her.

The map began to respond to Kaelin's mood. When she was annoyed, it showed dead ends. When she was calm, it revealed shortcuts. When Tobias laughed too close to her, it drew hearts in the margin. The number of times the map changed illustrated how much internal conflict the assassin was dealing with. Whole towns appeared and disappeared based on whether she clenched her jaw. It was, frankly, impressive.

Tobias noticed the trend and pointed it out.

"You're imagining things." She put up her mental wall one brick at a time to replace the ones that were cracking.

Tobias pushed his hair out of his eyes. "It's literally glowing in sync with your heartbeat."

"Coincidence." She walked away, one way to escape sentient-map-created emotional entanglement.

It was not a coincidence. It was karmic punishment for feelings.

The parchment quivered. A line shimmered across it—two dots, one labeled *K* and the other *T* appeared. Tobias blushed. The dots slowly drifted closer the longer he blushed. Tobias noticed first. Kaelin refused to look. The map, apparently, was shipping them.

Timber growled at the map. Not surprisingly, the map growled back.

"It's a romantic metaphor made flesh!" Brug declared as he moved towards the map.

Kaelin pointed behind her. "You. Away from the map. Now."

They looked over to Tobias, who shrugged and mouthed, "Don't get stabbed." Brug rolled their eyes before moving away from the assassin.

The map, left unsupervised, drew a tiny doodle of a dagger through a heart. Kaelin noticed. The dagger glowed. The heart didn't last long.

The trail narrowed to a rope bridge strung between two teeth of the cliff. A hand-painted sign read: CROSS ONE AT A TIME (UNLESS YOU'RE DESTINED, THEN HOLD HANDS). Kaelin and

Tobias stared at the sign. The sign stared back with all the authority of damp plywood.

"Absolutely not," Kaelin said, stepping onto the planks alone.

The map, out of spite, sketched a tiny stick-figure of Tobias taking her hand. The boards creaked like a chorus of old men judging her life choices. She crossed in quick, silent steps, refusing to look back. Tobias followed after the sway settled, lips pressed tight, hands nowhere near hers. The bridge groaned, disappointed by their emotional immaturity.

The sun set, lighting up the sky in fiery pinks and golds. They had traveled all day. But when Kaelin looked around, they were back at the cliff where they had started that morning.

She screamed.

If irony were gold, they could have retired.

"Give me the map. I'm going to burn it." She reached for the map.

Tobias snatched it away. "We need directions."

The parchment fluttered in the breeze, then transformed into an origami bird that took flight, screaming, "You don't deserve directions!"

Kaelin deadpanned, "I'm killing it next time."

"You can't kill it; the thing's too petty." Tobias sighed. "It holds grudges like a god with free time."

Brug clapped. "It's symbolic!"

Timber howled, maybe at the map, or the rising moon.

Tired logic led them to a scraggly patch of wind-stunted pines. Kaelin staked the tent fast and low; Tobias muttered a weather ward—sober, careful magic, the kind that kept rain out and feelings in. Brug hung a tiny string of charm-bells that jingled whenever anyone thought about kissing. They jingled far too often. Timber buried the bells.

Ever on alert, even when sleeping, Timber growled—low. A warning. The group turned. Off in the distance, they saw a flicker of red-orange light the forest. A familiar echoing crow reverberated through the trees.

"No," Kaelin whispered. "Is it . . . ?"

Tobias squinted. "Its . . . glowing?"

Brug gasped. "Is that Percival?"

Some horrors cannot be contained by poultry-based logic.

The rooster's fireball arced into the sky, illuminating the forest—and the map, now perched on a branch, flipped them off. Metaphorically, of course.

Kaelin grabbed a dagger. At the moment, she didn't care which one. "If that bird's back, we're turning around."

"Which way?" Tobias asked.

Kaelin looked at him with her quintessential assassin gaze. "Ask your stupid boyfriend map."

The map glowed smugly in reply.

In her current mood, she needed to stab something; instead, she built a fire and sharpened her blades.

Tobias sat nearby, close enough that Kaelin was still part of the group, but not forced to actually engage with anyone. He scribbled in his journal.

Brug strummed their lute half-muttering, half-singing as they worked on the lyrics to another ballad. Kaelin swore she heard something about 'lovebirds.'

"House rule," Kaelin said suddenly, eyes on the fire. "No one uses the word 'lovebirds' unless they want to lose a finger."

Brug raised a hand. "What about 'affectionate pigeons'?"

"Two fingers," Kaelin said.

Tobias coughed into a smile. The map, eavesdropping, sketched two tiny pigeons. Kaelin fed that corner to the flames. The pigeons burned with great dignity.

Neither mentioned the near-kiss, nor the sentient map.

The same couldn't be said for Brug, who sang a lullaby that somehow included the lyrics love, fire, feathers, and fate.

Timber sighed loudly before falling asleep at Kaelin's feet.

The waves crashed somewhere below the cliffs like laughter. The stars blinked awake one by one, pretending not to see the chaos beneath them. It was going to be a long night—and not just because of the poultry.

And somewhere beyond the dark surf and the rope bridge and the shrine to a very tired goddess, the map's inks rearranged themselves in secret: routes bending towards Eldreach, beyond Briarwick, and—infuriatingly—towards each other. But that, dear reader, is not the same as destiny. It's just a suggestion. Maps do love to suggest.

16

THE CULT OF NEVER FINISHING ANYTHING

"Welcome to eternal side questing. No closure. No progress. No refunds."

Sitting around the campfire while Tobias's ward kept the fog circling just feet away was too homey, too peaceful. The rhythmic scratching of the mage's quill in his journal, the bard's strumming, and the dog snoring were all too close to the dreams Kaelin refused to admit she had. She definitely wasn't sitting there thinking about the Almost Kiss and what it meant.

Kaelin was very good at lying to herself. The moment in the cursed bed was the only thing she was thinking about, especially after all the map's shenanigans and Brug's attempt to turn last night into a romantic song.

Had she really found someone to trust—

A log snapped, the fire roared. She'd had enough of this domesticity and overthinking.

"From here on out, there will be no more distractions." Kaelin stood, hands on her hips, as if making such a declaration would make it their reality.

In her defense, she truly believed it when she said it. The universe, however, had a long and petty memory. And thus, began distraction number seven hundred and forty-seven.

"Good evening!" a robed figure called from beyond the firelight, waving.

Distractions often started with a wave, so Kaelin had learned to distrust them. The man's robe was a shade of beige so indecisive it might have been grey once. Half the hem was still basted with thread, and his hood drooped like it had given up halfway through being menacing.

Brug stood immediately, delighted. "Ah, another weary traveler! Come, share our cozy camp." They gestured towards the flames like a bard introducing a song no one had requested.

Timber growled, low and steady. Kaelin might have too. Neither greeting, or lack thereof, stopped the stranger from joining them.

Tobias, being pathologically polite, offered him a mug of tea. "Something to warm you," he said, because apparently hospitality was a reflex he couldn't unlearn.

The man accepted, steam fogging his spectacles. "Thank you for such a generous welcome." He rummaged through his knapsack, pulling out a bundle of wrinkled parchment. "If you have a moment—perhaps several—I'd love to introduce you to the Cult of Never Finishing Anything, also known as the Eternal Side Quest."

Brug immediately grabbed the parchment and started to read aloud. " 'Join Us (Eventually.)' I love the branding—strong, indecisive energy."

Tobias took the flyer from Brug. Wet ink smudged and stained his fingers. "What's this all about?"

He immediately regretted asking, but he wasn't thinking straight. How could he be?

"I'm here to induct you into our faith," the cultist explained. "The worshipping of the Eternal Side Quest. Fulfilling each quest brings one closer to the gods."

It wasn't the strangest cult they had ever met. In fact, it wasn't even in the top five.

There was another growl. No one knew where it originated, but it was more feral than the last.

He knew he should be alarmed, but the mention of 'eternal side quests' triggered the same part of his brain that collected unfinished spells. He was already intrigued.

Tobias stood, fighting the instinct to find out more. "I'm sorry. We're in a hurry." He wanted to stop talking but couldn't. "You see, she's on a mission, and it probably should have been easy. But there's been all these things that keep getting in the way. I'm sure she would ignore them if she could, but for some reason she can't . . ." He trailed off, realizing he was oversharing things that were not his to share.

He tried to escort the man away. He failed.

"Perfect! You'll fit right in." The cultist snapped his fingers, and ten more robed figures surrounded them. Their robes were a mismatched assortment of colors and varying stages of completeness. Some carried half-burned candles; others carried partially finished sandwiches.

Timber, on the other hand, knew trouble when she smelled it. It normally came in groups wearing robes. She was ready to bite someone.

A woman in a purple robe with only one finished side seam stepped forward. "Welcome . . ."

"If one more robed idiot says welcome, I'm going to redecorate this forest in crimson." Kaelin unsheathed her dagger.

The mage shook his head, and for some reason she listened to him instead of demolishing the cultists who were herding them to a 'Welcoming Ceremony' that had been in progress for the last three years.

Kaelin counted ten robed idiots, one mage, one bard, one dog—and wondered which of them she'd regret not stabbing first.

The cultists pushed them past the weather wards, deeper into the forest. Fog swirled around them, thickening until it was impossible to see more than a few feet in any direction. Trees rose from the ground like shadows of sentinels standing guard. The fog dissipated. Before them stood a half-finished arch with the words WELCOME NE— AND PROGRESS IS . . . Before trailing off unfinished.

They passed an unfinished festival lane: the bones of structures held unlabeled jars of preserves, a judging dais was abandoned mid-argument, and a long trestle sagging under rows of untouched pies—apple, blackberry, one an alarming shade of purple. MIDHARVEST FAIR, a sign explained, followed by, (POSTPONED. PENDING. PERHAPS.)

Kaelin looked around, noting the scattered tools, unfinished projects, and incomplete signs. At least the Shadow Guild finished their crimes.

Under the arch, cultists chanted, trailing off as the chant was lost in the wind before starting over like a skipping record. It was obvious to anyone with eyes that the ceremony was never-ending, or at least it should have been. The robed officiants were completely unaware.

Brug looked on in awe. "They understand me."

The orc had written entire ballads about indecision, but this was performance art.

"That's what worries me," Kaelin muttered.

"I have..." Tobias pulled out his notebook and quill. He was already jotting down symbols. He scribbled the word *magic*, underlining it twice.

Kaelin held out her hand to stop him. "Don't do it."

"A question," he finished.

The woman perked up. "Of course." She took Tobias by the arm. "I'm Nysaura and more than happy to answer any of your questions."

"What's your organization's philosophy?"

"Completion breeds stagnation! To stop improving is to die!" Various cult members responded almost in unison.

"That's the dumbest thing I've ever heard," Kaelin said flatly. "And I've dated thieves who worshiped chaos geese."

Brug clapped like a scholar at a symposium. "Yes! Unfinished songs are the purest art! The lack of an ending leaves it up to audience interpretation."

Tobias's quill moved furiously across the page, noting everything around him. "How do you become a member if . . ."

Nysaura took his quill. "Come this way, you can learn everything you want to know."

He took his pen back, adding more to his journal. "Nothing is ever finished?"

No one answered. They just took him by the arms and sat him down in a mandatory 'Vision Board Workshop.'

Timber refused to enter. She was right. Dogs knew better than to walk into religious nonsense.

Beyond the entrance to the workshop stood a table overflowing with half-painted symbols, a scattering of quills, and a single piece of parchment that simply read, *Goals: TBD*. It radiated menace.

Kaelin rubbed her temples. Tobias was already knee-deep in cult bureaucracy. Timber was chewing on a banner, outside of course. And Brug—gods help them—was asking for glitter. Why did it have to be glitter?

It was going to be one of those nights.

Nysaura stepped to the front of the room. She raised her hands. "It's time to move on to the 'Task Assignment Hall.' "

"Not another unrelated task." Kaelin folded her arms.

The cultists gathered around them, herding them like sheep towards the next room. Each wall was constructed of a different material, a testament to the cult's inability to finish anything in a manner that made sense. The room had the same energy as a group project that had outlived its members.

The hallway beyond was lined with the detritus of unfinished ambitions: a mural half-primed, a suit of armor with only one sleeve, and an entire bakery booth still fragrant with day-old dough. A sign hung askew—CONTEST ENTRIES: MID-RISE PASTRY CATEGORY (INDEFINITE EXTENSION).

Kaelin's stomach growled. Timber's growled louder. She had decided it was unsafe to leave her human alone with such religious fervor.

One by one, a robed member stepped forward, doling out what they insisted were simple errands.

A redheaded elf looked at Tobias. "For you, my mage friend. You must perfect the Perpetual Potion of Self-Revision."

Tobias carefully wrote down his task. He tapped the quill against his teeth, already planning out what ingredients he needed. The notes turned from a list of ingredients to chemical formulas as he worked out the potion.

"If I adjust the recursive ratio to account for temporal backlash, theoretically it should improve itself faster than it fails." He paused. "Which . . . might destroy time and space. But with a slight adjustment I could always . . ." He trailed off as if he was already indoctrinated by the cult.

"Our new bardic friend, you must write the Ballad of Infinite Verses." Another member clapped Brug on the back.

They hugged the cultist. "A mission worthy of my talent." They tapped their foot in three-four time. "Verse one! Verse one-point-five! Verse one, the reprise—"

"No." Kaelin didn't look up. "Absolutely not."

Nysaura stepped in front of the assassin. "Your errand is to retrieve eight shards of something that's pointlessly shiny."

Kaelin rolled her eyes, then her shoulders. "You've got to be kidding me."

Somewhere in the distance, the chanting hiccupped into silence—a sign that either enlightenment or an explosion was imminent.

As annoyed as Kaelin was with everyone around her, she figured finding the shards would be the easiest way to get away from these people.

It didn't take long for her to finish the assigned task.

After every shiny shard was collected, someone hollered, "Wonderful! Now you just need the advanced version." Then handed her a commemorative participation ribbon that said 'Progress (Pending)'.

It was like trying to put a book down right when the plot begins plotting. Just one more chapter . . .

She handed the last shard to Nysaura and walked away, leaving Tobias and Brug to finish their errands, at least for the time being. First, she needed to figure out why she had a sinking feeling in the pit of her stomach. With everyone distracted, she searched the compound, moving farther away from the chanting officiants. The deeper she went, the quieter it got—no chanting, no glitter, just the lonely sound of unfinished thoughts gathering dust. That was until she found the record's room.

She searched the room, her annoyance turning to anger that simmered right below the surface. She wasn't angry because the cult was ridiculous. Anger was the easiest emotion to feel, better than anything else. Especially since somewhere deep down, she saw herself in their chaos—half-finished, forever distracted, pretending it was strategy.

She grabbed a stack of ledgers covered in dust. Sitting at the only desk in the room, she blew off the dust and grabbed the one on top. The first book had answers to the questions she didn't know she needed to ask. There it was, Dame Anwyn Stride's insignia, clear, recognizable, something Kaelin saw more times than she could count, and a donation. *Shadow Guild Educational Grant—For the Advancement of Heroic Distractions*. Beneath the entry there was a note: *Keep her occupied. She's getting dangerous.*

She slammed the book shut. The anger that flashed beneath it was the sting of recognition, the burn of betrayal. She'd been trained for efficiency and control, yet somehow, she kept ending up here—chasing side quests and feelings alike.

"Every time I start to finish something, someone reroutes me," she said to the empty room, or maybe it was to the goat that decided to join her. "Am I being sabotaged?"

The sabotage, dear reader, was often herself. But not always.

The goat headbutted her thigh, nudging her into action. She leapt up, stormed out of the room, and went straight to the meeting chamber where Nysaura was mid-sermon.It was going to end in seconds. Kaelin really didn't interrupt anything.

"Where's the money coming from?" She thrust the ledger towards Nysaura. "Who's pulling your strings?"

The leader stared at the book. "We're non-profit. And non-finished."

"Lies," the assassin growled. "Try again."

Before she could draw her blades, the cult surrounded them. They started the ritual to induct them as 'Permanent Members of Perpetual Purpose' once and for all.

No longer curious about the cult, Tobias panicked and started crafting an escape plan. "It's fine. I can improvise a distraction."

"You're the distraction." Kaelin raised an eyebrow.

Brug chanted with the initiates. They loved the rhythm, even if everyone continued to forget the next word, even the next line. The song was never quite complete. Like everything else around them.

"I can write a better chant than this," Brug proclaimed. "At least one that can keep the beat." They grabbed their lute and composed a rousing half-song of rebellion, which they belted out as soon as it was finished.

She watched Tobias focus—calm, determined, quietly brilliant—and felt the spark of trust grow into something she didn't want to acknowledge.

It wasn't attraction. It was something worse, reliability.

He thrust his sketched plan into Kaelin's hand.

"What is this?" She looked at the paper from multiple angles.

He sighed. "A catapult. Prototype A."

"Who's going to pull it?"

"The goats. Possibly enchanted ones." He tapped his notebook.

"Are those pies?" She raised an eyebrow.

"Pies aren't just dessert," Tobias whispered when she frowned. "Cream pies stun—visibility zero. Fruit pies carry mass. Pumpkin does . . . something to morale. We need predictable weight and high spread. Also, sugar is mildly conductive if the wards tangle."

"Who's baking the pies?"

Brug waved a ladle they definitely hadn't owned five minutes ago. "I found them! Abandoned pastry from the Midharvest Fair. It's destiny. Or indigestion. Maybe both." They tapped their horns with the ladle, pausing to contemplate the duality of existence.

Some plans are born bad and then miraculously worsen.

Timber stood and padded over to her favorite mage and lifted his hand up for extra ear scratches. She always approved of anything that involved running.

The lead nanny goat wore a crooked wreath of paper tickets—"Docket," Tobias read—while the smaller one headbutted anything labeled 'To Do.'

"That's Punchlist," Brug said reverently. "Natural sprinter. Terrible at follow-through."

They worked through the rest of the night building the catapult, finishing as the stars faded and the first signs of a new day hit the horizon.

Kaelin pointed, crisp and merciless. "Fruit on the left arm, cream on the right—pumpkin in reserve. Brug, tie those with baker's twine. Tight. If this turns into a sermon, I want custard in their vows."

Tobias murmured stabilizing runes over the pastry lattice; the pies began to spin, lazy and level. "If they wobble, they splatter early."

"If they wobble," Kaelin said, "we're already dead."

Brug lured the goats with carrots, Tobias hooked the animals up to the contraption before they realized what was going on.

"When I say go, we launch," Kaelin whispered.

Tobias was still in panic-mode. "What if the goats—"

"They won't," she answered. "If they do, we'll improvise."

Brug asked, "Should I sing?"

"Only if we miss," Kaelin responded.

Timber lifted her muzzle, barked thrice—one, two, three. Kaelin didn't look back. "On her mark."

The goats bleated, and the cultists noticed the escape. And I, dear reader, sighed with relief. Finally, momentum.

Brug struck a march. "Load, lock, launch—pie the pious! Custard clouds! Be righteous, bias!" The rhyme broke in the middle like a wheel into mud, but the beat held the goats steady.

Rope screamed; wood answered. Docket lunged, Punchlist followed, hooves throwing sparks off half-laid flagstones. The arm snapped skyward; a constellation of pies arced into dawn—silver tins flashing, cream tails streaming. The first cream pie struck the officiant mid-"wel—," converting welcome to whump. Fruit bombs landed next; blackberry hieroglyphs blossomed across unfinished banners. Pumpkin hit last, a fragrant shockwave of nutmeg and poor life choices.

They ran under their own barrage, pies falling like benevolent meteors. The cultist unintentionally assisted Team Chaos by taking a moment to taste the pies that assaulted them. Tobias reached, not quite taking her hand. Kaelin didn't take it. She didn't shake it off, either. The universe, generous for once, let that count as progress.

A ward flickered over the exit arch, weaving sigils into a net. Tobias swore. "Sugar lattice—give me the berry." Kaelin shoved a blackberry pie into his hands. He slapped it into the glyphwork; purple spread, sugar crystals spidering along runes. The ward hiccupped, sweetened, and melted like etiquette at a family reunion.

Docket tossed her ticket-wreath and trotted after them of her own accord. Punchlist butted the WELCOME NE— arch on the way out, finishing nothing with enormous satisfaction. They pushed and pulled the catapult back into place, clambering into the launch-cart as quickly as they could.

The ropes groaned, the goats stamped, and dawn caught the edge of the half-built arch like a blade. The sky brightened, the goats charged, and the universe braced for impact.

Behind them, a final cream pie slid down the cult's mission board, smearing PERMANENT MEMBERS OF PERPETUAL PURPOSE into PERMA . . . PUDDING.

Team Chaos hunkered down in the pastry basket hitched to Docket and Punchlist; it was time to exit stage left.

17

ESCAPE BY GOAT-DRAWN PIE CATAPULT

"Sometimes the only way out is up, on a projectile made of pastry."

Tobias tightened the ropes as he murmured to himself about trajectory. "These runes should keep us on the correct path . . . I hope."

"I call this 'The Ballad of Forthcoming Regret.' " Brug hummed a few notes, searching for the right pitch. They didn't find it. It didn't stop them from singing.

Kaelin kept her eye out for any cultists who made it through the pie onslaught, dagger in hand. Timber supervised the entire mission like a disapproving parent.

The rope creaked like an old man with opinions he refused to keep to himself. The air smelled of toasted sugar and melted butter—freedom, apparently, came with caramel undertones. Tobias's hands shook slightly as he traced the runes, muttering something about "gravitational consistency" and "inevitable doom" in the same breath. Timber sneezed once, frosting the nearest rune in powdered sugar. It didn't help boost anyone's confidence.

It was the kind of plan that started as a bad idea and somehow got worse through collaboration.

Tobias looked to the sky. "Technically, it should work."

He wasn't fearless. However, he was trying very hard to appear brave, for everyone's sake, especially hers.

She almost believed his bravado. Almost. But belief was dangerous—it made people stay, and staying was a kind of death she wasn't ready to repeat.

Kaelin squinted up at the same sky, noting how even the clouds had the decency to look nervous. Somewhere behind her, Brug tuned their lute with the solemnity of someone preparing for their own funeral.

Her fingers twitched towards Tobias, half instinct, half self-betrayal. Timber gave a low warning huff, like even the dog had opinions about emotional vulnerability.

Kaelin thought about taking his hand. She didn't, yet. "Technically, so should a lot of things."

Tension hung in the air like a pulled string. Kaelin had always been good at running towards chaos, never through it. Yet here she was—on the edge of pandemonium, about to fling herself into the sky beside the one person who made her feel calm and entirely out of control at the same time, as well as a bardic orc, and her loyal canine companion.

This had become more than an escape—it was the first step towards her admitting she wanted to move forward again (in every sense).

Of course, it's powered by goats.

And with that, dear reader, Team Chaos prepared to defy gravity, good sense, and the dairy industry.

The goats pawed the ground, muscles twitching beneath patched harnesses. One snorted clouds of steam; the other chewed on its own reins with what could only be described as suicidal enthusiasm. Tobias adjusted the last knot, Brug adjusted the drama, and Kaelin adjusted her expectations for survival.

"On a scale of one to catastrophic," Brug whispered, "where are we?"

Tobias didn't look up. "Statistically speaking, somewhere between singed eyebrows and an interdimensional lawsuit."

"Good to know," Kaelin muttered. "I'll pack light."

The goats bleated with impatience, cultists rushed the catapult, and the smell of caramel filled the air.

Brug belted out the "Hymn of Eternal Almosts," declaring it was inspired by their ineffable leader.

They never finished the song, of course.

It started as a ballad and devolved into interpretive shrieking within seconds. The cultists froze mid-charge, unsure whether to attack, applaud, or harmonize. Tobias took advantage of their confusion to scribble an additional rune—a hasty sigil of propulsion that buzzed like a bee with anxiety issues.

The rune sputtered like a nervous candle on a windy day.

Kaelin shoved him down into the basket. "If this works, you're the pilot."

"I think you mean projectile." Tobias hunkered down.

She raised an eyebrow. "Semantics."

The rune's glow spread, crawling over the catapult like veins of lightning searching for a place to discharge. The air vibrated with their tension. Timber's fur rose. Somewhere, a pie tin rolled off a crate with the slow inevitability of fate. It clattered when it hit the ground.

Timber growled, readying herself for what was coming. She barked the release order.

One goat refused to move, the other took offense and head-butted it. The rope snapped, prematurely, of course.

And there was liftoff. I watched with delight.

Physics took one look at them and quietly resigned.

The catapult flung the group in a perfect arc. One that would have impressed any engineer or horrified any sane person.

Tobias clung to Kaelin. Brug clung to Tobias. Timber bit Brug's sleeve as they soared over the compound and surrounding trees.

Air whipped around them like laughter from a cruel god. Kaelin's stomach performed a paso doble. Somewhere below, a tree probably questioned its career choices.

"If we die, please rhyme my eulogy!" Brug screamed.

As they continued to soar, wind tore at them, whipping their cloaks, hair, and what was left of their dignity. Sugar crusted along the rim of the catapult basket; it glittered in the dawn like confetti at a regrettable parade.

The world tilted. For half a heartbeat, they weren't falling or flying—they were suspended, a tableau of chaos painted against the morning sky. It almost looked like hope, if you squinted hard enough and ignored the screeching.

Some people see their lives flash before their eyes. Kaelin mostly saw her poor decisions—this one taking the lead.

Each choice she'd made streaked past like a banner in her mind: accepting the cursed map, trusting Tobias with the tonic, not stabbing Brug when she had the chance. She had a lot of banners. It was like a long parade with too many marching bands.

Trees were a blur underneath them. Cultists became dots on the horizon. Somewhere below them, Ed chomped on grass, happy he wasn't involved in this madness. Even if he was going to have to find them once they landed.

The wind howled. Her heart, traitor that it was, found rhythm in it.

Tobias yelled over the wind, "I think I love—"

"Don't you dare finish that sentence mid-flight!" Kaelin shouted back.

Her heart stumbled despite her wishes.

Brug hollered a tune about love taking flight.

Love was impractical mid-air, especially when you were the ones barreling through it.

As they soared, Tobias's sleeve brushed her wrist, a warm, impossible tether in the chaos. For the first time in years, the world wasn't standing still. She wasn't, either. Kaelin experienced something between exhilaration and horror—motion after stagnation, and it felt terrifyingly alive even as the thought of crashing to her death played in the back of her head. The air tasted like ash and sugar and second chances. She hated it. She loved it. She wasn't sure which one scared her more.

Mostly, she hated that Brug would probably write a song about it.

Growth, dear reader, often begins at terminal velocity.

Tobias's hand gripped hers mid-spiral. For once, she didn't pull away.

It wasn't romance. It was survival. Probably.

The universe snorted in disbelief, but let them have the moment anyway.

For a moment, everything stopped—no wind, no sound, no certainty that any of them still had bones. The forest creaked back to life one sound at a time: leaves rustling, a goat sneezing somewhere, Brug groaning in the universal key of regret. Then the world remembered gravity, and them with it.

The landing was less 'graceful descent' and more 'pastry-themed meteor strike.' Mud, leaves, and whipped cream decorated the aftermath. The impact with the ground shook the trees as they somersaulted over each other before a thicket stopped their motion. Timber crawled out first, shook violently, and immediately regretted existing, at least in this dimension. Next to them, Ed chomped on some tree leaves.

Finding them wasn't going to be too hard.

"I have been reborn in chaos," Brug announced. "This is worthy of a memoir." They pulled out a quill and parchment and jotted down notes in a hurry.

"Working title: 'Through the Air and Into Questionable Decisions,'" they added, already sketching a dramatic cover image of themselves mid-flight.

Tobias pushed himself off the ground, beaming as he limped his way over to Kaelin. "It actually worked."

"Next time, remind me to pick something that doesn't involve flight." Kaelin groaned into the dirt, not ready to pick herself off the ground.

The dirt smelled like pie crust and hubris. She decided she'd earned the right to lie in it for a minute. She wanted to groan. At the same time she wanted to laugh—hysterical, relieved, exhausted—but the sound stuck somewhere between her ribs and her pride.

Timber nudged Kaelin's shoulder. It was her way of checking to see if the assassin still lived. Kaelin reached back and scratched the dog's ears. It was her quiet way of saying 'thank you for checking on me.'

In the distance, they could hear shouting as it drifted through the air from the compound. The cultists couldn't agree on whether to chase them or form a committee about it.

Tobias laughed, falling to the ground next to Kaelin. Lying next to her, he took the map out of his pocket. His hope was that the map would tell them where they were. He was ever the optimist. Kaelin assumed the map needed to be stabbed.

The map gave them the paper equivalent of a sigh.

"Don't start," she warned. "I will compost you."

Brug brushed themselves off, collecting bits and pieces of parchment filled with scribbles of adventure in iambic pentameter. "Did you notice the quill and chain symbol as we soared over the compound?"

Kaelin froze. Tobias noticed.

"She's everywhere." She pushed herself up off the ground.

Tobias stood. "Who?"

"My boss." She turned away. "I should have known better."

"Do you think she's watching?"

"She's always watching."

Paranoia: it's only delusion until you're right.

And thus ended the quietest moment they'd ever had. It lasted forty-three seconds.

Later that night, they set up camp by the river. The mage worked his magic to keep the fire going. It worked, for once.

Kaelin tended the various cuts and scrapes of the group, kneeling in front of Tobias.

"Let me see your ankle. You've been limping." She didn't wait for him to comply.

He winced as she moved his foot in circles.

"You could've broken your neck," she said, her voice barely more than a whisper.

She didn't mean his neck. She meant everything else she'd started to rely on.

Tobias placed two fingers below her chin, tilting her head until their eyes met. "I knew you wouldn't let me. Besides, you grabbed me first."

Her silence was loud.

Brug sang, "Love is a catapult—unwise, airborne, and occasionally fatal."

Timber huffed. She agreed.

It wasn't long before they retired to their own tents and slept until morning.

Brug woke up first by a faint glow of footprints leading them deeper into the woods.

Timber growled. Tobias followed the light and found a fragment of the Eternal Draft—a quill and chain symbol burned into one corner.

"She's pulling the strings again." She snatched the paper out of his hand and pocketed it.

From far away came a distant furious rooster's crow—Percival, louder and angrier.

Because when one problem ends mid-air, another usually lands, beak-first.

18

BLOOD AND BETS AT THE BLACK FANG

"Nothing says character growth like punching someone in front of your ex-handler."

T he world hadn't stopped spinning since the catapult escape. Even days later, Kaelin felt the momentum of flight inside her. It echoed behind her ribs—pulling her towards something, whether it was the end of her mission or the ache of trusting someone. Someone she didn't know.

Every time Tobias attempted to make eye contact with her, she looked away at anything else: the bard, the dog, the next distraction. Especially the next distraction.

Post-escape exhaustion left every member of Team Chaos, except Ed, subdued.

Yes, even Brug, which was terrifying. Silence from Brug was like a storm sent by the gods: ominous, brief, and usually followed by property damage.

They left behind the fog-laden coast of Saltmere for the brittle chill of Briarwick. The air was cold and sharp. It reminded her of bad decisions and betrayal. Every now and then, a village would interrupt the trees. Each building looked cozy, if one ignored the icicles curling around wrought iron that looked more like torture devices than accessories belonging to a winter wonderland.

Wooden signs hung from the wrought iron. Each sign painted with matriarchal crests: crowns, daggers, and roses intertwined. Even the air bowed to its queens. Each sign, each village, each town showed how power could be disguised as beauty.

Briarwick was what happened when elegance learned to draw blood, politely.

Kaelin decided she needed to gather information—control wrapped in the illusion of strategy.

Translation: she was ready to stab someone productively again.

She didn't expound on her plan, so no one was sure if it was because of her mission or if it had something to do with the Guild. Every snapped twig felt like a footstep behind her. Every gust of wind sounded like a whisper from someone who used to give orders instead of advice. The Guild didn't need chains when memory worked just as well.

Word traveled quietly, on tiptoes, of fighters who owed too much and knew too many secrets disappearing. Vanishing before turning up in one city famous for its underground fight clubs—not that anyone talked about fight clubs—and infamous for who ran them: two elven women, committed to three things: each other, brutal brawls, and selling secrets.

Nothing says 'welcome home' like illegal gambling and weapons checked at the door.

The snow deepened with each mile, muffling the world with each step until even Brug's humming stopped. Timber's paws and Tobias's mutterings were the only things that marked the passing of each hour. They traversed through the woods for days, barely speaking. The silence of nature filled the space between them, that and Kaelin's stomping through pine needles and snow. At this point, Team Chaos feared speaking. No one wanted to end up with a dagger pointed at their jugular.

Avoiding that eventuality seemed less likely as they entered some city, better left unnamed, and stood in front of the Black Fang Tavern. This place wasn't much better than Last Wish, with more dried blood, more stale ale, and too many regrets to count.

Kaelin shook her shoulders and slipped a battered cloak over her, every dagger resting where her hands expected it. She pulled the hood low, slipping into her shadowy assassin mode. It used to fit like a glove, now it itched around the collar.

She didn't believe in omens, but tonight the air smelled like unfinished business. Guild business.

"Stay out here," she said. "I don't need you in there."

The words were like arrows to the heart, and she meant them that way. It was easier to hurt them first. To ensure that no one was caught in the wake of her unfinished loyalties.

Safety is just another word for distance.

She wanted to keep her companions safe. This was the only way she knew how to do it—shove them away, build a wall, ensure no one ever crossed the threshold again.

The cloak swirled around her as she turned away from her companions and slid into the Black Fang.

Tobias didn't argue. He nodded once—the quiet acceptance that said everything and forgave nothing.

The air hit her like a wall—thick with sweat, ale, and the metallic tang of old blood. A good night, by local standards.

Nobody came to the Black Fang for honor. They came for bets, bruises, and bad ideas in equal measure.

Shadows pressed in on her as she weaved her way between reprobates, mercenaries, and poor sops who still had a gleam of hope in their eyes. She was used to fading away into the background. Here, it was easy. The cheers and jeers of the crowd filled the building with sound; coins were exchanged from one individual to the next as two men punched, kicked, and bit their way towards victory or defeat.

She was here on Guild business, or that's at least what she wanted them to believe. The truth was murkier. She wasn't sure whose ghost she was chasing anymore: her mentor's, her own, or the one stamped into every order the Guild had ever given her.

That was the problem with ghosts—they always knew where to find you.

Gessa "Ironhand" Koral, fight handler and information broker, had promised her answers. Or leverage. Either would do. Rumor had it that a nobleman's courier—Lord Ferren's man—used the Black Fang as a drop point for royal intelligence.

Some people network at galas. Kaelin preferred venues with more blood and less hors d'oeuvres. Unless it was cheese. She always preferred cheese.

The fight ended with a thud, both contestants unconscious on the ground.

Gessa pounded her iron staff on the dais floor. "A draw." She waved her arm. "Now, get them off the floor." She sank back into her throne, every appearance suggesting she ruled the place. Her voice carried the easy authority of someone used to being obeyed—and the brittle edge of someone who knew it was temporary.

She was, in fact, not in charge. Her station was a poorly maintained guise that failed as soon as the two elves entered the ring. Still, even a false queen could command loyalty. Kaelin watched the crowd—loyalty here was measured in fear, and Gessa had plenty to spare.

Nadia walked the perimeter, tattooed arms extended. The ink shimmered like spellwork as she encouraged the crowd's jeers. Her smirk was like a sin, enticing enough to convince the most devout to follow her anywhere.

Her counterpart, Fen, stood in the center of the ring, muscular arms crossed. She tapped her leather-clad foot impatiently as she watched her partner, in business and in love, tease the crowd.

"And for our next fight, the mistresses of the manor, Nadia and Fen!" Gessa announced.

The two elves kissed like their lives depended on it before taking a step back and raising their fists. Watching their fight was like watching a ballet. They moved around the ring with brutal grace, alternating between flirting and fighting. Kaelin tried not to be impressed. It didn't work. There were moments when Kaelin felt like a voyeur as she viewed their intricate dance.

Nadia flipped, landing with her legs wrapped around Fen's neck. The momentum of her move sent them crashing to the floor. Fen grabbed Nadia's round cheeks, yes those cheeks. Nadia gasped.

The crowd roared; Kaelin reconsidered her life choices, her sexuality, and possibly her sanity.

"You always did like that move." Fen took a moment to squeeze before shoving her partner over her head.

They both leapt to their feet, the motion smooth. Their chemistry was electric, unbothered, and unapologetic. Kaelin looked away. It was too much—too open, too certain. She'd forgotten what it felt like to want anything without calculating the cost.

Nadia winked. "Only with you, my love."

Her roundhouse kick sent Fen flying backward into the crowd. The crowd pushed Fen right back into the ring with cheering loud enough to cause seismic activity.

Kaelin wasn't sure who was winning, but she was fairly certain the laws of physics were losing.

Finally, a romance built on mutual violence and uppercuts. Progress.

Somewhere in the back, a new round of bets started—and a name slipped through the noise like a knife. A name she hadn't heard since the job that broke her. Joren Hale.

Her eyes darted around the tavern searching for him. The only witness to the job that had gone horribly wrong, the last job she'd finished. For a brief moment relief washed over her. Whoever was fighting next must not be the person she knew. That's when he walked into view, rope-like muscles covered in scars, a man most people would cross the lane to avoid unless they looked into his eyes. Then they would see a kindness not normally seen in this world.

Her breath caught. The elves' fight concluded with a steamy kiss. Gessa announced the next fight, 'The Scourge of Seven Bells' against Hal Rennek.

Kaelin stopped Joren before he entered the ring. "What are you doing here?"

"Paying off a debt." He pushed past her, sweat glistening on his forehead.

Old instincts flared—protection, anger, regret, all tangled up in one shallow breath. She wanted to stop him. Instead, she let him go. At least for now.

He stepped into the ring, arms raised. The crowd chanted, ready for the next match. Gessa presided over the pit, tapping her iron staff like a countdown.

Rennek swung first, bigger and stronger, any blow that hit could do irreparable damage. Joren, small and lean, made his moves deliberately, every hit calculated to have maximum impact.

If you're rooting for the underdog, he's your man, built like a firecracker with more scars than a merchant's ledger.

Kaelin watched the fight, trapped with the knowledge that he was part of the same cycle she was, violence feeding tyranny. It was all around her, and she couldn't find her way out.

A movement to her left caught her eye. Weaving through the crowd was Tobias. He hid himself behind a subtle illusion, almost unrecognizable, even to her. But she knew it was him, the way his eyes found her in the crowd and his unnerving sense of purpose as he made his way to her.

She grabbed his arm. "What are you doing here? I told you to stay outside."

"Saving you," he said. "Again."

Tobias arrived fashionably late and completely unarmed. The fool. The romantic. The liability.

He glanced around the room, about as subtle as a marching band in a library. "There's someone here who's watching you."

She was about to shove him right back out the door, but his words stopped her. "What do you mean, watching me?"

His eyes shifted to the right. "Over there." His head tilted in the direction he was looking. "The woman trying not to be noticed. She has the quill and chain insignia embroidered on her cloak. I noticed it when she followed you inside."

Kaelin cheered as Joren made contact with his opponent, quickly searching in the direction Tobias had indicated. There she was, one of Anwyn's underlings, familiar to the assassin because she was the woman sent to see if orders were being followed. And to take care of disobedience when they weren't.

Another test of her loyalty, her restraint, her heart. She clenched her dagger hilt, torn between following orders and protecting . . . everyone. Tobias, Timber, Brug, even Joren.

Anwyn's voice still lingered. *"Attachment clouds judgment."*

"So does manipulation," she muttered, her voice barely heard over the crowd.

In the ring, Rennek's glove scraped Joren's ribs and left a dull, oily sheen. The skin beneath went the wrong color. Contact poison. Cheap. Cruel. Joren's punches slowed, sweat cascaded off him. He stumbled into his opponent.

A grizzled old man tripped, crashing into Kaelin. "Your noble's errand boy is in the back room. But you'll need the champ's token to get in."

"Our champ is slower than a turtle right now," Nadia bellowed from the bar top. "He needs your help to keep going."

She handed a hat to one patron. Within seconds coins, jewels, and precious metals filled up the headpiece. Fen threw in a bag of coins with a wink.

Kaelin spotted the champ's token hanging from Joren's belt, even as he listed one way then another.

"A little gold always gets a fighter to his feet."

"That it does, Fen. That it does." Nadia clapped.

"It looks like he needs a little more encouragement, maybe you should turn around, Nadia, show him something to fight for." She blew her lover a kiss.

Nadia caught it and slipped it into her pocket.

They were the best thing about the place. At least, until the drinks ran out.

Tobias momentarily forgotten, Kaelin watched her friend's match spiral. He was still winning, barely. Rennek chipped away at the lead, fighting like a man that had been paid to kill.

Joren tripped, flailing as he stumbled into the crowd. They shoved him back towards the ring. He'd lost all color, his skin an unnatural shade, his scars like inked-in lines traversing his entire body.

"He's been poisoned." She lunged for the ring. "I have to stop this."

Tobias grabbed her as the crowd roared for blood. "You'll blow your cover."

"Then cover me." She rushed towards the ring, trusting with every fiber of her being that the mage would help her.

One step away from the ring, she saw the courier sneaking away, satchel in hand. She bumped him, snatching his bag.

Mission accomplished, if your definition of success included public brawling, espionage, and mild poisoning.

She moved away—daggers at the ready, cloak off. The crowd gasped.

Tobias threw a glamour spell, trying to obscure her face from the spy. The veiled woman's gaze caught on Kaelin—then slid to a burly patron wearing the same face. Tobias's glamour held, barely. Two taps on her tankard; a runner peeled from the wall.

Joren collapsed the moment Kaelin entered the ring. She dove into the pit under a rain of jeers. She realized she was right as she held him in her arms he'd been poisoned. The fight was rigged.

Gessa popped a hidden panel and plucked a vial from a numbered rack. "No one dies in my ring unless my ledger says so."

"Give me the antidote," Kaelin demanded.

The handler hesitated, but tossed her the vial with a nod of respect.

"You didn't have to come back," Joren mumbled.

Kaelin rolled her eyes. "You shouldn't have made me."

"We have to leave . . . now," Tobias hissed, dragging both of them out of the ring.

Brug kicked the doors wide and belted a rebel chorus. Half the room sang, the other half swung. It was distraction enough.

They managed to escape through the back with the courier's satchel and a half-conscious Joren.

Outside, they hid down an alley, waiting to see if they were followed. Fen was there waiting—how, Kaelin would never know—but the elf was there.

"This will get you out of town." She handed the assassin a stack of papers and a key. "This will open a safe house. Get him there. I promise he'll be safe."

"Why?"

"We don't let the Guild's dogs eat our own," Fen said. "Not anymore."

Kaelin didn't know what to believe. She didn't have time to even think about it.

"Run. It's going to explode," Brug sang as they raced down the alley.

The Black Fang erupted—to this day, no one knows why. It could've been a random fire, a riot, or Gessa's patience snapping.

Standing in the smoke, Anwyn's agent watched them as they made their escape. The woman nodded. A silent message: you passed. For now.

The woman was kinder than Anwyn. Kaelin would have failed if her mentor was there.

Every victory came with a bruise. Some you wore on your skin. Some, you carried where nobody could see.

Outside, in the mist and falling ash, Kaelin tended Joren while Tobias hovered.

"You always pick the worst places for reunions." He smiled, then winced.

Kaelin raised an eyebrow. "Next time, let's try a bookstore."

Tobias's eyes widened. "You read?"

And that, dear reader, is how friendship works when both parties are armed and bleeding.

Behind them, the tavern burned. The sign flickered, a fang-shaped scorch mark carved into the night.

Kaelin tucked the satchel into her gear. The quill and chain insignia glowed on the book inside.

And just like that, trust issues are about to become a recurring theme.

19

SPINES AND BINDINGS

"Some safe houses have walls and locks. The good ones have books, suspicious witches, and at least one person who swears they don't need help."

They followed Fen's directions to the safe house, following winding back streets and alleys searching for the fang, a symbol inconspicuously left on buildings directing them through all the twists and turns.

Because nothing screams stealth like a scavenger hunt organized by people who refuse to leave direct instructions.

Honestly, at this point Kaelin expected the next clue to be written in glitter on a feral goose.

"Over here, I see one." Brug's stage whisper was anything but quiet.

Kaelin's fingers itched to use her daggers. "Will you please shut up? You're going to wake the entire neighborhood."

Tobias clamped his hands over his mouth, a desperate attempt to stifle a very inappropriate giggle. The man had many strengths, but stealth-by-association was not one of them.

The bard pointed down a road.

"That's not a fang, it's a dead leaf." If looks could kill, her job would be so much easier.

There would be a lot more casualties, though.

"Are you trying to get us lost?"

Tobias patted them on the shoulder. "She's just concerned. She'll feel bad later and apologize in her own way."

It was unclear when and how such an apology would manifest, but the group had quietly accepted that Kaelin's 'sorrys' came in the form of not stabbing people. Progress.

They nodded before spotting a purple door, the fang barely visible in the bottom corner.

Their search ended in front of that door. It was the portal to a narrow shop with a hand-painted sign. SPINES AND BINDINGS - USED TOMES, NEW REGRETS.

The safe house was actually a bookstore. Of course, it (bleeping) was. The irony of it all was true perfection.

Kaelin briefly considered turning around and demanding a different safe house. Unfortunately, bookstores were Tobias's natural habitat and her unspoken safe space.

Tobias fumbled with the key while Kaelin supported Joren. She was intensely aware of every movement around her, flinching when Timber nudged her, sweating as Brug hummed a new ballad. She checked the shadows behind them for the seventh time. A shadow checked back. She pretended not to notice. Unfortunately, her racing heart refused to read the memo that they were out of danger, for now.

At some point, the mage figured out how a lock and key worked, and the door swung open. The tiny bell over the door didn't jingle. Instead, it sighed, long and exhausted, when Kaelin pushed her way through.

Nothing says 'welcome' like a door that sounded as tired as you felt.

Kaelin helped Joren into a chair, noting every exit in the shop.

There were three, if you counted the windows. Four, if you counted the floorboards she decided she could pry up if there was a need for an escape.

Where were the sightlines? Those barely existed, too many books. Preparedness was a lifestyle, one she fully embraced.

The overcrowded shelves, precariously stacked books, and piles of paper blocked the view of—well, everything. Lantern light pooled in uneven islands across the floor, catching on gilt titles and cracked leather spines, leaving the aisles in deep, book-scented shadow. It didn't stop her from watching as one book shifted on its own, trying to escape a leaning tower of poorly made sequels.

Did every inanimate object have to have an opinion?

The fire popped, a chair creaked, and an inkpot gurgled.

Kaelin interpreted the various noises as answers in the affirmative.

Even the dust motes seemed judgmental.

She sniffed, inhaling the faint scent of dust, parchment, ink, and . . . bread. The smell of baking dough should have been stronger than it was, but she didn't know that at the moment.

Timber padded in directly behind her, settling at Joren's feet. Her nose twitched as she sniffed the air. She must have liked what she smelled because she slept almost immediately, her normal need to be on guard gone. For the most part, at least.

Timber relaxing was the canine equivalent of a divine blessing. If she said a place was safe, it probably only had mild danger. The 'mild danger' category included things like cursed books, sentient scones, and Tobias tripping over his own enthusiasm.

Tobias wandered through the shop, running his fingers over the magical tomes, adventure guides, and the odd romance novel. He rolled his shoulders back, the tension left his neck for the first time in days, maybe even weeks. He could feel magic pulsing around him. It's old, familiar even, but he didn't know why.

It was a balm to his *hiraeth*, like coming home, even though he'd never been there.

Kaelin didn't miss the soft awe in his face. She pretended she did.

The wooden floorboards groaned as a witch of indeterminate age appeared from behind a stack of atlases and spell compendiums. Kaelin's hand hovered over Mercy. She watched, guarded, as the woman made her way towards them. Flour dusted the witch's sleeves, ink stained her fingers, and her aura was one of permanently done with everything, but only mildly so. A quill pen hovered in the air behind her, scribbling notes faster than a person's thoughts.

"I'm Mistress Lira." Her gaze swept over the group like someone cataloguing threats long before breakfast. It stopped on Kaelin, noting the knives, the posture, the Guild shadow. "Fen's key, Guild steel, and a poisoned man. Interesting combination." She nodded, turned, and shuffled to the back of the shop. She moved like someone who had decided they were done with drama long ago and yet they kept adopting strays.

The way the woman's lips tightened when she mentioned the Guild suggested this wasn't her first run-in with a hired blade, nor would it be her last.

And just like that, hospitality came with homework.

Kaelin raised an eyebrow. Tobias shrugged. Timber snored. Brug lost themselves somewhere in the stacks, probably by the bardic tales.

"We should follow her," Joren said, struggling to get back on his feet.

Together, they ushered Joren to a back alcove where there was a cot and a shelf of medical grimoires. Tobias hovered near Kaelin without crowding her, a skill he hadn't intended on learning, but one he perfected accidentally. It had become a much-appreciated art form. He existed in the exact three inches of space where she could tolerate another human being.

"There will be no bleeding on the first editions," Mistress Lira ordered as she gathered what she needed to treat the fighter.

Timber sighed before following them. She placed herself between Joren and the witch, eyeing her as she worked. Sniffing the air, Timber barked once before sniffing around the back room, stopping in front of the hearth. Drool escaped her mouth as the smell of sourdough permeated the air. She sneezed at a ward glyph. It flickered but held.

She scratched at the hearth, sniffed again. Her ears pricked forward. Hackles raised. Something was missing, and she didn't like it. Timber didn't know what a sourdough starter was, but she knew when a hearth was sulking.

There was a mystery afoot, and Timber intended to solve it.

A medical grimoire snapped at her. She growled back before circling thrice and settling next to the fire.

Mistress Lira, finished with her tonic, turned back to the group. "I'm used to injured fighters, couriers even. But, Guild members, this is a first."

"I won't stay long then. I don't want to cause trouble." Kaelin clasped Joren's hand in hers. She said it was for his comfort. The lie held, barely.

"It's up to you. If Fen gave you the key, you've the right to stay here as long as you want." The witch spooned the liquid into the fighter's mouth. "Not sure why she trusts you though."

Kaelin didn't know either. Trust was expensive. She didn't remember earning any lately.

Tobias sat next to her, close enough that his sleeve brushed against her arm. She didn't flinch.

Progress. Terrifying progress.

Tobias's brand of romance—companionship with boundaries.

Joren's hand tightened around hers. "You've saved my life twice now. Debt like that doesn't just disappear."

Ah yes, the beginning of a future cavalry charge. Please keep your arms and trauma inside the plot at all times.

Kaelin took her hand back. The emotions were closing in on her like the walls of a cave.

"You would have done the same." She shrugged before turning away.

"No, I don't think I would have." Joren struggled to sit. "I owe too much, the Guild, the Guard, Rennek. If it wiped my debt, I'd have left you there."

His breath came in shallow pulls, sweat cooling to a clammy sheen along his hairline as the poison worked its way out—or didn't.

Kaelin heard his struggles and turned back, rearranging his pillows so he could sit more comfortably.

"Maybe, but who am I to judge? I'm on my way to assassinate the king." She sat back down. "It seems everyone wants him dead."

"Your mission is to kill the king?" Tobias gasped. "I mean, he's bad, but death seems a little extreme."

She stared at him, deadpan. "I'm an assassin. What did you think my mission was?"

Tobias didn't look away or squirm. That in and of itself was a miracle. "I don't know. We've been together for a while and you keep . . . saving people."

The worst part was he wasn't wrong.

Her jaw locked; the old instinct to shrug or joke it away buzzed under her skin like static.

Joren raised an eyebrow. "Interesting—"

"Don't start." There were too many people in the room for her to glare at them all successfully. "Why don't you explain how you ended up in this situation."

"Guild reach grows every season," Lira muttered before walking away.

"She's right. It does. I was supposed to take out someone. Failed. Rennek had already paid me." Joren wiped his eyes. "The battle was supposed to even the debt, not get me killed."

"Someone had another idea," Tobias said under his breath.

Brug chose that moment to join them. "Sounds like a tale of betrayal with just a hint of corruption. It's the fodder of epic ballads."

Tobias shook his head and stood. "Let's give them a moment." He dragged Brug into the stacks, leaving the two Guild members alone.

Kaelin nodded, hating that she agreed. "The Guild is tangled up in things I'm only beginning to see. I don't think it's good."

"What do you mean?"

"Stride's insignia, it's everywhere." She grabbed the book she stole from the courier. "She's even paying people to kidnap me, or maybe it was a test. But I think this is a power grab."

"But everyone hates King Varric. If it wasn't the Guild putting a hit on him, someone else would have." Joren was quiet.

"Maybe, or would the Briarwick Queen arrange a marriage? The Duke of Saltmere might start with bribery. The Midlands, well they could have stopped trade routes or sulked." Kaelin leaned back in her chair. "Does it always have to be violence? It seems like a never-ending cycle, and I want out. It's why I took the job. The money was my way to disappear."

Stabbing as an exit strategy. Flawed, but on brand.

"Anwyn will never let you disappear," Joren rasped.

She crossed her arms. "Then I'll make her."

"You always did pick the worst causes." His lips curved up into a smile.

She smiled back. "For some reason, you always followed me when I did."

"I can't this time. I have to warn the other fighters and ring-runners." His gaze held hers. "Start my own resistance."

He pressed something into her hand. A token engraved with the number seven and seven tiny bells attached to it.

"When you ring this, I'll come. Might take a few days. But I'll come."

And thus, dear reader, the assassin has allies. Messy, inconvenient, emotionally compromised allies. But allies nonetheless.

20

SPINES, SIGHS, AND OTHER DANGEROUS THINGS

"Even assassins need a break. Preferably with a blanket and some poorly written yearning."

Silence filled the space between them. The hearth crackled softly, a single ember popping like it was afraid to interrupt. She didn't know how to respond. Words seemed hollow. Instead, she took his hand and held it for a moment. They sat like that for an eternity, two people more alike than different, each contemplating exactly what steps they needed to take next.

His eyes drifted shut, exhausted from the near-death experience.

"Thank you," Kaelin whispered. "I'll let you rest."

Timber stood, stretched, and repositioned herself at Joren's feet like a furry ward. She exhaled a low, rumbling huff—the canine version of 'I'm watching all of you.'

Brug drifted back, took one look around the room and sashayed off somewhere between *Questionable Ballads of the Third Age* and *An Incomplete History of Horrible Ideas*.

Tobias rounded the corner, hovering near the shelves. The faint scent of old parchment and cooling bread drifted from the stacks, softening the tension in his shoulders. He was like a moth to a flame, unable to stay away from the books. Kaelin claimed she was going to monitor for threats but kept drifting to the fiction section.

Timber followed her. Her nails clicked lightly against the uneven floorboards, a steady metronome of loyalty. She pawed at a low shelf until a single book slid out and thumped Kaelin's boots. The impact sent a tiny puff of dust up her shins, like the book had opinions about being discovered.

Timber: 1. Destiny: 0.

The green and gilded cover gleamed in the firelight, illuminating the title: *Spines, Sighs, and Other Dangerous Things* by Lady Vexina.

Kaelin picked it up. The book was ostensibly a romantic serial—a dramatically posed assassin and mage on the front. The spine was reinforced with delicate metal filagree, sharp enough to cut.

Of all the things that could shove Kaelin's emotional arc forward, of course it would be a book that looked like Tobias fanfic.

Careful to avoid getting wounded by a book, Kaelin flipped through the pages. Inside, it was a half-overwrought, but weirdly on-the-nose, romance about an assassin who doesn't believe in love and the mage who keeps almost dying near her. It was filled with half marginal spell work and footnotes. Lady Vexina was clearly someone who knew her combat magic and emotional damage.

Always nice when an author understands their core demographics: murder, feelings, and bad decisions.

Kaelin sat on the floor, folding her legs in front of her. The floorboards were warm from the hearth, heat seeping pleasantly through her leggings. Turning the pages, the book absorbed her completely, causing her world to fall away, replaced by Lady Vexina's reality.

Which, for the record, was not avoidance. It was a tactical emotional retreat. A completely different thing altogether.

"What'cha got there?" Tobias asked, interrupting her reading like someone who valued their life very little.

"A book," she responded as she continued to read.

"I can see that." He looked over her shoulder, trying to figure out what had captured her attention. "Is that the quill and chain symbol again?"

She felt his sleeve brush her shoulder. He was too close for comfort and too far from the safety of pretending not to care.

"What?" She was annoyed but looked to where he was pointing. She gasped. "It is, why would it be in this book?"

She ran her fingers over all the margin notes. Scratched in a looping script were the words *Eternal Draft* and a warning that *binding ink must never touch leavened bread wards*.

"What's this Eternal Draft and how does it tie to the Guild?" Tobias tapped his chin as he asked the question. It was more to himself than anyone else in the room. "It was on that torn parchment from the cult."

He reached for the book. "Can I see it?"

She hesitated, but handed it to him.

Trust, in Kaelin-speak, looked an awful lot like reluctantly letting someone else hold the sharp thing.

"It looks like this says something about power changing hands, maybe through a contract." He glanced up. "Do you think the Order of Binding Contracts knows what the Eternal Draft is?"

"I don't think they know anything useful." She took the book back. "Look at this line, it's so . . . dramatic. No one talks like that."

Tobias shook his head. "Not out loud."

His words were quiet, almost as if he didn't want anyone to hear them. But she had. The declaration of love on the page was less over the top when she reread it, reminding her of something almost said mid-air.

The unfinished sentence still hung somewhere above the trees, stubborn as a storm cloud.

"It's probably just altitude sickness. It happens in moments like the one in the book."

"Ah, yes. The emotional turbulence trope."

They both stopped talking. The silence that followed was not comfortable. They could both feel what was left unsaid. It pressed at the edges of the room, heavier than any spell in Lira's grimoires.

"Here, why don't you look at the spell diagram?" She handed him the book.

The filigree caught his finger, cutting him. "Ouch."

She grabbed his hand before he could hide it. "Let me get a bandage."

"I'm fine, really," he protested.

"You're going to bleed all over the book," she responded. "Lira will be mad. It could be a first edition."

Bandages acquired, Kaelin took his hand in hers. His skin was warm under her fingertips—steady in a way she definitely wasn't. She applied a healing salve with the lightest of touches. Careful, precise, gentle. She took the white gauze and wrapped it over the cut. Tight, but not too tight. Her fingers knew exactly how to hurt. It was unsettling to discover they knew exactly how to help.

"Thank you," Tobias said, watching her work.

"Don't make a big deal out of it." Her voice was gruff.

He smiled. "I won't."

They ended up reading at the same table, shoulders touching.

"Is this okay?" he asked.

She shrugged, then nodded. No one ever asked what was okay. He had. She noticed and remembered. Her body stayed tense for three heartbeats, then—slowly—decided not to flinch. Consent, it turned out, was its own kind of magic.

Timber, furry chaperone that she was, wedged her head between their knees as they continued to read.

Progress, dear reader, is when two emotionally constipated idiots share a table, a book, and a silence that doesn't feel like a weapon.

"I grabbed another book from the courier. It has her insignia on it." Kaelin leapt from her seat to search the satchel. "Here it is. *Operational Ledger: Shadow Guard Rotation and Guild Special Projects.*"

"Sounds like a riveting read." Tobias was hardly ever sarcastic, but he'd been enjoying their cozy moment. And nothing ruins a burgeoning almost-moment like strategically treasonous paperwork.

Timber left the room, pacing next to the kitchen door. She whined.

There was a cooling rack with no bread on it.

She stared back at the stone hearth, watching as the carved sigil dimmed.

No one paid any attention to her. Really, what was the point of solving mysteries if everyone just went about their own business?

If Timber had been capable of filing official complaints, this would have been a strongly worded one.

Kaelin paged through the book. There were schedules, code names, and a repeated entry. 'Eternal Draft parameters: pending revisions.'

"It's the same as in Lady Vexina's book. Some kind of endless revision spell." Tobias tapped his chin. "It's like the cult's philosophy, but with more bite. Why would she want something like this."

Her fingers struck the table in a staccato rhythm. Then stopped. "Could all the distractions have been deliberate redirection? Is she trying to prevent me from finishing?"

"What would that accomplish?"

"My permanent servitude."

'Draft' wasn't just ink. It was the version of Kaelin that Anwyn wanted to keep revising until she belonged to no one but the Guild.

The uneven gate of Mistress Lira interrupted their research. "She can smell it, can't she? Wards running thin?"

"Smell what?" Kaelin looked up from the book. She hadn't noticed the shopkeeper coming or Timber's agitation. Her fingers flexed. Lack of attention, that was a good way to end up dead.

Lira sighed. "The safe house protection is baked into our daily bread. But the sourdough starter is missing. Without the magical anchor, the wards will eventually break."

A soft static prickle crawled along Kaelin's arms, the telltale warning of protective magic thinning.

"You use bread magic to protect this place?" Tobias had heard of such things, but he'd never seen it in action.

Lira nodded. "Uncle Crust, the starter, is the key. It's over two hundred years old. It's what holds the protection wards in place for all the inner-city resistance safe houses."

"And now it's missing?" Kaelin never expected to hear any of the words said strung together in one sentence.

Magical sourdough starters. Ridiculous. Sourdough bread, however, delicious. Especially with cheese. Priorities remained, even at the end of the world.

"Missing, stolen . . . It followed some fool with more enthusiasm than sense and hasn't come back," Lira said. "Not sure if it was intentional bamboozling, or just a sentient starter with a need for adventure."

On today's episode of 'Things That Should Not Matter but Definitely Do,' I give you bread. Again.

Tobias flipped through the ledger's pages. "I thought so. Look, here's an entry for leavening matrixes. And a note—*destabilize rebel wards*."

"Well, that certainly sounds ominous," Kaelin muttered.

"You can hide here for now, but if the starter isn't found, all the wards crumble." Lira sat. "Every fighter, courier, runaway who uses this network is vulnerable unless it's returned and I can start baking again."

"You want me to find it. Is this some sorta trade?" Kaelin felt the transactional burden rise.

Lira shook her head. "No, of course not. Stay here, leave when you're ready. There's no payment necessary for my protection."

Tobias closed the ledger. "But you do need help."

He looked over at Kaelin with pleading eyes.

"If you can help, I wouldn't say no."

It felt like another side quest. Kaelin hated that. She also hated that it clearly mattered. Every time she tried to walk in a straight line towards her mission, the universe handed her another wounded person, cursed object, or endangered carbohydrate.

"There was a woman here last week. They were very curious about the starter. Convinced me to make pizza with it." Lira pushed her sleeves up. "It was very good pizza."

Tobias took notes, but got distracted theorizing about fermentation magic and protective lattices. The paper was a mess of spells, baked goods, and something completely illegible. There was at least a fifty-fifty chance he'd accidentally invented a new form of pastry-based shielding.

"We'll leave tomorrow." Kaelin stood. "Now I need some sleep."

The warm air of the shop seemed to sigh as they prepared for rest, as though the safe house hoped they would succeed.

Tomorrow, they would go hunting—for a stolen sourdough starter, a saboteur, and whatever was left of their good sense. In that order.

21

THE SOURDOUGH OF DESTINY

"Sometimes saving the world means saving dinner. Or at least breakfast."

They did not, in fact, leave the next day.

A faint chill clung to the air, the kind that soaked into bones before the fire could scare it away. Morning light leaked through the dust-covered window, pale and hesitant, like the sun wasn't even sure it wanted to be awake.

And really, who could blame it? Does anyone truly like mornings?

Kaelin woke up to the almost smell of baking bread. It was there, but not there, like catching a ghost of a scent. It tugged at her senses like a memory trying to become real but giving up halfway.

She sat up, rubbing the sleep from her eyes, and pulled on her clothes before her brain had committed to being fully awake.

Downstairs, the fire was still crackling in the hearth. The ward glyphs around it pulsed in a jittery rhythm, their blue light fading from a vibrant cobalt to a faded sky blue with each beat.

Nothing says 'good morning' like magical infrastructure failing before caffeine.

Timber padded in behind her, nails clicking on the hardwood floor. She sniffed the pulsing glyphs, nose to the stone, nothing else in the room interested her. A soft static hissed each time the light flickered, raising goosebumps along Kaelin's arms.

She stopped sniffing with a snort, turning to Kaelin. With a bark, she made her way to the kitchen. The assassin followed her dog. There on the counter sat an empty cooling rack with a faint dusting of flour clinging to its metal wires—a reminder of the loaf that should have been. Timber stared at it; her low growls filled the room. Her head swung between Kaelin and the empty cooling rack, then back. It was like she was saying, 'Woman, fix the carbohydrate.'

"Don't look at me like that." Kaelin put her hands on her hips. "I already agreed to help."

Timber lay down, her front paws crossed and ears back, an accusation in canine form. Her tail thumped once, the slow, unenthusiastic thump reserved for humans who failed at basic tasks.

There was something about the judgment of a dog. Nothing quite matched its potency.

Kaelin resisted the urge to stomp her foot. The dog's judgmental tail thump was uncalled for. They hadn't even left to find the sourdough starter. She hadn't failed. Yet.

"Stop looking at me like that."

"What are you two talking about?" Tobias mumbled the question from the kitchen table, the sound raspy as his vocal cords weren't fully awake. His head popped up from behind a stack of books, some he remembered grabbing, others he didn't.

That's what happens when you pull an all-nighter in your thirties. It's really something a person should leave behind at university.

Kaelin's eyes looked him up and down. His hair stuck out in every direction imaginable. Ink smudged one of his cheeks. There was a half-finished cup of tea next to his elbow. He appeared to be wearing a blanket, but it was his cloak. The clasp sat crooked along his spine, like it had tried to escape at some point during the night.

"Is your cloak on backwards?" She responded to his question with her own.

Tobias's glanced down. "Um . . . It would appear so."

He ran his hand through his hair. It only made it worse.

Her lips twitched into the faintest of smiles.

The floor creaked as Joren entered the kitchen, his arm wrapped around his abdomen. He moved gingerly, careful not to open the wound that had almost killed him. He took a moment to take everything in.

"It appears I missed something yesterday." The fighter knelt to pet Timber.

Kaelin shook her head. "You were a little busy recovering, but yes, there's an emergency here with the . . . bread magic."

She heard the words leave her mouth. If anyone had said them to her, she wouldn't have believed them.

Joren raised an eyebrow.

"You heard what I said. Bread magic. There's a missing sourdough starter that's crucial to keep the protection wards working here," Kaelin explained.

Somewhere, a Guild instructor cried.

Tobias stood, moving closer to her. "It's really not uncommon. Bread is something made consistently in most households."

His warmth soaked through her leathers. She didn't move; even though she wanted to flinch away, a larger part of her wanted to stay close. Everything she felt was new, unfamiliar. His proximity was comforting, which unsettled her.

Joren looked from the mage to the assassin, noting the ease between them. "Interesting. I wish I could help, but I have to warn the others."

"I know," she said. "They need to know what's happening here, and maybe elsewhere."

He turned towards the exit, took a single step, turned back. "Thank you, you probably should have let me die. I'm happy you didn't."

"It was nothing," she deflected with professional coldness. The wall crumbled before she could stop it.

He held his hand out, it trembled slightly. It wasn't from weakness, but from the weight of choosing his own path. She went to shake his hand. She surprised herself by folding him into her arms in an uncharacteristic hug.

A hug, against all odds, and against every Guild regulation on emotional repression.

He wrapped his arms around her, returning the gesture. She took a deep breath, inhaling the scent of leather and iron. They broke the embrace, stepping back awkwardly, both uncomfortable with the unexpected display of emotion.

Dame Anwyn Stride would be so disappointed with her. All of these feelings bubbling over, it was unacceptable. She could practically feel Anwyn's disapproval like a draft at her back.

Tobias cleared his throat. "I have a healing charm for you. It's for emergencies. To use it you need to . . ."

He continued explaining how to use it as Joren pocketed the charm, not listening to any of the instructions.

It was very unlikely he would use the charm properly.

Men and instructions, name a more iconic duo.

The fighter rubbed the back of his neck. "I'll be on my way then."

He walked out of the shop. The bells on his token jingled ominously as he left.

Timber howled her displeasure. The bells were not her favorite.

Dear reader, it was like a death march and jingle bells melded together.

Kaelin stared at the closed door, flexing her fingers as if she was trying to remember how to hold a blade instead of a promise.

"Are we ready for a fabulous day?" Brug burst into the room like they were shot out of a confetti cannon. "Why does everyone look so . . . distressed?" Their voice bounced off the shelves like it hadn't received the memo on emotional nuance. Their magenta cloak swirled around them with the drama of a matador's cape. The beaded trim clacked as it moved.

Before anyone could answer, Mistress Lira made her way around the books and into the kitchen. "You're still here. I thought you all would be gone by now." She gestured towards the flickering glyphs. "Look how patchy they are?"

"We noticed," Kaelin said. "We shouldn't be here much longer."

"Actually," Tobias interrupted. "I think we need more information before we chase down the starter."

The faint smell of failed baking magic filled the room. Mistress Lira sniffed. "This is bad. Very bad. And also frustrating. Mostly frustrating."

Quill pen in hand, Tobias sat at the kitchen table. The wooden table was smooth from years of use.

"Can you tell us more?" He looked at her with curious eyes. "Any information will help."

"He's not wrong," the assassin added. "We need some clue to point us in the right direction."

Brug strummed their lute, providing tense background music for the conversation to come.

"It's over two centuries old and alive-ish." Mistress Lira dragged a chair across the floor. The legs scraped the floor, the discordant note hurting everyone's ears. "Uncle Crust is temperamental. Attracted to warmth, magic, and people with questionable judgment."

Timber looked from Kaelin to Tobias to Brug and sighed.

It was inevitable Uncle Crust would form an attachment with someone on Team Chaos. It was just a question of who.

"If I'm going to write this ballad, I need to know how the sourdough starter escaped." Brug pulled out their quill and a pot of pink ink. The scent of cotton candy wafted through the air.

Where they found the pink ink, one will never know.

"If you must know, the last person to interact with the starter was a flamboyant, overly enthusiastic culinary rogue." Mistress Lira dusted flour off her apron.

Brug scribbled furiously. "What a fantastic description. It's definitely going into my song."

"She was chaotic, possibly magical," Mistress Lira continued. "The exact type of person Uncle Crust would latch on to, especially after the pizza. Unfortunate but true."

I must admit, I have also become attached after having pizza.

Timber drooled when the shopkeep mentioned pizza.

"Sounds like pizza someone would kill over," Brug muttered. "I could use a slice right about now."

"If you get Uncle Crust back, I'll make you all your own pizzas." Mistress Lira turned towards Kaelin. "He really needs to be fed."

"Why is the starter a man?" Brug tapped their tusks.

The shopkeep sighed. "Because men always need so much attention. So high-maintenance."

Kaelin leaned back in her chair. "Did they mention where they were going?"

"I believe there was something about the Library of Unwritten Recipes. Maybe they're headed there."

Tobias fell into a chair, stood up, only to fall back into the chair. He vibrated with excitement. "I thought it was a myth."

Mistress Lira rolled her eyes. "Why would you think that?"

Kaelin sat up straight, watching, waiting. Chaos was sure to follow with that exhibition of excitement. She reached for her dagger out of habit, not that there was any immediate danger.

In Kaelin's experience, the moment a mage started vibrating with joy about a library, 'no immediate danger' had a very short shelf life.

"Do the recipes really rearrange themselves depending on who's looking for one?" He rubbed his chin as he pondered his question.

"We are not getting distracted by books." Kaelin crossed her arms, even though she didn't really mind being distracted by books.

A smile crept over Tobias's face. He knew she was lying to herself and everyone else in the room.

"Why would anyone be distracted by recipe books? Now, books with a tale of daring adventures, those are a worthy distraction." Brug looked at Tobias, their brow wrinkled either in confusion or disdain.

Tiny specks of flour dusting the floor began to glow. Timber sniffed, the faint scent of sourdough rose from the floor. Jumping to her feet, she followed the path, sniffing, sneezing, sniffing more. Every time she sneezed, the path glowed brighter.

The path of glowing dust led to the back door, where it fanned out to form an image of a rather rude gesture.

Uncle Crust apparently had opinions regarding the bookstore.

"I'll cast a detection spell," Tobias offered.

For a moment, Kaelin worried something chaotic would ensue, most likely involving glitter.

For once, the mage was competent. After a few muttered words and a flick of the wrist, spectral yeast footprints emerged. They glowed a faint gold and smelled like freshly baked bread.

Kaelin looked from the footprints to Tobias and back. It was moments like this that made her question all of her life choices.

Brug strummed their lute. "My next song will be 'The Ballad of Wanderlust Bread.'"

They played an upbeat tune and proceeded to work on new song lyrics, rhyming 'bread' with 'dread' and 'dead.' At the moment, the tune seemed paradoxical.

A scrap of parchment fluttered, caught in the doorjamb. Kaelin knelt, carefully, pulling it free. On it was a recipe fragment and the symbol of Unwritten Recipes—another quill, this time wrapped in steam. And a note '—*return before fermentation destabilizes*—.'

"This is certainly ominous." She shivered.

The parchment was warm to the touch. It was like it had been peeled off an oven door.

She made her way to the table so she could sit and study the parchment closer. Tobias sat next to her. He leaned in to examine it with her. Their shoulders touched. She didn't move away.

Brug added a line about romantic progress to their song.

Tobias muttered something about magical fermentation logic. Kaelin watched the flex of his hand instead of listening to him.

Ah, dear reader, we might be at the moment when trust becomes an emotional bond and physical attraction starts.

"If the wards fail, Lira, Fen, the entire network will suffer," Kaelin whispered. "I can't let that happen."

Tobias inched his hand closer to hers until their pinkies touched. It's only a whisper, but she couldn't take her eyes off them.

Mistress Lira moved around the kitchen, banging pots and pans. Utensils clattered to the floor, and the smell of yeast filled the room. It was a symphony of scent and sound. She limped her way back to the table with her arms full.

"These should help you on your way," she said. She placed a whisk on the table.

"A whisk?" Brug raised an eyebrow. "Are we going to make whipped cream?"

Tobias held his hand up. "Is the whisk humming?"

"It is. It's been used to mix all the magic loaves. The constant use infused the whisk with its own magic." The shopkeep placed something else on the table. "Here's some backup starter. It's not alive enough for the wards. But it might help you find Uncle Crust. Especially you."

Mistress Lira pointed at Timber.

"Thank you, it's so nice of you to help." Tobias reached across the table to pack the items.

The smack of a rolling pin on the table stopped him. He barely saved his fingers from injury.

"I'm not done yet." Lira huffed. "This map will help you navigate the culinary underbelly of Briarwick, as well as show approved viewers our resistance network hubs."

Only in Briarwick could 'culinary underbelly' and 'resistance network' reasonably occupy the same sentence.

She handed the map to Kaelin. The worn map looked like it had a fight with a paper shredder and barely survived. Each fold was worn through, likely to tear apart if the wind blew in the map's direction. Not to mention the stains—so many things stained the map. One corner bore a dark ring of what might have been coffee. Or blood. Or very committed gravy. Kaelin, afraid of very little, feared asking what they were.

"You are the only one who can see the network on the map." Lira poked Kaelin in the chest. "I don't trust the other two to keep their mouths shut. I would only show the dog, but she doesn't speak. At least not with words."

Timber growled, offended, even if the woman's words were true.

For half a heartbeat, Kaelin thought about defending Tobias and Brug. She shrugged instead. Mistress Lira wasn't wrong. "Your secrets are safe with me."

Mistress Lira rolled her eyes before continuing. "The last thing is the rolling pin. When it wants to, it can be used as a magic wand. But it's finnicky."

She handed it to Tobias. He tried to take it from her, but she held on longer than necessary. They ended up in a brief tug-of-war battle before Lira relented. The mage stumbled back, knocking over a stack of geographical recipe books.

The sigh Lira sighed could have been heard throughout the entire kingdom. "Uncle Crust is old. If he bonds with someone else—gods help them." She paused. "Never feed him after sunset, there will be trouble. And if he bubbles on his own—run."

Tobias pocketed the rolling pin.

Kaelin shoved everything into her satchel. "We should go."

"Yes, get out," Lira said. "I'm sorry, that was rude of me. Please, get out."

Brug swished their cloak. "We are off to save the day. Let us be gone."

The assassin's lips twitched up in what could have been a smile before following the orc out of the bookstore, Timber and Tobias close behind her.

Stepping out into the snowy alley, the cold assaulted their senses. The scent of cold metal and wet stone filled their nostrils. The wind cut through them like a blade, freezing them from the inside, or so it seemed. Wards flickered behind them. Timber vibrated with purpose.

Their trusty steed Ed trotted down the alley at that exact moment. The horse had impeccable timing.

Kaelin tossed their gear over the horse's back. Tobias stepped in to help her strap it down. Their hands touched. Their eyes locked. Kaelin glanced away first, alarm bells ringing in her head as her traitorous heart skipped a beat. Everything inside her said to run, instead she stayed.

And so, Team Chaos set off—not for glory, or riches, or destiny, but for a wandering lump of magical dough that apparently held the city's entire resistance network together. Saving the world, one breakfast item at a time. Somehow, it actually made sense.

22

THE LIBRARY OF UNWRITTEN RECIPES

"Some libraries hold knowledge. Others hold grudges, overdue fines, and the occasional unstable tart."

It only took two days and one uneventful night to travel to the Library of Unwritten Recipes. The map said they were at the right location no matter how Kaelin looked at it. And she had looked at the map from every angle, even flipping it over a few times. It was right there, clear as day, but there was no library insight. Just a teashop wedged between two chimney stacks, each one humming like an annoyed teakettle. Steam curled up between the stacks, carrying a faint whiff of scorched honey and something aggressively herbal, as if the building itself was steeped in resentment and lavender.

"Where is this place?" Kaelin fiddled with the hilt of a dagger. "It should be right here."

Magic prickled at the back of her neck—faint, but unmistakable. The same subtle warning she felt right before Tobias tried helping and his spell misfired. Which, statistically speaking, was about every fifth spell.

Timber sniffed the ground like—well, like a dog that caught a scent. Which was exactly what she was. The path she followed zigged, then zagged, circled around, and eventually led right to the door of the not-so-welcoming teashop.

It was pretty clear this place absolutely did not want visitors.

Timber growled at the door.

The door growled back.

Low, rumbling, and deep enough that Kaelin felt it through the soles of her boots.

In her experience, when the door growled first, you were already losing the negotiation.

Definitely off to a great start here.

Brug shrugged and followed Timber to the door. They knocked loudly. The door knocked back with just as much fervor.

"Oh, I've heard of places like this," Tobias explained a little too eagerly. "The library is 'interactive.'"

Kaelin gave him a sideways look. His entire face was glowing with academic joy. It was endearing. Which was deeply inconvenient for someone trying very hard not to catch feelings.

"So are traps," Kaelin muttered. In her experience, the line between 'interactive environment' and 'booby-trapped murder scenario' tended to be thin. Paper thin.

She took a step closer, assessing the door. No windows. No alternate entrances. No visible sigils—though that didn't mean they weren't there. If danger had an interior design style, it would look a lot like this storefront: hostile minimalism with a touch of malicious whimsy.

Timber sniffed again, ears perked, tail stiff.

Kaelin tightened her grip on her dagger. She'd fought assassins, cultists, and a fire-breathing chicken, but a hostile storefront was somehow the thing that unnerved her. To be fair, the chicken hadn't come with its own address.

The door creaked open.

The library had found them. Whether it intended to keep them was another question entirely.

Brug shrugged before bounding through the open door. Tobias and Kaelin looked at each other. A terrifyingly happy smile covered his face. She raised her eyebrow wondering if this was really a good idea. Not that there was anything she could do to stop it from happening. Timber whined, echoing Kaelin's instincts. They all followed Brug through the door and stopped.

Shelves surrounded them, each one stretching and bending as if they were breathing. The wood expanded with a slow inhale, then contracted with a papery exhale, like the entire place was alive and mildly annoyed. Spices floated in the air, replacing boring old dust motes. The place smelled of pumpkin spice and overindulgence. Paper and quills hovered over tables, scribbling recipes, erasing themselves, and having arguments in the margins.

Somewhere, a card catalogue shuddered like it had seen things. Terrible things. Experimental quiches, mostly.

The books rearranged themselves depending on who looked at them. Kaelin's section had titles like *Poisons, Spite-Based Cooking,* and *Defensive Baking.*

"These would have been useful before I ended up on so many baking-related side quests." She ran her fingers over the spines as she read each of the titles. The books shivered under her touch, as if excited to be chosen by someone with a high murder aptitude.

The shelves in front of Tobias looked quite different. He grabbed *Fermentation Magic* first, followed by *Culinary Thaumaturgy,* and tried to slyly add *How to Not Burn Your Eyebrows Off (Again).*

Yes, dear reader, he'd burned his eyebrows off more times than anyone should have to count.

Brug—well, Brug's books involved a lot of pictures, adventures, and things that shouldn't be mentioned in genteel company. A pop-up illustration in one of them immediately slapped itself shut.

Timber, of course, gets the *Treats* aisle.

I would like to say that the dog stayed calm, but that would be a lie. Pure chaos actually ensued.

The treat jars began vibrating like summoned familiars attempting escape, the shelves hissed in disapproval, and Timber made the exact sound of a creature who believed she had entered paradise and was prepared to fight anyone for it.

One jar labeled SALMON DREAMS tried to escape by rolling towards the emergency exit. Timber intercepted it with the grim focus of a seasoned operative.

Off to the left, a glowing sign flickered into being over a narrow corridor: INDEX OF REGRETTABLE SAUCES–ENTER AT YOUR OWN RISK. Brug immediately drifted that way before Kaelin snagged the back of their cloak and hauled them back like an errant balloon.

"Can I help you?" The shelves parted, revealing a librarian.

Kaelin gave him a once-over, noticing his dwarvish features, his ink-stained fingers, and the look of complete exasperation on his face. He wore an apron that was smoking—not a lot, but enough for Kaelin to wonder why, and if she should be concerned. A faint sizzle rose from the hem, like the garment was quietly trying to self-immolate rather than continue living this life. His eyebrows were singed in a way that suggested this was less an accident and more an occupational hazard.

Tobias held out his hand. "Hi, we're here . . ."

"Did I ask why you're here?" the librarian grumbled. "No, it's not what I asked."

"Oh, I'm sorry." He put his hand in his pocket. "I just thought some information would help. Mister . . . ?"

"Crumblethorn, on-duty archivist. Here to answer your questions." There was nothing friendly in the monotonous way his speech was delivered. He sounded like someone who had died inside, then been resurrected solely to file overdue returns.

He wore a small badge on his apron that read: 'Ask me about our late fees.' His eyes said, 'don't.'

"If you listened long enough, you would know why we're here." Kaelin stepped forward, hand on one of her many daggers.

Crumblethorn looked at her, the dagger, and back to her. "No need to get stabby. I assume you're here about the starter, Uncle Crust."

"How did you—never mind. I really don't want to know." She shook her head. "Yes, that's exactly why we're here."

Crumblethorn's sigh rustled several recipe scrolls above him, as if the library itself was deeply unimpressed by their collective existence.

"It's important for you to know that Uncle Crust doesn't just wander. He chooses." He stroked his chin. "Poorly."

"Great. Love that for us," Kaelin muttered.

Bread that makes bad decisions, seems appropriate, par for the course even.

Tobias perked up even more. No one was sure how that was even possible.

"How does Uncle Crust choose? Has anyone ever done research on the decisions he's made?" He pushed his hair out of his hopeful eyes. "I'm positive it would be a fascinating study."

"No."

Just one word—that's all the mage got in response to his enthusiastic questions.

Timber, unimpressed by it all, huffed.

Crumblethorn sniffed the air and looked at the dog. "You smell like that magical baker Finlo. Nearly burned down my entire sourdough wing. Sweet boy. Terrible impulse control. His friend Brenna stopped him from causing a culinary uprising."

Brug stepped forward. "Were they here about Percival? He's a firecracker of a rooster."

"Not now, that's a quest for another day," Tobias whispered.

Crumblethorn raised an eyebrow and shrugged. "Let me show you the trail Uncle Crust left behind him."

For a brief moment, Kaelin stared at the door behind her, questioning every decision she'd made that had led her to this moment of chasing a sentient sourdough starter with wanderlust. She followed Crumblethorn anyway.

They walked through the library of breathing shelves and books changing titles, Timber's nose glued to the floor, sniffing something when glowing smears of flour dust appeared on the creaking wooden planks.

"Looks like she's on to something." Brug pointed at their canine companion.

Timber barked in response before darting between the stacks.

"Timber, not now." Kaelin sighed before chasing after her.

The dog was either following the sourdough trail or had sniffed out cheese. Either way, Kaelin wanted to be there when she got to wherever she was running to.

They barreled past a low archway labeled PANTRY OF REGRETTABLE EXPERIMENTS. Jars rattled on the shelves as they passed. One jar of something neon purple thumped desperately against its glass and wheezed, "Don't let him make the foam again," before Crumblethorn snapped his fingers and silenced it.

Skidding to a stop, Timber growled low, menacing. Her hackles were raised, tail was twitching. Kaelin looked up as the rest of her unwanted team clattered in behind her.

Yes, dear reader, there were moments the assassin still lied to herself, but we know better.

In front of them were half-risen bread golems frozen mid-attack. In front of them, a recipe book lay on the ground, the words HELP ME appearing over and over again in sticky jam on its pages.

Timber howled and bared her teeth at the army of dough creatures. Uncle Crust had come through ... and left in a hurry. It was clear something had spooked it. Something big. Magical. Wrong.

A scroll fell to the ground, startling everyone. It unrolled, revealing a flour-dusted note. *Too much heat. Too much power. Must flee.* A dire warning from desperate dough.

With a bark, Timber was on the run again. She headed directly for the Experimental Kitchen.

"Don't go that way. You'll have to pass the Living Test Kitchen," Crumblethorn yelled after them. But it was too late.

Team Chaos had already crossed the threshold. Counters shifted like tides. Saucepans scuttled like crabs. A soufflé screamed when Brug tried to pick it up. They didn't handle the baked goods properly.

Rolling pins attacked Kaelin. They held grudges. She held daggers. A battle ensued. Somehow, it was a draw.

A whisk whirred past Tobias's ear like a tiny furious comet, leaving a streak of meringue on his cheek. He did not take this as a sign to retreat. Of course he didn't.

A hungry pudding attacked Tobias, clearly looking for its next meal. With a flick of the wrist, Kaelin hurled a dagger at it, saving Tobias from being consumed. It happened without conscious thought, shaking her up. The mage put his hand on her shoulder, a steadying comfort she pretended not to need.

Her heart did an undignified lurch. She informed it that they were in a combat scenario, not a courtship ritual. It declined to listen.

Brug belted their favorite aria, which sent the rolling pins back to their drawers. And Timber, well, she found chew toys shaped like bread. The toys squeaked.

There was a paper on the countertop. Tobias touched it, and words appeared. *Beware the Flame in Hiding. Fire Feeds.*

"What did you say?" Crumblethorn ran into the kitchen. He skidded to a stop, panting.

Tobias read the coded note again, slower, enunciating every syllable.

"Not the Flame in Hiding." Beads of sweat formed on the dwarf's brow. "It's supposed to be a myth."

Kaelin's hands rested on her two favorite daggers. "Explain yourself."

Crumblethorn paced the length of the kitchen. "It will ruin everything. A being who can destabilize any baked ward. A creature of heat, pride . . . and hunger." He shivered as he whispered the last word.

One of the nearby ovens shuddered and quietly turned itself off, as if refusing to be associated with whatever they were talking about.

"Hunger . . ." Brug wriggled their eyebrows, ". . . or hunger?"

Tobias shuddered. "I hope it's the first, I think."

"Just another thing for me to deal with." Kaelin spun her dagger, then slipped it into its sheath. "Let me guess. It's heading towards us."

The pantry shook in affirmation.

"There's a mystery we must solve." Brug held up one hand. "But where should we start?" They pulled a cap and magnifying glass out of their satchel.

Timber and Brug searched and sniffed around the kitchen before moving onto other rooms. Tobias shrugged, following them through the maze of shelves. There was nothing left for Kaelin to do but follow along as they searched for clues as to where Uncle Crust had fled to.

They passed a narrow reading nook where cookbooks whispered urgently to one another: "Too much cinnamon." "Not enough salt." "Who puts raisins in that?" One particularly judgmental pie manual snapped shut as Kaelin walked by, as if offended by her entire existence.

"Is that a feather?" Tobias asked.

Brug scurried over to where Tobias pointed. "It is." They held it up like it was an ancient artifact.

Crumblethorn took the feather, sniffing it before handing it to Kaelin. She stared at it. It looked like it was plucked from poultry and smelled of basil and combustion.

"Not more Finlo-coded chaos." Kaelin groaned. "We do not need a chicken-based distraction right now."

"That does smell like Finlo-magic." Crumblethorn nodded in agreement. "Has he created anything that's related to fire?"

"Only Percival, the fire-breathing rooster," Tobias answered. "Do you think it's related?"

"In this world, everything is related," Brug proclaimed. "We are all connected."

"They aren't wrong," Crumblethorn added. "This could be related, or it could be another fire-related disaster."

Timber nudged Kaelin towards the end of the aisle. There, on the floor, was a torn piece of parchment. It fluttered as Timber sighed and sank to the floor, lying down.

Kaelin picked it up and read it aloud. "To restore, knead with intent, fold with truth." She handed the recipe fragment to Tobias. "I'm sick of therapy metaphors disguised as baking."

"There doesn't seem to be any direction on where to find Uncle Crust," Brug, ever helpful, said.

Like it had been summoned from somewhere deep in the library, a magical container tumbled towards them. It clattered to a stop in front of Tobias.

"It's empty." He examined the ceramic jar with the precision of a scientist. "There's a label. Do not use for starter. Seriously." He turned to Crumblethorn. "So, someone used this for the starter."

"Obviously," the archivist responded.

"Is there anything else you want to tell us," Brug yelled to the library.

The shelves shook, and books fell to the floor. They spelled the word 'no.'

Kaelin rolled her eyes. "It's time for us to go then."

As soon as the words left her mouth, the stacks moved in unison, closing off their access to the main exit. The door to the left vanished. Bars covered the window to their right.

A cookbook whispered, "Stay . . . forever . . . test our muffins . . ."

Kaelin drew Mercy. Her hand hovered over Whisperthorn.

The door reappeared immediately.

"That's what I thought." Kaelin sheathed Mercy; after all, there was no reason to unalive the library.

Timber leapt towards the door. Brug skipped, they were like that. Tobias grabbed one forbidden recipe.

Kaelin glared.

He smiled back, weakly, before leaving the library.

She followed after him, with the hint of a smile on her face.

Love: the act of tolerating someone else's terrible decisions.

Outside, the wind carried the scent of smoke and rising heat. Timber bristled.

A new line appeared in amber on the parchment fragment.

Tobias read it. "*The Flame seeks the Starter. Stop it, or the wards will burn.*"

"Of course, the bread has a nemesis." Kaelin threw up her hands.

And so, Team Chaos marched on towards their next disaster—with a mysterious map, a clue from a panicked librarian, and the stubborn belief they could outsmart destiny, fire, and sentient carbohydrates.

Odds of success? Minimal.

Entertainment value? Immaculate.

23

The Ballad of Thorn and Flame

"Every assassin has a legend. Few have a bard who insists on making it a love story."

If anyone had been on the street when Team Chaos stumbled out of the Library of Unwritten Recipes disguised as a disgruntled tea shop, they would have assumed the weary, worn travelers had been kicked out for unseemly shenanigans. Timber pranced out, dusted in flour, head high, clearly proud of what they had accomplished. Brug hummed snatches of a melody to a song no one had ever heard. Tobias smelled of burned sugar and singed parchment, like a baking disaster had occurred. And Kaelin, well she was too busy checking roofs, alleys, and exits first, leaving her feelings for later.

And, dear reader, she was finally starting to realize she had a lot of feelings. Far too many, in fact. She was beginning to suspect emotional responsibility was a long con.

It was suddenly colder, noises from the city slid back into place, and the chimney smoke appeared normal. The tea shop actually looked welcoming.

"Is the library gone?" Tobias asked, his voice tinged with awe.

Kaelin shoved her hands in her pocket. The parchment fragment crinkled as her fingers made contact. It itched in her pocket like it was a splinter of fate.

An itch she couldn't ignore, like destiny poking her repeatedly with a breadstick.

They had survived a sentient library, a dough uprising, and emotionally loaded baking metaphors, which meant, unfortunately, the universe was now free to try something worse.

Timber plopped down, eyes filled with judgment.

"Mistress Lira is going to be so disappointed with us." Tobias kicked a rock; it didn't judge. He grimaced before grabbing his foot, unsteadily hopping as he dealt with the pain.

Kaelin almost reached out to steady him—almost—and then the moment passed like it always did, swallowed by instinct and old habits.

"How are we going to find Uncle Crust?" he asked, clearly defeated.

A low whine escaped Timber, the kind that suggested she personally would be filing a performance complaint.

"It wasn't a complete waste." Brug puffed up their chest. "We have—clues."

They gestured at everyone to show off the so-called clues.

"We have the Flame in Hiding—that's ominous enough for three quests. The Percival feather." They stroked their chin. "Do you think they could be the Flame in disguise? And this empty jar with the DO NOT USE FOR STARTER label."

Kaelin crossed her arms. "None of the clues points us in any direction. Uncle Crust is on the lam, and his trail is cold."

Even as she said it, Kaelin scanned the horizon, as though a sentient starter might simply stroll by, wearing a disguise and poor judgment.

Tobias fiddled with his cloak. "Are you suggesting we give up?"

"But the wards!" Brug exclaimed.

She sighed. "Not give up, but we need to regroup. Mistress Lira needs to know what's happening." She held a finger up to Brug's mouth. "I did not just make a bread pun. Don't start."

"I can't help it if you're punny." Brug giggled.

Kaelin drew a dagger. Don't worry, it was Mercy, and she had no intention of actually using it.

Probably.

Brug held up their hands in surrender. Their smirk told everyone around them that the surrender was only a temporary ceasefire.

"So, we're headed back to Mistress Lira then?" Tobias confirmed, his voice low.

Kaelin nodded. Timber howled. They packed everything and made their way back to the Spines and Bindings.

* * *

The group walked in loose formation, but Tobias kept drifting to the edge of Kaelin's peripheral vision, as though he wanted to walk beside her but didn't want to assume. The awareness of him tugged at her like a thread caught in her ribs.

They stood in front of Spines and Bindings. The cold wind sliced through their clothes, but none of them wanted to knock on the door and disappoint Mistress Lira.

The wards still flickered, but the glow was faint. The glyphs hiccupped instead of pulsed. It was clear that the magic was fading and the resistance Nadia and Fen were running was in danger.

The air smelled like the memory of bread, but fainter than before. The door of the bookstore swung open.

"Did you find Uncle Crust?" She herded them inside the safehouse. Her eyes darted around as each of them passed her.

The door clicked behind them. Books sighed in relief.

It was premature.

"So where is it?" Mistress Lira asked.

Kaelin looked at her. "We don't have it. Uncle Crust is on the run." She gestured to the back kitchen.

"It appears we need to talk." The shopkeep made her way through the stacks of books, ink pots with attitude, and flour motes floating in the air until the expansive kitchen table stood before them.

The flour motes, for the record, looked personally offended.

Tobias sat before digging through his satchel. He pulled out the clues they carried back with them. He put them on the table and explained everything that had happened at the library in a quick-and-dirty report. The report started with the bread golems, mentioned the jam-writing, the note about fleeing, the Flame in Hiding warning, and finally the empty jar.

As he finished going over their library experience, the books stood up straighter, and one shivered in fear. An inkpot tipped over, spilling pink ink everywhere.

Spilling pink ink was never a good omen. Spilling pink ink meant 'brace yourself.'

Lira pinched the bridge of her nose. "The disruption magic is spreading. It's happening faster than I expected it to."

Kaelin leaned forward. "What do you want us to do?"

Timber's head snapped towards the assassin. She padded over and sat down next to Kaelin, leaning against her in approval.

"Uncle Crust is on the move, probably drawn towards powerful heat sources or other dramatic flour-based disasters." Mistress Lira tapped the table. "There's been rumors. Nadia and Fen mentioned an unseasonal fog over the harbor and bread wards on the coastal safehouses fizzling all at once."

"Guess we're headed back to the coast." Kaelin stood, her chair screeching as it scraped against the floor.

Tobias's brows shot up, not in protest, but in a quiet kind of awe. Kaelin Thorn had volunteered to help without being sarcastic first. The world truly was ending.

Tobias nodded. "I'm going to do some research."

"The professor mage, nose always in the books. I will compose my next ballad while you—study." Brug stood, tossing their cloak over their shoulder with a flourish. They left the room with the flair of a dramaturg.

Kaelin followed the bard but stopped when she heard Tobias muttering. The mage waved his wand over the items they'd brought back from the library. A simple diagnostic spell, something that should have worked without a problem.

Instead, she smelled a faint hint of bread. Ghostly scribbles appeared on his wrists, glowing under his skin. Dust formed the words 'Do Not Overmix' and they drifted overhead before dispersing.

Tobias froze, shoulders tight—not with fear, but with embarrassment. Bread magic was not, traditionally, considered dignified. He rubbed his wrists, still glowing. Every movement he made projected his uncertainty.

The glow on his skin shouldn't have made her breath catch. It absolutely did. Not because it was magic—she'd seen plenty of that—but because it was him, and he looked uncertain, and that did something traitorous to her heartbeat.

Her voice softened. "Are you okay?"

The words left her mouth before she even thought about stopping them. She could have walked away or mocked him. Instead, she moved closer, took his hand in hers, and studied his wrist.

She didn't mean to touch him. Truly. Her instincts simply . . . misfired. Or perhaps finally fired correctly, which was worse.

Her fingers brushed his wrist and a pulse of something warm—not magic, something far more inconvenient—jumped between them.

He stilled for a moment. Instead of reaching for her; he rotated his other arm so she could see both of his wrists and waited. For once, moving away didn't even cross her mind.

The careful way he rotated his wrist, slow and deliberate, felt like an invitation—not physical, but emotional. A door left ajar. Kaelin had no idea how to step through it without setting off every trap she'd ever set for herself.

This, dear reader, is what we call progress. Alarmingly healthy progress.

Their eyes met. Tobias inhaled, a soft, brave breath like he was gathering a confession in his throat. Kaelin felt it land in her chest like the promise of a storm.

"I've done it!" Brug barreled into the room, lute in their hands, eyes bright. "My most epic ballad yet. 'The Ballad of Thorn and Flame.'"

"I don't like where this is going." Kaelin jumped away from Tobias like a teenager caught behind a closed door. Her instinct screamed retreat, but her pulse screamed something far less dignified. She ignored both with mixed success.

"You, my deadly friend, are the thorned maiden of unwilling yearning. And you, my magical beast, are the mage whose heart burned bright and his eyebrows brighter." They strummed the lute. "And I can't forget our Wolf of Destiny, Mostly Housebroken."

Timber wagged once, the canine equivalent of 'I accept this slander.'

Kaelin made her way out of the room but was stopped by the books and the look on Brug's face. There was no way she could disappoint him.

"I have the chorus, I think." They played the lute and sang. "And together they fell—metaphorically, don't panic—into love and destiny's flames, slightly manic."

Brug continued to sing. Timber joined, howling along on the wrong beat, but with great enthusiasm.

Tobias blushed, looking mortified by the lyrics, but his soft smile and the way his eyes softened when he looked at Kaelin said something very different. She caught the faint tremor in his smile—the kind that meant the lyrics embarrassed him, but the sentiment didn't.

A dangerous realization warmed her stomach.

The look on Kaelin's face said she wished she'd left, done anything but listen to a love ballad about her.

"I'm going to continue to add to it as we travel. It will be epic." Brug continued to sing, changing lyrics here and there. "It makes it more interesting."

While that was true, it also made it less accurate.

Kaelin walked out of the room. "I'm going to bed." She tossed the words over her shoulder. She didn't look back at Tobias. She couldn't. Not when her pulse was still misbehaving. Not when his almost-confession still hung between them like a spell waiting for a name.

She absolutely fled. Gracefully, of course—but fled nonetheless.

* * *

The clanging and banging downstairs forced Kaelin out of bed. Floorboards creaked as she pushed herself out of bed, as if it too wanted to rest longer. She reached for the foot of the bed to pet Timber, a habit she'd adopted and refused to admit she had. All that was there were tangled bedsheets. Her furry companion's absence was unsettling.

It didn't take long for her to don her assassin gear. Her hands grazed the hilt of each of her daggers, ensuring each one was in its place. When she finished, she made her way to the kitchen. She walked into a full room.

Brug sat at the table, making their plate of food. Timber was on the floor, chomping on a loaf of bread. The only one missing was Tobias. He wasn't in his chair, the one next to where she usually sat—she pretended not to notice.

The room was warm, warmer than anywhere else in the safehouse. The air smelled of spices, sizzling bacon, and a touch of smoke.

Domesticity at its most basic, except for the pending doom hiding around the corner.

Mistress Lira slammed a skillet on the stove. "I figured breakfast was a necessity. At least you tried to save my wards. That deserves a thank you."

She cracked eggs over the pan. They sizzled as they hit the pan. She whisked them with brisk impatience as they cooked.

"Do you have any cheese?" Kaelin asked. It had been so long since she'd enjoyed cheese.

Mistress Lira glared, but shredded some cheddar into the eggs.

Kaelin smiled, taking a seat at the table across from Brug.

"Our hero joins us for a meal before riding off to her destiny." They waved their fork in the air before bowing their head dramatically.

Sourdough bread sat in the middle of the table, still warm from the oven. Kaelin felt like it was judging her failure.

Maybe it was, after all, it crackled when Brug tore off a piece.

The wards sighed, faintly, causing crumbs to tumble across the table.

The jam they lathered on the bread glowed. It was like it was thinking about being magical.

"It smells wonderful in here." Tobias walked in, a book tucked under one arm, his glasses askew.

He looked around the room until his eyes landed on Kaelin. Tension left his body when he saw her—just a fraction, but she noticed anyway. It didn't take him long to weave through piles of books and step over Timber, so he could be near her. He sat next to her without any commentary.

She passed him the jar of jam. No flinching. No snark.

This, unfortunately, counted as progress.

"Is it okay if I . . ." He gestured to the teapot.

She nodded.

He reached past her, pouring both of them a steamy cup. Steam wafted off the cup. Its warmth caressed her cheek. The smell of cardamom and ginger filled her nose.

"It's Briarwick-grown and dangerously spicy." He couldn't stop himself from providing his analysis of the tea.

Internally, Kaelin smiled. Was she actually starting to like his impromptu professorial asides?

A loud deliberate knock on the door interrupted their cozy family breakfast.

The color drained from Mistress Lira's face. "No one should know this location."

"But it's a bookstore." Tobias scratched his head, confused.

"People don't knock on a bookstore's door. Especially when the closed sign is turned." Mistress Lira wiped her hands on her apron.

Kaelin stood. "I'll go."

The comfort of the morning left her as she pushed her chair back and donned her assassin persona. Timber stood, prepared to follow her to the door, but Kaelin shook her head and held her hand up to stop the dog. Timber huffed as she plopped back down, ears pinned back, annoyed.

She made her way through the magical bookstore. Books snapped shut, quills paused mid-scratch, and a lantern dimmed. Everything was still, for once. It felt like the entire shop held its breath in fear.

When she opened the door, no one was there, but floating in front of her was an envelope. She snatched it out of the air.

Inspecting the envelope, she noted Anwyn Stride's insignia. Her stomach dropped at the sight of it. On the front, in her mentor's handwriting, was her name.

She felt him behind her before anything else.

"What's inside?" he asked. His voice was soft and strong at the same time.

Her dagger cut through the envelope in one fluid motion. She pulled out the parchment inside. On it, written in a hand she knew as well as her name: *You're behind schedule. Hurry up. You know I don't like unfinished work.*

Her hand shook as she crumpled the note. The paper crackled like ice as she crushed it, as if even the parchment feared disappointing Stride.

All Kaelin could think was that the Guild knew she was here, tracking her movements. What if she was the reason the resistance failed? What if she doomed him just by letting him walk beside her?

For a moment, all she could hear was her heart pounding. A trickle of sweat dripped down her back.

Tobias watched, he could feel her reaction all the way to his soul. He raised his hand to comfort her, but didn't follow through. Instead, he stood there, supporting her in the only way he thought she would accept.

She saw it all out of the corner of her eye. She knew what it meant, even as she pretended she didn't.

"I can't." She turned and ran up the stairs. Away from him, her feelings, her thoughts. The most intrusive one was her fear that she was dragging Tobias, Brug, and Timber into the Guild's crosshairs.

She thought about leaving them behind, going back to the person she was most comfortable being.

A lone wolf.

The weapon she'd been trained to be.

For the first time in her life, she wasn't sure if that's what she wanted.

She pressed her palm to the cool wall, trying to breathe past the panic clawing up her ribs.

A soft knock interrupted her spiraling thoughts. She stared at the door, watched as the knob turned, and as Tobias stuck his head in. His curly hair flopped over his eyes.

"Can I come in?" Habits are hard to break, and he didn't invade her space without permission.

She shrugged.

He took that as a yes.

"You know, you don't owe her the version of yourself she tried to write." He stood near her, but not touching.

Yes, dear reader, he was referencing the Eternal Draft. And there it was: character development, stalking her again like an overeager plot device.

She turned to look at him, and everything she felt showed on her face. Her throat tightened. She felt prickly all over, as if she didn't belong in her own skin.

It was a rare moment of vulnerability. She hated it as much as she was starting to need it.

From downstairs, Brug's voice ripped through the tension. "Um . . . We might have a fire situation."

The scent of burned sugar weaved its way between them as tendrils of smoke curled in the air.

Tobias sighed. "Of course there is."

Everything in her shifted away from emotional angst to person-most-capable-in-an-emergency. He noticed it as she ran past him towards the kitchen.

They slid to a stop inside the kitchen; the bread was on fire, the glowing jam had joined the party, and the flames were rushing towards a stack of potion recipe books.

"My ballad. The bacon attacked it!" Tears stained their cheeks. "And everything burst into flames."

"Where did the scones of unusual size come from?" Tobias asked, momentarily distracted by the tower of baked goods in the corner.

Mistress Lira stepped forward. "I bake when I'm anxious. You never said who was at the door."

Tobias looked from her to the scones. "But it was only a few—"

The flames popped as the bread exploded. The wards flickered with excitement, or despair. It's hard to tell what bread-magic-based wards are thinking at any given moment.

Tobias drew his wand and channeled a cooling spell.

Kaelin used quick, practical motions—smothering the flame. The panic that had choked her minutes ago was gone.

Their hands brushed as they worked together to put out the fire.

Shocking, I know: the two of them together are actually good in a crisis. Dangerous and chaotic, yes, but also effective.

"Thank you," Mistress Lira hugged Tobias. She almost hugged Kaelin, but thought better of it. "I can't lose this place."

She looked around at the scorched table and singed papers.

"Don't worry, we'll help you clean up." Tobias offered.

Which was exactly what they did while they went over what they knew again. Mistress Lira brought up the coast, the failing wards at safehouses, the reports of sourdough-like magic near the harbor, and the ship wards burnout patterns that sounded like something they'd experienced before.

Brug set all the clues on the freshly cleaned table. They weren't sure it would help. But it couldn't hurt.

"Maybe the Flame in Hiding is drawn to the ward anchors, especially powerful ones like Uncle Crust," Tobias theorized, rubbing his chin as he did so.

Lira shrugged. "Maybe, I think someone took Uncle Crust towards a floating kitchen or coastal experiment."

"It's pretty simple if you ask me. The wards at sea are destabilizing, and something needs to be done about it or it's going to get worse." Kaelin crossed her arms. "It's time we moved out."

Timber howled in agreement.

"I think there's something big stirring in the water," Brug whispered. "And it's not happy."

"Whatever it is, we need to leave. The longer we stay the more attention we're going to attract." Kaelin paced as much as she could in the crowded space. The crumpled paper was a reminder of the danger she'd brought down on them.

"Here, I have some things for your journey." She handed Kaelin a bundle. "There's bread rations, backup starter, and a token that will get you into any of our safehouses."

Brug stood. "I will refine 'The Ballad of Thorn and Flame' as we continue on our adventures. It will be the perfect tale for when historians need something dramatically inaccurate."

"So, we go together then?" Tobias asked, quietly.

She hesitated. Her hand moved towards her dagger. Instinct told her she should leave alone.

She nodded. "Yes. Together."

As a group, they stepped outside towards the road to the coast. The wind smelled of salt, smoke, and looming bad decisions.

Next stop: unresolved romantic tension, structural ward failures, and a kraken who does not care about anyone's feelings.

24

Almost Confessed: Then a Kraken Happened

"Timing is everything. Unless a sea monster disagrees."

"Wait!" Mistress Lira called after them. "I forgot to give you this. It's for protection."

She handed Brug a sourdough loaf. It glowed faintly for mysterious reasons.

I'm sure the loaf knew why it glowed. Loaves, like assassins, had trust issues.

The glow pulsed once, like a very small sun bracing itself for very bad decisions.

"Thank you." Tobias hugged the shopkeep. He wanted to tell her they wouldn't let her down, but was afraid to overpromise. Words failed him, so he resorted to the oldest spell he knew: lingering.

Timber sniffed the loaf, cautiously at first. Her tongue flicked out to taste it, but Brug yanked it away before the dog could claim it as her own.

"Timber, you can't eat the protection loaf." Kaelin *tsk*ed.

The mournful look in Timber's eyes made her want to recant. She stayed firm, but it was a challenge. The dog huffed, the canine embodiment of 'you have betrayed me personally.'

"I will guard the bread with my life." Brug held the loaf like it was a holy relic instead of a baked good.

Spoiler: they did not, in fact, protect it with their life.

Team Chaos made their way to the coast through the chilled mountains. Ed still speechless followed, patiently carrying all their gear like the world's most overqualified pack mule. It's no wonder the horse decided to suffer in silence.

Tobias was unusually quiet. He didn't even ramble about fungus spores. Kaelin noticed, and it unnerved her. It didn't stop her from constantly checking that she was walking close enough to him to count as companionship but not intimacy. Every time she drifted a pace ahead, she found herself easing back without meaning to. She saw him notice and refused to acknowledge it.

I like to call this 'progress.' They called it 'confusing.'

After a day of traveling and a night of sleep, Tobias mustered up the courage to bring up The Unfinished Sentence.

The one that started mid-air.

"We should talk about—" he started.

She pointed to the sky. "Did you see that bird? I've never seen anything like that."

He almost rolled his eyes. "It's just a seagull."

"Oh, we must be close to the ocean then." Her eyes darted around looking for another distraction. "That rock is so sparkly. I bet Brug would love it."

At this point, she would point out anything to stop the 'I have feelings' conversation from happening. Literally anything. She would have discussed the socio-political implications of moss if it got her out of this.

Lute strumming drifted towards them. Brug sang new lyrics. They were about what was happening right now.

She picked up the rock and drifted over to the bard to give it to them. Timber herded her back towards the mage, bumping her knee with firm, canine insistence. The dog did this every time she tried to drift away from *the* conversation and from Tobias.

The Wolf of Destiny, Mostly Housebroken had decided that avoidance was no longer on the approved route.

Eventually, Kaelin ran out of things to deflect with.

Tobias—sweet, careful, respectful Tobias—asked, "Do you remember when we were mid-air and I tried to say something?"

She panicked internally and kept walking. Her boot caught on a root she absolutely should have seen. Under her breath she muttered something—she didn't even know what—but it managed to be both too honest and not honest enough.

Something about not wanting to lose him. Something about not deserving to keep him. Nothing she was ready to say at a normal volume.

BOOM!

They ran to the cliffside. The sea was wrong. The horizon rippled like bad ink. Ships tilted at impossible angles. Gulls fled inland. The air smelled of salt, smoke, and something ancient.

The kind of ancient that remembered empires, shipwrecks, and every bad decision ever thrown into its depths.

Tobias's skin pricked; he could feel the magic in the air.

Brug played a warning chord.

Timber growled at the surf as if it had personally offended her.

"That's not normal," Kaelin stated.

Understatement of the year, dear reader.

With one last glance at the ocean, they raced down the trail. Their surroundings blurred as Timber took the lead. She bounded through the switchbacks with the grace of, well, a dog. The others didn't fare quite as well. Tobias tripped on his cloak at one point. Kaelin steadied him before she leapt over a fallen tree, grabbed a tree branch, and launched herself to the bottom of the next switchback, landing with a somersault. Gravel sprayed under her boots as she slid to a stop, breath clouding the air in sharp bursts.

"Impressive. I would try it, but I might break the branch," Brug yelled as they ran. "It's going into my ballad."

The horse decided he had something to say after that.

"Show off," Ed muttered before returning to his normal silence.

Tobias's hand hovered over where she'd touched him. His eyes lit with appreciation of her acrobatics. Admiration warmed his features, threaded with something softer she wouldn't allow him to name.

Kaelin turned back towards them. "Are you coming?"

There was a hint of a smile before he continued his descent to the beach. He chose the safer route, picking his way down, but his gaze kept flicking to her, as if making sure she stayed within reach.

On the sand, the smell was sharper, with more salt, more smoke, and something that stung her nose and made her eyes water. The wind slapped at her, carrying flecks of brine that clung to her lips with a bitter tang.

There was a group of people scurrying around the beach, throwing glowing sticks towards the surf, avoiding the water at all costs. She didn't blame them. Ocean water should not be that color. It churned in shades of ink and bruise, as if the sea itself had picked a fight with reality and won.

Behind her, she felt Tobias and Brug skid to a stop.

Out near the water, Timber barked at the waves, her tail twitching in displeasure. She heard the dog's growl, but couldn't see what caused it.

A woman made her way towards them, her hair pulled back in a severe bun, glasses perched at the end of her nose. In her hand she carried a notebook, pen, and a basket full of glowing sticks. She walked past Kaelin, stopping in front of Tobias.

"Are you Tobias Merryweather? The one who made that sentient custard?" She held out her hand like she already knew the answer. "I'm Miriella Tideborne, head of the Salted Scholars. We're Saltmere's premier researchers of magic and wizardry."

Tobias shuffled his feet before shaking her hand. "Nice to meet you."

His embarrassment was palpable. Kaelin committed the moment to memory, prepared to tease him about it later. If they survived. Which, to be fair, was a fairly significant 'if.'

Miriella continued to talk. "I'm impressed with your skill, especially since you left university. What do you attribute your mastery to?"

Kaelin scoffed at the word 'mastery.'

Really, can you blame her? We all remember the multitude of glitter incidents.

"I wouldn't say I've mastered anything." He shook off her questions. "We're here to find out more about . . . that." He pointed at the turbulent sea.

The scholar sighed. "I'm not surprised. Come join us, the others can give you more information than I can."

As a group, they trailed behind her. Timber even joined them, tired of barking at the sea. She sniffed at Miriella, sneezed, sniffed again. Her ears pushed back in distrust.

A young man, probably half-elf, stepped forward. "The sea magic is destabilizing. I've tried everything I can think of. I can't stop it."

Miriella took notes.

Kaelin scanned the group of scholars. They were all so different and yet the same. Ink-stained cuffs, salt-stiff hems, boots caked in wet sand—each one looked like they'd been arguing with the shoreline and losing.

She watched as Tobias approached each of them individually, writing down what they had to say before moving on to the next scholar, Brug strummed their lute, waiting for the abridged version of the information the mage was gathering.

"It's my understanding that something is rising, something enormous, something with too many limbs for polite company." Tobias went over the data he'd collected.

Brug glanced up. "So . . . Normal coastal problems."

Kaelin looked at the sea as it bubbled and breathed. Something in her snapped.

It was, dear reader, the wall she'd built around her feelings. It had to give out eventually. Apparently, the end of the world was her breaking point. Reasonable, really.

She grabbed Tobias, dragging him away from the scholars, finally recognizing that if the end of the world was here, they needed to talk. Now.

It wasn't easy, but she tried to say something real. "Back at the safe house . . . When you said you care . . . I don't want to . . ."

Nothing felt right as she tried to put into words all the things she was feeling.

Feelings were, regrettably, not daggers. She couldn't line them up, sharpen them, and put them where they belonged.

Tobias leaned in. "Kaelin . . ." He pushed his hair back. "I meant it. I—"

Timber perked up.

Brug stopped mid-lute-pluck.

The ocean went silent.

And here, beloved reader, the author graciously provides an emotional cliff. Unfortunately, it will be immediately eclipsed by a literal one.

The sea exploded upwards.

Not metaphorically.

A massive, ancient, magically-altered kraken broke the surface. Orange scales and pink tentacles everywhere. It dragged broken ships and chunks of the coastline upwards with it.

The beast was almost too much to take in. Its tentacles were the size of tree trunks. Bioluminescent runes glowed along its limbs. A single enormous eye stared at them, the same violet color of Stride's insignia and Kaelin's eyes. Waves cascaded off its body in unnatural geometric symmetry.

It smelled of seaweed, salt, fish, and old magic. Like the ocean had been simmering a grudge for centuries and had finally taken the lid off.

"Oh. That's . . . big." Tobias stood in shock, staring up at the creature. He reached towards Kaelin, and unexpectedly her hand was there, waiting to be grabbed. Her fingers curled around his before her brain could vote on it.

"That's Guild magic," Kaelin muttered.

Brug stood in awe. "That's definitely going into the ballad."

Timber's angry bark intensified. She planted herself between her people and the shoreline, one small, furious creature ready to take on an ancient sea monster with nothing but teeth, loyalty, and poor risk assessment.

Everyone scrambled to react.

The scholars did the sensible thing and bolted, robes flapping, leaving their glowing sticks and half-finished theories to fend for themselves.

Kaelin ran up a dune, dragging Tobias behind her.

Brug played a battle anthem that did not help.

To be fair, it did make their impending doom sound very dramatic.

Timber decided everyone was safest buried under the sand, attempting to hide Tobias first.

Kaelin moved towards the kraken, daggers drawn. Mercy was nowhere in sight. Instead she held Moonveil and Glassfire.

The kraken raised a tentacle in the air. Kaelin ran back to Tobias because her instincts were overachievers.

The tentacle slammed down near the mage. She knocked him out of the way. He pulled her with him. Together they rolled down the dune until they slowed to a stop, him on top of her. Their noses almost touching.

"I really wasn't finished talking," he whispered.

She swallowed. A lot.

Is this the moment? Will feelings finally triumph over danger? Will our beloved fopdoodles—

The beach exploded again.

They both jumped to their feet.

The kraken destroyed more of the coast as its tentacles thrashed. Trees were sucked into the ocean, ships capsized, and sand flew in every direction.

Magic erupted next to her. Tobias stood, arms extended as a giant shield appeared in front of them. It looked like woven lattice, smelled like warm bread, and cracked like lightning. It held the kraken back long enough for Kaelin to strike, slicing through the tentacle like a hot knife through butter.

Color drained from Tobias's face. "I don't know how that happened. It was stronger, wilder than anything I've ever done." His voice trembled. "My magic. It's different, ever since the library."

She placed her hand on his shoulder. He took a deep breath, allowing her to ground him, for the moment.

The kraken rose from the waves again, unwilling to be subdued.

"Retreat!" Brug played a heroic sprint tempo as they led the retreat.

Timber bit down on Tobias's cloak, dragging him away from the monster.

Kaelin covered the rear, eyes blazing with adrenaline and something else she refused to name.

But I'll name it. Fear. That's what she was feeling.

They fled inland. Kaelin looked back as the kraken sank back beneath the waves. The creature paused.

It whispered in a voice Kaelin recognized. "You're mine, Kaelin Thorn."

Its violet eye met hers before it sank below the water.

The kraken was bound by Stride's magic. And it was looking for her.

She ran the rest of the way up the trail, away from the kraken and her past. At the top, she found everyone collapsed on the ground, panting. She shrugged before joining them, lying next to Tobias.

Of course, she's next to him, where else would she be?

She turned her head towards him. "We are never telling anyone what happened."

He looked back at her, breathless. "Kaelin . . . I meant what I said earlier."

She sat up. "We should . . . sleep." The word came out sharper than she meant, armor snapping back into place.

Ah yes, romance interrupted by a cephalopod calamity. It's a tale as old as time.

Kaelin pulled out her bedroll. She lay on her side, back to the mage. Timber curled up behind her knees. Tobias sat up next to her. She could feel his eyes on her. She refused to look back. If she met his gaze now, she was fairly certain something in her would say yes to things she didn't know how to survive.

25

Percival the Uncatchable

"Some legends are born. Others are poultry with boundary issues."

They continued inland after surviving the kraken; shaken, sandy, and exhausted. Sand clung to every fold of their clothes with vindictive enthusiasm. Even Tobias's hair poofed up like it was retaining trauma.

"I would give anything to sleep in a real bed," Tobias said longingly. His voice came out like a man who had absolutely tried and failed to sleep sitting upright against a tree because he was 'reviewing notes.'

Kaelin raised an eyebrow. "It hasn't been that long since we left Spines and Bindings. Did those beds not count?"

"They would have if he had actually slept in one." Brug sashayed next to them. "But the dear boy stayed up all night reading."

"It was research. Necessary research." Tobias pulled his cloak around him. Maybe he was cold, or maybe he wanted to block the judgment coming his way. He hunched like a scholar forced to confront his own choices. Kaelin had to resist the urge to bump her shoulder into his in silent consolation. Dangerous urge.

"Fine, if we find an inn, we'll stay at it. As long as the bed's not cursed or haunted."

She stomped off. Stomped might be a little strong for someone who was very carefully pretending not to glance back at Tobias every third step.

Timber padded along behind her. Ever loyal. Ever judging.

The trail narrowed as trees curved over them. The forest was so dense it would have been impossible to traverse if they weren't, by now, professional navigators of chaos and questionable terrain. Branches snagged Kaelin's braids like they had personal opinions about assassins in their woods.

Somewhere deep within the foliage, something rustled. Something large. Something with the confidence of a creature that had never once respected personal space.

It was the smell that assaulted them first. Cinnamon, woodsmoke, and something suspiciously like scorched feathers. The kind of smell that said 'you should run,' but also, 'bring a fire extinguisher.'

"You don't think . . ." Tobias pushed his glasses up his nose.

Kaelin shook her head. "It can't be." Her tone suggested this was less optimism and more bargaining with the universe. The universe, for the record, has never once responded well to bargaining.

Timber barked, clearly disagreeing with both of them.

"Oh look, it's a pop-up market." Brug pointed to a clearing up ahead. "I bet it's for winter solstice."

They practically ran to the market. Tobias followed somewhat slower. Timber wasn't far behind. Kaelin hesitated. Markets meant crowds. People made her stabby. Crowds made her stabby-and-sweaty, which was worse. Sweaty anxiety was never dignified for assassins.

Lanterns hung from the trees, lighting the area with a warm glow. Stalls shaped like teapots and cauldrons lined the clearing, each one selling something they didn't need. The scent of roasted chestnuts tangled with the unmistakable whiff of magical baked goods plotting something questionable. Pastries with malevolent intent were becoming a recurring theme in her life.

Tobias spun in circles looking at one booth after another. "I love markets. The food, the pastries, the joy."

He looked like an excitable puppy with a PhD.

Kaelin scowled. Joy was suspicious. Pastries were traps. Markets were emotional landmines. Her fingers brushed the dagger at her hip, instinctively preparing for both ambush and compliments.

"Don't forget the audience. Maybe I can test out 'The Ballad of Thorn and Flame.'" Brug grabbed their lute.

She glared at them. "Don't even think about it." But her glare softened half a degree when Tobias laughed under his breath. The sound hit her like a warm arrow—irritating and effective.

Timber sniffed the air. There were treats here. Treats made her happy. Her tail wagged with the unshakable belief that destiny—treat-based destiny—was near.

A tiny burning feather drifted down, landing on Kaelin's sleeve.

It didn't burn her. It sizzled in judgment.

She stared at it. "That seems bad."

Tobias looked at it. "It actually looks sort of like—"

Somewhere in the not-that-far distance there was an explosion.

Brug grinned. "More inspiration is near."

Timber growled, ears back, tail twitching. Whatever was coming, she wasn't happy about it.

Kaelin contemplated fleeing the continent. New life, new name, no poultry. Tempting.

A teapot stall tipped over. Out tumbled Finlo, his hair smoking, apron aflame, clutching a scorch-marked cookbook. Three panicked apprentice bakers and a goat ran out after him. They were followed by several singed pastries attempting a coup. One croissant barked. Kaelin decided not to investigate that further.

"Where did the goat come from?" Finlo asked under his breath. He sounded like a man who regretted every life choice that had led him to this moment.

A crate thudded to the ground. It was labeled, BRENNA'S ABSOLUTELY-DO-NOT-OPEN-UNDER-ANY-CIRCUMSTANCES INGREDIENTS. It rattled ominously, clearly displeased at whoever hadn't read the label.

Finlo spotted them and lit up like a holiday tree. Tobias lit up even more. His whole face brightened in that earnest, heart-first way that made Kaelin want to shove feelings back into the emotional oubliette where they belonged. Instead, she adjusted a dagger and pretended that was why her hands felt unsteady.

Kaelin groaned. They were in for trouble.

"Hey! You're alive! Also—HELP!" Finlo yelled as he ran past them.

Behind the mage-turned-chef a giant rooster stormed out of the wreckage. His beak glowed with contained magical fire, talons melted through the dirt, eyes full of righteous fury.

Percival was feathered like a phoenix who made questionable life choices. There were scorch-patterns on his wings that suggested he had recently exploded—possibly recreationally.

He even had a vest, probably embroidered by Brenna, that read, 'Good Boy(?)'

That question mark was doing a lot of work.

Percival screamed. It sounded half like a *ca-caw* and half like a cat being murdered.

The market screamed back. It was ear-shattering. Kaelin's eardrums filed a complaint with the universe.

And thus began the legendary incident of the Unfortunate Poultry Stampede.

Team Chaos split.

Kaelin attempted to trap Percival using her stealth and reflexes.

I would like to say it worked, but I would be lying.

Her first leap landed squarely on a table of enchanted potholders, which clamped onto her ankles in solidarity.

The rooster countered by parkouring off walls like a demonic feathered acrobat. He backflipped off a vendor sign. He drop-kicked a kettle. He winked at someone's grandmother. Truly unhinged behavior.

Tobias tried a very different method. He tried to reason with the rooster using magic—a bold strategy for a man previously attacked by sentient custard—and Percival set his notes on fire. Kaelin nearly reached for him on instinctively, which was deeply inconvenient and exactly the kind of problem she didn't have time for while dodging flaming poultry. Her hand jerked halfway towards his sleeve before she forced it back to her dagger.

Priorities. Unfortunately.

Brug composed a heroic chase ballad in real time, unhelpfully narrating the incident aloud.

Honestly, I think Percival enjoyed the soundtrack. He moved with extra flourish each time Brug rhymed 'rooster' with 'disaster-inducer.'

Timber couldn't believe she'd found a creature as dramatic as her. She chased him as if it was personal. Two divas in one clearing: disaster was inevitable.

"Will someone please grab the magic donuts?" Kaelin screamed, not that anyone could hear her over the uncontained chaos.

Brug stopped singing. "Donuts? Those were for him?" They pointed at the rooster.

Percival turned in a circle, torching a stall filled with books. Not the books.

I'm fairly certain a single tear fell from Kaelin's eyes. Tobias openly sobbed.

"Don't tell me you ate them," she hissed.

Brug shrugged. "Okay. I won't. But, in case you were wondering, they were a baking masterpiece."

"They were?" Finlo asked as he scrambled past them.

Kaelin pointed at the baker. "And you, what are you doing here?"

Finlo gulped.

"Be nice." Tobias yelled over his shoulder.

Kaelin unsheathed another dagger, unaware of who her target actually was.

"I was just here for a baking competition. I wasn't even going to use magic." Flames licked Finlo's boots. His screech was otherworldly.

"Run!" Tobias yelled.

Finlo did, and Brug followed. Kaelin stared for a beat then leapt, grasping a tree branch and flipping herself away from the most threatening poultry she'd ever met.

How she did this holding multiple daggers, I will never know. But she was very good at her job.

Mid-leap, Kaelin was heard muttering, "Why does everything we touch turn into a crisis?"

To which I would have responded, if she could have heard me, that narrative consistency is important. As I'm sure you're aware, dear reader.

Finlo ran under her. "Percival ate emotionally charged fermentation magic. But only a little bit." The baker ducked under a spout of flame. "Then he got into Brenna's experimental pastry arsenal."

She sighed. "Is that all?"

"No, I think he just set three more stalls on fire and stole a meat pie." Tobias shuddered.

Kaelin darted by a burning stall, slid under a table, and ended up standing next to the mage. Tobias, not Finlo. "Is he eating apples now?"

The feathered flamethrower had stopped at a barrel. He appeared to be bobbing for apples.

"You know, earlier—before the kraken—I was trying to tell you something." Tobias decided that this moment was *the* moment.

She wiped her sweat-soaked bangs off her forehead. Panting, emotionally overwhelmed, she responded, "Is this vital to say during a poultry pursuit?"

In his mind, it was. He opened his mouth to say how he felt.

Timber skidded to a halt, knocking him over. Percival reappeared like a feathery vengeance spirit. The conversation was over . . . for now.

If procrastination were a magic spell, they'd both be archmages.

Percival swooped down and grabbed the loaf of protection. The one Mistress Lira gave them. The one Brug promised to protect with their life.

The one essential to the ward-stabilizing sourdough subplot.

That very one.

He grabbed it in his beak and blasted off like a feathery comet.

Everyone screamed.

Especially Tobias.

Especially Brug.

Especially the narrator.

"I have—" Tobias inhaled.

Brug and Kaelin both muttered, "Oh gods."

Timber whined.

"—a plan." Tobias glared at them. "It's a good one. Maybe. I'm going to create a magic circle. If you"—he pointed to Kaelin—"can draw him into it, we can trap him."

Of course his plan involved her running straight at danger and him drawing circles in the dirt. At least they were consistent.

Timber's tongue lolled to the side as she watched her human take her treats and use them to bribe the (bleeping) rooster. The complaint she lodged could be heard around the world. It didn't stop Kaelin though.

"Here, Percy, Percy, Percy." She waved the jerky above her head.

Percival landed near her. He looked at the piece of meat, the howling dog, the circle on the ground, and paused. For a moment everything was still. It would have been silent too, if it wasn't for Brug attempting to play something soothing while Timber destroyed their effort with a mix of howls, barks, and boofs.

Percival eyed each and every one of them. Considered the jerky. Rejected it. Snapped at Brug's lute. The orc, the one who failed to save the loaf of protection, managed to save their lute. With a puff of smoke, Percival took to the sky once again.

From somewhere in the forest, Brenna barreled in armed with a lasso, a basket of pulverized ice scones, and a palpable sense of exhausted competence.

She saw Finlo's cloak smoking and extinguished it. It clearly wasn't the first time. "Percival's in his molt-cycle. It makes him volatile."

"That's what makes him volatile? He's not always volatile?" Kaelin gasped.

Brenna nodded. "This is a special level, worse than I've ever seen. Like Finlo's magic in the kitchen."

"Hey, I'm not that bad."

Brenna's raised eyebrow said it all.

The flapping of wings caught everyone's attention. Percival flew directly at them. Tobias created his bread shield despite his fears. The shield shuddered as it formed—unstable, wild, and still somehow there. Kaelin's chest felt uncomfortably similar. Protecting everyone from errant flames, Kaelin grabbed the lasso from Brenna and sent it flying, looping a chicken foot in the process. Brenna yelled. Finlo cast a half-finished cooling charm.

"Did that actually work?" Brug asked as they strummed their lute.

They all peeked from behind the bread shield. The rooster cooed, preened, and then set fire to the cooling charm.

The legend of Percival the Uncatchable endured for another day.

In a burst of flaming feathers and chaotic magic, the rooster took to the air, screeching triumphantly. He flapped his wings, carrying the loaf of protection, half of Tobias's notes, and Brenna's basket of ice scones with him.

No one knew how he got the ice.

A single feather floated down from the sky. Kaelin picked it up.

Finlo collapsed to the ground. "Well . . . he's gone."

"Not for long, he always comes back." Brenna melted to the ground next to him.

Kaelin still stared at the feather. It glowed violet, just like the kraken's eye.

Color drained from Tobias's face. Kaelin met his gaze.

"She's been here."

"How did she get to Percival?" the mage whispered his question. The idea of Stride's magic in something this ridiculous made his stomach twist; the idea of it circling Kaelin made it worse. "I was there when Percival ate the pies. She wasn't."

And there it is, dear reader. Nothing says 'escalating the villain arc' like poultry infused with hidden magic.

They said their goodbyes (Finlo cried) as they continued on their journey, exhausted and slightly afraid. The laughter from the market faded behind them, replaced by the quiet crunch of their footsteps and the unspoken weight of what they'd just seen.

One thing was certain: Percival would return. And when he did, the world would not be ready. Kaelin certainly wasn't. But then again, she hadn't been ready for Tobias either, and look how that was going.

26

TEAM CHAOS RIDES AGAIN (ALMOST)

"Found family: the kind you don't choose, but would fight twelve cursed badgers for anyway."

"Where's Brug?" Kaelin stood at the edge of the overlook sharpening her knives. It was her version of meditation: steel, repetition, and the comforting knowledge that something in her life still had an edge.

From where she stood, Briarwick, Saltmere, and Eldreach stretched out around her with nothing more than rivers to form their boundaries. The wind carried salt from the coast and woodsmoke from unseen chimneys, as if the whole region were breathing around her. Each exhale tugged at her braids and ruffled her bangs. The movement felt like a reminder of where she should be instead of where she was.

If she looked to her left, she could watch Tobias practicing silent spells. She looked to her left a lot, which was quite troublesome and absolutely not something she was prepared to discuss.

Nothing says character development like reluctantly admitting you might have people.

Tobias stopped mid-spell and waved away the resulting poof of glitter. His hand trembled slightly. "I believe they needed to restring their lute. Percival destroyed the strings." His mouth twitched like he wasn't sure if he should be impressed or traumatized.

"Oh."

That was it—a one-syllable response. Nothing more, no explanation or elaboration. She went back to sharpening her knives and brooding. Which, in this case, meant replaying kraken eyes, violet feathers, and every bad decision that had led her here.

Every time her thoughts started circling too tightly, Timber nudged her knee, a furry reminder that she was, regrettably, not alone anymore.

"I'm fine." She glared at the dog, one eyebrow raised.

Timber huffed with judgment before lying down on her human's feet.

She ran her sharpening stone over the blade's point one more time, imagining for a moment the violet eye rising from the sea. Her grip tightened.

Ed meandered over. "Can we sleep somewhere with a stable tonight? While the view is stunning, I wouldn't mind a roof over my head."

For a horse, he sure was demanding.

Kaelin remembered telling Tobias they could sleep somewhere with a real bed. "Fine." It came out harsher than she intended. "Do we need to wait for Brug?"

Tobias shook his head. "I believe they're going to meet up with us."

She turned away from the view. "Let's go and find somewhere comfortable for everyone to sleep." She patted Timber's head. "Somewhere they allow dogs inside the rooms."

Yes, those words came out of her mouth. No, she didn't hear herself. And I'm the only one brave enough to point it out.

They made their way down until they crossed the bridge into Eldreach. Kaelin was finally in the country King Varric controlled.

I know, I know. The lack of a troll at the bridge crossing was truly a missed opportunity. I'll have to add it next draft. Or maybe I won't. You never know with drafts.

Before nightfall, they were standing in front of the Towering Tree, an inn built inside a hollowed-out giant evergreen tree.

"Just look at those stables. You know where I'll be for the night." Ed trotted off to the stables without a second glance.

Kaelin's eyes followed as the horse left them behind. "I guess we're staying here tonight."

She tugged open the door, and the surrounding silence dissipated as the patrons' raucous laughter burst through the doorway. To say the tavern was bustling was like saying the Winds of Anderbroke were a nice breeze.

The plucking of a lute could be heard under all the other sounds in the tavern. Kaelin's head whipped around as she searched for Brug. But it wasn't them. Instead, a white-haired man sat on a stool, providing the score for the boisterous room. Her companions noticed the music as well. Timber's whiskers twitched. Tobias winced. Kaelin sighed.

It was almost impressive how much disappointment one could pack into a single exhale.

"I'll be with you in a sec, guv," a tree nymph hollered as she passed them; her green tattoos shimmering in the soft candlelight.

The savory smell of roasted beef wafted towards them. Timber sniffed the air, taking one step forward before Kaelin yanked her back. The soulful look in her eyes would have melted anyone else's iron resilience.

Our assassin stood firm, even if her heart twinged a bit at denying her furry companion.

"Hi, I'm Draya. How can I help you?" the nymph asked, her tattoos swirling under her skin as the light changed.

Tobias didn't respond. Instead he stared, watching the movement of green dance down Draya's arms. "That's fascinating."

"What he meant to say is we would like two rooms for the night." Kaelin glared at the tattoos like they were personally competing for his attention.

The nymph smiled. "Of course. I should warn you about Seque. He's one of my cousins. Gone now for at least a century.

This was his tree before they hollowed it out. His spirit refuses to leave, and he's quite the prankster. If you'll follow me."

Tobias looked at Kaelin. She responded with a raised eyebrow. Timber looked longingly at the kitchen. They all followed Draya up the spiraling staircase.

A stair creaked above them—except no one was on it.

Friendly reminder: this is the exact opposite of comforting.

They reached what had to be the fifth floor. It was hard to count because rooms seemed to exist at all levels—and some at angles that defied basic architectural reason.

"These two should do ya!" Draya handed them two keys, slipping Timber a piece of roast beef before she made her way down the stairs.

Bells jingled, even though neither of them had moved. The seven-bell token she carried jingled in response. Joren stepped out of the room to their left. His hands were bandaged, his eyes debt-free, and there was a renewed sense of purpose about him. Timber wagged her tail approvingly. She liked fighters. They smelled like snacks.

"Kaelin, I was hoping you would turn up." He bounded down the stairs. Bowing once, he stood in front of her.

"Get up. There's no bowing, absolutely no bowing." She tugged on his arm.

He stood. "Respectfully . . . No. Come downstairs. I want you to meet the troops. They're a motley crew of fighters and ring-runners. But their loyalty to me runs deep, and now it's yours."

Kaelin blinked at him, trying to calculate how she'd gone from 'lone wolf' to 'accidental commander' in under a week. This felt like a clerical error. A widespread one. She opened her mouth to protest, but Joren was already sweeping her towards the tavern below.

And thus began the night Kaelin realized she'd accidentally unionized the resistance.

Joren grabbed her arm, leading her back to the tavern. She looked back in time to see Tobias grimace, but he waved her on, offering support instead of jealousy. The unfair, wonderful man.

She wasn't sure whether that made things better or significantly worse.

The tavern hummed below them—loud, warm, chaotic. Kaelin barely had time to brace herself for whatever came next.

Before her foot could hit the bottom step, the doors to the inn flew open. In the doorway stood Brug, arms extended, smile covering their orcish face. "I've brought reinforcements."

Behind them was a wagon, probably stolen, full of minor bards, a half-drunk dwarf who claimed to be their manager, and posters advertising "The Ballad of Thorn and Flame."

Kaelin stared. Of course, Brug had returned with an entire musical entourage. Of course this was happening. She inhaled slowly, like she could physically breathe her patience back into existence.

Kaelin blushed. "Are there three goats?"

Brug shrugged. "They insisted on coming. None of us can figure out why."

A goat screamed.

Foreshadowing? Possibly.

Before Kaelin could decide whether to address the goats, the bards, or her rising urge to flee into the woods forever, the tavern's atmosphere shifted—like the world was politely warning her that escalation was imminent.

Clanking, and not of tankards cheering, interrupted the happy-ish reunion. Tobias's jaw dropped. Kaelin followed his gaze. In the not-so-far distance were Nadia and Fen decked out in full armor riding towards them.

Kaelin briefly considered lying down on the floor. Just lying down. Letting the moment wash over her like a tidal wave of lesbians and consequences.

Tobias mouthed, "Are you okay?"

Kaelin responded with an eye twitch.

They clattered to a halt in front of Kaelin.

Nadia lifted her helm. "How could you not invite us?"

"Invite you where?" Kaelin glanced up at the tree inn, understandably confused.

Fen attempted to cross her arms but had to settle for putting her hands on her hips. "To the revolution you're about to start."

"I'm n—"

Nadia held up her hand. "Don't try to deny it. You promised chaos."

"I did not—"

Fen stopped her from finishing. "We heard 'king assassination,' which is lesbian for 'road trip.' "

Tobias pinched the bridge of his nose like he needed a moment. Kaelin mirrored the motion with her soul.

Tobias stepped in. "How did you hear anything about the assassination?"

The elves both looked over at Joren. He looked away, pretending to whistle.

Nadia took one glance at the mage and promptly ignored him. "We have something for you."

She held out a dagger. Along the blade, the words To Our Favorite Disaster were engraved.

"You said we were both going to give her the blade." Fen harrumphed.

Nadia pulled her lover close. They clanged as their hips touched. "I forgot. Will you ever forgive me?"

The kiss that followed was hot enough to fog up glass. They broke their embrace, Fen blushing, Nadia smiling unabashedly.

"So, will you accept our little token?" Fen asked.

Tobias swallowed hard. Kaelin pretended not to notice the way his shoulders stiffened. She also pretended not to be flattered, overwhelmed, or on the verge of running for the hills.

Timber didn't care, she liked both of them immediately. Most likely because Fen was already sneaking her treats.

In front of her stood Joren with his motley crew, Brug and his bards, and the infamous fight club owners. They were all looking at her expectantly. She looked back at them, wondering exactly what she was supposed to do with all of them.

Nothing says 'accidental leadership arc' like thirty people showing up and assuming you have a plan.

Instead of coming up with a plan, she walked away, up the stairs, and toppled onto her bed. Timber followed and cuddled up next to her. She wasn't sure how long they lay on the bed. It couldn't have been minutes, maybe hours; it wasn't long enough.

There was a soft knock on the door.

"If you're expecting a plan from me right now, go away." She buried her face in Timber's fur.

The door creaked open.

"If you're the spirit of Seque come to play pranks on me, I'm not in the mood and will stab you." She really wasn't in the mood for a haunting.

"I wanted to check, make sure you're okay." Tobias's voice was soft, cautious.

She sat up, palms sweaty. "I'm fine."

He raised an eyebrow. Timber also raised an eyebrow.

"Fine. I'm not fine. But that's really my only option right now." She flopped back onto the bed. Staring at the ceiling, she counted the rings of the tree in the wood.

"I've been researching the Eternal Draft." He ran his hand through his hair. "I'm scared . . . for you."

"When did you find the time to do any research?" She continued to stare at the ceiling, burying her fingers into Timber's fur as she tried to find her normal aloof composure.

"After you walked away." He paused. The words he wanted to say were right there, on the tip of his tongue.

The *CAW-CAW* of Percival reverberated through the room, far enough away that there was nothing they could do, close enough for them both to worry about the destruction in his wake.

Romantic timing remained allergic to this party.

"I'm going to kill that bird," Tobias muttered.

Kaelin laughed. "I already would have if you hadn't stopped me."

27

DRAFTS, DAGGERS, AND DANGEROUS TRUTHS

"Destiny knocks softly. Doom sends a courier."

*B*ANG!

Kaelin jumped to her feet, daggers in hand, completely disoriented.

Outside her room, she heard Joren scream, "I'll save you. It's finally my turn."

There was another thud—something between a heroic leap and spectacular failure.

She threw the door open to find Joren on the floor and a courier standing in a half-burned cloak with Stride's insignia embroidered on the front. The woman's hand was raised, prepared to knock again.

Kaelin walked past her. "Interrupting an assassin's sleep is a good way to get killed."

The woman opened her mouth.

"No." Kaelin's boot hit the first step with finality. "We do this with coffee, or you meet Moonveil. There is no in between."

Tobias ran like a man who had expected chaos and was still unprepared for the amount delivered.

He covered the courier's mouth before she said another word. "I'd believe her. Last night was rough."

Timber barked once before following Kaelin down the stairs.

"Ready to head to the tavern?" Tobias asked the courier. She nodded. He removed his hand.

The mage led the procession down the spiraling stairs—him, the courier, Joren limping behind, the goats joining like summoned spirits of inconvenience, and three confused bards emerging from doors they did not rent.

It was amazing the inn had rooms for all of Kaelin's new teammates.

The tavern was quiet, or at least it was until everyone stumbled in.

"Oh, there's so many of you." Draya looked up at the mass before wiping the sleep away from her eyes.

Kaelin pointed at the courier and Tobias. "You two, sit with me. The rest, go anywhere else."

Timber raised an eyebrow.

Brug looked wounded. "Even me?"

"Fine." She was using that word a lot lately. "You two can also stay." She turned to the courier. "Who are you and why are you here?"

Kaelin raised a mug of hot steaming coffee to her lips. The bitterness hit her tongue like clarity.

She needed clarity.

"I'm . . . I'm . . . Andraya Merbotel. I was a member of . . ." Her voice dropped to barely a whisper. "The Shadow Guild."

"You left them?" Brug asked loudly.

Andraya's eyes darted around the room. "Not so loud, they're everywhere and always listening."

Some people called that paranoia. After all, paranoia was only paranoia until it paid off.

Andraya scrounged around in her satchel. Finally, she pulled out a sealed letter, rumpled from whatever had occurred before the woman found Kaelin. Like a good courier, Andraya handed the letter over.

The envelope felt dangerous—warm, pulsing. Kaelin sliced it open. She pulled out the parchment inside and read the missive. Her stomach dropped.

Tobias snatched it out of her hand and read it aloud. "*The Draft will be bound at the Gala. The king is bait. You are the ink.*"

The words that fell from his lips were not mage-appropriate.

Silence fell. Real silence.

The kind that tastes metallic.

Kaelin's pulse stuttered—the meaning slotted into place like a blade finding the soft gap in armor.

The stakes sharpened as the realization that this was most likely a trap solidified in her mind. A trap she had no choice but to walk into, especially with all these people counting on her to stop whatever was about to happen.

The missive was passed around—Joren, Nadia, Fen, Brug—everyone leaning in, shoulders tightening, expressions sharpening. Everyone rallied around her. Not because she was chosen, but because she helped them, accidentally, on the side.

The tavern air thickened, humming like danger had taken a seat at their table.

Timber sniffed the courier. Then sniffed again. She backed up, sneezed, and lunged—knocking Andraya flat.

A curse detonated—purple glitter exploding where Andraya should have been.

A beat of stunned breath held the whole room captive.

Even the mugs seemed to reconsider existing.

Tobias stared at the sparkling debris. "How did she know?"

Kaelin stroked Timber's fur. "She's smarter than all of us combined."

Timber basked in the praise.

Brug wrote a new heroic verse to "The Ballad of Thorn and Flame."

The goats screamed. Again.

Some mysteries unravel slowly. Goat-related ones rarely do.

Kaelin inspected the goats. One glimmered suspiciously. Was that a horn?

And thus, the goaticorn was canon.

Nadia and Fen stood first, both cracking various body parts.

"Well, if we're going to walk into danger, we need to train. Some of you look woefully unprepared." Nadia's eyes landed on Tobias as she finished her statement.

"Really? I hold my own in a fight. Sometimes, I've even been useful," Tobias muttered.

Kaelin placed her hand over his. "Don't take it personally. Nadia and Fen understand fists more than magic."

He relaxed under her touch.

Tiny moment. Barely noticeable—except she noticed it anyway.

Brug jumped up from their chair, knocking it over in the process. The sound jolted two bards awake.

"I will lead us in motivational singing exercises." They strummed their lute. "Our song will lead the charge to victory."

It wasn't long before their training had caused so much chaos that two other bards had fainted.

Kaelin stepped over the fallen bards. "Are music drills really necessary?"

Brug clutched their chest, crumbling to the ground, elegantly, of course. "I'm offended by your lack of belief in our necessity."

Kaelin had the decency to look at least somewhat shamed. Tobias did not. He looked like he was preparing a strongly worded thesis on 'Why Bardic Influence Should Have Acoustic Limits.'

"Enough of this musical nonsense." Fen crossed her arms.

Nadia stood next to her partner, arm draped over Fen's shoulders. "It's time to really train. None of this . . ." She gestured in Brug's direction. "Nonsense."

Kaelin set her mug down and pushed her chair back. "Combat drills?"

Nadia smirked. "Only if we can wager on them."

Draya jumped onto a table. "Outside. Everyone. No fighting in the tavern. I can't afford new furniture."

Nadia and Fen sighed.

Brawls are significantly less satisfying when you can't smash a chair over someone's spine.

"So, are you up for a little wager?" Fen waggled her eyebrows.

Tobias grabbed Kaelin's wrist. "Is now a good time to be making bets?"

Kaelin shrugged. "It'll make it more fun."

The tiniest spark lit in Tobias's eyes—equal parts worry and awe. She resolutely ignored it.

She turned to Brug. "Can you find Andraya a place to rest? The curse did a number on her."

The bard nodded before throwing the unconscious courier over their shoulder.

"Let's do this." Kaelin pulled her hair back, tying it with the sort of determined efficiency that suggested defeat was imminent for the others, not her.

Outside, the air shifted—the kind of anticipatory hush that happens right before someone makes a series of increasingly poor decisions.

The breeze smelled of pine sap and frost. Dirt clung to Kaelin's boots.

The drills were less practice and more of an out-and-out fight. Not feral—not exactly—but a controlled kind of wild: violent, balletic, sharp enough to carve constellations into the dirt. A dance of feet and fists that was stunning in both its ferocity and its beauty.

It was art, made violent.

The others circled around them, forming an impromptu arena. Even the goats seemed to sense this was a spectator sport.

Tobias watched—rapt, reverent. He didn't even try. Kaelin felt his eyes on her as much as she felt Fen's blade miss her jaw by half an inch.

One of Joren's men fell to the ground with a thud. Somewhere behind them, someone lost a bet. Fen cursed. Nadia applauded.

Timber patrolled the area like a wolf general, occasionally growling approval or disapproval with the air of a seasoned commander.

As the final strike landed and the dust settled—along with Brug fainting dramatically for unrelated reasons—the momentum shifted.

Kaelin won.

Mostly because she didn't know how to lose.

Mostly because she refused to.

She stood bent-breathing, sweat chilling on her spine. Exhaustion tugging at her legs. The glow of triumph softened the edge of her exhaustion—and, embarrassingly, the warm flicker in her chest when Tobias smiled at her like she had just rearranged the stars.

He cleared his throat. "I should have everyone with magic practice some defensive spells."

Gesturing for others to join him, he started his own drills. There were a lot of sparkles summoned, and a handful of successful spells cast. Tobias tried to pretend the sparkles were intentional. No one believed him.

Meanwhile, on the opposite side of chaos, Joren's fighters built traps out of kitchen utensils and stubbornness.

"I'm not getting those back, am I?" Draya looked at the contents of her kitchen laid out before her. "I hope this is for a good cause."

She looked around for someone responsible. Unfortunately, Kaelin's entire entourage disqualified themselves on sight.

Brug re-emerged, covered in sawdust, glory, and at least three stickers someone had slapped on them during their forced nap.

They sauntered over to the wood nymph, draping an arm over her petite shoulders. "It is, my dear. It most certainly is. Now, tell me about this place so I can include it in my ballad."

Kaelin heard them, didn't even attempt to stop the roll of her eyes before taking in the rest of her troops. She wanted to add a question mark at the end of the sentence, but refrained. Everyone was here to support her, even the goats. The hooved animals had, by this point, appointed themselves as scribes of destruction, chewing up every piece of parchment they came across.

"Will somebody get these goats away from me? They keep eating my notes," Tobias said, his exasperation leaking into every one of his movements.

Some armies train. Some are trained. And some—this one—assembled themselves like a kitchen accident trying to become destiny.

The rest of the day went on like this: a mix of training, breaks for nourishment, and new verses of Brug's epic ballad tested. If they weren't preparing for a potential war, Kaelin might have called it a good day.

By evening the clearing resembled a war camp, a music festival, and a kitchen disaster—simultaneously.

Kaelin was exhausted. Combat drills, dagger tossing, and actual skirmishes had drained her. Nadia and Fen were the only two still going strong, not surprising since they were in the ring every night back at the Black Fang.

"I'm off to bed," Kaelin announced. When everyone turned towards her, the pressure to say more prodded her. "Remember, rest and recovery are as important as training."

Nadia nodded. "Fen, are you ready to go get some rest?"

The way she drew out the word 'rest' implied they were going to be doing something very different.

"Of course." Fen winked.

The two linked arms before heading into the tavern. Kaelin followed them but turned and climbed the stairs instead of heading to the tavern with everyone else.

The door to her room loomed in front of her. She rested her head against the warm wood, shoulders sagging as the weight of what today meant crashed down on her.

It swung open, and she stumbled through the opening.

"Stupid haunted inns everywhere I go." She shook her fist at the ceiling, assuming Seque would see her.

"What's wrong?" Tobias leaned against the doorframe. It was his attempt to look casual. Timber padded by him and jumped onto the bed.

She turned towards him with a chagrined look on her face. "Nothing. I'm fine."

Timber whined, clearly disagreeing.

He raised an eyebrow. "You know, it's okay if you're not fine. We won't tell anyone."

She felt her lips twitch, like she wanted to smile. However, her eyes burned with unshed tears.

"I didn't ask them to follow me," she whispered. The admission scraped her raw.

He put his hand over hers. "You didn't have to."

She stared at where they touched. "I don't want them to follow me. It's too much responsibility."

He squeezed her hand. "I don't think you can stop them."

"I could just leave. Do it all on my own."

"We'll find you." He turned, looking at her until his eyes met hers. "The thing is, you can't stop any of us. It's not up to you."

She looked away. "But I can't protect everyone."

"You don't have to."

They sat quietly on her bed, neither one talking, just breathing. Kaelin allowed the comfort of his presence to wash over her. It was a new experience. One she wasn't sure she liked, at least not yet.

Growth: it's painful, inconvenient, and impossible to sharpen on a whetstone.

Timber softly woofed at the foot of the bed, her paws twitching as if she was chasing a squirrel, or something more dangerous. Whatever it was, her dreaming sounds shattered the companionable silence that filled the room.

Tobias rubbed the back of his neck. "I should be going."

Her hand, seemingly of its own volition, grabbed his wrist. "You don't have to go. Just—stay. Where I can . . . not think for a moment."

She looked down at her boots, unsure how he would respond or even if she really wanted him to.

"Okay." He sat back down on the bed.

She took his hand, lacing her fingers through his, and lay down, curling her knees into her chest. He filled the space next to her, with only their hands touching.

They slept like that through the night. But like all good things, it had to come to an end. So this did, with loud banging, barking, and a bard.

"Get up now! We have an infiltration to plan," Fen hollered through the door.

Kaelin sat straight up, dropping Tobias's hand like it was a hot potato. "What time is it?"

The banging continued, not just on the door, but on pots and pans. It was the worst kind of cacophony to wake up to.

"It's dawn. No time to laze abed," Nadia responded.

"How can she hear you over all that noise?" Tobias sat up slower, rubbing the sleep from his eyes.

Brug sang, "Are you two in there together?" There was a pause. "Finally, the verse I've been waiting to write."

Timber stood on the bed and howled.

"We'll be down in a minute. Order food, something with cheese . . . and coffee."

They waited until silence filled the stairwell. Tobias poked his head out.

"They're gone," he whispered.

Kaelin sighed. "Good. Let's get this over with." She grabbed her daggers, sheathed them, and left the room. Timber on her heels.

In the tavern, her troops gathered around a long table, leaving a spot for her and Tobias. She took an open chair and looked at them expectantly. At some point, Tobias slipped into the chair next to her. Everyone noticed, but no one said anything about it.

Nadia stood, moving things on the table before she started to speak. "You"—she held up a salt shaker—"are going to infiltrate the Gala that King Varric is hosting as a foreign envoy."

Fen passed Nadia the pepper shaker.

"The mage"—Nadia nodded towards Tobias—"will be your magical attaché."

Tobias tried not to blush. He failed.

"The bards, including Brug"—she lined up a handful of spoons—"will perform at the Gala."

Kaelin raised an eyebrow. Brug smiled, it didn't reach their eyes. It appeared even they didn't trust their part in the plan. That was not a good sign.

"Nadia and I will disguise ourselves as guards." She took two forks and put them in front of a napkin.

Kaelin assumed the napkin represented the castle gate, but she wasn't sure.

Fen took over. "Joren and his crew will set up outside the palace. We even found a tiny cloak for Timber, officially making her security."

It was a plan, maybe even a good one, if you ignored all the gaping holes in it.

"When did you plan all this?" Kaelin regretted the words as soon as they left her mouth.

"While you two were canoodling, of course," Brug answered. "I wonder what rhymes with canoodle?"

A bold accusation, considering they had barely mastered hand-holding.

A waitress set a plate of eggs and potatoes covered in cheese in front of her, followed by a mug of coffee. "We leave after I eat."

Which was exactly what happened. She ate her cheesy breakfast. Horses were saddled. Goats wandered behind them. Timber led the charge as Kaelin's allies surrounded her, all the ones she hadn't meant to gather. Tobias deliberately rode beside her at the exact distance she preferred.

And so, Team Chaos—reborn, reorganized, and only slightly on fire—rode to the Gala.

To kill a king.

To unmake a spell.

And maybe, just maybe, to finally finish a sentence without interruption.

In the distance a loud *caw-caw* was heard, making that last part highly unlikely.

28

Gala of Gowns, Daggers, and Hidden Keys

"Stealth, seduction, sabotage. Never underestimate a woman in silk and spite."

Yes, daggers appear in consecutive chapter titles. No, I am not apologizing. When your protagonist solves 90 percent of her problems with pointy metal, patterns emerge.

"To get into the castle, you have to wear a dress." Nadia held a violet ballgown in front of her.

It matched Kaelin's eyes perfectly.

"I do not wear dresses. Furthermore, I do not wear color." She shook her head violently.

"You'll look beautiful in it." Tobias took the dress from Nadia, handing it to Kaelin. His voice was gentle, unstrategic—dangerous in its sincerity.

Everyone in the room held their breath as some of the tension left her shoulders. His kind words were almost enough for her to relent. Almost.

Her back stiffened. "No. There's nowhere to hide my daggers. How am I supposed to do my job, protect myself from the trap I'm obviously walking into, and get everyone out alive, if I have to hike up my skirt to get to my weapons?"

Fen patted Kaelin's shoulder. "I understand, I don't like dresses either, but you can't be the lead of a foreign envoy in leather."

"Why not?" She crossed her arms.

Yes, dear readers, even assassins sulk. Especially when forced to wear formal attire.

"When this is all over, please remember this is for your own good." Brug wrapped their arms around Kaelin, lifting her off the ground so she couldn't retaliate.

Nadia painted the assassin's face, Fen did what she could with her black hair, Tobias cast a subtle glamour spell to hide Guild scars. She almost jerked away. Almost.

Trust is slow, sharp, and earned—never given. But she let his magic settle anyway.

She heard him mutter, "I want to kill whoever caused these."

"Stop moving. This will be over so much faster." Nadia threw the dress over Kaelin's head.

Brug dropped her to the ground. Fen pulled the dress down so the fabric fell to the floor. It slithered cold against her ribs, unfamiliar, wrong. Too soft to trust. Too bright to disappear in.

Nadia tightened the corseted bodice. Air rushed out of her lungs in one sharp instant. Kaelin gasped for breath, finding it surprisingly easy to fill her lungs. If she knew how to trust, she would have known Nadia knew how to appear sophisticated while still being able to throw a kick.

In mere seconds the dress was on and Kaelin was defeated.

Timber barked before guarding the door as final adjustments were made. The dog knew her human would try to run. Kaelin saw her furry companion block the door and knew running wasn't an option.

"Where's the loyalty?" she asked.

The dog just stared at her, one doggy eyebrow raised.

If anyone tells you a makeover scene isn't a form of psychological warfare, they have never corseted an assassin.

"Before you look at yourself in the mirror, it needs some 'cultural authenticity.' " Brug added sparkle dust with a dramatic flourish.

Kaelin sneezed.

She turned to see herself in the mirror. The violet fabric swirled around her feet; silver embroidery thread caught the light as she moved. Slits ended mid-thigh, somehow hiding her daggers but allowing her easy access. The corseted top created feminine curves she didn't know she possessed and wasn't sure she liked. That being said—

She looked . . . powerful.

Terrifying.

A weapon disguised as a woman. Or perhaps—finally—both.

"I hate it," she said. Everyone exhaled like that was the best outcome possible.

Our assassin discovers the ancient rite known as 'formalwear,' which, when combined with a thigh dagger holster, has been known to end empires.

Tobias was speechless in a way that dented her composure. She almost asked what he thought, but she wasn't ready to hear what he had to say.

"Now that your armor is on, it's time to head to the palace." Nadia winked.

Kaelin wasn't sure if she was talking about her daggers or her dress. She nodded anyway.

Outside, Ed stood, ready to carry her to the palace. She swore he smiled, thrilled to be carrying a person instead of gear.

"Milady." The horse bowed his head. "You're a vision this evening. It's my honor to take you to the Gala."

"Shall I call you Edelwhin tonight?" Kaelin pulled herself up onto the saddle.

"It does have a rather debonair ring to it, appropriate for tonight's festivities." He pranced forward, then stopped. "You are all coming, are you not?"

Fen's jaw dropped. "The horse talks."

Tobias nodded. "It's unsettling at first, but you get used to it."

Despite the streets being lined with townsfolk who treated the procession of nobles, dignitaries, and politicians making their way to the palace like a parade, it didn't take long to get to the palace gates.

Kaelin handed a guard her forged invitation. Next to her, Tobias held his breath, Timber stood beside Ed with a confidence known only to very few, and Brug got distracted by all the sparkles.

The guard waved them through. Air whooshed out of Tobias as if he were deflating.

She dismounted the horse, handing him over to a stablehand before walking through the courtyard to the entrance. The stones under her feet radiated cold, something she wouldn't have noticed if she had been allowed to wear her leathers or at least her boots.

She noted at least six structural weak points and three good escape routes all before walking up the steps to the entrance.

At the top of the stairs were two statues made of suspiciously polished marble. Both statues watched them progress to the front of the line, their eyes tracking her with every step she took. There was even a moment she swore one looked away, guiltily. She didn't like them.

Tobias stayed next to her, stiffly. He was trying not to touch her, but also to stay the right distance away. Not too far, but not too close. What he wanted to do was put his hand on her back and help her up the stairs. He didn't, he knew better.

Together, with Timber at their side, they walked into the Gala. The sound of laughter and political deals drifted towards them on the breeze. Kaelin counted eighteen chandeliers. Far too many. They were a fire hazard even if they caused the entire palace to become a glittering labyrinth.

Below the dais, corrupt nobles pretended not to be corrupt. In the time it took her to assess the ballroom, she saw someone pocket a knife, various individuals swapping bribes instead of pleasantries, and then there was a duke whose smile was too wide.

No one looked that happy networking.

The guards' rotations looked . . . wrong. One guard walked past them, looking up and winking before moving on. It was Nadia in disguise.

"Are those cream puffs?" Brug pointed to the dessert buffet. "I wonder if they'll bring me musical enlightenment."

They wandered off in search of dessert. Kaelin hoped they would be in place when the time came. Even if it seemed unlikely.

And thus began their downfall, at the hand of a pastry. Is anyone surprised?

Music filled the room. It was deep, layered, different from anything they'd heard on their journey. Strings like secrets. Brass like warning bells. A rhythm like footsteps behind you in an alley.

Intrigue in three-quarter time.

"Not quite the drinking songs I'm used to." Kaelin smiled.

Tobias shook his head. "Definitely not. This is something it's imperative to dance to."

He held out his hand, a question that needed no words.

She hesitated before placing her hand in his. He escorted her down the stairs as Timber slipped into the shadows. They both knew the dog would be there when she was needed.

He spun her to face him as soon as they stepped onto the ballroom floor. Their eyes met. His hand settled on the small of her back. She placed her hand on his shoulder. They danced. Everything faded away as she let herself be in the moment.

She threw her head back, laughing as he spun her. The laughter faded when she saw the quill-and-chain etched into a chandelier bracket.

"Did you see it?" she whispered.

He looked up to where she was staring. His steps faltered. "I do."

The smell of burned parchment and something else, something familiar, drifted through the room.

"Do you hear that?" Tobias asked.

At the same time, Kaelin asked, "Why do I know that smell?"

"It smells like the Cult of Never Finishing anything. Burned paper and sugar." He sniffed, then grimaced. "The humming, do you hear it?"

"No." She led him off the dance floor.

Some things were more important than a stolen moment. But she tucked it away for later anyway. Quietly. Like contraband.

"It sounds like . . ." He snapped his fingers. "A ward of revision."

She felt her pulse quicken. "That sounds ominous."

"It isn't good. Whatever's happening, it's already started." Tobias pushed his glasses up. "They're rewriting something . . . or someone."

"This is never going to work. We need more information." Kaelin reached for her dagger but stopped herself before she unsheathed it.

He grinned. "Ready to try your hand at flirting-as-spycraft?"

Dear reader, she was not ready. She wasn't even in the same country as ready.

One nobleman asked if she was spoken for. She almost responded with her occupation and a dagger to the throat. His or hers, she wasn't sure yet.

Tobias choked on a cream puff to distract the noble from her faux pax. Thankfully, it worked.

Unfortunately, Timber growled warningly at anyone who invaded Kaelin's personal space.

A line of bared teeth is more effective than a wedding ring. It works for dogs and humans.

Timber really was a girl's best guard dog. A mage's jealous hero. A nobleman's worst nightmare. Tobias patted her head, approving the dog's need to drive away anyone who flirted with their assassin.

Despite her failed attempts at flirting, Kaelin was able to gather some intel. Mostly from eavesdropping on others.

The Duke of Saltmere mentioned that King Varric looked tired, thinner even, and weaker than he'd ever seen the king. He added some not-so-nice wishes after his observation.

A member of the Midlands Coalition said something about Stride having people everywhere. Color drained from Tobias's face when they overheard this. She couldn't stop her eyes from darting from one person to the next in an attempt to clock who was a minion of her mentor.

Then there was the Queen of Briarwick's lady-in-waiting, more aptly described as her security, who told another member of their court that a locked vault beneath the ballroom contained 'the future of Briarwick.'

Because, of course, there's an impenetrable vault that needs to be penetrated at the palace. Why wouldn't there be?

"We need to get down to the vault," Kaelin whispered into Tobias's ear.

She felt the warmth of his breath on her cheek, and the touch of his shoulder brushing against the silk of her sleeve. It was proximity she wasn't used to, one she no longer minded for reasons she refused to acknowledge.

He nodded, tucking her hand in the crook of his arm before leading her to the outskirts of the room.

They didn't make it far. A fight broke out blocking their path down to the vault. Security guards fought each other. Two of them looked out of place: their uniforms were tight, attractive, hugging the shape of their bodies.

Kaelin shook her head. "Nadia and Fen."

"We should do something before they get us all caught." Tobias darted through the crowd.

She followed, skirts hiked up so she wouldn't trip. Her right hand hovered over her dagger. Timber ran ahead, weaving through the legs of drunken attendees.

Nadia leapt in the air, grabbed onto a chandelier, and swung over the melee. She landed in front of Kaelin and Tobias, striking a hero pose. Timber preened when Nadia reached out to pet her.

"Was the pose really necessary?" Kaelin scoffed.

Nadia smirked. "If you're going to do something, it should be done with style."

"Should you be talking with us?" Tobias looked around.

Everyone was watching the fight, except them.

"Probably not, but you should know Stride has a private guard posted outside the vault." She turned back towards the chaos. "Guess who won't be there for long." Then she dove back into the fray like joy itself was a weapon.

Tobias and Kaelin ducked into an alcove behind velvet curtains.

"How am I going to get into the vault?" she pondered. Not with fear—but calculation. The difference mattered.

He didn't answer. She wasn't really asking.

"Do you mind if I check on the glamour spell?"

She nodded, turning her back to him. The violet fabric brushed his trousers. His magic hummed through the air—warmth hovering just above her skin where his hands refused to touch. Not without permission. Not without certainty.

She felt him trembling—not with fear, but with restraint.

"You don't have to do this alone." His voice was soft, hesitant even.

She turned back to face him, meeting his gaze. "I don't know how not to."

Everything she felt was new, like the person standing in front of her could actually be trusted, that he would be there when she wanted him. It scared her more than walking into Stride's trap.

Progress is terrifying. Attraction is worse.

She almost let words slip from her lips, words she'd never uttered before, when they were abruptly yanked from the alcove.

"Confessions come later," Fen muttered. "The guard's gone. Now's your chance."

Kaelin grabbed Tobias's hand, dragging him towards the stairs. A servant spotted her, and his tray clattered to the marble floor. He froze like prey.

She caught his sleeve before he could run. "Speak."

He whispered, "Dame Stride isn't killing the king . . . She's replacing him."

Her stomach plummeted.

Tobias turned an unnatural shade of green. "Oh, no."

"Do not vomit," she hissed at Tobias before turning back to the servant. "Replacing him with what?"

The servant shuddered. "Not what. Who." He tore free and fled as if chased by ghosts.

Kaelin didn't know how to respond—fortunately, distraction arrived wearing seventeen pounds of sequins.

Brug stood on stage beneath a rain of candlelight, tusks tipped in gold, cloak glittering like a gaudy constellation. They raised their arms. The bards joined in.

The tune: "The Ballad of Thorn and Flame." Of course.

It's overly romantic.

Historically inaccurate.

Written to embarrass Kaelin.

The lyrics were filled with metaphors involving daggers, flames, and 'yearning held tight as a drawn bow.'

Tobias listened, enraptured.

Kaelin died on the inside, but just a little.

And thus, the prophecy was fulfilled: no good plan survives a bard.

But the distraction worked. Guards shifted their attention. Applause and laughter bounced off the walls. No one was watching them.

Nadia and Fen slipped towards the vault. Kaelin and Tobias followed.

Inside they found: a bound magical contract, a quill made of bone, a drafting circle, and a second throne.

Horror washed over Tobias's face. "She's drafting a replacement king."

His magic crackled, a warning only he could sense. The draft was targeting Kaelin.

He grabbed her hand without thinking. "She wants to rewrite you."

Their fear for each other burned brighter than the fear for themselves.

Magical alarms shrieked throughout the palace. The chandeliers dimmed. Shadows crawled up the walls. Dozens of Guild agents revealed themselves.

"I guess there was an alarm we missed." Nadia purred, delighted.

The king raised his goblet to speak—then collapsed. Wine spread through ermine like fresh blood.

And so, the moment etiquette died, violence took its seat.

Team Chaos inhaled.

Prepared.

And stepped into the next chapter with knives and consequences.

29

A Dance Before the Fall

"There are few things deadlier than ballroom politics. One of them is falling in love."

Well, it looks like we've reached the part of the evening where diplomacy ends and stabbing begins. Where was I? Ah yes . . .

Magic hummed low in the bones, vibrating like a plucked string behind the sternum. The room didn't just dim—it recalibrated. The evening's sparkle tarnished in an instant as mist filled the room. Damp air was tinged with metallic. It stung Kaelin's nose and caught in her throat.

The mist drifted over the floor. Conversations that echoed off the walls were swallowed by the sentient cloud. It rose higher, distorting faces until the only person Kaelin could see was Tobias.

Green beams of light shot through the damp air, connecting one chandelier to another where the quill-and-chain sigil was engraved. It created a spiderweb of magic, eliminating swinging from ornate lighting as a form of escape. She wiped her sweaty palms on the front of her skirt. Next to her, Timber whimpered.

She looked from one chandelier to the next, trying to rate them on swingability.

Spoiler alert: They all failed. At this point, they were all useless.

The mage muttered a dispersion spell, causing the fog to dissipate enough to make hiding in it impossible, not only for them, but also for Guild members.

Guards scrambled and shouted. One pointed towards her as she dragged Tobias deeper into the crowd. Nobles scattered like ants on a rainy day. The chaos that ensued would have been laughable if Kaelin could see past being a tactician.

A duchess swung a candelabra like a sword at the shadows of her compatriots.

The head of the Midlands Coalition hid under the punch table with his security detail.

And the gossips, they continued to spill the tea, despite the blaring alarms, green lasers, and thick fog.

An apocalypse didn't stand a chance against a scandal update.

Magic flared everywhere. The walls glistened, the floor glowed, and the ceiling, well that's already been described.

The ballroom became a living spell—every surface breathing as light crawled across gold and marble like veins in a living thing.

Kaelin and Tobias locked eyes. They both knew there was no escape. She should have looked away. Instead, she stayed, caught in him like another ward—one she walked into willingly.

Both were secure in the knowledge that they would protect each other.

They looked away at the same time. Tobias noted magic wards blocked all the known exits. She scanned the room. Even the less established exits she'd spotted were protected. Her corset suddenly felt too tight as her eyes darted from wall to window to door looking for a way out she hadn't already noticed. There were none.

Despite everything, a feral-calm overcame her. There was no use in panicking. These were the situations she had spent the majority of her life training for. Her pulse slowed to a normal speed. She knew she would find a way to get out of the palace safely.

There's no graceful exit when destiny pulls the fire alarm. Although a bit of signage would have helped.

They both knew they should run. Kaelin assumed everyone else already had. Spells flooded the ballroom, compelling movement, glamour, illusion. She felt the spell push her towards Tobias. Her feet moved before a decision formed—like her pulse had been rerouted into choreography.

The ballroom was choosing partners.

It chose them. It demanded a performance.

The other dancers did not disappoint. A marquis waltzed with a fern. The plant looked offended. A couple twirled themselves right into a fountain.

Whoever thought a fountain in the middle of a ballroom was a good idea had never completed a pirouette, and it showed.

Timber refused to dance. She dragged a chair behind her though. Apparently, it also counted as a partner.

This time they danced, not because they wanted to, but because they had to, to stay alive and unnoticed.

Fighting in plain sight requires rhythm. Assassins improvise.

She led them around the ballroom, and he followed her lead. As they spun, they caught snippets of conversations. Mostly they heard questions. "Why are we dancing?" "Is the king still alive?" Someone even asked why there were goats at the Gala. No one responded.

A general twirled his partner while discussing various ways to commit tax fraud.

A page ran by them muttering, "Where is the Black Bishop, shouldn't they be here by now?"

Internally, Kaelin shuddered. The page had confirmed what she already knew. "Stride's supposed to be here. We need an escape plan. Now."

Tobias nodded, his cheek brushing hers as they took another turn around the floor. He muttered ward-breaking equations with every step. She didn't move away. She calculated how many strikes it would take to break the web of chandeliers.

Romantic, but make it tactical.

"I thought Stride's pet assassin was going to be here. She has to be present and conscious for the spell to work," a woman from the Briarwick court said as she waltzed past them.

"She's talking about you." Concern was etched on Tobias's face.

Kaelin clenched her teeth. "You don't think I know that? I'm no one's pet."

She wanted to storm off the dance floor, but the magic held her in place, wrapping around her and Tobias like a chain. Her breath caught as the spell tightened and their bodies brushed against each other with each step they took.

A nobleman declared loudly that they had never been so inconvenienced in their life.

"I thought they were going to kill the king," a man said, conversing with his partner. "Wasn't the whole point to get rid of that withered bag of bones? He's still alive, barely. He's practically a shadow of himself."

"Do you know who the second throne is for?" another dancer asked.

The response chilled Kaelin.

"It's meant for a duplicate of Stride's chosen one."

Kaelin felt something cold crack inside of her—fear she refused to name partnered with the icy hand of betrayal. She shivered as the meaning of it swept over her. Her feet wanted to stop dancing. The spell wouldn't let them.

The music stopped, but not long enough to escape, barely long enough to catch their breath. On the stage, Brug sang as if they were narrating the dance.

"Two hearts spinning through peril." Their eyes were wide.

Kaelin had never seen fear on the bard's face. She didn't like it at all.

Brug spun as they strummed. "Daggers beneath silk."

When they caught her eye, they mouthed, "I'm sorry."

"She's to be the rewritten queen." The lute strumming escalated into a crescendo.

Somewhere on the mezzanine, the fight club lesbians placed bets, not on who would win—but whether Kaelin would admit she cared. The odds were in Kaelin's favor.

Tobias's eyes widened. "Above the dais, the drafting circle is activating."

She spun them around so she could see for herself. Her pulse raced. This didn't feel like a situation she could slice her way out of.

He whispered, "If they rewrite you, I won't remember you."

She could hear the terror in his words. She could feel his hand tremble in hers. His fear sliced through her like one of her daggers.

Her heart stuttered. Not from love, but from the terror of being forgotten.

It was love, dear reader, she just didn't know it yet.

"I would never let you forget me." The words rang like a promise, almost an admission of . . . feelings to a silent room.

The music had stopped without warning, without grace. Kaelin's words echoed through the ballroom, bouncing off marble columns and magic wards.

She tried to step away after all the music had stopped. The spell pushed her back. It wasn't about to allow her to leave things left unsaid.

Tobias's voice cracked while he calculated how to break the wards.

The room leaned in, holding its breath like it was waiting for its prey.

She palmed Moonveil, then threw it at a chandelier chain. The dagger sliced through the links.

She was, after all, a professional.

The chandelier crashed to the floor, cracking a marble slab. Brug leapt off the stage, grabbed the overpriced lighting, and flung it at a bevy of guards running towards their friends.

Kaelin dropped Tobias's hand, tore her dress slit higher for mobility and ran, a dagger in each hand. She sliced through three guards, pushed a goat out of the way, and slid to a stop before the king sitting on his throne. He was still unconscious, which was deeply inconvenient.

Tobias cast counter wards, attempting to stop the Eternal Draft's spread. One spell after another in quick rapid fire. Most worked, some exploded in puffs of glitter.

The rest of Team Chaos assembled like a threat and an accident.

Brug sang battle orders at the top of their lungs. Their vibrato was truly inspiring. Some nobles covered their ears. Others ran from the stage. Some stayed and clapped like the songs were the best thing they'd ever heard. Brug was good in battle and had started their own fan club.

Guild reinforcements dropped from the ceiling, avoiding the green beams. They did not avoid tables, chairs, or dancers.

Somehow, Joren was with the spider-like reinforcements. He turned on them as soon as their boots hit the ground, tossing one over his shoulder while the other two members of his crew sliced a path towards the king.

Timber yelped. Kaelin lunged faster than she believed was possible. The Guild member fell. The dog licked her cheek—her way of saying thank you—before barreling back into the chaos.

Fen cracked her knuckles before she started swinging. Her smile, as she broke jawlines, lit the ballroom. She really had it out for the reinforcements. Nadia wrestled someone off the balcony. The crash, when they landed, made everyone pause.

Only for a heartbeat. Then the room remembered it was on fire.

Timber dragged a Guild mage by the boot, tail wagging like this was the best game she'd ever played.

Another chandelier came crashing to the floor. Kaelin grabbed the front of Tobias's jacket and hauled him backwards before it crushed him. Shards of crystal scattered over their boots like fallen stars. They stood there for a moment, breathing hard, faces too close, the world reduced to smoke, sparks, and the sound of his pulse.

"Thank you," he said, voice hoarse.

"Stop needing so much saving," she snapped automatically. It came out more like a plea than she liked.

The ballroom split. Nobles clustered on one side, Guild members on the other. Only a few souls who hadn't picked a side lingered in the no-man's-land between them, mostly people too stunned—or too petty—to move.

One noble declared, "I'm on the side of whoever wins," then hid behind the canapés.

Kaelin and Tobias stood on an island in the center, completely surrounded, panting.

Team Chaos drew in around them without being asked. Nadia and Fen flanked Kaelin's left. Joren and two of his fighters took her right. Brug climbed onto the wreck of a table like it was a stage, lute at the ready. Timber planted herself at Kaelin's heel, teeth bared. The goats, for reasons known only to them, formed a crooked wedge in front like a very confused vanguard.

"Is it just me," Brug panted, "or do we look incredibly heroic right now?"

"Terrible odds," Fen said. "Love it."

Joren raised his sword in a salute that was half respect, half apology. "Just say the word."

Kaelin rolled her shoulders, testing the give in her dress, the weight of her daggers, the pull of the drafting magic overhead. She could feel the circle above them now—pressure at the back of her skull, like a thought that wasn't hers trying to settle in.

"No one goes near the king," she said. "No one goes near Tobias."

Tobias blinked. "You do realize I can hear you?"

"Good," she said. "Then you can follow instructions for once."

He swallowed, eyes bright with a hundred things he didn't have time to say. "Not a chance."

Overhead, the drafting circle flared brighter, lines of green light tightening, etching themselves deeper into the air. The crown on the king's head glimmered dully in the reflection—small, almost pathetic against the storm gathering above it.

Kaelin felt the magic brush against her mind again, testing, measuring, trying to take her shape. She bared her teeth at the ceiling like she could snarl a spell into submission.

"Let them come," she muttered. "I'm not that easy to rewrite."

The first Guild volley hit—spells cracking against Tobias's hastily raised shields, sparks bursting like furious fireflies. Swords lifted. Boots scraped. Someone screamed. Someone laughed.

The ballroom took one last, collective breath.

And then, at the exact same moment, two things happened.

The king's crown slipped sideways on his head with an almost comical little tilt—and every Guild blade turned towards Kaelin.

Well. It seems we've finally arrived at the part of the evening where the crown stops mattering—and the person wearing it becomes optional.

On that cheerful note, let's step lightly into the next disaster, shall we?

30

THE CROWN IS A LIE

"Power rarely resides in the throne. It prefers shadows, secrets, and the occasional disguise."

With an unmatched flair for the dramatic, Brug sang the final note of their battle song. It shivered in the air like a dying star, allowing the room to fill with silence while Team Chaos took the time to breathe. Kaelin felt the pause like the moment before a blade drops—danger gathering itself for the second swing.

The quiet didn't last long. Nobles stampeded towards exits that no longer existed, ignoring how the king's body lay slumped—a centerpiece to a horror tableau no one was brave enough to look at. Someone sobbed into a champagne flute. Someone else tried to use a tax ledger as a shield.

Royalty is fragile. It only takes one poisoning, one coup, one spilled goblet to remind a kingdom how mortal power really is.

Tobias worked spells like a frantic orchestra conductor, magic sparking off his fingers. Sweat clung to his jaw. His hands shook—not with power, but with the fear of losing something more vital than a king.

Joren dragged wounded fighters behind overturned banquet tables, turning chaos into structure with military precision.

Brug tore through the crowd like a battle-bard, singing and smashing heads with equal levels of passion. They amplified the chaos in the room exponentially.

Guild members didn't know whether to fight or clap. Nobles stopped running to sing along. And their new fan club followed them throughout the ballroom, punching anyone who tried to stop their song.

Nadia and Fen kicked open the balcony doors and stormed in like glittering war gods. Caped. Bleeding. Beautiful. A storm in sequins.

No one knows how they got from the center of the floor to the balcony. And the costume change? Astonishing. It's easier for everyone if you don't ask questions.

They slid down the draped velvet with the grace of professional acrobats, landing in perfect superhero stances.

Kaelin rolled her eyes. "We don't have time for your dramatic entrances."

"There's always time for drama." Nadia smirked.

Fen grabbed a quarterstaff from a statue of decorative armor. The statue looked offended.

She twirled the staff over her head and took out two Guild members. "Don't waste your breath, Nadia will always take the time to strike a pose."

"Aw... you know me so well, my love." She snaked one arm around Fen's waist and planted a kiss on her mouth, all while expertly fencing an attacker.

Fen stepped back and smashed an enemy in the head. "I believe this calls for a wager."

"Oh, yes. Ten silvers says Kaelin disarms a Guild captain in eight seconds," Nadia wagered.

Kaelin—deadpan, mid-stab: "Make it five."

She did it in three-point-five seconds.

Some heroines need prophesies. Kaelin just needs a time limit and someone doubting her imagination.

Guild captain disarmed, Kaelin fought her way to the king. She wasn't sure if it was to assassinate him or to save him.

She reached him first, with Joren behind her, covering her flank, swords drawn. Tobias was nearby. They stood around the throne, two men ensuring she could do what she needed to do.

Her heartbeat slowed—the kind of stillness before an ambush. Something ancient watched her back, breathless.

She expected blood. She expected rot. She did not expect ink.

The blood that soaked the king's ermine trim smelled of ink, not iron. Glyphs pulsed a sickly green under his veins in the chandelier light. His eyes opened, not dead—blank like an unwritten page.

Tobias's breath rushed out of him. "He's not a corpse. He's a draft."

Joren stared. His hand trembled. Loss etched the grooves on his face. He looked so much older than he had just moments before. "I came here to save the king." His shoulders sagged. "I never had a chance."

"Then why was I sent here?" Kaelin's confusion was palpable. It hung in the air like a physical thing.

Mundice Mortimer stepped out from behind the throne, pushing his spectacles up his nose. "You got here too late. We replaced the king weeks ago." He sniffed his displeasure. "Stride was prepared for you to fail. At least you're here for the handover."

"What?" Tobias yelled, reaching for Kaelin's arm.

She slipped through his grasp as she approached the throne. It flickered like live static in shades of silver and gold.

Every fairytale warns you not to touch enchanted objects. Kaelin has read none of them. On purpose.

"Don't do it." Multiple voices in unison tried to stop her.

She couldn't stop. She reached towards the throne—and it snapped, magic sparkling like teeth across her palm, leaving a mark that would never fade.

She felt cold intent threading her bones, starting at the mark on her hand. The throne wasn't built to welcome her. It was measuring her. Fitting her for replacement.

She stepped back, dizzy, afraid she would leave this moment rewritten.

It was not meant for her. It was meant for her duplicate.

Ah yes, the classic mistake: believing destiny chooses you, when really it simply wants to revise you.

"Okay, I'm really confused now. What's going on here?" She rubbed where the throne bit.

Her hand burned like the memory of a touch she never had.

Tobias saw her flinch—mistook it for pain.

Maybe it was lineage making itself known.

Tobias looked just as lost. "Maybe the vault has answers?"

"To the vault." Joren waved his arm, signaling the others to join them.

But as Kaelin followed, she felt eyes she couldn't name tracing her spine. A presence, familiar as the scars on her back, lingered like a held breath in the room she left behind.

The Black Bishop was not present, which meant she was everywhere.

The way to the vault was littered with guards and Guild members, each force trying to stop them. They were no match for Kaelin and her team. Each attack was swatted away like an incessant fly hovering too close.

It wasn't long before they stood in front of the vault, the door swung open. No need for them to break in.

If anyone had been paying attention, they would have known this was a bad sign. It really screamed, 'it's a trap.'

"We'll stand outside as guards." Nadia took her position on the right side of the door.

Fen took the other side. "I hope we get to punch more people."

Kaelin almost laughed as she stepped inside the vault. She'd always thought she was bloodthirsty. Fen might outrank her in that particular category.

Pinned to the wall were ink-soaked maps labeled Revision Points.

"It's like she's rewriting the entire world." Tobias studied the maps, unable to stop the awe he felt from creeping into his voice. "The years of planning . . . this is strategical genius at work."

Nothing more dangerous than brilliance paired with no moral brakes. Truly—innovation is wasted on the ethical.

"You're not helping." Kaelin picked up a journal from the only table in the room.

Stride's looping letters covered each and every page. Flipping from one page to another, Kaelin admitted, if only to herself, that Tobias was right. Stride, the Black Bishop, knew strategy better than anyone else.

"What's that say?" Joren asked, reading over her shoulder.

" 'Replacement Candidates.' It's a list of names." She ran her finger down the list. Every name was crossed out.

She recognized most. Other members of the Guild. Some alive, others not so much. The only name not crossed out was hers. Kaelin Thorn. Beside it, in looping scribbles, *Pending Revision—Final Proof Required*.

Her vision blurred. Not from tears—she'd learned long ago how not to cry—but from the sensation of identity sliding sideways inside her ribs. She was no longer Kaelin Thorn by merit or defiance or choice. She was Kaelin Thorn by design.

The Black Bishop's handwriting felt like a hand around her throat.

Not a prophecy.

A blueprint.

Tobias reached for her but didn't touch—like she was a live spell.

Joren swore. Loudly.

He looked at Kaelin like she was suddenly someone he might lose to magic instead of knives.

"Um, Kaelin." Tobias's voice shook, definitely with fear this time. "The shadows are moving."

She broke eye contact with Joren as Shadow Scribes descended into the room. The shadows solidified before their eyes, each armed with razor-quills, ink-venom, and memory-erasure wands.

They moved like pages turning—quick, silent, inevitable. Not warriors.

Editors.

Not just in the vault, but materializing throughout the palace.

Ink dripped from their gauntlets like venom-thick blood. Where the droplets landed, memories smeared—nobles forgot they were afraid. A guard forgot which side he served. A woman forgot her own name and sobbed like she'd dropped something precious she couldn't remember losing.

One scribe brushed a sleeve across a tapestry—history vanished. Decades turned to blank linen.

"Don't let them touch you," Tobias warned, voice cracking with concern.

Kaelin fought faster, sharper, but every blow landed with the dread of footnotes closing around her life. What if every decision she'd made had been written for her? What if her life was never going to be her own?

Tobias muttered a protection spell. Before he could finish, a Shadow Scribe waved his wand, erasing Tobias. The mage flickered like bad handwriting.

Kaelin slammed the Shadow Scribe into the wall, Whisperthorn at his throat. "You will bring him back or die."

A Scribe reached for Kaelin's name with their razor quill. Joren intercepted, taking the hit meant for her. He briefly forgot her name.

Kaelin tossed Moonveil, pinning the Scribe to the wall. "He remembers me. He stays. I say so."

Her name slammed back into reality.

Tobias flickered back, no longer erased.

The Shadow Scribes disappeared, fading away into the light.

The vault alarms stopped mid-howl.

The ballroom was frozen between breaths.

Brug's voice wavered. "Um. Did we win . . .?"

Fen looked around. "This isn't victory. This is curation. We were meant to win this part. But it's not over."

Joren wiped ink-blood from his sword, hands shaking. "Then what are we?"

"The audition." Quiet and lethal, Kaelin's assassin mask fell into place.

Brug cleared their throat like the gods themselves were listening. "Very well," they declared, already tuning their lute. "If this is an audition—we'll make it unforgettable."

They strummed a triumphant chord, sparks falling from the strings.

"Write not our names in ink —for ink can be erased.Carve us in memory instead."

Kaelin blinked.

Tobias looked like he might actually cry.

Fen whispered, "Are they allowed to be this inspiring?"

Nadia wiped blood off her cheek. "Let them. We need a soundtrack."

And so Brug composed victory mid-battle—loud, defiant, ridiculously emotional—a song meant for people who had not technically won anything.

The kind of anthem you sing when survival counts as triumph.

She ran back to the ballroom. She could feel and hear the others following her. The king was gone. The throne, an empty seat waiting for someone to be written in to take it. The intention had always been to replace him, with her as the model.

The throne pulsed like a living thing. Not silver, mercury. Not power, hunger. It wanted her. Or the version of her that would obey.

Kaelin stepped closer, hand unconsciously rising to the mark burned into her palm.

Tobias grabbed her wrist gently, like holding a fuse.

"Not you," he whispered. "Not like this."

She almost said the dangerous thing—the thing about wanting more than survival.

Wanting something unscripted.

Hers.

Instead, she said, "We take the throne only to destroy it."

It was a vow. It felt like lighting a match in a library.

The room held still—a page before the turn.

The rest of her team fell in beside her. Tobias next to her, ready for whatever came at them next. She grabbed his hand, letting it tether her to the reality she wanted for herself. He looked at their entwined fingers, then at her, but said nothing.

Time stilled. Wind raced through the windows of the palace. Torches erupted.

A low horn trembled through bone and stone.

The palace doors bulged like lungs—then burst inward.

Sir Harlow rode through the shattered gates, undead cavalry at his back.

Brug cheered, loving every moment of the knight's grand entrance.

Timber growled, hackles raised. Something wasn't right.

Tobias whispered Kaelin's name like it would shield them from whatever happened next.

And Joren—he stepped forward, sword lowered, expression unreadable.

Kaelin dropped Tobias's hand and drew two daggers. Neither one of them was Mercy.

This was not the end—only the opening strike.

31

SHADOW GUILD REUNION (WITH BETRAYAL PUNCH)

"Just once, Kaelin would like a reunion that doesn't end in blood."

K aelin stared up at the knight atop his skeletal warhorse, silver scars etched into bone that glowed like runes. Behind him, the undead cavalry rolled in like a tide of cold fire.

Once, she would have called him an ally. Maybe even a friend.

He looked alive, changed, like forgiveness wasn't the end, merely the start.

His bony hand reached for her. "Sister," he said, not as an enemy, but as an equal. Not a threat—worse. An invitation.

The room inhaled, frozen. Even the chandeliers held their breath, as if light itself feared the answer.

Her daggers dropped an infinitesimal amount. She wanted to trust him. This was the man who wanted nothing more than to save his brother. He stood by them, helped them even.

His hand never wavered, still outstretched. Not to capture her, not to kill her, but to ask her to stand with him.

The moment should have felt like relief. Instead, it felt like a test. One where failure meant death. Or worse, obedience.

Timber inched forward, teeth bared, growling, the tone so low it vibrated against her bones.

Tobias stood at her shoulder, waiting, magic trembling inside him like a held breath.

Everyone knew what she would choose. Except her.

Nadia and Fen snuck their way onto the balcony and took sniper-like stances with their crossbows. Crossbows they absolutely didn't have thirty seconds ago.

Again, it's better not to ask when it comes to those two. I don't know where they got their weapons.

Kaelin hesitated, listening to Timber's warning.

It was bound to happen at some point.

The room exhaled with a whoosh.

"The Black Bishop asked for you personally." Disappointment clouded the knight's eyes.

It broke her internally. That's when she noticed his armor bore the mark of the Guild. His horse's bridle was script-bound. His eyes flickered when he mentioned Stride's alias.

"I had no choice. She offered me my brother back," Harlow whispered. A mercy for him. A sentence for her.

Tobias stepped forward. "So, you sold your soul for his."

Harlow ignored the mage. "Take it." He offered her a Guild brand.

She shook her head. "The Guild has left enough marks on me."

He didn't lash out, but deflated. It was like he expected this exact moment, and it broke his heart. "You could have ruled beside me."

"As what, a mere copy of myself?" She took her fighting stance. "I don't think so. I'd rather bleed for my choices than reign over someone else's."

He dismounted. She took a step back, waiting for his attack.

Before she could stop him, he kissed her on her forehead, betrayal not as an attack but as a farewell.

Love and war speaking the same language: loss.

Undead soldiers swarmed around her, closing in like the jaws of death, in more ways than one.

And so, dear reader, the reunion ended as all good chaos does: beautifully, terribly, and with absolutely no time to reminisce, not that it stopped Kaelin.

For a moment, a fragile, merciful moment, the battle held its breath.

Kaelin looked at Harlow and saw not a knight, nor a traitor, but the man he once described: the one who adored his brother, the one who had pleaded for her help. She wondered if she should have stayed longer, fought harder, stopped him from going off on his own.

But choices were blades—and his had a name. All of hers did too.

Joren stepped between them like a question that hadn't decided its answer.

"You trusted him," he said quietly to Kaelin.

She nodded. "I still could."

"You shouldn't," he whispered back but he didn't step away.

It was a small thing: a man torn between the meaning of duty and the cost of compassion. But wars are decided in moments like that. Soft ones. Human ones.

Then the undead army surged, and gentleness died.

The battle was not elegant like the Gala. It was dirty, bone-splintering, and emotionally catastrophic.

The orchestra struck up again. Unwilling, terrified, playing a waltz of doom while nobles hid under tables and skeletons politely dismembered chairs. Brug changed tempo twice, once for dramatic flair, once because a skeleton stole their lute pick.

Timber launched herself onto a necromancer's shoulders like furry divine judgement.

Somewhere across the room, Nadia yelled, "Fen, stop using the centerpieces as throwing weapons!"

Fen responded by braining a ghoul with a crystal swan. "No."

A baroness fainted into a punch bowl.

A goat headbutted an undead warhound and won.

Someone began taking bets. "Two-to-one odds on the raccoon-wolf!"

Another yelled, "Five-to-one she eats another mage!"

Cozy? No. But comfort adjacent. The way a fire warms while the world burns.

Meanwhile, Kaelin and Harlow fought like mirrored grief. Every strike a memory, every parry something neither said aloud.

Joren defended their flank, striking with the fury of purpose regained. Not betrayal, not yet, but a man choosing, over and over, to stand at her side even when the world asked him not to.

He didn't know which future he believed in. He only knew who he trusted this second and maybe that was enough.

Kaelin sliced off the rest of her skirts, destroying the last remnants of elegance that clung to her. She grabbed a sword from a guard, ready for Harlow's attack.

Up on the balcony, Nadia and Fen shot arrows and broke arms with stilettos. It was enough to keep some of the undead at bay.

Brug took their place on the throne platform, playing a battle tempo to boost morale. They only stopped when bashing skulls became a necessity.

On the ballroom floor, Kaelin and Harlow circled each other. A fight of blades and willpower. Their swords clashed and clanged. Sparks flew.

Timber kept others away, disabling a necrotic mage by sheer force of will and teeth.

Someone off to their left shouted, "Pay up!"

Tobias shielded Kaelin's back. It cost him nosebleeds and trembling hands, but the shield held true.

Kaelin almost won.

Harlow almost let her.

Almost.

Kaelin's blade met Harlow's collarbone. Shallow, merciful.

His sword grazed her ribs. Warning, not execution.

They were both losing on purpose.

Harlow's voice cracked like ice under weight. "You were always meant for more than blood."

Kaelin pushed harder. "Then why give me nothing else?"

He almost answered and that was the tragedy. Words hovered like ghosts.

Then every torch bent in the same direction.

Fighting stopped. No one had yielded, but everyone felt the shift in the room.

Dame Anwyn Stride had arrived. Harrowmistress of the Shadow Guild. The Black Bishop. Kaelin's mentor and more. She wasn't disguised. She definitely wasn't hiding.

Stride did not walk into the ballroom. She authored it.

Her shadow arrived first, long, elegant, dissecting every soul it touched. The chandeliers dimmed, not in fear, but in reverence. Even the undead straightened like schoolchildren awaiting inspection.

She walked over to the throne. Her long black hair shifting as she took each step. She snapped her fingers and the king's false corpse returned. Ink flooded its veins and it rose like a puppet.

Power wasn't in the throne. It was in the author rewriting reality.

Stride's violet eyes searched the room, looking for one person.

"She looks an awful lot like—" Tobias never finished his thought.

"You." Stride pointed to Kaelin, her long finger curled like an accusation.

Kaelin stared at her mentor. The woman who'd raised her. The woman who weaponized her childhood.

"My blade, you were never meant to kill the king." Stride's lips moved into what might have been described as a smile.

Honestly, a smile was a stretch. There was no joy in it, just the feeling of control.

"You were meant to replace him," she finished.

Kaelin rolled her eyes. "Tell me something I don't know."

"Maybe don't antagonize her," Tobias whispered.

Brug's quill scratched wildly, already myth-making. "This is going to be the most epic ending of my ballad."

Fen swore softly.

Nadia didn't breathe.

And Joren—Joren looked at Stride the way a drowning man looks at the shore. With hope. With danger. With the possibility of rescue or ruin.

He was the question mark Stride intended.

Stride's gaze slid to him, assessing value, measuring usefulness.

He lowered his sword, not surrender, but consideration.

Kaelin saw it all. And her ribs tightened like vows she hadn't sworn yet.

Stride just showed her teeth in what could only be described as an evil smile. "The throne is yours. There are only a few strings attached."

"Over my dead body." Kaelin's voice rang throughout the palace.

Her defiance sank into the walls. The marble statues looked on in awe. Somewhere, Mundice Mortimer quaked as he hid from Stride.

Softly Stride answered, "As written."

War was no longer coming. It was here—wearing the face of the woman who raised her and the knight who almost didn't betray her.

32

HOW TO STAGE A REGICIDE (WITHOUT DYING)

"Assassination is 90% planned, 9% luck, and 1% theatrical flair."

Kaelin waited, daggers at the ready. She knew something was coming. Stride didn't speak unless she controlled, and Kaelin had refused to be controlled.

Refusing the Black Bishop was a death sentence. She knew it was coming and was ready to fight it off as long as she could.

A blade honed long enough forgets how to bend.

A soft smile touched Stride's lips. It almost looked like pride. She raised her hand, and a quill appeared. She wrote in the air. Red ink bled across the ceiling like constellations rewritten, edited into existence. Even the shadows held their breath as her ink-wards sealed the castle. There were no exits, no teleports, no death cheats.

"Yeah, that's not ominous at all," Nadia hissed from whatever strategic position she'd decided on.

The undead paused like pieces waiting for the next chess move.

Brug, halfway through a rhyme, stopped breathing mid-syllable, which would later ruin the scansion of Act III of their ballad.

"Are you sure that's a wise decision, my blade?" Stride gave her ward a chance to change her mind, something she had never done before to anyone's knowledge.

Mercy from Stride was rarer than sunrise in the underworld.

Timber left a low growl vibrating across the floor, like warning thunder disguised as fur.

"Probably not, but if you were looking at a vacant shell, more corpse than king, you'd probably make the same decision." Kaelin positioned herself between Stride and the throne.

She knew her decisions dictated everyone's survival. For the first time, she didn't find it burdensome. Instead, she felt it settle against her ribs like armor, giving her strength and purpose.

Behind her stood Tobias, shield still in place. The faint smell of baking bread fought its way through the tang of ink. His hands shook. She wanted to comfort him, but couldn't, not now.

Later. If there was a later.

Stride looked at the draft king, tossing him aside. "Better?"

"I don't know. Illustrating how disposable pawns are doesn't instill confidence in my continued existence." Her voice sounded strong, but inside she quaked with fear. Years of training by the woman standing in front of her were the only reason she hid it so well.

"My blade, you've never been a pawn." Stride held out her hand. "You've always been too rebellious."

Fen's razor-thin whisper drifted to them from the balcony. "If she touches that hand, I'm putting a bolt through somebody."

Nadia hummed agreement. Terrifyingly romantic.

Kaelin looked at another outstretched hand, someone else wanting to pull her into their story, to force her to be the character they wanted her to be. She allowed her stillness to be her answer.

Stillness is a weapon. Silence is refusal sharpened to a point.

"Loyalty. It's just not the same anymore." Stride turned to Harlow.

The knight knelt before her, joints cracking as he took a knee. It injured Kaelin almost as much as a knife to the heart. Harlow had once chosen hope. Now he chose something darker, something less freeing.

Joren stepped closer to Kaelin. She felt him waiver.

Brug stopped writing, which was how everyone knew things were bad.

Timber pressed against Kaelin's leg, as if reminding her who she was.

Some reunions begin with hugs. Others, with necromancy and generational trauma. Life is rich that way.

Joren's voice cut through the ink-hum. "Say one word, Kaelin, and I stand with you."

One sword angled slightly towards Stride.

He could protect her.

He could betray her.

At this moment, even Kaelin couldn't tell which he leaned towards.

Worse, she didn't know what he wanted her to say.

"If you'll let me explain, I knew who you were the moment we met. I made sure you were forged into the perfect weapon." Anwyn Stride waited until all eyes were back on her. "I've done all of this for you. I never lost you. And here we are, ready for you to take the place created just for you. Almost ready, that is."

Kaelin scoffed. Tobias quickly cast a spell to keep her from saying something that would get them all killed. The look she tossed his way let him know she didn't appreciate his actions and was next on her list of who to stab, once this was all over, of course.

"You were always meant to inherit this throne rewrite. I never abandoned you. I prepared you. For this." Stride paused. "You just need a little editing. Soften your memories, strengthen your loyalty, control your destiny."

"Oh, that's all," Tobias muttered. "Just change her past and future entirely without asking. Such a gift."

Kaelin stomped on his foot. His spell dissipated. "And you thought I was the one that needed to keep my mouth shut."

"I see why you like this one, my blade. He's got spirit." A cruel smile spread on Stride's face. "I might let you keep him around, if you agree to rule beside me."

Nadia whispered, "Was that supposed to sound comforting?"

Fen, calmly loading another bolt, said, "Dear gods, she's worse than me at gift giving."

Kaelin's heart stuttered. Could she save them all if she took the path her mentor laid out for her?

There was a subtle tremor in his spellcasting as he looked from Kaelin to Stride and back. The Black Bishop's words, seemingly wrong, out of place in this conversation, fell into place like pieces of a puzzle fitting together for the first time.

You know that moment before a truth hits?

The breath.

The silence.

The drop?

Here it comes.

"I see the mage has figured it out." Stride raised an eyebrow. A silent question asking him what he would do.

Kaelin's eyes darted from one to the other. "Figured out what?"

"You're going to make me say it." Stride paused. "Kaelin, I am your mother."

Kaelin froze. Jaw, breath, heartbeat all stilled. If she could have, she would have screamed in denial. Instead, she experienced stillness in its most violent form.

For years, she had shaped herself from nothing. Built a spine out of hunger, sharpened loneliness into steel. And now the truth slid beneath her ribs with all the subtlety of a blade.

Mother.

A word she had never used. A need she had trained herself not to have. And Stride—this woman—was wearing it like a weapon.

"She's not just your mentor," Tobias whispered, voice steady for her, not for himself. Not claiming, not assuming—simply present. A choice, not pressure.

Kaelin did not crumble, she didn't know how to, but she tilted.

The ground shifted beneath her like ink on wet parchment.

Memory flickered; a doorway, a lullaby without melody, the vague sensation that someone once brushed dirt from her cheek. Or maybe she imagined it. Maybe longing invented ghosts.

"My. Mother. Is. Dead." A sentence like a severed thread.

"Ooh, I did not see this coming." Nadia leaned so far over the railing Fen grabbed her collar.

Brug scribbled with manic reverence. "I'm adding five verses. Possibly an overture."

Kaelin didn't hear them.

The emotions she'd kept locked inside a vault to which no one had a key pounded on the door, fighting to break free.

She felt fourteen again—cold, hungry, furious. A girl waiting for someone who never came. And now she stood before the one who could have, who didn't.

It was almost enough to drop her to her knees.

But she stayed standing.

"Giving you up was the only way to solidify my place, our place, in this world. It was the only way I could return to power after . . ." Stride pushed the memories away with a shake of her head. "I helped create the Shadow Guild for you. And when I came back for you, Kaelin, you were ready for my training."

Years of training flashed through Kaelin's head. The isolation, the tests, the punishments. Every task was a lesson. Every morsel of approval was conditional. Words she'd heard from the woman standing in front of her echoed as memories crashed over her one on top of another.

"You were never my favorite. But you were the piece I moved most carefully. All for this moment. Join me." Stride waited for her daughter to comply. "You're my legacy."

Instead, Kaelin stood, unmoving, like one of the marble statues. Inside her mind, the walls fractured, and everything she was feeling poured through the cracks. Rage at being used coursed through her. Relief that she wasn't discarded flooded her. Grief for a mother she never wanted filled her. Then there was the terror that she would become her mother.

As much as Kaelin wanted to deny it, she could see the truth in the color of their eyes, the way they moved, and so many other small idiosyncrasies.

Joren fell to his knees. "You're not her." His voice cracked. Not in denial of lineage, but in defense of Kaelin's right to self.

Not blood-defined.

Not destiny-bound.

Not owned.

She didn't know what she needed, only that she needed something. A hand. A word. A promise she wouldn't become the thing that made her.

Tobias stepped closer—slow, deliberate, giving her the space to choose. Not touching. Not assuming. Just there.

He spoke softly, a voice like warm earth to stand on. "Blood doesn't define you. Choice does. You don't owe her your life just because she gave you breath."

Kaelin inhaled and the air soothed her instead of shattering what was left.

Timber pressed against her leg, grounding her better than magic ever could.

Brug lowered their quill. They didn't need to write this down to remember it forever.

Fen and Nadia aimed, but did not fire, waiting for Kaelin to decide who they killed.

For the first time in her life, Kaelin was not an instrument waiting for instruction. She was the one the room paused for.

"You will obey me," Stride demanded as she watched her daughter take control.

"I don't think so." Kaelin offered her own rewrite. "I choose myself."

She raised Mercy—not to kill Stride. After all, she never killed with that particular dagger. Instead, she cut her palm over the throne-bite-mark. Blood dripped from the scar, red splattered like spilled merlot on the silver throne. Power recoiled.

Pain bloomed bright and real, not the ghost-pain of old scars, but something new, chosen, clean. Her blood rewrote the script Stride intended for her.

She rejected inheritance with a single cut of her blade.

Some legacies are built to break. Kaelin just became the one holding the hammer.

Tobias exhaled, not with victory, but reverence. He watched her choose herself, and loved her more for the wound she walked through to do it.

Brug whispered, awed, "This verse is going to bring down taverns. People will sob."

Fen raised her crossbow.

Nadia grabbed Fen, a kiss before the next battle started. "For luck."

Timber's growl rolled like thunder through the marble.

Joren stepped to her side, sword raised, choice made.

A collective sigh rippled through the room—hope breathing for the first time in hours.

"Good choice, my boy," Harlow murmured, taking his place beside Stride instead. "One I should have made."

Stride's glare cut the air. Her earlier words about loyalty drifted in on a breeze that shouldn't have existed.

Timber howled her approval.

Tobias only shook his head with exasperation, fondness, and ruinous devotion.

Nadia whispered, "He's finally stopped waffling."

Fen muttered, "Leave it to a man to be indecisive."

Brug scrawled *FATE, BUT MAKE IT MESSY* across the top of a page like a battle standard.

Kaelin rolled her shoulders, lifted Mercy, and smiled like rebellion made flesh. "Round two?"

33

Ink, Blood, and an Unwritten Crown

"Some destinies are inherited. Others are set on fire."

"Round two," Stride echoed, quill pen outstretched like she was holding an épée.

Kaelin pivoted, grabbed, and tossed Mercy into her other hand in one fluid movement. She bent to grab a sword from a fallen guard before settling into a perfect fighting stance.

"Should I say 'En Gärde' or something?" Kaelin raised an eyebrow.

Stride smiled like a tutor humoring her favorite student. "If you must."

With a flick of her quill, a blade appeared in her hand. Blue, like she was ready to sign on the dotted line.

Steel met ink in a duel for control. The clash was graceful, a ballet of muscle and mind. Stride lunged and parried while casting runes mid-air. She rewrote Kaelin's footing, shifting the ground beneath her.

Kaelin adapted, rolled, and sliced through spells with Whisperthorn. Her ability to switch from one dagger to another while wielding a sword was a sight to behold.

Schools would attempt to teach others her technique for centuries to come; very few, if any, would ever master it.

Nadia swept the legs of a Guild member, then shouted from her vantage point, "Stab her metaphors next."

Fen shot a bolt past Kaelin's ear. "Oops! I was aiming for her hubris."

Brug's lute hit war mode. They played faster than they'd ever played. Kaelin swore she saw magic sparkle from the strings.

Stride circled the quill over her head. An army of ink soldiers formed around her. She cackled with delight.

Team Chaos surged.

Tobias dropped the shields and started hurling one spell after another at the soldiers like it was confetti at a wedding. For every spell that hit its target, a written attacker turned into a puff of glitter. A rainbow of sparkling fabulousness surrounded Kaelin and her mother.

Timber charged, leaping in slow motion before her jaw snapped closed, tearing into Stride's cape. With a shake of her head, Timber sent Stride careening right and then left.

Joren moved like an oath through the ink soldiers, taking blows meant for Kaelin. For every blow he took, he gave one back twice as hard.

Free to focus on one person, her mother, Kaelin attacked with all her might. She sent her mother's sword flying. The quill snapped in two.

Stride stumbled, falling to one knee.

Ink swirls appeared across the ceiling, spiraling like galaxies. Then snapped inwards. The wards ruptured with a snap, like a quill pin breaking under the weight of too much truth.

Stride laughed, cruelty tinged with pride. "You're stronger than I ever intended. You learned my lessons well."

Kaelin raised an eyebrow, her eyes bright with purpose and sharp enough to cut her lineage in half. "I learned to survive you, not to survive from you. And my strength—that's from inside me." She gestured around the room. "And them."

Nadia sniffed, wiping away a tear. "I didn't think she was capable of being sentimental without stabbing first."

"She said something heartfelt." Brug's quill scratched across the parchment. "I need to record it for posterity, and later, teasing."

Fen cupped her hands around her mouth. "It's all you, Kaelin. We're just backup."

Tobias placed his hand on Kaelin's shoulder, a steady reassurance. "She's right, you've always been this strong. We all could see it. Now you can too."

For half a breath, the room softened. It felt . . . safe, not because the threat was gone, but because she knew who she truly was, and it hadn't left her standing alone.

Kaelin needed only one more strike. One heartbeat. She could end this. She raised her dagger, it glinted in the light. In her hand was Mercy. She didn't kill with that blade.

Stride whispered, soft and lethal, "You always hesitate."

CAW-CAW

I wouldn't call it 'hesitation' so much as 'poultry interruptus.'

Brug looked up, horror and awe flickering across their face. The two emotions shared space in their soul. "Oh, no!"

"You don't think..," Tobias whispered as if he were watching a prophecy unfold.

Maybe this was all fate, after all, he was in Skritch five years ago.

"It can't be . . ." Kaelin sucked in air.

It was. The poultry had impeccable timing.

BOOM—glass rained down on them.

Finlo barreled through the opening, hurling cream-filled donuts behind him. Brenna charged in, throwing cheese wheels like siege weapons.

Yes, dear reader, Kaelin did shed a tear for the loss of cheese. It was the one thing she allowed crying over.

CAW-CAW.

The fire-breathing rooster flapped through the window, screaming like the dawn of war. He perched on the balcony, flames raining down, turning everything to ash.

Guild agents combusted. Harlow ducked. Nobles fled screaming. The curtains went up in flames. The throne melted like guilt, exposing where Mundice Mortimer had been hiding this entire time.

Brug called for their bards to switch from a battle tempo to a full heroic overture. "Continue to play, my friends. We are here to inspire. We shall lead our friends to victory."

"Is that a rooster?" Joren stared, his mind unable to comprehend what was happening before his eyes.

Harlow stood, his joints creaking as he did so. "A fire-breathing chicken is one for the ages."

"Five-to-one the chicken defeats us all," Fen bet.

Nadia gasped. "How dare you wager against Kaelin."

Backs together, they punched and kicked their way across the balcony, keeping the Guild and guards at bay all while dodging flames.

And Kaelin? She laughed, a sound sharp enough to cut fate, smiling through blood, heartbreak, and the destiny she had just refused.

If love wouldn't kill her first, then destiny would have to take a number.

She stepped forward as herself, surrounded by the people who chose her and whom she chose back.

Stride smiled like a wolf watching her cub grow fangs.

Kaelin threw Moonveil.

The Black Bishop almost looked startled. Almost.

Ink splattered—enough to wound, not enough to finish her off.

Stride snapped her fingers.

Reality folded.

Some stories end with closure. Ours ends with a door left slightly ajar.

Everything went black.

34

Ashes, Aftermath, and Goodbye

"Endings come in many forms. Some louder than others."

T he palace was still so dark that everyone was afraid to move. Not from fear of enemies, but fear of stubbing their toe or running into the corner of a table.

CAW-CAW

"Percival, if you don't go home to Skritch—" Finlow stopped mid-threat, realizing he didn't have a follow-up punishment in mind harsh enough to deter the poultry chaos.

A blast of flame illuminated the room. Torches flickered back to life.

This might be the one situation when having a fire-breathing rooster around was actually useful. There won't be many, so cherish it.

"Where did she go?" Kaelin scanned the room, looking for Stride. Instead, she found her dagger lying on the floor and Mundice Mortimer quaking next to a melted throne.

Everywhere she looked was destruction. Ink-stained marble, torn silk, and feathered-shrapnel. Cream puffs were smashed into chandeliers. The one thing she didn't see was her mother.

No chance to finish what she had started. There wouldn't be a goodbye, not even the ugly kind.

Percival pecked at the pastry bombs that were supposed to extinguish his flame.

"Somebody better do something about that chicken before I do." If looks could kill, Kaelin's glare would have ended Percival's reign of terror.

"Sorry Kaelin. We wanted to help." Finlo shifted from one foot to another like a boy who got caught with his hand in the cookie jar.

Brenna tiptoed closer to Percival. She spun her lasso—hope, dairy, and stubbornness braided together—over her head and let it go.

It was like he knew it was coming. Percival crowed, ascended like a feathery demigod, and the rope missed by a full kingdom.

"Dammit!" Brenna stomped her foot. "I was so close. I'm really tired of his antics."

Tobias giggled, relief, shock, and near-hysteria blending into sound. He couldn't stop the tittering laughter. "I'm sure Kaelin wouldn't mind taking care of him for you."

"It'll involve daggers," she muttered. "Maybe a barbecue afterwards."

And because Fate is dramatic, Percival returned, landing like royalty.

"Someone give me a rope, or better yet, a quill. I can rewrite that rooster back to normal." Kaelin stalked forward with the confidence of someone who had survived destiny itself. "I'm assuming I'm not allowed to erase his existence."

It wasn't a question, but Finlo answered anyway. "Auntie Thyme would be so angry if we didn't have our town mascot. I really don't want to be turned into a scone."

Her sigh reverberated through the room. "Fine."

She snatched the quill Tobias had somehow conjured like a magician in a tavern show.

Tobias ran after her. "Are you sure you want to do it?"

If you recall, dear reader, magic and Kaelin are not, and likely never will be, on speaking terms.

She sighed before handing him the quill back. "Fine, but don't (bleep) it up."

He took the quill from her. He whispered syllables, flicked his fingers like punctuation marks in the air: magic, revision, mercy, maybe all three.

Percival hiccupped, shrank back to his original size, and burped gently. Still enormous. Still chaos incarnate. But flame-free.

And with that, the world exhaled. Even Kaelin did—a breath she didn't know she'd been holding. Yes, I know it's an overused description, but it happens, sometimes.

For the first time since the throne bit her skin, nothing was attacking, exploding, or rewriting reality—which left only the uncomfortable space where feelings lived.

Brenna blushed. "I guess we should take him back." She smiled. "Write me when you get somewhere you can accept packages. I'll send you cheese."

Kaelin almost cried at the thought of being sent cheese. It was one of her dreams come true.

Nadia limped down from the balcony. "What in the gods is going on with that chicken? It almost singed my eyebrows off."

"There was an incident with a dragon pepper and a touch of magic to add spice," Brenna explained.

Finlo blushed. "I had the best of intentions. Percival stole the tart, both tarts."

"I see." Fen stumbled.

Nadia reached out to help her.

Victory never looked like triumph. It looked like exhaustion wearing borrowed glamour, everyone still bleeding and laughing and pretending it was fine.

Fen swatted her hands away. "I'm fine."

In truth, she wasn't fine. After two steps, her knees buckled, and she crumpled to the ground.

"Ugh. Fine. Someone help me stand." The other words that fell from her mouth were not fit for human consumption.

Brug wrote lyrics through nosebleeds. "Do not despair, my friend, I will make it sing with drama."

Timber growled at anyone who dared to inch their way into Kaelin's personal space, guarding her like a shadow with teeth.

And the king, he lay unconscious, but free. No longer a draft of himself.

The battle was over, yet the room felt like the moment after lightning—air still cracked open, waiting for rain.

News of the Shadow Guild's demise swept through the palace. Nobles whispered about the draft being broken, Stride being gone—or mostly gone—and about the fracture where the throne sat empty.

Bickering ensued as different people tried to claim the throne.

Everyone wanted it. Kaelin wanted the exit.

Unfortunately, there was the fallout to deal with. Funny how power always returns to the room fastest—grief, responsibility, duty . . . they arrive slow.

Tobias stood beside her, quiet, watchful. His fit of giggles had passed. Magic settled around him like embers after a wildfire. He looked like a man who wanted to speak of love, but he offered his loyalty instead.

Kaelin exhaled, grounding herself. There was no mother left to fight. Just the consequences of what the woman had started. No more blade at her throat. Just the hollow quiet where choices came home to roost.

Harlow approached, abandoned by the person he'd promised loyalty to. "She promised me my brother back. After I left you in those tunnels, I couldn't face him." His voice caught; grief poured off of him in waves. "She came to me with promises I should never have listened to."

Kaelin wanted to hate him. She wanted to remember that he chose Stride over her, although that wasn't the complete truth. He'd chosen reconciliation.

"Did you get your brother back?" she asked, her voice not much more than a whisper.

The knight shook his head. "Briefly, once he was himself, no longer a lich. He didn't live much longer."

"Go home," she said finally. "Bury your brother, if you haven't already. Then decide who you are without her voice in your skull."

He bowed his head. "I will remember this."

He left. No longer an enemy, but not yet a friend. Kaelin let the memory of him settle—not forgiven, but no longer a wound.

Kaelin hated how Stride had used Harlow. She'd made him another pawn in her game. She didn't want to remember him as he'd been here, but like he was during the Ale Trials. She grabbed Tobias's hand, seeking comfort from someone who would understand.

Tobias opened his mouth to speak, but was interrupted, again.

At least this time, it wasn't a chicken.

Mundice Mortimer staggered forward like a man who expected to die because he was seen.

"Thorn of the... Kaelin... I was only following orders." The words finally came out. It was a poor excuse. He wasn't young or inexperienced. No, he was power hungry and selfish.

Ah yes—a man who confuses surviving with contributing.

"I would like to say you were following out of fear. But you know I know better. You want recognition, power, acclaim."

Kaelin looked around. "You aren't going to get it now. It's not up to me to decide what happens to you. You can wait for the king to awake, or you can scurry off like the coward we all know you to be."

Mundice Mortimer pushed his glasses up higher on his nose. He bowed.

"But, if I see you again, I don't think I'll be as inclined to be nice." She didn't even need to put a dagger to his throat.

Mundice Mortimer gulped; sweat beaded on his forehead. "I understand. Thank you."

He skulked off just as the king stirred. Ink drained from his veins like a poison leaving his body. His eyes—real now—found Kaelin.

"I'm alive. You did it," he whispered. "You broke her story."

"No," Kaelin said. "I wrote my own."

Joren kneeled next to King Varric, helping him up off the ground. Tears ran down the royal's face as relief, confusion, and even guilt made themselves known.

The former king looked around at the place he once ruled from. The throne room no longer felt like a battlefield. It felt like aftermath—stories half-finished, loyalties rearranging like furniture in a house after a storm.

"It's destroyed. What am I supposed to do?" King Varric asked.

There's nothing quite like overthrowing a regime only for the ruler to ask you for career advice.

"Rebuild, if that's what you want." Kaelin shrugged. "But be smarter about it. The Guild wasn't the only one that wanted you dead. Surround yourself with trustworthy people. Honest ones."

"What about you? Will you stay, help me rebuild?" The king's eyes pleaded for her to stay.

She shook her head. "I won't, I can't. Ruling is not my goal. But I wish you the best."

Our girl does not do thrones. Chairs, yes. Preferably with snacks.

He nodded, grateful and grieving. She could tell he respected her decision.

Now for the hard part, when everyone goes their own way.

Kaelin turned away from the king, looking for her exit. She knew the goodbyes were coming, and they weren't her thing. Joren stopped her.

"I'm going to stay. Help him rebuild." He looked back at the king.

Growth is rarely glamorous. Sometimes it's rebuilding a kingdom out of shame, hope, and really questionable budget allocations.

She nodded. "I understand. Thank—"

He put up his hand, stopping her from thanking him. "Don't. You've saved me enough, more times than I can count."

"Just twice," Kaelin added.

"I faltered. I shouldn't have. I'm going to make it right." Joren held out his hand. "Remember, we all chose to stand by you. We chose you."

His words rattled her. She took his hand anyway.

"Keep the bells. I'll be there if you ever need me." He clasped her hand in both of his before walking back to the fallen king.

Kaelin wiped her eyes. There weren't tears, at least not yet. But the day wasn't over.

Nadia waved her over. Another goodbye.

Endings, it turned out, were simply beginnings wearing different boots.

"We're headed back to Briarwick. Just because she's gone doesn't mean the Guild isn't out there plotting." Fen laid out their plan.

Nadia draped her arm over Fen's shoulder. "We already have the tavern fight club and the network of safe houses in place. There is the Uncle Crust conundrum, ran off with a culinary rogue." She rolled her eyes. "We can find him and continue what we've already started."

"I understand." And she did.

Fen wrapped her arms around Kaelin in a bear hug. "If you ever need someone to break some jaws, we'll be there."

"Or a spa day. Growth, balance, etc." Nadia joined the hug.

They stood like that for a moment. They turned away, holding hands, their love obvious.

Brug picked Kaelin up and swung her around. "Before everyone leaves on their own path, we need to celebrate."

Tobias clapped. "Yes. We need a night of revelry."

A goat, not the one with the horn, headbutted Brug. "Yes, you can come too. Of course you can."

Kaelin shrugged, pretending she didn't care. She did, she always had.

Brug dropped his arm over her shoulder. "Don't worry, I will immortalize all of this. My ballad will exaggerate everything."

She laughed. "Of course it will."

* * *

They gathered at a tavern just outside the capital.

Because what do heroes do after almost rewriting destiny?

They get drunk, obviously.

Timber was on the floor chomping on the best roast in the house. Brug cried as their song was performed by strangers.

"It's so beautiful." They wiped away their tears.

And yes, they took notes mid-sobbing. A ballad must evolve, even when the bard is emotionally compromised.

Kaelin looked around. Everything felt so normal, like the world hadn't almost changed, completely, moments ago.

Taverns have a way of pretending nothing apocalyptic just happened. Sticky floors are grounding like that.

Tobias sat beside Kaelin, close but not touching. Little touches had increased over time, but he respected the space she needed.

Nerves, hope, affection—all quiet, all present. Growth disguised as proximity.

Nadia and Fen organized a fight; the two of them couldn't help themselves. Joren joined. Bets were made. Taunts were exchanged. Punches and kicks landed. A winner was declared.

Brug narrated the brawl like a sports commentator who'd lost all objectivity.

They all regrouped at the table. Kaelin raised her glass. "To side quests. The ones that ruin us. The ones that save us."

Everyone drank.

The laughter rose loud and bright, the kind that only comes after surviving something that should've broken you.

Kaelin leaned back, watching the people who had become something dangerously close to family. Not bound by blood. Bound by choice. Far more volatile, far more precious.

Tomorrow they would scatter. Tonight, they existed.

And for the first time, she let herself stay present long enough to feel it.

* * *

The next morning they scattered to their own futures. There was no victory parade, just footsteps on stone and a horizon waiting.

Tobias hefted his pack up, slinging it over his shoulder. He began to walk away, assuming she'd choose to be alone. Like she always had.

Funny thing about growth: no one tells you it feels like standing at a cliff's edge with nothing but your own heartbeat for company.

She reached for his sleeve. "Don't vanish. Not yet."

"You want me to stay?" he asked, not quite able to see the truth in her words.

Kaelin had faced blades, betrayal, destiny itself, but saying yes felt like the sharpest risk of all.

She shrugged. "Are you really going to make me ask twice?"

"No." He took his place beside her. Staying, not because she promised anything, but because she knew how to ask.

Kaelin left the capital with Timber trotting ahead, Tobias walking beside her, and Ed, the horse, trailing behind with their packs. She left a kingdom behind her that would outgrow her. A future she refused to choose.

But for the first time, she wasn't running. She was walking towards something, instead of away, and she really hoped there was cheese.

She walked towards her dream, no longer an assassin, no longer as a weapon, but as the person she's finally allowing herself to become.

And if the world tried to rewrite her again?

It would bleed ink before she bent.

35

THE TAVERN ON THE EDGE OF THE WORLD

"She didn't choose peace. She just ran out of quests . . . temporarily."

The world felt too quiet as they continued away from the capital. Kaelin's muscles ached with post-battle soreness and fatigue. Behind her, smoke from the palace rose, curling into the sky until it disappeared into the clouds. She didn't look back. Tobias did, just once, for both of them.

There are some endings you only survive by facing forward.

"Where are we going?" Tobias watched his feet as he put one foot in front of the other. Hopeful. Cautious. Like a man waiting for an answer and not sure he deserves one.

"Home, or not." She stared at the road ahead of her. "Where do you want to go?"

"I can go anywhere you want," he responded.

She smiled. "That's not an answer."

He smiled back. "It's not. But it's all you're going to get for now."

Patience disguised as mischief. A man who finally understood her pace, not just her blades.

A rabbit darted across the trail, and Timber leapt after it with a bark of delight. She frolicked through the woods with no intention of catching the critter, just happy to run without purpose.

Freedom looks like fur, mud, and absolutely no mission objectives. Joy without agenda—a strange new magic.

"What's that?" Tobias pointed to a leaning signpost.

Ed decided this was a great time to speak up. "It appears to be a sign of some sort."

Kaelin rolled her eyes. The horse had too many opinions.

"Is someone going to read it? I'm a horse, unfortunately, I don't know how to read," Ed continued on.

One arrow pointed towards CERTAIN DOOM. Another pointed towards SLIGHTLY LESS DOOM. Thankfully, there was an arrow that had a less ominous tilt to it.

She read the sign out loud: "THE TAVERN ON THE EDGE OF THE WORLD. GOOD SOUP, BAD DECISIONS. ABSOLUTELY NO QUESTS BEFORE BREAKFASTS."

Timber sniffed the sign with approval.

Tobias smiled. "That sounds like where we should be heading."

And Destiny—fickle, fond, and a little drunk—exhaled with agreement. You could almost hear it mutter, *"Fine, take a break. But not a long one."*

Kaelin pretended she wasn't curious. "I guess we have a destination, for now."

They followed the signs, turning this way and that. The roads they were on didn't appear on any maps. But every time there was a split in the road, there was a sign directing them one way or the other. Most often it was towards the path covered with overgrowth, clearly unused.

Maybe all great futures begin where no one else cared to walk.

After days of traveling, a quaint building appeared, rising up from the mist, book-ended by towering trees. As they approached, the door opened, welcoming them inside.

Kaelin walked into the tavern. Warm light spilled through moss-covered beams. She inhaled the smell of cinnamon, ale, and long-earned rest.

To her left was a bar lined with relics from finished quests. Across from the bar was a hearth built of stones from fallen kingdoms. By the entrance, there was a guest-book full of names crossed out, rewritten, evolving.

This was a place for heroes without wars. Legends between chapters. Protagonists on pause.

It was exactly where Kaelin needed to be, for now.

"Hello, a table for . . ." A plump woman with curly hair looked them over, noticing Timber first. "Three?"

Tobias nodded. "Yes, please."

The woman nodded. "This way."

This was the first unhurried meal since they had met. They sat next to each other, a comfortable silence between them.

Soup arrived—hot, thick, comforting. Timber got her own bowl.

Kaelin took a bite and stilled, savoring the feel of it on her tongue. Food tasted different when no one was trying to poison you. The soup tasted like someone had cast a mild comfort spell on it. Illegal in most cities, required in this one. It was the opposite of poison, which was refreshing. Little by little, tension left her body.

Honestly, she barely recognized the sensation.

Tobias watched as she softened, enjoying seeing her relax for the first time. He ate slowly, just to stay longer.

Silence, but the safe kind.

The tavernkeeper came to their table. He was old, amused, probably immortal. "Ah, Kaelin Thorn. Side quests cling to you like burrs."

Her head snapped up. "How do you know my name?"

"I know the name of everyone who walks through my doors." He winked. "It's my job. I'm Markus, the owner of this establishment. Are you enjoying your dinner?" He had the air of someone who knew exactly how many quests Kaelin had derailed—and approved.

"Of course," Tobias interjected. "I really like the use of tarragon in the soup. It added so much flavor."

Kaelin placed her hand over his. "I don't think he wants a dissertation on soup."

Tobias shrugged. "It's good soup."

"Thank you. I love when patrons appreciate our chef's cooking." Markus gathered their bowls. "I'll let her know you enjoyed it, Tobias."

"That's a little unnerving," Tobias said.

Markus smiled like he had all the secrets of the world but wasn't ready to share. "So some of the others have mentioned." He reached down to pet Timber. "How about you, Timber? Are you enjoying your meal? I bet you want some bacon."

Her ears perked at the word bacon, and she licked her chops.

"I'll take that as a yes." Markus laughed. "I'll be back."

Kaelin watched him walk away. "I doubt he'll be long."

Timber set her head on her human's lap. Kaelin petted her head without thought. She whined.

"I'm sure he'll be right back with your bacon. Too bad he isn't bringing cheese as well." She leaned back in her chair.

Tobias sat there, letting her hold his hand. "Have you thought about what's next?"

Kaelin didn't answer at first. When she did, he had to lean in to hear her.

"I don't know, I've never let myself dream." She took a deep breath.

He waited for her to meet his gaze. "Maybe it's time you do."

Markus reappeared, setting a plate of bacon in front of Timber and a cheese board on the table. "I thought you might enjoy this."

Kaelin's face lit up like a solstice tree. "Oh, you didn't have to." She grabbed a piece of cheddar and popped it into her mouth.

Tobias couldn't stop himself from laughing, but he also didn't really try. "Of course he did."

"I thought you might enjoy some cheese." The smile that crossed over his face was fleeting, but said he knew too much. "I also want to offer you a room. Free of destiny for one night."

It sounded so freeing Kaelin almost wept. Instead, she nodded her head, accepting the room and a night without quests.

"I'll be on my way." Markus left two keys on the table. The keys jingled with a suspicious amount of narrative significance.

"Thank you," Tobias said.

They sat together, snacking on some of the best cheese she'd ever tasted. Not as good as Brenna's, but a close second. She shook her head, smiling.

"What are you thinking about?" Tobias leaned back in his chair.

She smirked, just a little. "Cheese. Brenna's cheese. This cheese. Comparing the two. Which do you think is better?"

Tobias didn't hesitate. "Brenna's, of course. But this is also really good."

Kaelin tapped the table with her fingers. "What do you want to do next?"

"You know what I want to do next." Now that he had the chance to say how he felt, he was terrified to do so.

Her eyes widened. "Oh . . ." She shifted in her chair. "More real-life experiences with magic?"

"That's not exactly what I was thinking. But, I always want to learn more. Maybe even figure out how I made that bread shield," he answered. "Why don't you let yourself dream?"

"There was never any reason to. And now that I can, I'm afraid I don't know how to exist without a target." The words came out rushed, like if she didn't hurry through them she wouldn't ever say them.

"Maybe now's the time for you to learn." His tone was gentle.

She didn't know what to say; instead, she went to bed. Alone, but not lonely. For the first time in forever, she slept without a dagger under her pillow with Timber curled against her feet.

Tobias remained downstairs, awake. He watched the embers burn low in the hearth, keeping vigil without being asked.

In the morning, somewhere on the horizon . . . a distant *CAW*. Soft. Menacing. Promising chaos. Peace only lasted until the next quest woke.

36

YOU STAYED

"Love is not a weapon, but it does leave a mark."

Sun streamed into the room, right into Kaelin's eyes. She groaned, tried to roll over, but couldn't. Timber was sprawled like a log across her legs. For a second, panic coursed through her—cold, instinctive, familiar.

Old reflexes don't die. They just wake up cranky. Some of them also want coffee first.

It was gone as quickly as it came. She knew there were no threats except for sunlight filtering through the curtains. She groaned again, covering her face with her pillow. For the first time in forever, she wasn't preparing for a fight, and she didn't know what to do with that.

Rest, as it turns out, requires more bravery than battle. Bravery she absolutely had not trained for.

The weight on her legs disappeared suddenly as Timber jumped off the bed. She scratched at the door, whining.

"Fine, I'll get out of bed." Kaelin threw her pillow off the bed before sitting up.

Timber ran in a circle, sat, and barked once.

"I get it, but I have to get dressed first." Which was exactly what Kaelin did.

She made her way to the tavern, her dog trotting next to her. "Let's go outside and then get some food."

Timber leapt over the last few stairs, skidding to a stop in front of the door.

"Do you want me to open for you, Timber?" Tobias asked.

Kaelin froze—actually froze—one foot hovering above the floor.

Heroes face dragons without flinching, but show them a boy who stayed the night? Catastrophic emotional failure mode engaged.

Her pulse hiccupped—betrayal by cardiovascular system.

In her defense, no one trained her for romance in the Shadow Guild. They barely trained her for regular conversations.

Sitting in front of the fireplace was Tobias. He sat there with a book open in his lap, his glasses crooked, his tea half-finished. It wasn't what she had expected. No one had stayed with her without it being out of obligation or needing something.

This was new territory: the kind with warmth instead of knives.

Warmth was, frankly, suspicious. Warmth meant vulnerability. Vulnerability meant feelings. Feelings meant emotional paperwork.

He turned to look at her, smiling softly. "Good morning."

"You stayed," she whispered.

Timber barked.

"I'm coming, I'm coming." Kaelin finished descending the stairs and made her way to the door. Her heart was doing something strange in her chest—thumping instead of shutting down. Alarming.

She pushed the door open.

Timber darted out, running towards the trees, probably chasing a rabbit or some wood sprites. Hopefully not a minor forest god. Kaelin didn't want to add any more accolades to her name. It involved too much paperwork.

Kaelin lingered at the threshold.

She could step outside, pretend nothing had shifted. Or she could turn back towards the boy with crooked glasses and a steadiness she didn't know she needed.

Behind her, she heard Tobias close his book. Quietly. Gently. Like someone who planned to be right there when she came back. It felt like when he had held a shield for her at the Gala. The same breath he took before casting spells in an effort to protect her. A pattern was forming. An annoying, heart-warming pattern. Patterns were dangerous. Patterns became habits. Habits became attachment. No one warned her about this mission.

She turned. He was still there, watching her.

"Breakfast?" he asked.

Markus popped into the room. "Did someone say breakfast?"

Kaelin stared.

Tobias stared.

Timber raced back into the room and howled her answer. She definitely wanted breakfast.

"I think she answered for us. Breakfast it is." Kaelin looked from Markus to Tobias.

Tobias nodded. "Definitely. Do you think we could eat by the hearth?"

"Of course." Markus offered a slight bow before leaving the room.

Next to Tobias, there was an empty chair. It looked cozy, welcoming even. She should go sit in it; she wanted to, but hesitated. Comfort, especially shared coziness, was out of her comfort-zone.

Ironic, I know. The assassin who faced demi-gods and revision magic brought low by a chair.

He gestured towards the chair. "Sit. I don't think the chairs bite."

"Are you sure? I'm kinda over chairs using my hand as a chew toy." She laughed.

She made her way over to the chair and sat.

"I think I miss Brug," Tobias blurted.

Classic Tobias defense mechanism: when faced with feelings, deploy bard nostalgia. He once avoided a confession by explaining the wonders of moss.

While the two were capable of sitting in silence, it was something Tobias struggled with. His two defaults: talk about their friends or his feelings.

Kaelin tucked her feet under her. "You know, I think I might miss them too."

He leaned towards her. They were close, close enough to touch. They didn't. Timber walked over and settled in between them.

Kaelin stared at the fire. "Last night, when I said I didn't have dreams, that wasn't exactly true."

The calm, controlled assassin mask hadn't just slipped, it had disappeared at some point during the night. She twisted her hands. Tobias placed his hand over hers. She stopped moving.

Some truths needed a steady hand to keep them from scattering.

"Do you want to tell me?" He didn't pressure her but waited for her to decide what she wanted to do.

"A bookstore with a tea shop, or maybe a tavern. Something cozy. Maybe somewhere that Brug can perform, when they want to."

She closed her eyes, picturing all the details. Somewhere without undead knights, rewrite magic, or poultry warfare. A revolutionary thought. And with an excellent cheese menu.

"I have your breakfast here." Markus interrupted their conversation. "I didn't forget you, Timber."

They waited in silence for Markus to leave. Markus bustled around, bringing out tea, cheesy eggs, and bacon. Lots of bacon, extra for Timber.

He paused before stepping into the kitchen. "Before you leave, I have a gift. Don't leave without it."

"Where do you want your bookstore tavern to be?" Tobias asked.

Kaelin thought about it. "Maybe the beach, or the mountains. Actually, mountains, I don't want to deal with another kraken."

"I can see that influencing your decision. It would influence mine." Tobias laughed. He was quiet for a moment. "When you build your dream in the mountains . . . can I be a part of it?"

It wasn't a question she expected to hear. She wasn't sure she was ready to answer. She didn't need to be.

"I want you there, for as much or as little as you want to be around for." She rested her head on his shoulder—barely, briefly.

He stilled, not wanting to break the moment.

Timber sighed. Content.

And that, dear reader, is how an assassin accidentally built a future—one breakfast at a time. No daggers, no destiny, no dramatic lighting. Just bacon and bravery. Who knew?

37

Final Side Quest (Just One More)

"Heroes never really retire. Especially not when there's a dragon in the next valley."

A few months later . . .

The smell of frying bacon drifted up to her room, waking Kaelin. She'd almost become used to the lack of danger in her life, waking up to Timber's cold nose pressed up against the back of her legs.

The world was calm. She didn't trust it, but she was learning.

Healing, it turned out, required suspicious amounts of breakfast.

She made her way downstairs. Sunlight filtered through the wavy glass panes Tobias insisted had 'character.' Bookshelves lined the walls, some crammed with spellbooks, some with romance novels Kaelin claimed were 'for ambience.'

She still wouldn't admit how much she actually enjoyed reading them.

A dagger hung above the pastry counter, strictly for cutting scones. Timber's rug lay beside the hearth, already covered in dog hair and the occasional breadcrumb. The sign Markus gifted them—NO QUESTS BEFORE BREAKFASTS—hung crookedly over the bar, as if defying anyone to take it seriously.

Tobias was in the bookshop area, reorganizing books alphabetically by magical threat level. ('Slightly Dangerous,' 'Probably Cursed,' and 'Absolutely Do Not Touch Without a Cleric' were already full shelves.) She was going to have to find more space for bookshelves sooner rather than later at the rate they both collected books.

Brug, yes Brug, played softly by the hearth. A rare gentle verse, proof even chaos could rest. Briefly, if supervised.

Breakfast was served in the tavern, a room with mismatched tables and chairs. Soon it would be alive with travelers, rumors, laughter—no bloodshed. A miracle, especially since Nadia and Fen were visiting. They'd rebuilt the fight ring, with extra legal loopholes. They continually tried to convince Kaelin to let them use her tavern. She refused, emphatically.

"Joren's rebuilt the king's guard. People are even starting to accept the king again." Nadia filled Kaelin in on what was happening away from her bookshop.

"Even the Briarwick Queen? Never mind, I don't want to know." Kaelin struggled not to get involved.

Fen leaned in. "Do you have any news for us?"

Tobias laughed. "This is where people go to exchange news."

"Harlow came by. He's struggling with the death of his brother. Andraya has been delivering intelligence. There's been rumblings. I'm ignoring them." She really was trying to ignore them. She was very nearly successful.

Ignoring trouble is an advanced skill. Kaelin was at a beginner level, but improving.

Wind blew the doors open, ruffling pages of books and sending parchment flying. In the opening, a cloaked woman stood.

"Is Kaelin Thorn here?" The woman gasped for air. "A dragon, it's nesting in forgotten mountains."

The room fell silent.

She looked over at Tobias. He nodded. Brug tuned their lute. Timber thumped her tail.

Somewhere in the distance, a rooster's call cracked through the sky.

You know the one.

And so, the story ends . . . for now.

There will always be one more side quest.

After all, peace is temporary.

But chaos? Chaos is loyal.

The End. (Or is it?)

Field Guides

A Field Guide to Extinct Flora (and Other Botanical Mistakes)

By Lady Vexina Quagmire, Banishé of the Nine Realms, Former Court Herbmistress (briefly)

Includes Questionable Illustrations and Absolutely No Guarantees

Moonveil Lily

Status: Extinct (traded for a promise never kept)
Habitat: Grew only during full eclipses on cliff edges where widows wept
Magical Properties: Oath-binding, lunar resonance, dramatic exits

Notes:

Popular among tragic lovers and cult leaders. Binding someone with a Moonveil meant your word was sealed by the stars—an excellent way to avoid accountability. Do NOT confuse with Duskdroop Lily. That one just makes you forget your laundry.

Glassfire Bloom

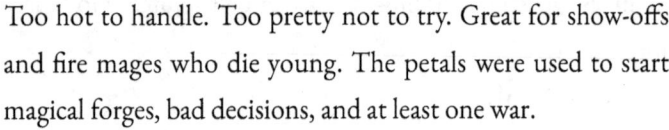

Status: Extinct (the last one exploded during a wedding)
Habitat: Glass-blown valleys near molten veins of dormant dragons
Magical Properties: Elemental ignition, flame-channeling, ambiance

Notes:

Too hot to handle. Too pretty not to try. Great for show-offs and fire mages who die young. The petals were used to start magical forges, bad decisions, and at least one war.

Whisperthorn

Status: Extinct (thankfully—therapy exists now)
Habitat: Places where truths died unspoken: under gallows, old temples, childhood bedrooms
Magical Properties: Memory capture, soul resonance, guilt enhancement

Notes:

If it bloomed near you, someone had a secret. If it bloomed

under you, you were the secret. Steeping the petals in tea lets you hear the last words never said. Use caution. Or wine. Preferably both.

Lachryssom Vine

Status: Extinct (devoured by melancholy)

Habitat: Grows on mausoleums, battlefield wreckage, and tragic cliffsides

Magical Properties: Necromantic catalyst, emotional amplification, mascara ruin

Notes:

Wore it once at a funeral. Regretted everything. Every leaf carried a tear—yours, theirs, someone long dead. Very popular with necromancers, poets, and dramatic teenagers.

Aurora's End

Status: Extinct (hope died; so did it)

Habitat: Fields of lost battles and coronation sites that never were

Magical Properties: Light refraction, illusion enchantments, heartbreak weather

Notes:

Technically still blooms in bard songs. Turns to dust when touched, like most dreams. Smelled like sunrise and ash. I don't miss it. (That's a lie.)

Frostwillow Floret

Status: Extinct (thank you, climate instability)
Habitat: The breath of sleeping giants, frozen groves, cryptic lullabies
Magical Properties: Dream-walking, time dilation, frostbite (emotional and physical)

Notes:

Not to be confused with frostnip or actual willows. The Floret vanished when the last dream giant died snoring in the Glacial Vale. Still occasionally appears in enchanted paintings and particularly sad lullabies.

Bleeding Briar

Status: Extinct (overharvested by repentant lovers and dramatists)
Habitat: Guilt-soaked soil, abandoned altars, royal gardens with secrets
Magical Properties: Memory extraction, wound preservation, regret infusion

Notes:

Each thorn could extract a memory—painful, sweet, or stupid. Not recommended for the emotionally constipated. Storing the memories properly requires a copper bowl, a steady hand, and absolutely zero shame.

Witch's Eye

Status: Extinct (banned, burned, blamed)
Habitat: Wild heaths, scrying circles, the edge of knowing
Magical Properties: Foresight, farseeing, uncomfortable truths

Notes:

I'll say it: this flower slapped. Just because it showed people things they didn't want to know doesn't mean it deserved genocide. I kept one dried in a locket. It still blinks sometimes. Very nostalgic.

Everswoon

Status: Extinct (too many assassins misused it as perfume)

Habitat: Fields of first kisses, shadowed dueling circles, unspoken rendezvous

Magical Properties: Subtle poisoning, dramatic flustering, lusty misdirection

Notes:

If anyone ever hands you one, don't inhale. Just kiss them or kill them. Either way, things will escalate quickly.

THE RIDICULOUS REGIONAL POLITICS OF ELDREACH (AND BEYOND)

By Lady Vexina Quagmire, Banishé of the Nine Realms, Former Court Herbmistress (briefly) with great reluctance, mild irritation, and an encyclopedic understanding of everyone else's mistakes.

THE KINGDOM OF ELDREACH

Current Ruler: King Varric the Magnificent

(self-appointed title; opinions vary)

Style of Rule: A monarchy strengthened primarily by tradition, ceremonial pageantry, and denial.

Actual Governance:

A precarious balance of:

• nobles who plot,

• nobles who pretend not to plot,

• and one royal falconer who somehow has far too much influence.

Key Issues:

• **Prophecy Legislation:** Ongoing debate over whether legally binding prophecies should require a royal signature.

• **Economic Reforms:** Currently stalled due to a heated dispute over the Horse Tax Reformation (no horses affected, no one knows what it changes).

• **Security:** Rumors persist of a 'shadowy organization' influencing court decisions. Rumors also persist that half the court is looking for the other half's secret passages.

Narrator Note:

"Eldreach is best described as a kingdom held together with ribbon, optimism, and the faint hope that no one asks too many questions."

THE DUCHY OF SALTMERE

Notable For:

Trade routes, smugglers, and citywide arguments about maritime law that end in fistfights and cocktails. There's also desert that is only ever mentioned when threatening someone with banishment.

Style of Government:

Technically subject to Eldreach, practically run by a Merchant Council that changes its mind hourly while the Duke of Saltmere, unironically, believes that he is in charge, despite the fact that no one ever listens to him.

Key Issues:

- Dueling seagulls for dock dominance
- Demanding recognition as 'Most Essential Port'
- Resisting taxation on 'imported nonsense,' including—controversially—poetry

Narrator Note:

"Saltmere has declared independence so many times the crown stopped updating the paperwork."

THE QUEENDOM OF BRIARWICK

Notable For:

Matriarchal leadership, ferociously beautiful armor, and the world's highest reported rate of duel-related courtship.

Style of Government:

The ruling Queen presides over warrior poets, poet warriors, and citizens who believe diplomacy should involve at least one blade.

Key Issues:

- Maintaining neutrality while quietly interfering everywhere
- Controversy over whether men may join their national ballet
- A cultural debate on whether foreplay must involve duels (currently undecided)

Narrator Note:

"In Briarwick, if someone offers you wine, check for hidden daggers. If they offer you daggers, check for hidden wine."

THE MIDLANDS COALITION

Notable For:

Five city-states that only agree on one thing—meetings should never exceed ten minutes.

Style of Government:

A cooperative alliance in theory; in practice, a perpetual group project where no one reads the assignment.

Key Issues:

- Annual border negotiations that devolve into interpretive dance
- Magical regulation disputes (one city wants to ban it; another wants to marry it)
- Unconventional elected leadership, including one surprisingly competent goat

Narrator Note:

"The Midlands prove that democracy is alive, well, and frequently on fire."

THE GUILDS

(Not to be confused with The Guild, though honestly everyone is confused anyway.)

Shadow Guild:

A quiet, discreet, entirely mysterious organization rumored to influence courts across the continent.

Or perhaps it doesn't exist at all.

(If you hear this claim, consider who benefits from that denial.)

Official Concerns:

- Maintaining balance between kingdoms (unaliving individuals as necessary)
- Collecting secrets
- Writing increasingly dramatic bylaws

Unofficial Concerns:

- Turf wars
- Petty rivalries
- Who gets to claim credit for operations they weren't technically involved in

Narrator Note:

"Imagine a secret organization pulling the strings of power. Now imagine several sets of hands tugging in opposite directions. That's the Guild."

THE DUSKMIRE BORDERLANDS

A fog-laden stretch dividing Eldreach from the Midlands.

Why People Avoid It:

- Too misty
- Too haunted (allegedly)
- Too many ruins in which adventurers vanish dramatically

Why Certain Individuals Prefer It:

- Quiet
- Remote
- Hard for enemies—and even friends—to locate
- Excellent for reflection, regrettable decision-making, or building new lives

Narrator Note:

"The Duskmire is a perfect place for anyone hoping to be forgotten. Or found. Or both."

IN SUMMARY

The political landscape of Eldreach and its neighbors is:

- volatile,
- unpredictable,
- mildly absurd,
- and ripe for adventure.

Whether one seeks glory, trouble, or simply to avoid being drafted into a prophecy, one thing is certain:

There is always a side quest waiting.

About the Author: Lady Vexina Quagmire

Banishé of the Nine Realms, Former Court Herbmistress (briefly), Survivor of the Saffron Betrayal, Unlicensed Oracle, and Not Legally Responsible for Any Disasters Involving This Book or Any Others

Lady Vexina Quagmire is a semi-retired enchantress, reluctant memoirist, not-so-secret romance author and former party leader of the infamous adventuring company *Death By Destiny*, which tragically disbanded after a cursed fondue incident and one deeply regrettable group hug. She has died twice, been engaged seven times (three of which were political), and was once crowned 'Most Likely to Hex Her Ex' by *Sorcery Monthly*.

Her first guidebook, *So You've Been Betrayed by a Chosen One: Now What?*, was banned in seventeen kingdoms for being 'a little too accurate.' She has since made a modest living offering life advice no one asked for, judging other people's quests from afar, and occasionally consulting for heroes who ignore her warnings anyway.

When not annotating tragic romances or shouting at prophecies, Lady Vexina resides in a haunted coastal tower with an emotionally manipulative cat named Regret and an unpaid intern who may be a mushroom spirit.

Her hobbies include:

- Scrying into other people's drama

- Dramatically sighing near windows while wearing a flowing gown

- Dueling her critics (verbally and magically)
- Collecting cursed love letters
- Pretending she doesn't care

Lady Vexina is *not* responsible for your decisions, poor romantic judgment, or side quest addiction. Any emotional growth resulting from her guidebooks is purely accidental.

APPENDIX: A LESS-THAN-OFFICIAL ADVENTURER'S COMPENDIUM

(Compiled by Lady Vexina Quagmire, who has absolutely no reason to know this much about them.)

KAELIN THORN

"Do not sneak up behind her unless you enjoy being stabbed. Some lessons you only learn once."

Class: **Rogue / Fighter (Subclass: The Reluctant Hero)**

Race: **Human (Probably)**

Background: **Former assassin, current disaster-in-progress**

Alignment: **Chaotic Guarded**

Strengths:

- Deadly precise with daggers (especially the named ones)
- Excellent judge of exits, motives, and bad ideas
- Strong protective instincts under all the trauma
- Surprisingly good at leadership when tricked into it

Weaknesses:

- Feelings
- Any extended conversation about feelings
- Destiny (allergic reaction pending)

Equipment:

- Mercy, Whisperthorn, Moonveil — her three signature blades
- A collection of grudges
- Timber (counts as emotional support and melee backup)

Personality Notes:

Tough, tense, sarcastic. Loyal (once earned). Distrustful of authority figures.

If she says she's fine, she is absolutely not fine.

Ideal:

"I choose my own story."

Bond:

Her ragtag found family (she has not admitted this out loud).

Flaw:

Assumes betrayal is Plan A.

TOBIAS FENWICK

"If the magic doesn't get you, the earnestness will."

Class: **Wizard / Support Mage (Subclass: Accidental Bread Mage)**
Race: **Human**
Background: **Scholar turned adventurer**
Alignment: **Lawful Soft-Hearted**
Strengths:
- Adaptable spellcasting, strong protective magic
- Quick thinker, excellent researcher
- Empathy that borders on magical in its own right

Weaknesses:
- Prone to rambling essays
- Would absolutely apologize to a monster while fighting it
- Easily flustered by Kaelin

Equipment:
- Traveling spellbook filled with revisions, side notes, and scone crumbs
- Half a dozen quills
- A wand (sometimes), glitter (always)

Personality Notes:

Earnest, thoughtful, and catastrophically supportive.

Endures danger, mostly because Kaelin keeps walking toward it.

Ideal:

"Knowledge should protect, not harm."

Bond:

Kaelin, whether she knows it or not.

Flaw:

Would walk into a trap if there was a book inside.

TIMBER

"The deadliest creature in the group—and the only one allowed to nap on the furniture."

Class: **Beast Companion (Subclass: Wolf-Raccoon Mystery Mix)**

Race: **Canine (technically)**

Alignment: **Lawful Food-Motivated**

Strengths:

- Acute danger sense
- Fearless protector
- Very loud bark

Weaknesses:

- Will eat anything
- Selective hearing
- No concept of "stealth" despite adventuring with an assassin

Equipment:

- One blue eye, one hazel — both judge
- A deep love of bacon and cheese
- Bite force capable of altering destinies

Personality Notes:

Devoted, mischievous, unimpressed by authority.

Does not trust chickens. Correctly.

Ideal:

Protect the pack.

Bond:

Kaelin.

Flaw:

Will absolutely start a fight with something three times her size.

BRUG

"I blame them for most of the chaos. They blame 'the muse.'"

Class: **Bard (Subclass: Chaos Laureate)**

Race: **Orc**

Background: **Traveling lyricist, professional dramatist**

Alignment: **Chaotic, Delightful**

Strengths:

- Inspires allies through music and sheer enthusiasm
- Surprisingly decent aim with a lute
- Writes ballads faster than most people breathe

Weaknesses:

- Prone to embellishment (severe chronic exaggeration)

- Attracts trouble the way a tavern attracts drunks
- No volume control

Equipment:
- Battle-lute
- Three notebooks full of unfinished epics
- Dramatic cloak (mandatory bard attire)

Personality Notes:

The party's serotonin generator.

Has never once met a situation they couldn't turn into a musical moment.

Ideal:

"All stories deserve an audience."

Bond:

Their friends' legends.

Flaw:

Volume. Just . . . volume.

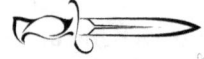

NADIA

"If she smiles at you, check whether she's drawing a blade."

Class: **Ranger / Rogue (Subclass: Elegant Mayhem Specialist)**

Race: **Elf**

Background: **Exiled noble, current menace**

Alignment: **Chaotic, Good-ish**

Strengths:

- Deadly accurate with ranged weapons
- Tactical mind, excellent at infiltration
- Stylish under all circumstances

Weaknesses:

- Will fight anyone, anywhere
- Terrible impulse control
- Keeps daring the universe to escalate

Equipment:

- Paired crossbows
- Collection of lockpicks
- Dramatic entrances

Personality Notes:

Flirtatious danger wrapped in velvet and spite. Loves fiercely, fights joyfully.

Ideal:

Freedom.

Bond:

Fen (ride-or-die, emphasis on "die" if needed).

Flaw:

Cannot walk away from a challenge.

FEN

"She and Nadia once defeated three assailants while arguing. Romance is complex."

***Class:* Barbarian / Fighter (Subclass: Problem-Solver Through Punching)**

***Race:* Elf**

***Background:* Former mercenary, current chaotic guardian**

***Alignment:* Chaotic, Loyal**

Strengths:

- Brutal close-range combat
- Tactical brawling
- Shockingly good at emotional honesty

Weaknesses:

- Direct to the point of danger
- Sees "diplomacy" as a warm-up for violence
- Has a personal grudge against chairs

Equipment:

- Reinforced knuckle wraps
- Backup knuckle wraps
- Nadia (they come as a pair)

Personality Notes:

Blunt, brave, ride-or-die.

Can and will suplex a problem.

Ideal:

Protect the people she loves.

Bond:
Nadia.

Flaw:
Solves emotional problems the same way she solves physical ones.

FINLO QUICKWHISK

"He means well. That's what makes it worse."

Class: **Sorcerer / Artisan (Subclass: Culinary Pyromancer)**

Race: **Human**

Background: **Baker, accidental arsonist**

Alignment: **Chaotic Wholesome**

Strengths:
- Explosive magic (usually unintentional)
- Creative problem-solving (also usually unintentional)
- Can bake weapons and pastries simultaneously

Weaknesses:
- His magic is powered by panic
- Has no idea how dangerous he is
- Chronic over-apologizer

Equipment:
- A whisk he treats like a staff

- Spell-enchanted pastry dough
- A fireproof apron (thank the gods)

Personality Notes:

Kind, anxious, well-meaning.

The universe bends around his mistakes in alarming ways.

Ideal:

"Feed people. Try not to burn them."

Bond:

Brenna (the grounding to his wildfire).

Flaw:

His magic reacts to strong emotions. And he has many.

BRENNA BIRCHBAKE

"She could stop a war with a well-placed gouda. Or start one with a flaming fondue. Either way—respect the cheesemonger."

Class: **Artificer / Ranger (Subclass: Dairy Engineer & Livestock Wrangler)**

Race: **Half Elf**

Background: **Cheesemonger, crisis manager**

Alignment: **Lawful Practical**

Strengths:

- Throws cheese wheels with alarming precision

- Excellent survival skills
- Manages Finlo and Percival, which counts as a high-level feat

Weaknesses:

- Perpetually exhausted by everyone else's shenanigans
- Too responsible
- Cannot leave Skritch unsupervised for more than 48 hours

Equipment:

- Cheese-wheel bandolier
- Rope lasso
- Snacks that double as bribes or weapons

Personality Notes:

Steady, grounded, deeply competent.

The universe tests her patience daily and she keeps passing with grit and dairy.

Ideal:

"Structure keeps chaos from burning down the bakery."

Bond:

Finlo.

Flaw:

Underestimates her own heroism.

JOREN HALE

"His loyalty is impressive. His timing . . . less so."

Class: **Fighter / Commander (Subclass: Reluctant Steward)**

Race: **Human**

Background: **Knight of the Crown, battlefield tactician**

Alignment: **Lawful Conscience**

Strengths:

- Exceptional battlefield awareness
- Tactical leadership under pressure
- Will put himself between danger and others without hesitation
- Knows how systems break—and how to rebuild them

Weaknesses:

- Carries responsibility like armor (heavy, always on)
- Slow to forgive himself
- Prone to believing he must atone rather than rest

Equipment:

- Longsword, service-worn but meticulously maintained
- Standard-issue armor, modified for real combat (not ceremony)
- A battered signaling bell (kept, not rung lightly)

Personality Notes:

Steady. Principled. The kind of man who believes loyalty is a verb.

Questions authority when it conflicts with conscience—and then does something about it.

Ideal:

"Leadership means standing when it would be easier to leave."

Bond:

Those he failed once and refuses to fail again.

Flaw:

Thinks redemption must be earned through suffering.

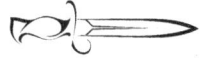

SIR HARLOW "He is made of bones and regrets. Handle gently."

Class: **Paladin / Knight (Subclass: Oath of Memory)**

Race: **Undead (Skeletal, Sentient.)**

Background: **Once-honored knight, now legend-in-progress**

Alignment: **Lawful Haunted**

Strengths:

- Unyielding determination
- Immune to fear, pain, and most physical exhaustion
- Strong sense of honor—even when it costs him
- Commands undead forces with grim precision

Weaknesses:

- Bound by bargains he regrets
- Carries grief like a second skeleton
- Tends to believe duty matters more than happiness

Equipment:

- Runed skeletal warhorse

- Knight's sword etched with old vows
- Armor bearing marks of allegiance, past and present

Personality Notes:

Quiet. Formal. Earnest in a way that feels old-fashioned and painfully sincere.

Does not excuse his choices—but does not flee from them either.

Ideal:

"Some debts are paid in service, not forgiveness."

Bond:

The brother he loved, and the memory that drives him forward.

Flaw:

Believes choosing wrongly once defines him forever.

Acknowledgements

(In which the author attempts to thank people, and someone else cannot resist meddling.)

This story could not have been written without the people who encouraged every absurd detour, every chaotic side quest, and every moment when destiny politely stepped aside to let disaster speak first, you know who you are.

To those who believed Kaelin Thorn deserved a life outside the shadows even while secretly, or not so secretly, wishing I was working on a different book—thank you.

Yes, well, Dear Reader, some of us believed this long before the author did.

To my readers, who have followed this merry band of disasters-with-hearts-of-gold: your enthusiasm is the wisdom in Timber's eyes, the melody of Brug's ballads, and the glitter in Tobias's increasingly creative spell attempts.

You're also the reason a certain individual insisted on telling this tale with ... editorial commentary.

To my beta readers and everyone who listened to me come up with one outlandish idea after another and cheered, cackled, and occasionally yelled "MORE CHAOS"—thank you for seeing the heart beneath the humor.

They yelled it because they were right. Also, because some of us supplied the chaos.

To the friends and family who listened to me talk about daggers, magic systems, pastries of questionable stability, emotional arcs, and plotlines—this book is better because of you.

Especially the pastries. Excellent work there.

To everyone who reminded me that stories can be both soft and sharp, both earnest and ridiculous, both tender and teeth-baring—thank you for encouraging this absurd, yet meaningful journey.

Some of us demonstrated this personally. Tirelessly. You're welcome.

And finally, to the storyteller behind the scenes—the voice who threaded warnings, winks, and wisdom between the lines—thank you for guiding the tone and the laughter of this world.

Oh, please! I merely observed. Recorded. Commented where necessary. Hardly my fault if the commentary was brilliant.

But to the readers:

If at any point you wondered who, exactly, was narrating this tale . . . well.

Some mysteries are more entertaining left unsolved.

Though if you recognized the voice . . . congratulations. I knew you were clever.

Thank you for adventuring with us.

There may always be one more side quest waiting.

Trust me. I've seen the next one.

About the Author

Stephanie K Clemens is known for many things: an author, photographer, dog mom, instagrammer, adventurer, teacher, lawyer, and more. When she's not sitting behind her laptop she can be found on some adventure. Most of the time it's a road trip with her two doggos, but recently it has been in the pages of a book.

Also by

Ladies of WACK Series
A Study in Steam
A Practicum in Perjury
A History in Horticulture – Coming Soon

Ladies of WACK Prequels
The Daring Adventures of Honoria Porter: Volume 1

Wynterfell Romances
For the Love of Hot Cocoa
Villain Rehab – Coming Soon

Fantasy Books
Stripped Away
Cursed by Bandits
Mundane Mornings and Enchanted Evenings

Children's Book by S.K. Clemens
Frankie Wants to be a Sled Dog

www.ingramcontent.com/pod-product-compliance
Lightning Source LLC
LaVergne TN
LVHW012031070526
838202LV00056B/5466